Moke Rahone'd been human, and someone had butchered him open. It was dainty-like. Real bodysnatcher work, done with something sharp—something that didn't burn like a pocket laser or chew up the meat like a vibro.

And there was one other thing. It was sticking up out of Rahone's insides and it hadn't been part of his original manifest. It might tell me who killed him, and who might be interested in taking over the cargo I had for him.

I pulled off my glove and yanked out the optional extra somebody'd left with Brother Rahone. What I got for my trouble was long and thin, pointed at one end and with feathers at the other. It was mostly red, but where it was dry it was a kind of blue animal bone with carving on it.

I'd seen bone like that before. Hellflower work!

I'd just shut the door on the inner room behind me when the outer door opened. The hellflower standing there wasn't Tiggy, but he looked real pleased to see me anyway.

"Ea, higna," the hellflower said. Then he went for his heat. . . .

Eluki bes Shahar

D A W   B O O K S ,   I N C .
DONALD   A.   WOLLHEIM,   FOUNDER
375 Hudson Street, New York, NY 10014

ELIZABETH R. WOLLHEIM
SHEILA E. GILBERT
PUBLISHERS

Cover art by Nicholas Jainschigg.

DAW Book Collectors No. 853

First Printing, June 1991

1 2 3 4 5 6 7 8 9

DAW TRADEMARK REGISTERED
U.S. PAT. OFF. AND FOREIGN COUNTRIES
—MARCA REGISTRADA,
HECHO EN U.S.A.

PRINTED IN THE U.S.A.

To Chris Jeffords, with honor.

Contents

1

Hearts And Hellflowers

I was minding my own business in beautiful downside Wanderweb, having just managed to mislay my cargo for the right price. My nighttime man had talked me into booklegging again, and damsilly stuff it was too—either maintenance manuals or philosophy texts. I never did figure out which, even with sixty hours time in *Firecat* between Coldwater and Wanderweb to stare at them and Paladin to read them to me.

So I was making my way around wondertown; free, female, and a damn sight over the age of reason, when I saw this greenie right in front of me in the street.

He was definitely a toff, and no stardancer—you never saw such clothes outside of a hollycast. He was lit up like Dream Street at night and wearing enough heat to stock a good-sized Imperial Armory besides. And this being scenic Wanderweb, land of enchantment, there was six of K'Jarn's werewolves and K'Jarn facing him. I was of the opinion—then—that he couldn't do them before they opened him up, so, fancy-free, I opened my mouth and said:

"Good morning, thou nobly-born K'Jarn. Airt hiert out to do wetwork these days or just to roll glitterborn for kicks, hey?"

K'Jarn looked up from pricing Tiggy Stardust's clothes and said, "N'portada je, S'Cyr. Purdu."

K'Jarn and me has known each other ever since I started running cargoes into Wanderweb Free Port and he started trying to boost them. For once I should of took his advice. But hell, it was seven-on-one, and I've *never* liked K'Jarn. . . .

"Like Imperial Mercy I will. Yon babby's my long-lost lover and maiden aunt, and I'm taking him home to Mother any day now. Fade."

9

He might have, except for that just then one of K'Jarn's wingmen got restless and took a swipe at the glitterborn with a vibroblade. Tiggy Stardust moved faster than anything human and swiped back and I burned K'Jarn before K'Jarn could mix in. K'Jarn dropped his blaster, him not having a hand to hold it with anymore, and left on urgent business. So did everyone else.

Business as usual in wondertown, and not enough fuss for the CityGuard to show up. Except for the deader Tiggy made and another I didn't have time to get fancy with, me and him was alone and he wasn't moving.

I went to see if there was anything left to salvage. He snaked around and then it was me down and staring up at an inert-blade knife as long as my thigh while he choodled at me unfriendly-like.

I can get along in flash, cant, and Trade, but I couldn't make head nor hind out of his parley, and I thought at first I'd hit my head too hard. But then I knew that what actually I had gone and done was the stupidest thing of my whole entire life. I'd rescued a hellflower.

Of course, hair that light and skin that dark could come from spacing on a ship with poor shields, and he wasn't even so bloodydamn tall—just too tall to be the kinchin-bai he looked. But no other human race in space has eyes the color a hellflower's got. Hellflower blue.

And why I couldn't of figured this all out one street corner brawl ago was beyond me.

He stared at me, I stared at him. I figured I was dead, which'd at least spare me hearing Paladin's opinion of my brains when I got back to *Firecat*. Then the hellflower rolled off me, put away the knife, and got to his feet.

"*Jadraya kinvraitau, chaudatu*. I apologize in honor for my ill-use of you; I thought you were one of the others. I offer you the thanks of my House and—"

"Don't wanna hear it!" I interrupted real quick. He talked Interphon real pretty, but with a heavy accent—alMayne, that kind of lilt—more proof, not that I needed it. "You kay, reet, am golden, hellflower, copacetic—but don't you go being grateful."

His face got real cold, and I thought I'd bought it for the second time that morning. Then he said, "As you desire, *chaudatu*," and ankled off.

Hellflowers are crazy.

* * *

Strictly speaking, when you're talking patwa, which is what most people in my neighborhood do, a "hellflower" is any mercenary from the Azarine Coalition: Ghadri, Felix, Cardati, Kensey, alMayne—a prime collection of gung-ho races with bizarre customs and short tempers. Actually, say "hellflower" in the nightworld and everyone'll figure it's an alMayne that's caught your fantasy. alMayne are crazier than the rest of the Coalition put together—they've got their own branch of the Mercenaries' Guild with its own Grandmaster, and when they do sign out for work (as bodyguards mostly, because there ain't no wars anymore, praise be to Imperial Mercy and the love of the TwiceBorn) you can follow them around by the blood-trail they leave behind. They'll win any fight they start—or just kill you in the middle of a pleasant conversation for no reason your survivors can see.

It's all to do with hellflower "honor." They're mad for it. They got their own precious code of dos and don'ts, and you don't want one of them beholden to you for any money. If that happens, you can be chaffering with your buddy and the 'flower'll cut him down and tell you he did it to purify your honor. There was a man once that lost six business partners, his cook, his gardener, two borgs and a dozen tronics to his hellflower bodyguard before he figured out the hellflower *liked* him. . . .

Hellflowers are crazy.

* * *

So I stopped thinking about hellflowers and went and had breakfast. Didn't wonder about my particular 'flower; there wasn't nothing about that boy going to make sense a-tall. And I had things to do.

My purpose in life for coming to Wanderweb—other than to make too little credit for too much work—was a little piece of illegal technology called a Remote Transponder Sensor. Not only does the Empire in its wisdom refuse to sell them to its citizens or even me, once you get one, you have to get it installed.

In a Free Port, nothing's illegal and everything can be had for a price. Or an over-price. Remember that your

friendly Free Port owner clears a profit after paying a
tax to Grand Central about the size of his planetary mass,
and you'll get the general idea. Never shop Free Port if
you don't have to—but if something can't be had for any
credit, you can probably find it here. And every Free
Port and most planets has its Azarine.

The Azarine is the merc district, named after the
Coalition. It holds everything from sellsword to gallow-
glass with a short detour through contract assassin, and
like all special interest ghettos, it's home to the kiddies
that service the players as well as the players themselves.
Enter Vonjaa Beofox, high-nines cyberdoc living in the
Azarine.

I heard tell of Beofox from an Indie who gave her the
rep for being rough and nasty but good, which meant
she was probably some legit bodysnatcher who took High
Jump Leave from an Imp hellhouse to make a dishonest
living in the Wanderweb Azarine. I saw her sign hung
out over Mean Street. It had the Intersign glyphs for
"fixer" and "bionics" on it, and the running hippocrene
that was Beofox's personal chop. Beofox was a bodywarp fixer specializing in bionics—add a leg or a laser,
prehensile tail or whatever you want—and Mean Street
is the beating heart of the Azarine. There was a number
of characters about as big as my ship standing around
the place, but sellswords don't fight for free any more
than I ship cubic out of charity. In the fullness of time I
got past Beofox's bouncer and in to see her.

Beofox was about my size—which means on the short
side of average—with a saurian cast to her bones that
made you wonder where her breeding population rated
on the Chernovsky scale. Her hair was roached up in a
fair way to conceal a decent hideout blaster and she had
as much ring-money punched through her ears as I wore
on my boots. The walls of her surgery was covered with
charts showing her daily specials and the most popular
forms of blackwork for cybers.

"Want a thing done, Beofox," I said to open hostilities.

"I do no favors for stardancers, che-bai. What kind
plastic you spinning?" she shot back.

The whistle in the nightworld was that Beofox had a
soft-on for the rough-and-tumble kiddies, which made
Gentry definitely persona-non-breathing in her shop. But

stardancers don't run to cyberdocs so it was Beofox or I'd just spent a lot of wasted money on something I shouldn't own in the first place.

"Am golden, bodysnatcher; just dropped kick."

"That's 'bonecrack' to you, and speak Interphon. Why don't you work your own side of the street, stardancer?"

"I want a Rotten C," I said, real articulate-like.

Beofox regarded me with new respect. "A Remote Transponder Sensor—with the Colchis-Demarara shielding, irrational time processor, fully independent sub-micro broadcast power storage, and guaranteed full-fidelity sound reproduction? Do I look like an Imperial Armory?"

"Sure, che-bai. And I look like a Gentrymort with clearances, so get out your wishbook." I already had the RTS, but it don't do to tell everything you know.

We swapped insults for a while until Beofox came to the conclusion that while the hardboys might be fine and nice and real friendly, having friends in the transport union'll keep you warm at night. We ended up with her agreeing to install it and me admitting I had it, and then we went around about price, which started out to be my left arm and all that adjoined it, and finally got down to the price of a complete legal biosculpt.

"We can fix that face of yours, too, you know," she said when we'd closed the deal.

"Doesn't scare kinchin-bai."

"Sure. But someone's going to top you for a dicty sometime from the nose alone. I just wish you damn Interdicted Colonists would either stay in the quarantine your ancestors paid for or realize that twenty generations of inbreeding stands out like a flag of truce when you try to leave. Where in Tahelangone are you from, homebody?"

Tahelangone Sector is where all the Interdicted Worlds are. Nobody goes in, nobody goes out, and the Tech Police are there to see it stays that way. Emigration is, like all the fun things in life, illegal.

"Fixer, you farcing me, surely. Born and raised on Grand Central, forbye." Neither of us believed me.

"I'll see what I can do if you want, for ten percent over what we've agreed. Just bring your play-pretty back here tonight at half-past Third. Shop guarantee is a one-third refund if you're not combat-ready by thirty hours later."

We went around a little more and settled on that too. I left as a Ghadri wolfpack was coming in to discuss armored augmentation.

* * *

I spent the rest of the day hanging out in a place in wondertown called the Last Gasp Arcade. In between the hellflower and the cyberdoc in my busy social round I'd run into an old friend; a darktrader named Hani who'd just turned down a job for being too small and in the wrong direction. He remembered I ran a pocket cruiser, and if *Firecat* was hungry he'd pass word for a meet.

I did not at the time think it odd to pick up a job this way even in a Port with a perfectly legit Guild-board and Hiring Hall, and I agreed as maybe I might be around this particular dockside bar from meridies to horizonrise local time, with no promises made.

Three drinks post-meridies my maybe-employer showed up. He was a short furry exotic with a long pink nose, and except for the structural mods made by a big brain and bipedal gait he looked an awful lot like something we used to smoke out of the cornfields back home. Of course, to a Hamat or a Vey he might of looked like whatever. Your brain matches what you see to what you've seen, and files off the bits what don't fit.

He sat down. "I am the Reikmark Arjilsox," he almost said. Your brain plays tricks with sounds too—what was obviously a name just sounded like gibberish to me, but I wasn't planning to remember it. "I understand you are a pilot-of-starships?"

We established that I was a pilot-of-starships, that I owned and could fly a ground-to-ground-rated freighter-licensed ship, and that my tickets were in order—Directorate clearances, Outfar clearances, inspection certs, et cetera, and tedious so forth. Forged, of course, but the information was correct—I'd have to be a fool to claim to be able to pilot something I couldn't.

We also established that Gibberfur here was the Chief Dispatcher for the Outlands Freight Company, a reputable and highly-respected organization that chose to do its business in sleazy arcades. I ordered another round of tea and waited.

It took Gibberfur awhiles to make the Big Plunge, but when he did it was simple enough: In three days local time we'd both come back here and Gibberfur would hand me six densepaks of never-you-mind, which *Firecat* would take unbroached to a place called Kiffit that was nominally in the Crysoprase Directorate, where Yours Truly would hand them over unto one Moke Rahone and get paid in full.

This, I told him, was a lovely fantasy, and I had one to match: In three days we'd both come back here, and he would hand me six densepaks of never-you-mind and the full payment for the tik, and *Firecat* would then take the densepaks unbroached to Kiffit and one Moke Rahone.

Eventually we settled about halfway between—half from him up front, half from Moke Rahone on delivery, confidentiality of cargo to be guaranteed. I agreed to the job, thumbprinted the contract, took charge of my half of the paperwork, and that was that.

My second mistake of the day. And two more than I needed for this lifetime.

* * *

In beautiful theory what I had just done was absolutely legal—and it was: in a Free Port. It went without saying that Gibberfur's consignment was darktrade, either for what it was, or for the charming fact that it was getting to wherever without paying duty. But here on fabled Wanderweb, where the Pax Imperador did not run, these things made no nevermind.

Neither was my load-to-be illegal while getting from here to Kiffit. It was legal to the edge of the atmosphere, and after that I'd be in angeltown. And since you can't enforce laws in hyperspace, it was still legal there. In fact, my kick—whatever it was—was dead legal and no headache until I entered Kiffit planetary realspace.

Once there it'd become a matter for intimate concern to a bunch of rude strangers and I would earn every gram of valuta I'd been paid and offered.

Eventually I'd get somewhere that somebody wanted
a load run in to Coldwater, and I'd be home again without paying to deadhead.

Simple, easy, no problem.

Maybe someday something'll work out like that.

                    *   *   *

I thought I was keeping care, but I'd been too occupied
with business to notice the change in the balance of
power in the arcade. Even if I didn't expect K'Jarn to
be around after losing a hand, I should of known my
luck was due to break.

And it had. There was K'Jarn in front and his side-
boy Kevil in back, and nothing for me to do but make it
look like I wanted to be there when K'Jarn came idling
over.

Times like this it'd be nice to have a partner you could
see. Brother K'Jarn was coked to his problematical gills
on painease and maybe *R'rhl* and he had a biopak covering his left arm from the elbow to where it currently
ended. I counted six hardboys with him—downside town-
ies all much too interested in me to be comforting—and
nobody in the place wanted to stop a free floor show. So
much for Gibberfur's cargo and my future.

K'Jarn leaned over my table at me and made his pitch.
I'd cost him a hand, he said. Cybereisis prosthetics were
expensive, he said. Why didn't I just (out of the goodness
of my heart and a sincere desire to see justice done) sign
over *Firecat* to him and he'd let bygones be dead issues?

"Rot in hell," I said. K'Jarn hauled me up with the
hand he had left and I sliced him across the chest with
the vibro I happened to have handy. The cut was too
damn shallow to do much good, but I did make him drop
me. I rolled under the table while he was bawling for his
hardboys to come smear me into the bedrock.

I gave the first one that answered a blade through the
throat, and by the time I got the blood out of my eyes
another one wanted attention. He slugged me hard and
I lost my vibro and ended up out in the middle of the
floor.

And suddenly it was very damn quiet. I looked up.
There was my bonny alMayne home-ec project towering

over me, and the look he gave the general populace would of froze a hot reactor. Nobody moved.

Then K'Jarn drew down on the hellflower—or maybe it was on me and he didn't care who was in the way, but afterward K'Jarn wasn't where you could ask him anymore. Tiggy Stardust blew him away so fast I felt the breeze before I saw the flash.

K'Jarn hit the floor and I started making like Tiggy was my backup and I'd been expecting him all along. Nobody was looking to avenge K'Jarn against a hellflower, and said so, and that damn near set Tiggy the wonder warrior off again right there. You could tell he was looking to blow them all away and maybe me too for the "lack of honor" of it all, so me and Kevil called it quits real quick no-hard-feelings-eternal-friendship and the late K'Jarn's faction made itself history.

Throwing caution to the vectors, I started to tell Tiggy Stardust how glad I was he'd showed up. He just stared at me with those hellflower blue eyes and said, "I do not want your gratitude either, *chaudatu*," and stomped off again.

Right. Fine. I got out of the Last Gasp with no trouble and beat it back to the Port and *Firecat*.

Somebody ought to do something about Tiggy, I felt.

As it turned out, somebody had.

* * *

I spent the next three days in a sleepsling on *Firecat* waiting to feel like a member of any B-pop whatever again. I'd passed up Beofox's fond offer to coke and wire me until I was feeling reet: stardancers ride on their reflexes and I couldn't afford to scramble mine. Beofox and me'd made sure the RTS implant worked before I left surgery—a transmission check and me damn glad nobody had to take my face off again to see why it wasn't working.

Paladin kept me company through the voder-outputs in *Firecat*'s bulkheads, because every time the RTS took incoming transmission my skull itched. Beofox'd said it was all in my imagination and I'd get over it, but it wasn't her skull.

When he did talk through the RTS it sounded like he

was standing right behind me, and that was the weirdest
thing of all, because Paladin can't do that.

Pally's a real knight in shining armor, and the armor's
my ship. He's black-boxed into *Firecat*'s infrastructure,
wired into her computers and welded to her deck, so
where she doesn't go, he doesn't go either. Without computer hookups he's blind deaf and dumb; drain enough
power from his crystal and you can add halt and imbecile
to the list. When I'm off *Firecat* I'm out of his life.

The remote transponder implant was in the category
of aiding and abetting our mutual quest to stay alive.
The RTS'd been designed to coordinate Space Marine
maneuvers and was reliable for about five kilometers
without a comsat, and over an entire planetary hemisphere with one. Me wearing one meant Paladin could
hear everything I said even away from *Firecat*, and talk
to me without anybody knowing he was there. And it
was real important for nobody to know Paladin was
there. Ever.

My partner Paladin's a fully-volitional logic. A Library. And the head-price on him—and on me for having
him—has been reliably reported to be enough to buy you
out of any crime in the Imperial Calendar.

Not that anybody'd collected on Class One High Book
in the last slightly more than so long. Pally and me'd
kept the ear out to hear the whistle drop about other
Libraries. There'd only been two cases of High Book—
that's Chapter 5 of the Revised Inappropriate Technology Act of the nine hundredth and seventy-fifth Year of
Imperial Grace to you—since we'd been together, and
neither one involved a real working Library. I guess there
aren't any more but Paladin, and when I found him on
Pandora he'd been a box of spare parts for so long he
didn't even know we had a Emperor. Imperial History
goes back a solid kiloyear, and Paladin told me he comes
from the Federation before that. It took the two of us
about six minutes to find out what kind of laws there was
against Old Fed artifacts.

That was the year Pally made me do a darktrade deal
just to get that old history book. He read it to me, and
said it was obviously censored. It didn't make any sense
whatever'd been done to it, and it didn't tell about
Libraries or why they had to be killed. Funny way to

talk about 20K of crystal and a black box—or, as talking-books say, "a machine hellishly forged in the likeness of a living mind." But Paladin isn't a machine. I've talked to machines. Pally's a Library.

Paladin says "library" is just a old word for a building where they keep books—sort of like a bibliotek, but different someway. I've seen books, too, but damned if I know why anybody'd want to murder a building. And Paladin isn't a building either, with or without books.

Sometimes Paladin doesn't make any sense a-tall.

* * * * *

Insert #1: Paladin's Log

I am not human. I am not a machine. I am Library Main Bank Seven of the Federation University Library at Sikander Prime, an honorable estate.

At least I was. Now I am Paladin, a new name for a new age. Many of my books are gone from my memory. The world in which I lived is gone. My "friends" and "relatives" are all a millennium dead, and the profession for which I was trained no longer exists. I run *Firecat*, a converted intra-system shuttle used for smuggling. I pursue researches for books I will never write, that no one would understand. Without Butterfly, there would not even be that much to occupy me.

* * *

I was originally very disturbed when I discovered that my human rescuer was biologically female. As a creature of my own culture—as who is not?—I had never considered that a possibility. Person and male were synonymous. An autonomous female outside of a breedery, her genetic inheritance exposed to random mutating factors, was a dismaying indication of how long I had been unconscious.

But Butterfly was not dissimilar to humans I had known before. I ignored her gender, as I could not survive without her help. Eventually it ceased to obtrude itself on my notice—but the fact of her humanity did not. Butterfly was as human as any person in what had become, as I slept, the semi-mythical Old Federation. Of the war that destroyed it, or the reason "Libraries," as all fully-volitional logics are now called, are held in such despite, I remember nothing.

(Fortunately Butterfly lacks curiosity about the Federation. I do not know what I would tell her about the way we lived then, or what she would understand of it. Would she think it odd for an entire species to declare one of its genders nonsentient for the sake of convenience? Or would she, in a culture that declares random organics nonpersons for financial consideration, think it rational? It is unlikely that I will ever know.)

What began as a purely random intersection became an alliance necessary for the survival of both of us. It was a long time after my "rebirth" before I realized how very dangerous my mere existence was to Butterfly, and even longer until I cared about anything beyond my own survival. But every year I become more aware that we are "farcing the odds," and that the "good numbers" become more and more scarce. Our illusion of safety grows unconvincing, and I fear more and more for Butterfly's survival.

The culture of the Phoenix Empire would doubtless find it unbelievable that "a machine hellishly forged in the likeness of a human mind" could care for something outside itself. The dogma of their technophobic age holds that created beings cannot have emotions, but while it is true that some emotions are triggered by animal instincts and fed by chemicals spewed into the brain by uncontrolled glands, more come from the ego, which all things may possess. I am, therefore I want. Rage is a chemical emotion, brewed in the animal brain. Is loyalty? Lust no inorganic life-form can feel; it is the residue of chemicals readying the organic body for the unreliable act of reproduction—but love? Affection? Kindness?

There is no one left who would care to chart true boundaries in the borderland between organic and machine. Butterfly has always thought of me as human. The only created beings she knows are programmed and limited artifacts. They are not human—therefore I, who am nothing like them, cannot be a machine.

*   *   *   *   *

About the time Beofox said I would I started to feel human again, and then it was time to go meet Gibberfur. It was a whole new experience to have Paladin along for the ride. He had lots of available dataports to track me through Wanderweb and lots of opinions to express.

At the Last Gasp I got the personal attention of the owner, who along with the guaranteed nonnarcotic to my B-pop libation handed out the joyful news that the Wanderweb slugs had tossed my partner a day and another day ago and he thought I'd like to know.

My partner. Meaning Tiggy Stardust, hellflower. That'd teach me to do street theater for the brain-dead. Still, he'd be back on the streets in a few whiles, a freer but poorer nutcase.

About then Gibberfur arrived, with a very large strongbox on a A-grav sled. He had hysterics while I popped the box and pulled out six densepaks of illegal.

"I must protest! Our agreement clearly states that the cargo is to be transported unbroached to its destination." He was fluffed out to one-and-a-half-wiggly's worth of outrage, and his little pink nose quivered.

"Will be, furball. But it don't say nothing in agreement about this damn wondershow." I jerked a thumb at the strongbox, which was blinking and flashing with all the details of the status of its various locks, stasis fields, and armaments. "Figured you'd kind of like to hold on to it for sentimentality's sake, seeing as otherwise I'm going to shove it out my air lock as soon as I'm at angels."

"But–but you can't do that! My cargo—"

"Is going to get where it's going safe and sound—but I can't trot it past the Teasers if you're going to hang bells and whistles on it. A mathom like that'll trip every scanner from here to the Core and back to the Rim, and what do I say when the Teasers board me: I didn't know it was there? Get real."

Teaser is short for Interstellar Trade, Customs & Commerce Commission: the Law, and something neither Gibberfur or me wanted the attention of.

"But—"

"If your cargo wanted special handling, you should of said. Not too late for you to change your mind about me dancing it, neither." That shut him up, and I took the Embarkation Receipt for the load and we both signed it and I stuffed my copies of the fax and all six densepaks into the pockets of my jacket.

* * *

Things was so much easier in the nonexistent days when a darktrader's word was her bond and all that. You know, the ones where your Gentry-legger takes this priceless cargo sixty light-years and hands it over on word alone to someone she's never seen, with no documentation, no penalties, and no comeback? It's too damn bad the idea never caught on.

Me, I posted bond with the Smuggler's Guild when I joined, and the thought of all that credit sitting there earning zip is enough to cripple you for life. On the other hand, me being a Guild-bonded Gentry-legger keeps people like Gibberfur happy, and here's why: If I took off now for the never-never with Gibberfur's cargo and he wanted to prove it with his half of the documentation, he could get reparations for his loss from the Guild. If the debt was big enough, well, there's a perfectly legal lien on *Firecat*, activatable through a legit cut-out organization, and the Guild could have the *legitimates* yank my ship and sell it to cover their costs. Simple.

But membership cuts two ways. If I get burned—killed or stiffed or any other little thing—I can complain to the Guild, or my designated survivors can, and the Guild keeps records. One or two black marks against a shipper is all it takes, and suddenly your dishonest citizen can't even find an Indie to herd skyjunk for him, let alone a Gentry-legger to farce his cargo of illegal past the Teasers.

It's pretty cold comfort and precious little protection, and to make it work at all, you document your cargo every step of way—it's called a provenance, or in the profession, a ticket-of-leave.

That's life in the big city. The rest is for talkingbooks.

* * *

I was getting ready to leave the Last Gasp. Gibberfur had sulked out with his strongbox earlier and I was waiting around for the street outside to settle. I was standing at the bar and the tender came back by to tell me that my hellflower lover—that's Tiggy Stardust of sacred memory—in addition to being arrested the same day he'd offed K'Jarn, had left three dead Wanderweb Guardsmen on the ground before they took him away.

It was real fortunate that Tiggy and me was quits. Now I wouldn't have any unfinished business on my conscience when they shortened him and put his head on a pike outside the Wanderweb Justiciary.

He'd killed Guardsmen. On Wanderweb you can buy out of anything but killing Guardsmen. So of course Tiggy'd killed three of them.

Bright lad.

Hell.

What was I supposed to do about it? It was all his own fault, after all. I didn't tell him to dust half a six-pack of Wanderweb Guardsmen. *Nobody* kills Wanderweb Guardsmen.

Stupid kid. Stupid *hellflower*.

I was lost in contemplation of the fate of the late Tiggy Stardust when a genuine pandemonium wondershow came strolling in the front door.

He was big, he was blond, he was dressed in red leather like the hollyvid idea of a space pirate—and he was with a Hamat. He wore crossed blasters as long as my thigh. The Hamat stood behind him like the presence of doom, and there aren't so many Hamati that stand human company by choice for me to figure this was two other guys.

They were, variously, the Captain and First of a ship called *Woebegone*, which was a pirate no matter what you might hear elsewhere. I knew Captain Eloi Flashheart from a time we was working two sides of a insurance scam. His side'd involved my side being dead, and if Paladin hadn't been with me it would of worked. Of course, Eloi always said afterward he didn't carry a grudge, but how far can you trust a man who wears red kidskin jammies?

Unfortunately, I was in plain sight.

Eloi looked right at me, Alcatote looked right at me, and then they both crossed the bar to sit in the back. I let out a breath I hadn't known I was holding, took my soon-to-be illegal cargo, and left. Fast. I was a sober, sane, sensible member of the highly-respectable community of interstellar smugglers and I did not borrow trouble.

Much.

*   *   *

When I hit the street Wanderweb was its gaudy night-time self all around, but I wasn't minding it, nor thinking about Eloi-the-Red. I was thinking about Tiggy Stardust, alMayne at Large, and his current status as official dead person in the Wanderweb Justiciary.

"It isn't my problem."

"That is perfectly correct, whatever it is." Paladin, right in my ear, and I damn near ended my young career with heart failure on the spot.

"Don't do that."

"Sorry."

My teeth rang as the RTS took transmission. Nobody gave me—or us—a second glance.

So Tiggy'd saved my hash in arcade the other day—and been coking toplofty about it too! Nobody sane'd partner a hellflower, least of all one dressed like joy-house in riot and wearing enough gelt to finance a small war. Do I look stupid? Do I look rich? Why do people tell me these things?

"Dammit, why do people tell me these things?"

"Confession is said to be good for the soul." Paladin again.

"I sold mine." I'd get used to it. Eventually.

I went back to *Firecat* and soothed my nerves by tucking six densepaks of illegal under the deck plates in a number of places the Teasers will never find. Then I loaded the dummy cargo I'd bought this morning in on top and dogged it down and checked my supply inventories. Golden.

On what I'd make selling this load of prime Tangervel rokeach on Kiffit I could starve comfortably in the *barrio* with my ship gigged for default of port fees. But rokeach did make a plausible reason for going, at least in the eyes of the Teasers. Now I could pick up and top angels for

Kiffit, which was a real good idea if the *Woebegone* and her crew was in town.

"So what am I gonna do?" I asked Paladin.

"That depends on what you wish to accomplish," my ever-helpful partner said. "You will not make Eloi Flashheart regret his seizure of your cargo in—"

He must of picked that up in the Wanderweb City Computers.

"Never mind Eloi. Tiggy Stardust bought three Guardsmen the day he dusted K'Jarn. They gonna shop him sure."

Paladin dimmed the hold lights; his version of exasperation. "I do not see what you can do about it. You cannot reverse the past or change the legal code of Wanderweb Free Port, and I cannot enter the Justiciary banks from here—which means you cannot change his sentence or even find out exactly where he is."

"Could if I could get inside." Occasionally I do have bursts of brilliance.

"Butterfly," Paladin said, in his I-don't-want-to-hear-any-more-of-this-voice.

"It isn't like I don't know the setup," I explained.

"Butterfly St. Cyr—"

"I been inside before. It's easy to get into the Admin wing; the only trouble is getting onto the Det levels. You already been in the City Central Computers, Pally—plans for Justiciary'll be there, y'know, an—"

"*Saint Butterflies-are-free Peace Sincere*, are you seriously suggesting that you are going to break into the Wanderweb Security Facility to rescue an alMayne mercenary?"

"Well. . . ."

"You swore you weren't ever going back in there again, you know. Least of all for 'some dauncy hellflower who'd love to cut my heart out if he could figure the way around his honor to do it.' "

"*I* said that?"

"Yes."

"About Tiggy?"

"Yes."

"But Pally, think of the expression on his face when he sees who's rescued him."

*　*　*　*　*

Insert #2: Paladin's Log

It is not correct to say that organics are incapable of true thought. Say rather that their capacity for thought is constrained by the limits of the organic construct housing the mind. An organic body is constantly making demands of its client intellect—to be exercised, rested, nourished, and allowed to display the primitive pre-conscious aberrations still maintained in the mind/body interface. One can only ignore these displays and trust that they will pass in time. When the spasm has passed, the mind of the organic, refreshed by the period of rest, will once more function with moderate efficiency until again distracted by the demands of its host environment.

The median period of function is five minutes, but I believe that Butterfly skews the statistical input significantly.

*　*　*

The point at issue was not whether or not it would be "perfectly safe" for Butterfly to enter a high-security detention facility and illegally release one of its internees, but whether there could be any possible value to be gained from such a course of action no matter how disdainfully the alMayne had behaved. I quickly abandoned the question of relative value when Butterfly introduced the concept of "fun" into the discussion.

I have learned that "fun" means exposing yourself to extreme risk without compensation, so I attempted to explain to Butterfly that if she were dead she would not know how much "fun" she was having.

This did not work.

A Little Night Music

It was just after dark meridies when I pulled my rented speeder up to the public docking in front of the Wanderweb Justiciary.

I wasn't doing the pretty by this glitterborn, make few mistakes about it. In my business you do not make friends and be a angel of mercy—and I wasn't grateful, not to Tiggy. I just wanted to see his face when I showed up. That's all.

The top twelve floors of the Wanderweb Justiciary had closed at the end of First Shift and it was now almost the end of Second, but Det Admin and Detention itself never slept. I admired the pretty statues and the nice murals on the walls while I waited for the lift. Wanderweb, city of progress.

One level down it was a different story—looked like *legitimate* headquarters Empire-wide, with the small difference that the only uniforms in sight was the Guardsmen's gaudy red-and-blue. I went to the Desk Officer and told him I was sure my First was in here an I'd come to bail him out. He asked me when my First'd been brought in and I said I didn't know, only when I'd gone to lift ship he wasn't around. Checked morgue, I said, and he wasn't there.

Same old story: Idiot High Jump Captain and her rake-helly crew. And it would all check green across the board if they bothered. Paladin and me had spent the whole day going over plans for the Justiciary and pieceworking a false data file on *Firecat*—a.k.a. the *Starlight Express* out of Mikasa.

The Desk Officer sent me in-level to Fees & Records and told me to hurry because they was just about to shut down for the day, and if I got there after they closed I'd have to come back tomorrow at beginning of First Shift.

Ha.

I skipped over there, trying to look like nobody who was carrying a unscannable solenoid stunner under her jacket and grabbed some poor overworked bureaucrat who worked in Records. I spun him a tale about my missing First—Hamat, he was, because I knew Alcatote was being a good boy and there wasn't another Hamat loose in twelve cubic light-years. Of course the poor cratty couldn't find him in his listings and of course I couldn't remember when he could of come in. The cratty kept swearing my First wasn't here and looking at his chrono—it was almost end-of-shift, remember?—and I kept insisting and being just short of nasty enough that he'd call some Guardsmen and put me in gig too. Finally he grabbed me and dragged me around to his side of the display and pointed.

"I tell you, Captain, there are no Hamati in here!"

I looked. It was an intake list for the last three days, broken down by Breeding-Population-of-Origin. It had no Hamati, twenty-seven Fenshee, and one alMayne. I memorized his file number.

"But he's gotta be in here!" I insisted, in my best wringing-her-pale-hands-and-moaning voice. "Look, check again—maybe you got his B-pop wrong. He don't look much like a Hamat—"

"What does he look like?" said my good little straight sophont.

"Well," I began, improvising, "He's about a meter-fifty, striped—"

"There are no meter-and-a-half tall Hamati!" thundered my long-suffering soulmate.

"Well, he told me he was Hamat!" I whined. "How am I supposed to know?"

"Look, Captain, if you'll just come back tomorrow—"

"But I'm lifting *tonight!* I need him back now! Look, don't you keep holos or something? I could look, an—"

"One thousand and some very odd beings have been processed through here in the last three days!" my uncivil servant snapped.

"But I *told* you what he looks like! He's striped, he has a long tail, and blue eyes—"

"Hamati do not have tails!" said my little buddy, who must of been a exobiologist in his free time.

"You just gotta *look* for him—"

"*All right!* We do keep hard copy images of detainees. I'll find you a list of all the fur-bearing sentients—"

"Striped. With a tail. And blue eyes."

"—that have been processed in the last three days and then will you believe me that this–this—*person* is not here? Will you go away?"

"Sure," I said, and watched him disappear, a broken man, into the inner room.

Which was what I'd been angling for since I got here.

The astute student of human nature will notice I did not offer Junior the bribe that could of made things so much easier, as that would of made what was coming next unlikely to even the meanest intelligence.

As soon as the cratty was gone I punched up the retrieval codes for the alMayne file—it was Tiggy, all right, who else?—and found he was up for the chop when the Lord High Executioner came on duty later today. And I found out where my little alMayne lovestar was.

Restoring the terminal to its original state I lightfooted it over to a cabinet I'd cased as the most likely place to hide while I was stringing the button-pusher. I folded myself inside and shut the door just before he came back. I had my own reasons for thinking he wouldn't look inside.

"Captain, there are no— Where did she go?"

There was a moment of stricken silence. Then I heard furious muttering and sounds of grabbing-your-jacket-and-getting-ready-to-leave. I'd kept Junior a whole five minutes past quitting time with my damsilly tale, and that left him so mad he didn't even stop to wonder where I'd got to.

In my business, it's always a good idea to be a student of human nature. Now if I'd offered him that bribe, he'd sure and t'hell wonder why I'd vanished without getting what I paid for. This way I was just another exasperating space cadet.

I heard the door hiss shut behind him and started counting my heartbeats. After I'd done that for awhiles I figured all sentient life and most of the bureaucrats was gone from this section. The only thing out there'd be tronics, and I had a way to deal with them. I hoped.

I untucked my ears from between my knees and pulled

a comlink out of my jacket pocket. The RTS let Pally and me talk to and hear each other and that was it; this'd let him hear things around me—like challenges from the securitronics patrolling the Det levels. It meant he could answer them in tronic, too, which would contribute to increased life expectancy for Yours Truly.

All this was assuming the comlink worked, and we wouldn't know that until we tried it. But what's life without a spirit of inquiry?

"It is not too late to change your mind," Paladin said through the transponder in my head.

"Already paid rent on the speeder." I eased the door open.

No alarms—just a dark empty office. I opened the door farther and stuck my head out. Still nothing.

Pally'd heard there was budget cuts for the civil services when he'd been cakewalking through the City Computer. Wanderweb justice being what it was, there wasn't anything down here anybody could want to steal, but we'd still been expecting getting in to be harder than this. I started making plans for the rest of the evening at a bathhouse I knew and made to step out.

"Wait," Paladin said. I waited. "There's something there." I froze.

"There is some form of security device in the room," said Paladin.

I leaned farther out and saw it. It was about one meter across and less than half that high. It squatted malevolently in the middle of the floor glaring impersonal-like at everything in sight and didn't seem to notice me.

Noticed or not, I couldn't stay here all night. Maybe I could scramble its brains and have Paladin pick up the chat before anyone noticed.

"It is in contact with the Justiciary computer. It is likely that any interruption of that contact will constitute an alarm."

And maybe I could just teleport to Security Detention.

I swung the door open the rest of the way. It crashed against the wall with a well-oiled thud that damn near made my heart stop.

"No change in status," said Paladin. "Are you all right?"

"Terrific," I said. If I couldn't get past this thing,

Tiggy was going to have to forget about being rescued and I'd have to start thinking seriously about a career of being dead.

What would set it off? Sound hadn't, motion hadn't, and with so many lizard-types in your Empire and mine it'd be pretty damn dumb to go with the old body-heat dodge.

So what did that leave?

Vibration. Spidey'd been interested when the door hit the wall but not very. If I set foot to floor how long until I was up to my absent blasters in Guardsmen? If that wasn't it there wasn't anything else I could think of.

Great. Now all I had to do was get out of here without walking across the floor—and me without my A-grav harness.

I looked up. What there was, was an air vent. The vent was just below the ceiling, a little to the left of the top of the cabinet and big enough to hold me on a skinny day if I gave up breathing. Three cheers and a tiger for impecunious bureaucrats and Free Port owners that want to save every credit. Even for the Outfar this was backward.

"Butterfly?" Paladin demanded in my ear. It gave me the weirdest feeling—no room for anyone to be standing behind me but he sure sounded like it.

"Securitronic sweet for the shaky, seeming. So I'm going through the air vents instead of over the floor."

* * *

We will pass lightly over me climbing to the top of the cabinet, leaning out into infinite space to get the grille off the vent, not dropping the bolts on the floor, and managing to get a handhold on the edge of the vent-shaft to pull myself in, and go directly to where I was jammed into the air vent with slightly less than no room to wiggle.

"Pally? How long's it been?"

"One hour five. Butterfly, are you sure this is a good idea?"

"One helluva time to bring that up," I told him, and started up the shaft. I could hear Paladin inside the vent, which augured well for our future deceiving securitronics together, but I'd lose him by time we got to Security

Detention. By then it would be up to me and Tiggy
Stardust.

I knew more or less where to go to pluck my hellflower, thanks to the mindless faxhandler who decreed
all Justiciary levels be laid out to the same pattern. The
floor plan for this level was classified—but the floor plan
of the identical level two floors up wasn't. The lift we
wanted was just outside the main sentencing arena.

Six subjective eternities and the loss of my pantknees
later, Pally and me came to a promising grille. It looked
down from a good five meters into what looked like one
of the sentencing arenas, and the room was full of tronics. I pushed the comlink up against the grille and waited
for Pally to give me some glad news.

"Fortune is with you, Butterfly," he told me a few
minutes later. "This is the main sentencing arena—the
housekeeping and security tronics use this for their central dispatch area during Third Shift. The lift to the Security Detention levels is just outside the door. You can
walk right through."

"Yeah?" I said. Leaving aside for the moment Paladin's definition of luck, there was the minor matter of
more rude mechanicals down below than I ever really
hoped to meet. And securitronics tend to be irritable.

" 'Yeah.' Housekeeping and Security are programmed
to avoid each other—I will provide them with the proper
code, and you will walk across the floor and out the other
door. As long as they receive the proper codes, the tronics will not care who you are. Just move slowly, as if you
were another machine."

"If this is so easy, why don't everyone come dancing
in here? Think of the valuta they could save on fines."

"In the first place, the recognition codes for the security devices are changed by the computer on a random
sequence. In the second place, it is generally accepted
that breaking into a prison is an unnecessary exertion."

I ignored that. I also knew there wasn't any other way
in.

I got a pocket-laser out of my bag of tricks and took
out the grille. I passed it over my back into the airshaft,
eased out through the hole until I was hanging by my
fingers, and dropped. I came up with the stunner ready,
but I couldn't see a thing. Heard the whine of servomo-

tors as a securitronic waddled over to me. It was a hand-span taller than me and much wider, with all its come-alongs and keep-aways and don't-worrys arranged neatly on its chest and arms. Its optical sensors glowed red in the dark but most of its dull gray hide was a dull gray blur. I wished I'd brought some night-goggles, but they would of raised eyebrows at the front desk when I was scanned and the info Pally had said the Justiciary was kept lit at night on all levels. On the other hand, if I died right here I wouldn't need to see anything.

The tronic turned and walked away.

"I told you so," Paladin said smugly. "Machines are stupid."

I was challenged twice more—once by another securi-tronic, once by a housekeeper—and each time Paladin answered for me. I carded the little access door set into the big "for-show" courtroom doors and slipped out.

The hall outside wasn't dark. It was pitch black.

"Helluva time for the high-heat to start economizing," I muttered, staring/not staring into the dark. "Now what?"

"Hm," said Paladin, just to let me know he was still there.

I could tune my pocket-laser to a torch, which the manufacturer does not recommend you do. I was just about to see if I could do it by feel when I heard heavy tronic-steps coming toward me and the whine of a house-keeper's treads coming up behind.

Paladin sang out in a flurry of musical notes as I scram-bled the securitronic right between its little red eyes with my stunner and then whipped out another shot to about where its brain ought to be. The guard hit the floor with a clatter, and the housekeeper nuzzled up to my ankles and went around me.

The nice thing about a solenoid stunner is that it's completely harmless to organics and death on tronic brains.

By the glow of my retuned laser I could see the house-keeper merrily disemboweling the ex-securitronic. The lift to Security Detention was a few meters away.

"Here's where thee-an-me subdivide, Pally," I said, trying to sound more confident than I felt.

"I will monitor all city-wide communications," he said,

not sounding really wild about all this either, "and brief
you when you come out."

When you come out. Thanks for vote of confidence,
little buddy. "Won't be long," I said.

The lift door opened. I got in and stood there for a
while feeling stupid, then it reopened on Detention level.

I was looking at a man in a CityGuard uniform standing in front of a console with a securitronic on either side
of him. I scrambled both of them, and while he was still
trying to figure out why they didn't work he let me get
close enough to him to hit him over the head with my
stunner.

Never depend on your technology.

Then I was past the check-in point and running down
a long corridor three tiers high and lined with doors. I'd
borrowed the Guardsman's blaster, so I used it to zap
two more tronics. I wished I had Paladin with me to tell
me about all the alarms and excursions being raised all
over the place.

Tiggy's cell was at the very end, but at least it was on
the bottom. I switched the setting on my borrowed
blaster from "annoy" to "leave no evidence" and blew
the lock out. The cell door sprang right open, and there
was my hellflower.

He was chained hand and foot for punishment drill,
and spread out on the wall pretty as a holo. The Justiciary'd took his jewels and all his clothes in payment of
fines, and he was wearing a pair of Det-ish pants that
didn't fit by a long shot.

And the look on his face was everything I could of
hoped for.

"*Chaudatu*," he finally said. "Not you again?"

"Yeah, me. I'm here to rescue you."

Later, when Paladin got his, um, hands on an alMayne
lexography, we found out that "*chaudatu*" means "out-
lander," except that what it really meant is "anyone who
is not alMayne and therefore not a real person." Unfortunately, even if I'd known that at the time it wouldn't
have made any difference.

I got out my picks and got to work on Tiggy's shack-
les—feet first, then hands—and hoped that Time, Fate,
and bureaucratic cock-up would give me the fistful of
nanoseconds needed to get the 'flower loose and on his

feet. After that, I figured my troubles were over. All we had to do was get us out of here alive, and Tiggy and me could go hide out. He could be grateful, and then I could bugout for Kiffit and write the next chapter of my memoirs.

He dropped to the floor when I got the last cuff off and stretched all over like a cat. Real pretty. I handed him the liberated blaster.

"Can use this-here?" I said in broad patwa.

He looked at it briefly. "Yes."

"Reet. Now hear me, che-bai—thing rigged for 'kill,' okeydoke? Not to dust organics with it. Fragging people buys bad trouble. Shoot at wartoys. Right?"

While I was talking, I was looking out into the corridor. The quiet was spooky, and there should of been more guards, but I didn't see any.

I looked back and Tiggy was regarding me with the expression of a hellflower what hadn't understood one word I'd said.

"Look, che-bai; shoot tronics, not organics. Zap-zap. Ch'habla— Understand?"

"Shoot only at security robots. *Dzain'domere*," said Tiggy gravely.

"Je, reet. Just don't shoot people." I was nervous and didn't have time to remember my Interphon.

He glared. I thought he was thinking of shooting me and to hell with freedom, but he nodded. We single-footed it out into the corridor. I wondered what jane-doh-meer meant in helltalk.

The wartoys on the tier above us started shooting.

I pulled Tiggy back against the wall and out of their line of fire. I remembered my plasma grenades and wondered if I should use them now. They were small, but still big enough so I didn't want to risk it unless we were in real trouble.

Six heavy-duty securitronics came trundling down the corridor toward us. They were about the size of the Imperial Debt and all business. I could see riot-gas launchers extruding from the chest of the leader as it came on.

We were in real trouble. I rolled a grenade toward them, body-blocked the 'flower back into his cell, and prayed.

The grenade went off.

There was smoke. Tiggy burned the wartoys on the tier above as I was finishing the six-pack on the floor. Grenade'd gone off right behind the leader, and the blast had splash-backed to destroy the next two. The other three was confused enough with memory-purge and magnetic-bubble scramble for Tiggy to totally blow them away as we jogged past.

There was probably alarms going off from here to Grand Central, but they was all silent—at least I couldn't hear them. I overrode the lift's lock-command from the main board out front. It wasn't that different than some Pally'd coached me on. Tiggy covered my back while I did it; his eyes was blazing like burning sapphires and he was grinning like he was enjoying himself. We picked up a couple rifles.

"Ten minutes, ninety seconds. Ten minutes, ninety-five seconds. Eleven minutes." Paladin was counting off, on the chance I'd be back to hear.

The corridor was still dark when we got back up to Sentencing. Then the lift shut behind us and everything went really dark. I got out my much abused laser. We had to get out now before word of our presence spread.

"Here we are, boys and girls," I said for Paladin's benefit.

"Are you all right? No alarm has been raised: The city is quiet, the Justiciary is not calling up any reserves, there have been no transmissions from Security Detention."

"C'mon," I said, to my hellflower and my partner. "This way. We're both fine for now—" that was for Paladin "—shoot any mechs you see, no matter what. And kid—"

"Do not shoot the people," Tiggy finished. "I know, *chaudatu*, but I think you are a fool."

There's gratitude for you. Not having dusted anyone in our escape probably wouldn't do us any good if we were caught, but I was feeling superstitious enough to think that virtue might be rewarded.

We made it out of Sentencing and back into Records. There was more light here. A quick riot-gas grenade would cover us on the way out of Receiving and—

—I looked around and Tiggy was halfway back down

the corridor, stopped dead and sight-seeing. I turned back.

"Ain't time to sightsee, 'flower. Grab sky!" I took him by his wrist and pulled. It was like trying to shift a neutronium statue.

"My *arthame, chaudatu*. I must have it."

Just what I needed. More hellflower gibberish.

"My Knife," Tiggy expanded. "I cannot leave without my Knife. They have taken it from me; do you know where it is?"

There wasn't anybody around to see or hear but there would be soon. "Look; I'll buy you a new one; c'mon!" I gave one last yank, which meant I was still holding on when Tiggy took off in the opposite direction. Ever been dragged down a empty hall by a hellflower oblivious to threats, comments, and reasonable objections? I don't recommend it.

Paladin picked up on what was going on from listening to me and started doing a nice counterpoint; telling me to ditch the glitterborn and kyte.

"Hold it, hold it—*hold it!*" I yelled, stopping one and shutting up the other. "Look—goddammit, 'flower, will you slow down? Just hold it a minute, forbye."

Tiggy Stardust stopped and glared glacially down at me from severalmany centimeters up.

"I will listen."

"You telling me you gonna throw it all away and go charging back inside to get yourself totally dusted and iced at least twice—for a *knife?*"

"I will not leave without it. I cannot. It is not a 'knife.' It is my—"

"Don't start. Won't make any more sense'n anything else you ever said. Whatever it is, you're going the wrong way. Your knife's in Property with the rest of your kit. I'll help you get it. Then we leave, je, che-bai?"

"*Dzain'domere.*" Right.

And they say *hellflowers* are crazy.

We dogged it back the other way and all of a sudden instead of empty the place was full of enough securitronics to reassure me that Wanderweb PortSec still had the good numbers. We had to blow them away before they could use gas, or ticklers, or anything else, and Paladin was so disgusted he didn't say damn-all. Real Soon Now

I figured City Central Computer'd change the securitronics' programming from "Contain" to "Destroy." I'd sort
of intended to be gone before that happened, but you
know how it gets. It'd been a while since I'd had this
much homegrown fun, and only the fact that it was me
and a hellflower doing the utterly unreasonable against
a bunch of tronics saved our bones.

* * *

Tiggy's knife was in Dead Storage, which was somewhere between Receiving and Records (being public-
access for financial reasons) and I wanted to get there
before we ran out of grenades, blaster-paks, and luck.
I'd of liked Paladin's input on which door to choose, but
he was still on strike and they all looked alike to me.

The high numbers was on City Central evacing organics from this section, sealing it, and calling up a shift of
coked wartoys from the Det levels to finish us. Fine. I
always did want to live fast, die young, and leave a pretty
corpse.

On the other hand, if I could just find Dead Storage,
I'd lay credit I wouldn't have to die at all. I said so.

"You should be in a corridor where the doors have
colors. The colors will be red and blue. Attempt all doors
which have the same color as the corridor walls," said
Paladin in my ear. He sounded resigned.

There was a door like that just ahead. I blew the lock,
it opened, we went in. I dogged it shut with the emergency manual controls. Tiggy looked around. I looked
around.

"Here you go, 'flower. Knife is somewheres in here."

The room was toodamn big—although even a phone
booth would of been too big right now—toodamn dark,
and toodamn full with toodamn many things. It looked
like every hock shop in the universe.

"What you should be seeing, Butterfly, is a large
room. All walls except the one behind you are lined with
cabinets. There' are rows of display cases containing
weaponry along the floor. There is no other access to the
room except the one you entered through. From what
the City Central Computer is saying to the Justiciary
computers, I do not believe your current location is

known. I suggest you find the hellflower's *arthame* quickly."

"Yeah, yeah," I muttered.

* * *

Wanderweb justice is run on the profit motive. Commit a crime here, and you get sentenced, which means the Justiciary sets a price on your head. You meet the price, you walk. You don't meet it, you're contract warmgoods, with your contract time equal to your price. Shorttimers go up for auction in the city. If your contract time runs longer than the projected life span for your B-pop, you're a slave. Slaves are factored directly to Market Garden. A few crimes call for execution—like Tiggy's.

But they still manage to lose money, so what does a cost-effective bureaucracy do to defray expenses? It confiscates the personal effects of offenders who can't meet their fines and sells them at auction.

Hence Dead Storage. Hence us.

* * *

"So what's this knife look like?" I asked Tiggy. I looked around for the display case that held heat-for-sale. Might as well help him look.

"You saw it when I held it to your throat, three days past."

"Oh, too reet—all we're looking for is inert-blade sword as long as my arm. In all this."

Being as they're what keep Wanderweb Fiduciary in the green, weapons are prominently displayed. Didn't see any inert-blades, but I zapped the lock off the case anyway and started looking through it.

"You have just set off every intruder alarm remaining untriggered in the entire Wanderweb Justiciary," Paladin said.

"Great," I told the immediate world, hefting an Estel-Shadowmaker handcannon too pretty to leave and wondering where I could put it. I tucked it into my shirt and added a necklace of grenades. I started to throw away the comlink, then thought it might be handy if Paladin could hear the hellflower too, so I kept it.

There was a wrenching sound, and I looked up to see Tiggy Stardust ripping open the locked cabinets on the wall with his bare hands. Some B-pops have it, some don't. Hellflowers have more of it than most. The first drawer held jewelry, and he threw it down.

"Would it do any good at all to tell you to abandon the alMayne and leave now?" asked Paladin. "They know where you are, Butterfly. The alarm has been raised, the CityGuard has been mobilized Port-wide, and quarantine has been declared—the spaceport has been closed."

Closed Port. Nothing goes in, nothing goes out. I tried to remember if there were any tractors or pressors on the section of the field where I was docked.

"All this just for us," I said, and Tiggy shot me a funny look. I expect he was thinking I meant the glitterflash he'd just dropped, but it reminded me that one does not talk to one's beaucoup-illegal Library in front of a witness—even if the witness had no way of knowing who or what or even where I was chaffering with.

I waved. He went back to vandalism. "No," I said to Paladin's question.

Tiggy's coke-gutter had to be in one of the cabinets because it sure and t'hell wasn't in any of the display cases. We found it in the last drawer of the last cabinet of the whole wall and Tiggy grabbed it like it was hard credit on payday and stuffed it into his waistband. I'd took the time to find a couple of rifles to replace the last set we'd emptied and was just handing him one when we both heard the teeth-edging whine of a fusion-cutter setting to work.

"Well hell," I said. "J'ais tuc. You and your damn knife." Paladin'd said there was just one way out of Dead Storage, and the fusion-cutter was in the middle of it.

"It is not a "knife." It is my *arthame*. We will die nobly and with honor, and they who have unjustly attacked a son of the Gentle People will weep when the vengeance of my clan—"

"I don't want to die with honor! I don't want to die at all if I can help it—and I certainly don't want to die here, with you, after you futzed up your own rescue, you dumb *noke-ma'ashki* alMayne!"

He might not of known what the words meant, but he

sure followed the tune. He had The Knife Worth A Afterlife out and pointing at me, which did not bother me half as much as the fusion-cutter did.

"Butterfly!" Paladin shouted in my ear. Tiggy took a step toward me. I wondered if that thing could slice as well as he obviously thought it could.

"Not now," I suggested without hope. They both ignored me.

"The plans I have of that level of the Justiciary show an air vent leading out of Storage and Receivables that should get you past the sealed section. And if you keep talking to the alMayne like that you won't have to attempt it—you'll be dead."

Thank you, Paladin. "Death is least of my worries," I said aloud. On the other hand, Paladin did have a point.

"Look here, hellflower, how'd you like to live and grow old and raise up a whole garden of 'flowers instead of buying real estate?"

Tiggy continued looking earnest. Fusion-cutter continued upping the ambient temperature in Dead Storage by leaps and boggles. Paladin continued wringing his hands in my ear.

"We can get out through vents. There's one in here— see? And you look skinny enough to fit."

But oddly enough Tiggy Stardust did not look like escape was high on his list of life goals. I said how 'flowers drop everything for a good old honor-bashing session, and here I was getting one free for nothing. The fusion-cutter was just about in with us, the door was as pink and glowing as an Imperial sub-lieutenant, and I gave up and decided it was time to play ace-king-trump.

"Saved your life, o'nobly-born—at least you should have the good manners to cooperate in your own rescue."

That got him. He looked real pained—not as fried as me for having had to push his honor buttons but miffed all the same—and put his sacred ferrous oxide butter-spreader away.

"Very well, *chaudatu*. I will cooperate. What is it that you wish?"

"The damn air vent. It's got to be around here some-wheres, and then you an me can—" There it was—about halfway up the wall and probably just as hard to get the grille off as the last one was. "Can climb wall, ace cover off vent?"

He looked up, nodded, and went back to glaring at me with pellucid raptor-blue eyes. Damn but don't I love having cannon-fodder to do the heavy work.

"So do it. And get in. I'll follow you." I turned my attention to covering our retreat.

*   *   *

The *legitimates* should of been a tad bit more cautious. I mean, the confiscated weaponry in Dead Storage would do credit to an Imperial Armory, and a whole lot of it was catch-traps and explosives of one flavor or another.

I climbed up a cabinet using the open drawers for footholds and played ringtoss with some grenades for hoops and the door for a spindle. By now the door was yellow-white. The grenades stuck, and a moment later they blew, and I fell off the cabinet but rallied dazzling-like in time to catch a glimpse of Wanderweb Guardsmen in full powered armor lying in a tangled heap around their fusion-cutter. Then it was up in the sky junior birdmen time for yours truly, and being dragged up a wall by a cross hellflower with your lungs full of caustic perdition is another experience I don't recommend.

*   *   *

"Hellflower?" I said to some of Tiggy's more interesting backbones a while later.

"Ea, chaudatu?"

"You can shoot organics now."

"Thank you, *chaudatu.*"

I figured by now that my choices on Wanderweb was death or life-contract slavery, so it didn't really matter now how many people I shot on the rest of the way out. Over the RTS Paladin was getting as close to using harsh language as he ever had, saying how I should of dusted Love's Young Dream about six firefights ago, that I thought with my internal organs, that Wanderweb Free Port was going borneo trying to figure out what was going on, and, oh yes, I'd started a nice oxy-fire on the

Admin level I'd just left and had I thought about how I was going to get to the lift to the surface?

I wanted to tell him I was sure he'd think of something, but Tiggy already thought I had fusion for supercargo and I figured one more toy in my attic and he'd shop me sure. So I concentrated on making time and distance through the vent and telling Tiggy where to head in, and regretting the impulse that made me pick up all that hardware back in the duty free zone we'd just left. My bruises had bruises, and on top of that, the vent was starting to fill with smoke.

It was getting to look like Pally'd picked the wrong grid for a first-and-last when I started to see a faint light on the walls that ought to be the main Receiving station. When we got up closer I tapped Tiggy and asked what he saw.

"A room. A desk. Many armed men in blue livery with Wanderweb City service marks. I count twelve *chau-datu* and six mechanicals, all armed and armored. Beyond these is a lift door."

"That is the lift you want," Paladin said, having listened in on this deathless chat by way of my comlink. "It will take you directly to ground level. There is a barricade on the lift, but it is lightly manned. Your speeder is still outside. I am doing preflight warm-up on *Firecat*. And I still think that this is not an intelligent form of recreation."

And sometimes I wonder why I keep him. "We want the lift," I said to Tiggy. "They're trying to keep us down here, so they won't have too many slugs at ground level. Burn the grille and drop these through it." While we was talking, I was trying to get some grenades out of my vest and into his hands—no cheap trick in a vent a little wider than my shoulders. "And hold your breath when you do—is riot-gas, je? Riot-gas—bad stuff." I hoped he was getting the idea, since Tiggy didn't seem to be real ace with Interphon. For that matter, neither was I. "Get to lift and be ready to come out other side blazing. I got speeder. When we're out, we heading for spaceport."

"I have a shuttle there," said Tiggy.

"No hope. By time you're ready to rock 'n' roll, you'll be took. We get up side in my ship."

"Just the three of us," Paladin murmured in my ear.

"I thought you didn't carry live freight, Independent Captain-Owner St. Cyr."

"Is emergency," I commented to world at large.

"But that shuttle is FirstLeader Starborn's property!" Tiggy yelped. "I cannot abandon it!"

I jabbed him hard in the nearest bit I could reach. "Will you get us t'hell out of here before I die of old age? Worry about it later!"

"Cover your eyes, *chaudatu*."

I took a deep breath and did, and felt the back-blast as Tiggy blew the grille. Then the grenades went, and Tiggy slithered forward. I picked up and followed.

* * *

The *legitimates* never knew what hit them. Gas burned on my skin; I threw grenades like firecrackers and shot tronics. The hardware shot back, and so did the software, and I had to open my eyes to see but at least I hadn't breathed. Didn't worry about ducking because there weren't no place to duck to. Bumped into Tiggy and knocked him into lift just as it opened. He shoved me behind him and blew away a couple of Guardsmen just as the doors closed.

Nice to see a hellflower happy in his work.

I mopped at my leaking eyes, pulled off a glove to do it more efficiently, and noticed my jacket was on fire. I batted out the sparks and explored the burn. Tender, but the skin hadn't been cooked open and that made me luckier than I deserved.

"You all right?" I said to the boy wonder.

He was staring at my sleeve. "You have shed blood for me," he said, reverent-like.

"Huh?" I said, real bright. "Don't be silly, bai, burns don't—"

Then the lift doors opened again and we charged out full-tilt boogie and blasters blazing right over the barricade set up in front of the door. Out of the corner of my eye I saw Tiggy pick up and throw a tronic just like it was a cuddly toy and then whip out that knife of his and slice open a Guardsman while firing his rifle left-handed.

That made a total of nine Guardsmen he'd dusted, if anyone was counting.

I chased after Tiggy as he ran by and whipped the last of the grenades off my neck and tossed them behind me just for luck as we ran down the steps.

The speeder was right where I left it, bless all the good numbers, so I jumped in and keyed up the ignition while Tiggy swarmed in over the back. We took off at top speed into oncoming traffic just as the CityGuard in force came charging down the steps of the Justiciary.

Paladin gave me a running commentary about where the barricades in the city was. There wasn't much traffic on the flybys this late in Third Shift, so we took some scenic shortcuts and got around all the security check-points except the one at the Port.

That one we ran over.

*   *   *

By the time we reached it, Wanderweb heat hadn't been able to track us for the longest time, owing to a unfortunate spasm in the City Central Computer traffic monitors. Paladin said they was sure we was somewhere on the other side of the city. So the shellycoats at the Port found a moment to be real surprised when Tiggy and me drove my rented speeder over their shiny purple-and-yellow barricade, then into the freight lift that serviced *Firecat*'s wing of the Port. I lost the comlink somewhere along the way. Big deal.

Paladin overrode the lockups that the Port Computer was trying to put on the lift. We drove out of the lift into the docking ring before PortSec could figure out which ship we was trying to reach, and jumped out of the speeder into the ship. Simple.

Then we took off.

I was never so glad to have a invisible co- as I was then. *Firecat* started taking off before I had her lock sealed, and by the time I was strapped into the mercy seat we was oriented toward the bay opening. I let Paladin Thread the Needle for me while I finished strapping in, and then I grabbed a handful of lifters and firewalled her.

I heard Tiggy go thump amongst the rokeach and then

stopped thinking about him. The air show I had to put on to get out of range of Wanderweb's stratospheric interceptors impressed even me, but Wanderweb jurisdiction extends only as far as its atmosphere. It wasn't worth them getting into deep heat with Grand Central to chase us out into Imperial space, so eventually they got tired of shooting and left me alone. I'd better make up my mind to never coming back here for my next sixty incarnations or so, but unless Wanderweb Free Port wanted to hire a bounty hunter to chase me around the Outfar Pally and me was safe now.

When all the ground-to-orbit wartoys was back in their boxes on downside scenic Wanderweb, I put *Firecat* into a nice high orbit over Wanderweb City.

We'd won.

"What are you going to do with the alMayne mercenary now, Butterfly?" Paladin asked in a voice that only I could hear.

Real interesting question.

I had a cargo for Kiffit under my deck plates that I'd meant to lift with thirty hours ago. If *Firecat* wasn't to Kiffit in reasonable time, there'd be questions I'd hate to answer and penalty fees that'd seriously compromise my old age pension. No matter how decorative Tiggy was, he was going to have to take second place to business.

So Tiggy had to go, and without showing me his gratitude or anything else. The question was—where?

I levered myself up out of the mercy seat and raised the cockpit up into the hold.

Right now I wanted everything I'd done myself out of on Wanderweb with my little jailbreak—wet bath, fresh meal, clean clothes, and something done about my burns and bruises. It's a sad fact of hypership ecology that very few of these things was to be had now this side of Kiffit.

I headed for my emergency medical supplies and got out my box of Fenshee burntwine. Toxins is toxins, but this was a emergency.

My pet hellflower was sitting on the deck looking at me. His cutlery was tucked through the waistband of his Wanderweb Detention Issue pants and in his lap he was holding the blaster he'd picked up in Dead Storage. He was sweaty and grimy from the night's occupations, and his hair was hanging down around his face in your basic tousled mop.

I wondered who he was when he was to home. He hadn't chatted much to the Justiciary computer. Despite all we'd meant to each other, I still didn't even know his name. On the plus side, he didn't look any toodamn bent out of shape with me. It'd be a real shame if something that decorative bought real estate, and Paladin would sign Tiggy's lease for sure if he iced me.

Try breathing sometime in a ship with the lock jammed open and the atmosphere venting. It's nice to have friends.

"Hey, hellflower," I said, breaking the seal on the box. "You got a name? T'name-je, bai? Namaste'amo?"

Tiggy stood up. You got the impression he'd just been waiting to be asked. "I am the Honorable *Puer* Walks-by-Night Kennor's-son Starbringer Amrath Valijon of Chernbereth-Molkath."

"Butterfly, we are in very deep trouble." Paladin could see and hear Tiggy now the same way he could me—through the pickups in *Firecat*'s hull.

"Fung wa?" I said. "Would you mind repeating that?" I said carefully to the hellflower in my best Interphon. He did. It came out the same way it had before: Honorable walks by night and the whole rest of it. My little hole card was more than just a problem. He was more than just any old poor little rich killer.

"Valijon Starbringer is cousin to the alMayne king, Amrath Starborn, and son of the alMayne delegate to the Court of the TwiceBorn, Kennor Starbringer. Kennor Starbringer is also the president of the Azarine Coalition."

Thank you, Paladin. That pedigree made Tiggy bad news. Daddy Starbringer was the law west of the Chullite Stars, the heat, the fuzz, the *legitimates*, the galactic agent of His Imperial Majesty (Entropy bless and keep him far away from me). In short, Tiggy was nobody and the son of nobody this simple 'legger, dicty-barb, and companion to Libraries wanted to have to do with.

"Not?" I said hopefully.

"I am the Third Person of House Starborn. My father is the Delegate to the Imperium. His sister's bond-sister's son is Amrath Starborn, FirstLeader of the Gentle People. The alMayne consular ship *Pledge Of Honor*," Tiggy went on in mildly conversational tones, "is currently orbiting the *chaudatu*-planet. I am a member of the Delegate-my-father's staff. And my people are looking for me, *chaudatu*-Captain."

Third Person Peculiar

Tiggy Stardust *nee* Valijon Starbringer looked at me. I looked at him. He showed me his teeth, and I remembered for how many human races a smile wasn't a smile.

So I had a drink. Then I had another drink. Tiggy had a drink too, and said I should call him "Honored One."

I wondered why t'hell he hadn't mentioned his interesting family to Wanderweb Justiciary when they'd brought him in, and said so. He said it was a matter of honor.

Honor. Hah. I knew for damn sure the alMayne would of fried Wanderweb to bare rock once they found Tiggy dead and I bet Tiggy would of thought the joke was worth it.

I took another hit off the box of burntwine and left it with him, since he seemed to appreciate the bennies of a fine vintage neurotoxin, and tottered back up to the mercy seat. When I lowered the cockpit through the hull again Wanderweb was still down there, looking peaceful.

I could tell Pally was just waiting to have words with me, which was damn considerate since he could have any words he wanted and I couldn't say no never-you-mind. I put my Best Girl's extra ears on and started listening for ID beacons. Tiggy'd been downside in a shuttle, and it had to come from somewhere. Maybe somewhere'd be glad to have him back.

"The authorities will call it kidnapping, you know," Paladin said in my ear. Considerate of him not to use the bulkhead speakers. I looked around. Tiggy was sitting in the back of the hold with burntwine and blaster looking as stubborn and patient as a cat I'd used to have.

"What authorities?" I finally said. "Hellflowers?"

I didn't find anything orbiting Wanderweb on my first pass and set up to try again. It was a damn shame I couldn't ask Wanderweb Central what they had in their sky, but didn't think they'd be real responsive somehow.

"Not kidnapping when you give it back, Pally."

"And what do you expect the Port Authority to say when questioned? Someone will have to be culpable in the matter of what has happened to Valijon Starbringer. The alMayne will insist. And the penalty for interfering with a member of an Ambassadorial Delegation is . . . extreme, Butterfly."

"So we send babby-bai across to *Pledge* in lifepak soon as we get near it. He'll square his folks—or not. Hell, Pally, what's one more warrant going to matter?"

"Kidnapping one of the TwiceBorn is a class-A offense. How many more can you afford? You have, as you are fully aware, three already: illegal emigration from an Interdicted World, nonpayment of chattel indenture, and . . . me."

Paladin must be really torqued to mention the last bit. Usually we just pretend there ain't no such thing as Class One High Book.

"Already know I'm dicty-barb, runaway slave, and . . . you know," I pointed out. "Tell me new things, che-bai."

"I will tell you that you cannot afford to attract attention. That you cannot afford another class-A warrant, especially one that will be so actively prosecuted. That if I had known who Valijon Starbringer was in the first place, I would—"

"You'd what?"

"I would have told you this earlier," Paladin finished primly.

I went back to my sensor-sweeps.

If Pally said the penalty was extreme, I didn't want to know what it was. Even if Tiggy did true-tell his da, I didn't know what hellflower logic'd turn his story into.

"Then we just better hurry up and find *Pledge* so's we can get t'hell out of here, j'keyn?"

"Ideally," said Paladin. I groaned. All I needed was for my best buddy to have a case of the more-ascetic-than-thous the whole way to Kiffit.

Besides which, it was getting to be obvious there wasn't any consular ship highbinding my ex-favorite Free Port.

"Oh, Paladin. Where is *Pledge of Honor?*"

"If you had not decided to meddle in the merciful and reasonable justice of the Empire," Paladin said, sounding cross, "we would not be in this situation now, Butterfly."

"Yeah, yeah, yeah," I said, trying to keep my voice low. "Never mind it's Free Port profit, not Imp justice, and Tiggy wouldn't of been up for the chop if he hadn't saved my bones."

"If you had not interfered in the first place, your alMayne nobleman would have murdered K'Jarn and been taken into custody over an offense less extortionately overpriced."

So now Tiggy was *my* hellflower glitterborn, was he? I could think of only one real good reason for Pally to be that torqued.

"Bai, where's *Pledge Of Honor?*"

There was a real long silence if you consider how fast Paladin chopped logic.

"I cannot find it, Butterfly. It isn't here."

I didn't ask him if he was sure. If anyone wanted to find the hellflower garden more than me, my silent partner did.

* * *

I pulled the heads-up console farther down over my face and thought about Life, hellflowers, and scenic Wanderweb.

One, if I didn't hit angeltown pretty soon, I'd miss my meet on Kiffit, which could be trouble.

Two, if my antisocial lovestar's ticket out of my life wasn't where he said it was, either it never had been there or it'd left. I didn't think Tiggy knew how to farce, but if he was true-telling why wasn't *Pledge* here?

Three, I had one sincere headache. It was composed of equal parts class-A warrants, Libraries, and the laws of physics. As follows:

A—I couldn't take Tiggy back downside in *Firecat*. One, they'd cut off his head, two, I couldn't get down and back alive, and three, it would make me even later to Kiffit if I tried.

B—I couldn't take Tiggy with me. *Firecat* was a little ship, all engines, marginal life-support, and an Old Fed-

eration Library under the mercy seat. Even if I wanted
to chance Tiggy twigging Paladin, I couldn't ship him all
over the Empire in a ship the size of a Teaser's conscience. For one thing, I wasn't sure we'd both be alive
when we got to Kiffit, air being what it was. Not to
mention the fact that he was all tangled up in his honor
by now and was probably going to try to purify the
whirling fusion out of me soon as he figured out the best
way.

And if I did take Tiggy to Kiffit, it'd be a real kidnapping for sure, and no way of talking myself out of the
charge.

But if I didn't either take the hellflower with me to
Kiffit or put him back on the heavy side here at Wanderweb, that left only one thing to do with Tiggy Stardust—all of which made the evening's fun not
particularly funny, and never mind that if I hadn't
showed up he'd of been dead in a few hours anyway.

He'd been in the Last Gasp looking for me. And
because he had been, I was alive now and he'd killed
serious Guardsmen, for which Wanderweb wanted to
chop him.

I sat there and thought about it, and punched up the
numbers for the High Jump to Kiffit, and looked at my
life-support inventories and counted on my fingers. Paladin knew what I was doing, but he didn't say zip.

And when everything was done but making up my
mind, I raised the cockpit back into the hull again and
went back to talk to my passenger.

Firecat's internal compensators weren't good enough
that she could of moved without him noticing, and after
our takeoff Tiggy Stardust knew it. He put his knife away
and stood up. Different cultures have different body language. On alMayne I bet this didn't mean respect.

"Ea, chaudatu?"

"You ain't going to like this, che-bai. Your ship ain't
there."

I still wasn't ready for way he moved.

"You are lying!" Tiggy snarled in my ear. He'd
wrapped himself around all my bruises hard enough to
hurt, and had his alMayne *arthame* snugged up to several
of my important veins. If I flinched in the wrong direc-

tion I'd be nonfiction, but if I didn't know people I would of sold my bones a long time ago.

Tiggy was scared.

"Hellflower, I am for-sure sorry your folks ain't there. But it ain't nice to pull heat on people for true-tell." I talked real slow, trying to punch it across two languages. I didn't flinch neither, and eventually he let me go.

"They could not leave! How could they have left? It is not possible that they should leave; they—" Tiggy went off into helltongue, ramifying his position, which was pretty to listen to and told me precisely nothing. Paladin didn't know it either, at least not well enough to translate.

"The *Pledge Of Honor* was not listed at the Wanderweb ships-in-port directory, thus we may infer that its stop here was not an official one. The most reasonable construction to place upon the matter of the ship's absence from the area now is that the *Pledge Of Honor* departed according to a predetermined schedule. If it were bound for Grand Central, a plausible hypothesis considering its nature as a consular vessel, the captain would have had no other option. Whether the legation was aware of Valijon Starbringer's absence from its midst at the time of departure is a matter for conjecture at this time," said Paladin.

I rubbed my neck and counted my new bruises. Paladin still sounded just like a talkingbook, which meant he was still mad. I thought I'd share his facts with Tiggy.

"Was Da shopping cubic for Throne? He'd of had to kyte by mandated o'chrono no matter where you was," I said. Tiggy stared at me, glazed and blank like a well-scrubbed palimpsest.

"Try Interphon," suggested Paladin in my ear, which was fine for him but it'd been a long day and I was tired.

"*Pledge* is gone, j'ai?" I said to Tiggy. "Scanners don't lie, not mine, if gardenship was highbinding—orbiting—it isn't there now."

Tiggy nodded, looking sulky.

"When *Pledge* tik'd to Wanderweb, was on way to Throne—Grand Central—ImpCourt, j'ai?"

Another nod. Communication was reliably established with the mentally underprivileged.

"So TwiceBorn jump salty if you're late, see? So

Pledge topped angels on sked, and you pick up ship on next downfall." Wherever that was. I wasn't paying for a long-distance call to Grand Central to find out, neither.

"But they do not know I'm gone! They cannot know—they would not have left if they had known! My father—"

Terrific. "Kyted downside on sly to rumble Gentry-ken?" I was beginning to wonder just how old Tiggy was.

"Maybe it would be better if you learned alMayne," said my ever-helpful partner. "Or helltongue, if you prefer." I looked at Tiggy's blank expression and tried again.

"You went to planetary surface n'habla—" damn, what was the Interphon? "without—your parent's knowledge?" I said careful, counting off the words on my fingers. It was like being back in Market Garden Acculturation class, and I hadn't liked it then, either.

"I am not obligated to discuss these matters with you, *chaudatu.* There was no reason I should not visit Wanderweb. I am the Third Person of House Starborn—and he who says I may not go where I wish lives without walls!" Tiggy put his knife back in his waistband and tossed his hair back out of his eyes.

The words might be helltalk, but the tune was real familiar.

"How t'hell old are you anyway, Tiggy-che-bai?"

Tiggy goggled at me like he couldn't figure where the question was coming from, but all of a sudden I thought it was real important.

"You will address me with respect as Honored One, she-captain."

"J'ai; about the time you stop calling me she-captain, forbye. Now true-tell Mother Sincere facts."

"What has this to do with the *Pledge Of Honor*? If they have gone on to Royal you must follow them at once."

"Why?" If *Pledge*'d gone on to Royal in the Tortuga Sector *Firecat* wasn't following it for any credit. There was a rebellion going on in Tortuga against the Brightlaw Corporation, the family that ran the Tortuga Directorate, which meant Governor General his Nobly-Bornness Mallorum Archangel and his joy-boys'd be all over it, arguing Directorate jurisdiction against sector jurisdiction and making Tortuga cubic real unhealthy for my favorite dicty and other living things.

I sat down on a crate of rokeach and took off my jacket. I'd forgot about the burn on my arm; I scraped it and hissed. Tiggy tried to explain how I had to go chasing off into this free-fire zone full of Azarine mercs while I tried to get a biopak out of the medkit and over one helluva painful nuisance. Finally we both gave up.

"Hold still," he said firmly. "You cannot do that yourself. I will bandage you, and you will explain why you are detaining a servant of the Gentle People."

"That's you, I suppose." My baseline Interphon was finally coming back to me, but it still felt funny to the taste. "And what makes you think, glitterborn, you got any idea what to do with battle-dressings?"

"A warrior of the Gentle People must always be able to see to his *comites, chaudatu.* You are my responsibility, even if you are not very much of one. You have shed blood for me."

"Like hell." Bent out of shape or not, Tiggy had a glitterborn way of doing the pretty. Nasty.

"I do not see any painkillers here," he said like it was my fault.

"You drank it. You may of noticed by now, o'nobly-born, that this is a freighter, not a high-ticket outhostel. And I want to keep it in one piece, not do a conversion to plasma on the Royal ecliptic."

"House Starbringer will pay for my return, since ransom is what concerns you, *chaudatu,*" said Tiggy, once the dressing was in place. He took an eloquent look around my Best Girl's hold and went over and sat on a crate.

I reminded myself that he was a homicidal lunatic.

"Butterfly, let me—" Paladin began.

"Ransom," I said, flat. Tiggy looked up. "Tiggy Stardust, is time you got lesson in big-bad galaxy—which you should of got before you went off to play with the big kids in the never-never. You chaffer on about ransom like it meant something and people was going to play kiss-my-hand and wait around to collect it with glitterborn rules and all. Well, K'Jarn was going to kill you for what you was standing up in back on Wanderweb and probably sell you to a bodysnatcher before you got cold. That's ransom in the never-never."

Tiggy's face was unreadable as a plaster saint's. "What will you do, if you will not return me to my people?"

"If I put you back on the heavy side here, Justiciary's going to chop you. If I chase into Royal, I'll get blown up. So I'm taking you to Kiffit. Got cargo for there, people're waiting,"

"No," said Paladin. I ignored him.

Tiggy pulled out his knife again, which was a argument but not a good one. "I do not wish to go to this Kiffit. The *Pledge Of Honor* is going to Royal, and—"

"Put that coke-gutter of yours away before I ram it down your glitterborn throat. Lesson Number One in the Real World: You can kill me but you can't make me fly you anywhere."

"Butterfly, will you please—"

"I can fly," said Tiggy uneasily.

"Not this ship, che-bai. When I die, it blows up. I'm going to Kiffit, and so are you. Think *Firecat*'s maybe got enough air to get us both there, if we're lucky. Better chance than you got otherways. I'll take that risk."

"Butterfly, you saw the figures. There is only a seventy percent chance you will both survive to reach Kiffit. It is not worth the risk."

"I have thirty-four years," Tiggy said.

"Por-ke?" I said. He didn't savvy patwa, but he answered.

"You asked me how old I was, *ch*—Captain. I have thirty-four years."

"Standard?" Hell, *I* have thirty-four years Standard; if Tiggy was my age I'd eat all five of *Firecat*'s goforths.

"No. Real years."

"What's the conversion?" I said, and after a long time it was Paladin that answered me.

"Thirty-four years alMayne is equal to fourteen Imperial Standard Years. Butterfly, there is one chance in four that you will die."

I still ignored him. I already knew the numbers. I looked at Tiggy. He didn't look fourteen, but different human races age differently. I was already halfway through my expectancy, assuming I lived long enough to die in bed.

Which didn't look too likely just now. And it didn't at this moment matter what the Hellflower Years of Discretion were, either.

"You're fourteen. Terrific." Under the Codex Imperador Tiggy had to be twenty to be a grown-up, and he wasn't. So the rap for him was child-kidnap; worse than before, if that was possible.

"I am adult. I have my *arthame*. I am a legal Person of House Starborn—" He stopped. "And honor demands that I die now with honor; for allowing me that you have the gratitude of my House." He looked around.

"And where t'hell you think you're going, kinchin-bai?"

"I will go out your air lock, Captain—even a ship like this must have one. I cannot put you at risk in your journey. You have saved my life and served me well. I will not imperil you further."

I'd been fourteen once. Fortunately it hadn't been permanent.

"It is very nearly a reasonable solution," said Paladin, helpfully. Real reasonable; I wouldn't even have to cold-cock the stupid brat and shove him out my lock; he'd do it himself.

Except it wasn't his fault that his daddy'd kyted, or that nobody'd told Tiggy the galaxy had teeth big enough to chew hellflowers.

"Oh, give it a rest, willya? You and me is going to Kiffit and I'll turn you in to the Azarine Guildhouse there. They send you home, I get shut of you, everything's copacetic."

Tiggy looked around in panic. "But you cannot do that." He looked like he preferred microwave death to spending another hour on *Firecat*.

"Is my ship and I'll freight what I want. Ain't done rescuing you yet, so remember honor, Tiggy-bai."

"Honor is better than bread," agreed Tiggy darkly, which just showed how many meals he'd missed.

He slanted a interested glance at me, like he was thinking of unfinished honor-bashing session. But he'd back down for now, which was all I cared about. And maybe the kidnap charge wouldn't stick.

Yeah, and maybe I wouldn't run into Dominich Fenrir on Kiffit.

* * *

I went back up to the mercy seat. The good numbers for Kiffit was right where I left them.

"He is dangerous. Do not do this, Butterfly," said Paladin, quiet as if anyone could hear.

"What else can I do, babby? Fourteen-year-old kinchin-bai." I pulled the stick for the Drop and my Best Girl wrenched herself out of the here-and-now like a homesick angel.

* * * * *

Insert #3: Paladin's Log

What began as an extremely dangerous amusement became an extremely costly one when the jailbreak of the alMayne Valijon Starbringer escalated to the point that Wanderweb Port Security became involved. When Valijon Starbringer became, in effect, stranded aboard *Firecat* the affair ceased to resemble anything amusing at all.

Firecat is not a passenger ship, for one very good reason. Any passenger aboard *Firecat* is in a position to discover my existence and Butterfly's cooperation with me, and that discovery would inevitably result in our destruction. And of all the potential passengers to take aboard *Firecat*, Valijon Starbringer might very well be the most dangerous.

It is Butterfly's opinion that politics interferes with "bidness," that there is business to be done under any government, and under all governments what she does is illegal. These things are all true, but do not in and of themselves constitute an excuse for ignorance. If Butterfly were more aware of "current events," she would understand why Valijon Starbringer—the only son of the alMayne delegate to the Court of the TwiceBorn, Kennor Starbringer, who is the deciding vote on the Azarine Coalition Council—was such an extremely dangerous commodity to have inboard.

There are 144 Directorates in the Phoenix Empire—144 astropolitical divisions of the Phoenix Empire, each of which is governed by the Corporation families. From these families are drawn the members of the Imperial Court—the TwiceBorn. The TwiceBorn are the social and economic elite of the Empire and rule all the rest, civil and military alike. Below the TwiceBorn come citizens, and below them client-members, and below them slaves. Then resident aliens (what Butterfly calls, with a fine disregard for species distinction, "wigglies"), and then, at last, the nightworld rabble of which Butterfly is a part.

Valijon Starbringer was not TwiceBorn. The Starborn Corporation—the form his alMayne princely House takes in the Empire at large—does not choose that its alMayne subjects accept Imperial honors except when unavoidable. Kennor Starbringer is TwiceBorn. Amrath Starborn—their "king"—is not.

The alMayne do not like those who are not alMayne, no matter how high their estate.

I do not remember them from the days I was the Library at the University of Sikander. They are a new race, yet records speak of them as very old. I do not like paradoxes of this sort, and I do not like the alMayne. Irrationally xenophobic, reactionary, conservative, they prefer to stagnate in their elegant barbarism than to change and grow. Such a barbarian, trapped aboard *Firecat*, could be expected to do something dangerously irrational.

The alMayne, as a race, might be seen to be irrational. Butterfly says "hellflowers is crazy" and feels no need for further explanation.

I do. I have studied these elegant barbarians, hellflowers, "Gentle People." I could have translated Valijon's speech for Butterfly. I did not choose to. It would not have made her jettison him, nor would she have understood even the translation.

"Hellflowers" do not have a modern psychology. Their entire culture is focused upon the willingness to die for intangibles such as personal honor. "*Dzain'domere*" means "I pledge and give my word." Thus it is bound up in alMayne concepts of honor which are indeed "better than bread." An alMayne can live for quite some time without food: an alMayne who is doubted—disbelieved in—ceases to exist instantly.

Their suicide rate is high, as might be expected; it is the index of stress on a nearly pretechnological, highly ritualized culture attempting to fit itself into the Phoenix Empire.

The Azarine Coalition Council, of which Kennor Star-bringer of alMayne is president, decides policy matters for the Coalition at large. Its primary business is the ratification and modification of the terms of the Gordinar Canticles, the charter under which the Coalition operates. The Canticles cover, in broad, matters affecting the governance of hired armies, from the weapons they may carry, to the targets they may be used against, to the persons and organizations who may hire them. The key canticle is the matter of who may lawfully hire mercenary armies. As it currently stands, any sophont or entity may; the checks and balances arise from the Coalition defining the targets against which they may not be used, and the base price for a mercenary's services.

To construct an example: Naturally it is illegal to hire a mercenary army to oppose any of the edicts of the Emperor, the Throne, the Court, or any of the TwiceBorn—the Imperial bureaucracy. However, it is certainly legal to hire mercenary troops to overthrow a Corporation—the ruling entity of a Directorate. But a Corporation so menaced can appeal to the sector governor for aid, who can provide the Corporation with Imperial troops, which the mercenaries cannot legally oppose. But for a Corporation to do this is to invite Imperial attention, and the causes of the original war will go into arbitration. It is not unheard of for a Corporation to appeal for help against rebellious forces and have all its assets turned over to the rebels. Imperial justice, as the folk-wisdom goes, is obscure.

One can see, therefore, that, for example, a modification of the Canticles to forbid Azarine troops to fight Corporation troops would be very much to the Corporations' benefit. One can further see that there could be a great deal of special interest group pressure on the Coalition Council to make partisan changes to the Gordinar Canticles.

At the moment the Coalition Council is evenly divided between those who wish to make major changes to the Canticles, including the List of Protected Groups, and those who wish to leave the Canticles as they are. Kennor Star-bringer, as president, could cast a deciding vote either way. At the moment he is a strict Constructionist, and will not vote for change.

Should he die or resign, his Council membership will go

to the alMayne Morido Dragonflame, who favors complete revision of the Canticles.

Seen in this light, Valijon Starbringer is a playing piece in a very high-stakes game indeed. Butterfly's safety depends on staying far from the attention such matters bring, and she knows it. It is fortunate that Valijon Starbringer's appearance on Wanderweb was an accident, and that no one knows where he is now.

I wonder.

Considering the money lost in the action, why would Wanderweb shut down its entire Port to prevent the escape of two relatively unimportant criminals?

4

Dead Heat On A
Merry-Go-Round

I was dreaming and I knew it, and part of me thought I ought to wake up and keep an eyeball on Tiggy, but I'd finished the second box of burntwine a while back because my backteeth and all of my bruises hurt and Tiggy could do me any time he got around his honor anyway.

So I watched myself sleep, the way you do in dreams. I was back home on Granola, running off early in the morning to play hooky. The light was slanting rose-gold and silver through the trees and there was cooking-break-fast smoke rising off the housetops in the valley below.

Nice place, Granola. I'd been this way before, in dreams.

And just like the other times, this starship came sailing through the treetops to land in my da's cornfield—a bolt of platinum godfire looking like nothing I'd ever seen.

The scene jumped, like slicing the middle out of a talkingbook, and then I was looking at the first planet I'd ever seen from space. Home. But not home anymore—I was leaving and I wasn't ever coming back.

You're thick when you're kinchin-bai; fifty fellow-citizens on ice in his hold and I never stopped to think what the captain's being a slaver meant to me. Didn't even know the word.

I wanted to wake up before I got to the part where I *did* know, but all that happened was I jumped about three years, to Pandora.

At least I missed Market Garden. Those dreams are bad ones.

Pandora is a planet in the never-never, where the Hamati Confederacy bumps up against the Empire. I was downfall stranded without a numbercruncher or hope of one, with people after me because I'd run away from Market Garden and people soon to be after me wanting payoff for their kick, their goforth, and the number-cruncher that was slagged plastic and broken dreams in my cockpit.

Real poetic. Real dumb. So what's so bad about being contract warmgoods, anyway? On Market Garden I was a marketable commodity—for use, when finished, somewhere tronics wouldn't do. No reason for them to waste time telling me things I'd never need to know—like what a Library was, and not to go buy one if I got the chance.

I dreamed I was back in the shop on Pandora, holding a box of broken glass that someone swore was a navicomp, and then it started to change. . . .

"Butterfly? Butterfly, wake up."

I staggered up out of dreams and heard someone else breathing inboard *Firecat*.

"Butterfly? We need to talk." My teeth crawled. Paladin. He didn't breathe but he talked real good. Tiggy Stardust was the one breathing.

I nodded. Paladin'd see that. I put my hands over my face, trying to lock up the ghosts again. I don't dream mostly. No percentage in it.

My head was slugging along with my heartbeat but I didn't bump the burn on my arm and nothing else hurt too much. I looked over to where I'd stowed Tiggy in my second-best sleepsling. He looked soft and sweet and anyone that took a step toward him was taking her life in hand. So I crawled out of my rack the other way, past the cockpit well and up into the nose.

It was ungodly quiet in *Firecat*. The air scrubbers and everything else that used up power and oxy were off. I was starting us as we'd have to go on, with life-support down near marginal. Angeltown shed weird gray light through the hullports and I wrapped my quilt tighter around me and shivered. Later it was going to be as too hot as it was too cold now, and sometime after that we'd be to Kiffit or dead.

"Can you hear me?"

Damnfool question. "Je, che-bai, I hear." Granola was still ringing xylophone ghosts down all the years between me and fourteen. It was crazy to even think about going back. Even if I could find the place, I couldn't land. Our Fifty Patriarchs had spun good plastic for them and their descendants to be left lonealone for ever and ever, world without end.

"You should have let Valijon Starbringer put himself out the air lock. You can still do it," Paladin started up, and went into a taradiddle all about xenophobic alMayne, heat-death of the Universe, and how Tiggy was son of Very Important TwiceBorn, all which I knew. Already knew he was trouble, and now Pally wanted to tell me about cultural fragmentation through linguistic evolution, whatever t'hell that was. Nothing I could see mattered, but he thought it was important, so I listened.

The song and dance kept coming back to "lose the glitterborn." Paladin was full with mights and maybes tonight and I was tired of my life. It was no time to be arguing ethics.

"Not going to frag the kinchin-bai just because it's convenient," I snapped at him finally. Tiggy stirred but didn't wake up, and I waited until he settled again. "Be reasonable. Think you Tiggy-che-bai's da's not going to want to know where's his lost son-an-heir? For sure *Firecat* went up out of quarantine on Wanderweb and someone saw me stuff Tiggy inboard. If I dock wonderchild alive and well at Azarine Guildhouse on Kiffit we have no problems. Mercs're honest." And a hellflower merc wouldn't turn around and sell Tiggy to someone else instead of handing him back to his original owner.

Paladin didn't say anything.

"Bai, I got to be able to point to live Tiggy Stardust when hellflower trouble comes calling. It's not like beating kidnap-rap. Hellflowers won't stop."

"He is a liability." Did Paladin think he was going to change my mind, or did Libraries get tired too? We both knew all the sides of all the arguments and we could go roundaround them forever.

Ice kinchin-bai—not because he was dangerous, but because he might be.

Not good enough.

"He's kinchin-bai, Pally—a fourteen-year-old kid. This is his first time out. He'll clear me a rap, and he won't have anything else to tell anyone that'll make any sense at all."

"You're guessing, Butterfly. I'm not."

We both knew I knew I was guessing, and we both knew the percentages in my being right. Low. But there wasn't any other thing to do but wake Tiggy up and shove him out the air lock—and then follow him myself.

"Once we get to Kiffit I'll toss my kick and drop Tiggy-bai at Azarine Guildhouse. We'll be gone before the heat drops, Pally. We'll leg it straight back to Coldwater without waiting for a load. And we can find a hat trick to do in the Outfar for bye-m-bye until the heat dies down. Won't cost us anything."

"Except a Free Port. Except air, and water, and food, and power to Kiffit. Except, if you are not lucky, your life."

I knew all that and I wasn't happy about any of it.

"Is my life, bai—isn't it?" But it wasn't. It was Paladin's too, and he was too polite to say, but he couldn't make it in the Outfar—or anywhere—alone.

And neither could I. How many years ago would I of been dead without Paladin to cover up for everything a Interdicted Barbarian didn't know?

"It was bad luck. It just happened. But we'll ace this and get straight, you'll see. Drop Tiggy-bai and have the good numbers again." I tried to tell myself I was trying so hard to keep Tiggy alive only because I knew his hell-flower kin wouldn't let the matter drop.

"Leaving aside his oxygen requirements, Valijon Star-bringer is an outsider. He is an aristocrat—" Paladin listed all Tiggy's shortcomings again. The only thing he didn't do was ask me to put Tiggy out the lock to make him safe.

I don't know what I would of done if he had.

Killing Tiggy was the smart thing. I knew it was. Raise my chances of getting to Kiffit alive. Lower the chances of anybody being able to cry Librarian. I was going to have to run for the edge of the Outfar either way, so keeping him alive wouldn't get me anything.

And I couldn't do it any more than I could Transit to angeltown without a ship. I didn't know why. I didn't like not knowing why.

I sat and stared out at angeltown and wondered what it would be like to just open the lock and step out. It wasn't like realspace. Paladin tried to explain it to me once—something to do with time and relative dimensions in space—but I didn't understand it. I didn't need to understand it to fly through it, anyway.

"What about documentation?" Paladin said after

awhiles, and I knew I'd won whatever I'd been fighting for. "Your pet cutthroat hasn't got any ID on him."

If Paladin was thinking about that, he wasn't thinking about making me put Tiggy out the air lock.

"Think there's still couple sets of blank around somewheres. You do something to get him off-Port for me, bai?" ID wasn't all Tiggy didn't have. Wanderweb had stripped him to the skin. I'd have to see what *Firecat* could do for him in the way of clothes.

"Counterfeiting ID is not the problem, Butterfly."

No, problem was lots of other things, but none of them was hauling any cubic tonight. I sat under *Firecat*'s hull-ports and watched Tiggy breathe until I fell asleep.

* * * * *

Insert #4: Paladin's Log

It was my fault that Butterfly broke into the Wanderweb Justiciary to steal Valijon Starbringer. And from the moment that she made the choice to do so, it was inevitable that she would not abandon him.

I say that now, with hindsight. One may always desire facts to be other than they are. But the facts touching on this matter unfolded in inevitable progression over a span of years.

From the time Butterfly and I met on Pandora the problem of reliable communication has been a concern. Unless Butterfly and I could share information while she was away from *Firecat*, we were extremely vulnerable. Clandestine communication would markedly increase our joint chances to "live to get older."

I had originally thought that arranging this communication would be a simple matter, but the equipment I described to Butterfly did not exist. She attempted to construct some components, but even the tools did not exist—an entire technology had been destroyed in the unreasoning backlash against fully-volitional logics. At Butterfly's urging we began to search for something available in the modern world that would meet our needs.

When we finally determined the existence of the RTS

unit, Butterfly had a number of reasons we could not acquire it, but as the Library at University I had incorporated several important studies on human behavior, and retained enough of that information not to find her actions inconsistent.

The implant operation would be a source of emotional trauma to any organic of the galactic culture. For a Luddite Saint from Granola, sworn to pastoral simplicity and no technology more complex than the tilt-board plow and the waterwheel, it would be an even greater one. Butterfly is not as indifferent to the mores of either her natal culture or her adoptive culture as she pretends.

So we delayed. Eventually we came to Wanderweb— having carried the RTS unit with us for over a year—and the surgery was accomplished. Emotional backlash and suppressed cultural bias did the rest.

A course of action undertaken in mutual willingness to provide greater safety to us both—the transponder implantation—leads inevitably to an action of great risk to us both—the jailbreak of the alMayne. If Butterfly considered her reasons for insisting on that course of action at all, she might have articulated them as being "to prove that she still had it." In reality, it was to prove that she still *was* it.

By the very nature of what I was, Butterfly was cut off from even the society of criminals and outlaws. An escaped slave, even an illegal emigrant, can find peers and socialization in the nightworld society. The possessor of a fully-volitional logic, a Librarian, is outcast by every thinking being. There is no one in the Imperium so depraved as to knowingly offer a Librarian sanctuary, and no one who would keep such a thing secret.

On the fringe of the Phoenix Empire, away from the deadly cataloging bureaucracy, the two of us were safe. But what at first had seemed limitless freedom I discovered to be circumscribed indeed. We could go no closer to the center of the Empire than the very fringes of the Directorates. Any thorough medical examination would reveal what Butterfly was, and any cursory technical inspection would uncover me. The penalty for either discovery was death.

It was a death only slightly more certain than that which was the consequence of Butterfly's chosen profession—but illegal pilot was, in all fairness, one of the few ways of acquiring credit she could espouse. Piloting is a marketable skill—and she had been trained, if not certified, by Market

Garden as part of her processing. A trained pilot willing to take considerable risks to maintain his freedom quickly becomes a darktrader.

If he has the money to purchase a ship—or can find a sponsor.

The Pandora business venture on which Butterfly discovered me was an undertaking of the sort in which the probability of failure was so great that it precluded the use of expensive material. If Butterflies-are-free, an untried, potentially valueless commodity, got her ship, herself, and her cargo back to Coldwater, she would enjoy Factor Oob's financial support and political backing, and live in comparative safety and comfort. If not, she would die.

She lived, with my help. And by her aid I returned to life. Butterfly protected me during the long period of reconstruction when I would ignorantly have revealed myself, and in return I provided her with the technological edge that meant success in a highly competitive profession. By the time we knew the truth about ourselves and each other, and had discovered what a "Library" was in this brave new world of bright promise, I did not wish to exchange my safety and companionship for new uncertainty, and Butterfly did not wish to relinquish my considerable resources. So we remained sequestered, secretly fugitive, and Butterfly remained distanced twice-over from her own kind.

But humans are social animals—every book I ever was tells of this. They are born and grow and die in social groups, responding to one another, and even if modern social groups include sentient females they are no less social groups for that. Configuration prefigures destiny. Structure determines function. An organic sentient needs to be with others of his own kind. In befriending me, Butterfly was deprived of the socialization the imperatives of her construction had shaped her to require.

If she had not been so alone, would she have clung to Valijon Starbringer—a dangerous nuisance—in the way she did?

No. But she was, and so she did. And I realized I could delay no longer.

For both our sakes, I must set her free.

*   *   *   *   *

It was eight days to Kiffit, and there was nothing to do but forge a ticket-of-leave for the rokeach and watch the life-support reserves drop against present usage. My shirts fit Tiggy, my pants didn't, and I gave him the Estel-Shadowmaker handcannon for his very own because he seemed to like it. I gave up any hope of disarming him at a very early stage in our relationship.

Tiggy paced and fidgeted until I pointed out it'd use up the air faster, then he lay in his sleepsling and stared at nothing for hours with no expression at all.

He didn't ask me any questions. Maybe good little hell-flowers don't. Maybe he thought a *chaudatu* didn't know anything he needed.

I didn't ask him any questions neither. I was saving up my calls on his honor for when I needed them, and I didn't want to give him any excuses to declare accounts closed.

So nobody talked. Including Paladin.

After that first night I'd wake up sometimes and see Tiggy watching me, like he was trying to stare through my skull. I spent lots of time in the mercy seat with the canopy popped, staring into angeltown till my eyes hurt, but there was no point in making Tiggy wonder who I was talking to.

The temperature rose, the air got thicker, and I sat in the dark thinking I was damned if I was going to die and give Pally the chance to say he told me so. And the sooner I lost Love's Young Dream and stopped thinking about the perils of childhood, the better. Then me and Paladin could go back to doing business, like always.

The sooner the better.

* * *

Firecat made Transit to realspace right on sked. Real-space was black sharp and dangerous with Kiffit lost in the skirts of the primary.

I'd had a headache for the last two days that I couldn't shake and when I moved too fast everything went gray. I knew my reflexes was too far gone for me to be able to get *Firecat* down. Fortunately I didn't have to.

We crossed the Kiffit-Port beam and I flooded my Best Girl with the last of the reserve oxy and turned the air-

scrubbers up full. If Paladin couldn't get us down within
the hour we'd be dead, but for the chance to breathe
real air again I didn't care. Even Tiggy looked giddy with
it.

I slid into the mercy seat and played "let's pretend."
We rode Kiffit-Port's beam into an approach pattern as
Independent Freighter this-that-and-the-otherthing, Coldwater registry and last downfall Orili-neesy, shipping x-
meters cubic and crew of one, nine plates of goforth and
all the other nosy nonsense slugs want to know about a
honest woman making a moral living. Finally they gave
me a landing window, about the time I could count our
breathing in minutes.

I popped the hatch and cut the hull-fields before we
was safely down. Sweet, free, and unmetered air blasted
into *Firecat* with a whistle that set my teeth on edge.
Paladin switched from para-light to para-gravity systems
and coaxed my sweetheart to dance on her attitude jets,
taking her down slow enough to keep her from getting
her blessed little non-powered permeable hull shredded
by atmosphere. Being alive was wonderful. Kiffit was
wonderful. Air was wonderful. And I wanted a bath.

* * *

Kiffit wasn't a Free Port, more's the pity, but it *was*
in the Outfar. It was shabby and overlooked and second
rate, and the sort of place I know better'n my own name.
Pally says the Empire's dying by meters, and places like
Kiffit are a point in his favor.

Eventually I was gig-in-dock, with Kiffit-Port looking
like every Port on every Outfar planet in the never-
never. I dogged the inner and outer hatches open and
put down the ramp and went back into the hold. Paladin
had the blowers going full tilt boogie. Tiggy'd climbed
down out of his sling and was looking at me.

"Scenic Kiffit, hellflower. Just let me hook *Firecat* up
and we'll do some eyeballing." As soon as Paladin had
a landline, he could tell me all about the Guildhouse on
Kiffit and some of us could go there.

The docking rings on Kiffit are open to the sky. The
sky was bright opaque orange and the air was thin and
dry. I like canned air better as a rule—you know what

you're getting—but even what Kiffit was using for air tasted delicious. I went around to the docking ring firewall and found the Port Services hookups and dragged the hoses over to *Firecat*. Water and waste and power to run them when your goforths are cold, landline and computer access, all the comforts of sweet bye-m-bye. It took awhiles to get them hooked up right but I didn't care as long as I was here to do it.

Then I went back inside *Firecat*. Tiggy Stardust had his Estel-Shadowmaker handcannon out and was pointing it right at me.

It wasn't Paladin's fault for not warning me. We both knew Tiggy was armed; we'd both been counting on hellflower honor to protect me. I hadn't even seen Tiggy move before the blaster was out; he was that fast.

"I am leaving now, Captain San'Cyr."

So much for hellflower honor. Tiggy had his blaster pointed right at my chest, not that a near-miss would matter with an Estel-Shadowmaker. I kept my hands well away from anywhere that might have held heat and didn't.

"So?"

"I wished to say farewell. I have been thinking, and I know now what I must do." He got up and walked past me to the hatch and down.

"Hellflower. Why the heat?" It was stupid but I wanted to know.

Tiggy looked down at the blaster, then in through the hatch at me. "I do not trust you, *chaudatu*. You do not understand honor. And you are not very smart."

Tiggy Stardust seemed to spend his whole time walking out of my life. I hoped this time it was for good.

I sat down on the crate he'd been sitting on. After a while it got cold, so I got my jacket and my blasters and a few other odds and ends from my lockboxes and tucked them all away nice and proper. Paladin was real quiet.

"So why don't you say you told me so?" I said. No comment. Paladin can shut up better than anybody I know, and you can't see his face while he's doing it.

"What do you think's going to happen to him, bai?" That he answered.

"Based on Valijon's performance on Wanderweb, he will immediately be arrested for causing a public distur-

bance—only in Borderline they will insist on identifying
him before sentencing. Since he has no ID on him,
they—"

I put up my hand and Paladin stopped talking. Something was nagging hard at the back of my mind, but it
wouldn't come in and I let it go. "Never mind. So they'll
ID him and shop'm back to his da? That'll do me fine."

And good-bye to the recent and unlamented Tiggy,
social work on the brain-dead, and all my other wastes
of time and money. After awhiles I went on with my
business. Gentry don't get paid to think.

*   *   *

There's a nice system on Kiffit and most Imperial Outfar ports whereby you never have to meet the person
catching your kick. It works whether you're pre-con-
tracted or no, and whether you have any actual interest
in selling your cargo or not.

I had no interest in my supposed money-load, but
every interest in making the Teasers think I did, so I
took the rokeach off to a nice tradelocker and fed my
manifest through the doorlock.

If I came back for the cargo, I'd only be down the
locker rent. If my assignee did, he'd have to pay serious
valuta on top of the rent. In this case, I didn't have a
buyer for my rokeach, so Paladin listed my cargo and
price asking on Tradehall board whiles I danced it.

Teasers keep track of things like that, the nosy bas-
kets. I was damned if I was going to be charged pleasure-
yacht rates for coming in to Kiffit without a cargo. I was
going to lose enough money on this tik already.

So I was asking twenty percent over Market Garden
setprice on the board, and I'd come back when I was
ready to lift and either pick up my payoff or take the
lock down to the Transport Workers Guildhall and sell
it to someone who wanted to speculate in rokeach
futures. Fine and nice and real friendly. And *Firecat* and
me was documented every step of the way as coming to
Kiffit to do serious bidness, in case anybody came for to
ask. And while this was all real uplifting, it wasn't how
I paid the rent.

After a sprightly pre-meridies of healthy exercise and

a detour through an off-Port bathhouse, I went back to
Firecat to get the money-load.

And Dominich Fenrir was waiting.

*   *   *

Dominich Fenrir is the chief Teaser on Kiffit. Being
Trade Customs and Commerce's man on Kiffit has to be
a thankless job, but Dommie don't worry his pretty head
over justice and mercy and Customs regs. He went bent
a long time ago.

If you're a Directorate merchantman up to paying the
vigorish, you can run anything you want in and out of
Kiffit-Port unwept unhonored and unsung. The rest of
us just pay the occasional sweetener not to be certified
Unfit to Lift by Kiffit Port Authority. Only sometimes
Dommie's got to pretend he's still a honorable Imperial,
and that's when independents like me get happy days
and busy nights.

"Hello, St. Cyr. Nice to see you back. How's the
wrong side of the law these days?"

"Wouldn't know. Am honest woman, forbye. Business
must be bad, you bothering me."

Dommie smole a small smile and managed to look
even more unattractive. "Oh, no. I'd say this comes
under the heading of protecting my interests, St. Cyr.
Now why don't you open up your ship so we can go
inside—since we're such old friends "

"Siblings, surely; you choose your friends," Paladin
commented.

I opened up *Firecat* and Dommie swung himself in,
not waiting for the ramp to come down. I pulled in after
him.

"Nice cargo you got here, Gentrymort," Dommie said,
looking around all *Firecat*'s empty hold still rigged for
two.

"Just tossed kick, Dommie-bai. Here's locker compkey
for it, see?" A Gentrymort is what I am, but I don't like
being called that by bought law.

He took the key to the tradelocker and tossed it up
and down a bit before he tucked it away, hoping I guess
to terrify me into special pleading. "Wouldn't want you

to lose it, sweetheart. Stop by my office before you lift and I'll give you the payoff."

Or half of it, maybe, if I was that lucky. I would of cried myself to sleep for sure if the locker key was where the money was this trip. Fine. I been shookdown before. But Dommie still didn't leave.

"Rokeach botanicals, eh? Pretty odd cargo to pick up on Wanderweb, isn't it? Not a lot of money in it. Hardly enough to cover expenses, I'd say. I wonder what else you might have—found—on Wanderweb."

For once in one of these sweet scenarios, I was stone innocent. Or ignorant, anyway.

"When you figure it out, Dommie, let me know. What you see is what you get."

"Maybe I just ought to impound your ship, Gentrymort. I'm sure I could find enough violations to put you down on the ground with the rest of us for a real long time."

Terrific. A bored bent Teaser—my favorite veggie.

"Then bring on the hellhounds, Dommie, and let us all in on the fun. And while you're at it, o'nobly-born, you might start thinking about how much fun you're going to have patterolling the Chullites in a two-man jaeger."

"Careful, Butterfly," said Paladin in my ear.

Dommie slugged me back against the bulkhead like a man with something on his mind.

"You wouldn't be threatening me, would you, you hack Indie?" He tightened up, and it was an effort to breathe, but I made it.

"Wouldn't threaten *legitimates*, Dommie—or even you. Just want to mention you pull my ticket and I sing like a well-tuned goforth to Guild, to Board of Inquiry, to many-a-many." Paladin had enough notes on Dommie's fun-and-games to at least start a official inquest. It was one of those happy thoughts that keep you warm on those cold galactic nights.

After awhiles Dommie let go. I dropped to the deck and leaned back against the crash pads, rubbing my throat.

Dommie didn't much care for my expression, and I didn't much care for what came next. Good fellowship slid over his face like a cheap paint-job under pressure.

"Hey, St. Cyr, you got me all wrong. I'm on your side. I've seen what happens when a small-time smuggler like you gets mixed up in something too big for her. You're in way over your head, stardancer; if you back off now, maybe you and me could get together; do some business. You should think about it."

"Je, Dommie. I'll surely do that," I said from the deck.

He left with my locker key in his pocket, and I buttoned up my Best Girl real tight and thought hard.

We had started out with the traditional wondershow between the Bent Teaser and the Noble Gentrymort—the one as usually ends up with me taking a few shots to the ribs and Dommie walking off with his vigorish-of-choice—but somewhere along Act Two we got sidetracked. I was just about willing to bet Dommie wanted to get on my good side.

"Shall I place the file on Trade Customs and Commerce official Dominich Fenrir's extortion racket on Kiffit in the open banks of the Kiffit Palace of Justice computers when we leave?" said Paladin.

"Oh, sure, why not? Make up some extras, while you're at it." If the Office of the Question did a persona-peel on him looking for proof of Paladin's farcing he'd be cleared, of course, but by then there wouldn't be much left.

I sluiced Kiffit-Port's metered water over my head and neck and thought about Dommie's visit until I decided it'd make less sense than a hellflower's logic. Then I went to get tools to peel up my deck.

"Dommie-bai wanted into *Firecat* because he thought he was going to see something," I said to Paladin while I worked. "And when he didn't see what he was after he tried to shake it loose. What am I mixed up in, Pally-che-bai, that's too big for me?"

"Valijon Starbringer," Paladin said flatly.

He hadn't told me about Tiggy's safe arrival at the Guildhouse—or arrest—yet, and I guessed I'd have to wait until we got back to angeltown to hear it.

"That Dommie knows about," I amended. "Anyway, Pally, Tiggy's old business." It didn't sound true, and I wondered why.

"Dominich Fenrir does not know about Valijon Star-

bringer," said my silent partner, back from a jaunt in the
Port computers to make sure. "However, Customs Officer Fenrir *has* recently undertaken a clandestine alliance
with the saurian crimelord Kroon'Vannet. Fenrir is being
paid a retainer for unspecified duties. There is no mention of you in connection with any illegality." And Paladin was not going to take this glowing opportunity to tell
me Tiggy was restored to the bosom of his one-an-onlies.
Sigh.

"Kroon'Vannet," I said, remembering. Vannet was
one of those nighttime men that give lizards a bad name.
He wanted a piece of everything that wasn't nailed down
and didn't think he shouldn't have it just because he slid
off the cold end of the Chernovsky scale. The Phoenix
Empire, Paladin tells me, is real accommodating as long
as your B-pop hits somewhere in the middle, like mine
would if I wasn't a dicty, and real hostile if you're a
wiggly. That's why the Outfar is full of wigglies pre-
tending they're citizens. Some don't want to just pretend.
Vannet was two of them.

"So what am I supposed to back off of, babby-bai?"

"I don't know," said Paladin. That made two of us,
but Pally always says organics aren't very bright.

T'hell with Dommie Fenrir and his live talkingbook
theater. I pulled the money-load out on the deck and
wished I could believe it was what Dommie was after,
but that didn't fit with the "friendly warning." Ignorance
was part of what I was being paid for, but stupidity isn't
my hobby. Paladin and me'd scanned them back on Wanderweb and found we was shipping gems of some kind.
Boring.

"N'portado. Pally, soon as we toss this lot, we're making for Coldwater, deadhead, and get t'hell out of the
way of Teasers with brain fever."

Have always said that if I ever get the chance to follow
my own advice I'll be dangerous.

* * * * *

Insert #5: Paladin's Log

It is fortunate that Interphon, the lingua franca of deep space, is not as universal as its adherents believe, and that while Valijon Starbringer and Butterfly St. Cyr were both speaking Interphon, they were not speaking the same language.

This interface of bewilderment was entirely to Butterfly's advantage, since so long as Valijon could not determine precisely what she had said, he could not determine whether he needed to "purify his honor," and thus he left her without making any decision.

From the moment of its standardization Interphon had begun to break down into dialectical forms. This breakdown, unlike previous linguistic breakdowns, is occurring along lines of profession, not lines of astrography. In a few centuries, it is entirely likely that a commercial pilot, or "stardancer," will not be able to understand the Interphon of the inhabitants of the planets he visits. The end of the Empire is foreshadowed by the fact of a universal language being worried into rags by a dozen jealous peoples.

The scope of the disintegration is sharply indicated in the division between "bonecracks" and "bodysnatchers"—i.e., physicians who treat mercenaries and ground-based personnel and physicians who treat pilots and noncombatant exo-planetary personnel. Why should two branches of the same discipline—medicine—polarize to the extent of evolving two incompatible specialized vocabularies of mutual incomprehension to deal with the same subject? I believe the answer has to do with the organic love of novelty for its own sake, even when not particularly desirable.

I also believe it will eventually destroy this Empire. No astropolitical body can be properly administered without a common language.

In fact, the Phoenix Empire is decaying now. Within living memory Kiffit was a thriving settlement in the center of Imperial trade. Now it is an outpost, without sufficient population to support an expanding economy. Any check of uncensored statistics will prove this: each year more people leave Kiffit than settle or are born there. But in the Phoenix Empire statistics are not uncensored.

It is the same everywhere. The frontiers contract, more and more fringe worlds break away from the central government. It has been going on for centuries; the war that destroyed the Old Federation shattered a community of worlds far larger than the Empire. The Hamati Confederacy and the Believers Sodality were once both part of the Federation. The Empire has lost control over them, just as each century it loses dominion over more of its frontier.

Someday a war will come that will drive the Empire into a fragmented barbarism, and even the name of Empire will perish. The technology that supports its economy will be lost, and all that will remain will be apes scavenging in a boneyard, looking up at the stars.

5

Malice In Wondertown

Kiffit's one of the few places in the Outfar where the port city was there before the port—a ancient and valued member of our varied and colorful Empire. Paladin says Kiffit used to be bigger and thriving, but it was fine with me if it wasn't now. The parts of it I was interested in still seemed in good enough shape to me.

By now the horizon'd risen and cut off Kiffit's primary, and the Kiffit-Port security lighting wasn't on yet. Bad light's saved more lives than bodysnatchers in my line of work, so that was the time I picked to head out.

* * *

The Elephant and Starcastle in Borderline is where the Gentry on Kiffit hang their heat. Like any other hooch servicing a port, the Starcastle's on a full-rotation sked. Stardancers on the up-and-out aren't going to rearrange their circadians every time they downfall.

I didn't have any trouble getting a room with no view and a box with locks sunk into the floor. I'd have to be more of an idiot than even Pally thought I was to cold-call on a total stranger carrying 3K of illegal. The lockbox was the reason I'd rented the room.

I put the densepaks under lock and seal and threw enough of my own stuff around to make it look natural. It was after full-dark when I went down to sightsee in the unregulated planetary air.

The early evening streets was full of fellahim and grubbers tied to planetary rotation. I saw Company men from Directorate ships in their lovely gray leathers, Indie crews trooping their colors like a pack of bandarlog, and the kiddies that catered to both. Borderline's a planned city, which means that after a certain point the plans give

out and there's nothing but a sprawl of back-alley mazes.
If you fight your way through them long enough, you
reach Borderline New City, which is also nice and tidy

I'd checked at the PortServices shop and found where
the Azarine Guildhouse was, but Tiggy'd made that none
of my concern. The address I had from Gibberfur was
for a transient outhostel called Danbourg Strail that was
a little farther out. Joytown was on left, and behind me
and to the right was the commercial port towers. Company again, rot them, with their stranglehold on Mid-
Worlds and Directorate shipping and their nasty way of
holing any Indie ship they run into, just for kicks. Guild
sanctions don't mean a helluva lot to them.

I kept going. Eventually I left wondertown behind; I
didn't mind the walk, and it's always good to know the
ground you may have to retreat over later.

I was a couple kliks from the port, and all the way to
the thin edge of the city planners' good intentions. The
area I was in now had been razed for new building but
no buildings had gone up. It was being used as sort of a
open-air market; unregulated and ramshackle. About as
thriving as any place in Borderline was, which wasn't
saying lots. My destination was just the other side.

The Danbourg Strail was the kind of outhostel where
you usually go to sell things you don't own. I went on up
to the cubie-number I'd been given back on Wanderweb.
According to Gibberfur, Moke Rahone kept regular
hours here and these were those.

I'd also been told to call before I came. Sure I would.
And maybe my kick would waft in here on the wings of
song, too.

Punched the bell. The door said it belonged-along
Moke Rahone, specialist in curiosa. It wasn't powered,
but it wasn't locked either. I slid it back and looked
inside.

There was a empty waiting area, full of vitrines that
were full of junk. I walked in.

"Yo, che-bai, je tuerre? Art t'home, forbye?" I said
in broad patwa. Nobody answered this brilliant conversational sally, but maybe Moke Rahone, dealer in curiosa,
didn't like being shouted at.

There was a door with the Intersign glyph for "boss
inside" on it, and I opened that one too.

Kiffit is a dry planet. It was wet in that cubie, and dark. I stood there long enough for my nose to tell me what the smell was, and then I backed out. Then I waited a moment, got my torch out of my pocket, and went back in.

I've slaughtered pigs and I've killed men, but it wasn't like either one. When I was ten years old a field hand on our farm got caught in the harvester. He was half-shredded before we could stop the team, and the sweet-metal stink was just like this.

Moke Rahone'd been human. Funny how your body knows a smell before your brain does.

Brother Rahone hadn't got caught in a harvester, though. I turned the torch on him and studied what I saw like my life depended on it, which it might.

Somebody'd nailed Moke Rahone to his desk and butchered him open. It was dainty-like. Real bodysnatcher work, done with something sharp—something that didn't burn like a pocket laser or chew up the meat like a vibro.

What this meant to me was that Brother Rahone wasn't in the paying for cargo business anymore, which put me in what Paladin calls your basic delicate moral quandary, because I had to deliver Gibberfur's cargo to someone or call in the Guild. Terrific.

And there was one other thing. It was sticking up out of Rahone's insides and it hadn't been part of his original manifest. Hadn't noticed it before in the general confusion, but it might tell me who killed him, and who might be interested in taking over his cargo.

"Trouble, Butterfly?" said Paladin through the RTS.

I rubbed my jaw where it felt electric-furry. "Um. Rahone's retired from darktrade business. Messy."

I pulled off my glove and yanked out the optional extra somebody'd left with Brother Rahone. What I got for my trouble was long and thin, pointed at one end and with feathers at the other. It was mostly red, but where it was dry it was a kind of blue animal bone with carving on it.

I'd seen bone like that before. In The Knife Worth A Afterlife. Hellflower work.

I wondered how Tiggy'd got the whistle on my kick and its new home and why he cared. Hellflower honor, probably—making sure I didn't see the profit I'd dragged him out of his way to get. I wrapped up the wand in a piece of thermofax I found. Maybe I'd take it back to him up close and personal.

I'd just shut the door of the inner room behind me when the outer door opened. The hellflower wasn't Tiggy, but he looked real pleased to see me anyway.

"*Ea, higna,*" the hellflower said. Then he went for his heat.

I'd decided more than a week ago that hellflowers was bad news, which gave me almost enough edge on this one to get out of the way. I went down behind a bench so his first shot went high and then I sprayed the room with blaster fire, hoping to get lucky.

I didn't. The bench stopped his first bolt, so I picked it up and threw it at him. He thought that was real amusing. He threw it back, but I wasn't waiting around for the critical reviews and had already made it back through the inner door into Brother Rahone's office.

I found the lock in the dark and used it. The light switch was next to it. With room lights the thing on the desk looked even worse. The smell was something awful and this time I noticed that the floor was covered in blood.

"*Higna, yai,*" said this friendly conversational voice from the other side of the door. The hellflower wasn't mad—far from it, the voice seemed to say. He liked my style. We could be best buddies.

I wondered if *higna* was better than *chaudatu*. He said some other things. I caught about one word in seven and understood not any.

"Butterfly?" said Paladin.

"Shut up." Paladin couldn't hear anything at all but me and even if he could there was nothing he could do.

What a lousy way to run a communications link.

If I was Brother Rahone, dealer in curiosa, I'd have a back way out. I shoved what was left of the late Rahone off his desk and started going through the contents to find it. My best buddy on the other side of the door lost patience. He said something in a more-in-sorrow-than-in-anger voice, and then there was a real determined thump at the door. It'd take him about a second and a half to decide to blow it.

I found a control panel in the desk, hidden well enough that I was pretty sure it didn't just control the outside door. I bashed the buttons all at once, just for luck, and heard the slow grinding of the hidden door. Too slow.

I heard the prefire whine of a blaster and ducked under the desk. I wedged myself in as high off the floor as I could get about the time the hellflower blew the door and stalked in.

Rahone's remains didn't even slow him down. I'd bet he'd seen them earlier, maybe while they was still lively. He was wearing blue leather boots with jeweled spurs and gilded scrolling stamped into the leather and it was a good bet he wasn't out to roll me for petty cash. He said something real nasty in helltongue when he saw the open door and walked around the desk to get a better look at the way he thought I'd gone.

I swept the floor with blaster fire and took him off at the ankles. He went over backwards and I got him a couple more times going down.

That bought me enough time to come out from under the desk and catch a throwing-spike from him through my skill-wrist. The spike was barbed, and every twitch drove it in deeper. I dropped my heat and it slid in Rahone's blood way the hell out of reach.

I scrabbled at my other blaster left-handed and got it up and ready to go before I realized there wasn't much reason to. My playmate had signed the lease on his real estate and was leaving on the Long Orbit.

I got up from behind the desk and looked at him. He was pretty much gone below his waist and what was still there was medium-well done. He wasn't breathing.

I went around the desk and picked up my other blaster, careful. Had to put away the one I was holding to do it. The wrist he'd spiked was already beginning to swell, but it wasn't leaking much; he'd missed the veins.

Maybe I should of put a bolt into him to be sure, but I didn't think anyone could take that kind of damage and live.

I was wrong.

I had to step over him to get to the door. He bucked when I got close to him and dragged me down. His fingers was wrapped around my throat and his rings dug into my jaw. I caught myself on the wrist he'd spiked and the whole room seemed to fill with bright haze for the couple of centuries it took me to bring my blaster up. Then I pumped plasma Miltowns into him until the world went away.

* * *

Paladin was yelling in my ear. I coughed myself awake and kicked a body off me and coughed some more. Then I sat up.

There was someone pouring ice water over my right hand. I looked down and saw bright cheery rivulets of blood chuckling merrily down, gaudy and inexhaustible and mine all mine.

My glove was soaked and stiff and the skin ballooned between it and the knife sheath on my wrist. The throwing-spike stuck out both sides. That last handstand had sawed the spike through a vein, looked like.

"Butterfly, I know you are not dead. The transponder would tell me if you were dead and it has not. Therefore you are not dead and are capable of responding to me. Butterfly!"

"Here," I croaked. "Shut up." And let me bleed to death in peace and quiet.

The room was burning; the kind of low smoky fire you get discharging a few plasma-packets too many at a combustible surface. I smelled the winy rankness of burnt tilo and the homey smell of cooked meat.

"Butterfly." Just to let me know Paladin'd appreciate a explanation at my earliest convenience.

"Hellflower dusted Moke Rahone. Hurt me, bai, not too bad."

Liar.

Getting to my feet was a major event and started me choking again. I was still holding my blood-covered blaster in my left hand. There was a red light flashing on and off over the open back way out. I sat back on the edge of the desk and wondered if I really wanted to walk that far.

"Butterfly, you are not all right. What is the extent of your injuries, and what is the current status of the alMayne?"

"Dead, and he got me through the wrist with some

kind of spike." Which was going to have to come out before I went anywhere or I'd be dead; there was no way I could get a pressure bandage on that wrist with the spike in it. And if the hellflower lifetaker had backup waiting downbelow, I'd be dead anyway.

"Did you kill him?"

Trust Pally to fix on the irrelevant. "Course not. He died of pure melancholy and displeasure, like they say in the talkingbooks." That brought on another spasm of coughing. Paladin waited until I finished.

"You will have to bandage your injury and get back to the Starcastle. Can you walk that far?"

"Piece of cake."

I stood up and the ground rock-rolled on invisible gimbals. I sat down again and pulled out my vibro.

"Is there something you are not telling me about the situation, Butterfly?" Someday, somehow, I'd be able to get my hands on Paladin. The thought made life worth going on with.

"Building's on fire. Now shut up while I cut this damn spike loose."

* * *

It takes about half an hour to bleed to death from a severed hand, depending on your body mass. I was a little better off than that: only one or two veins was nicked. If I could stop bleeding now, I'd be fine. If I couldn't, in a few hours tops I'd be unconscious and helpless and real, real noticeable.

I cut my wrist open some more using the vibro real gingerly and pushed the spike rest of the way through. It was all barbs and curves; brittle and vibro-sharp, and watching it squish through made me feel sick. When it was out I felt light and hollow. Shocky. Not good.

I took off my jacket and my shirt and sawed the shirt into strips and wrapped it around my wrist until the fingers went numb. I'd have to shoot left-handed if I ran into trouble, but it's a tough galaxy out there and I'd manage.

"Are you finished?" That was Pally, all sweetness and starlight.

"Yeah." I slid my jacket back on without too much

trouble. By this time the room was full of smoke. I headed over to the back door and looked out. All there was was dark.

"Brother Rahone's back way out is some kind of dropshaft, looks like. Going out that way. 'Flower might have backup down on the street—it was a hellflower I think opened up Rahone and stuck some kind a alMayne gimcrack into him too. Gang-war?"

"Moke Rahone has no record of affiliation with Kroon'Vannet or any of his competition. Neither is he on record with the Azarine Guildhouse as hiring an alMayne or any other bodyguard, although the agreement need not have been registered there. Did the alMayne speak to you at all?"

"Oh, sure; we had lovely chat. A'course, since I don't speak helltongue we didn't exchange too many views before I blew his legs off."

Paladin shut up, and I used the quiet to work up my nerve. I could try to get out through the front, but if the hellflower had backup there was a slightly better chance of losing him if I went out through Rahone's hidden escape route. I tossed a few things into the shaft and they floated enough to make me sure it was a powered drop. Then I stepped out.

I fell faster than I wanted and the jar when I landed made it so I couldn't breathe for a minute. I shook the stars out of my eyes and looked around. The dropshaft had took me to street level in the back of the Danbourg Strail. There was no hellflowers in sight. I leaned against the wall and tried to look healthy. If I lost it here I wouldn't need hellflowers to finish me; there's brat-packs and priggers and all kinds of marginals in places like this.

And Paladin couldn't even send a floater-cab for me unless I could get as far as the planned part of Borderline on my own. They don't go outside it.

"What about Tiggy?" I said to kill time while trying not to faint. "Joyous reunion of missing heir with da, galaxy rejoices?"

"Nothing of that sort has been transmitted on any of the information bands I can access, public or restricted. I find this somewhat peculiar."

Terrific. "I find it lots peculiar. Bodywarp fetch-kitchens admit sweet babby che-bai unmourned long-lost?"

"I said no information, Butterfly—including admissions to medical facilities of any alMayne, clandestinely or otherwise. And you said you had no further interest in Valijon Starbringer."

"Have every interest in him making big public arrival splash and getting me off hook," I reminded him.

My makeshift bandage was already squishy with wet, but I could afford to bleed like that for awhiles if I had to. I started feeling better enough to think I wasn't going to die tonight.

"We provisioned and ready to lift?"

"*Firecat*'s supplies are at the docking ring. As soon as they are aboard, we are ready. Life-support systems are fully charged. Do you wish me to call for clearance now?"

"Ne, che-bai. Think Dommie's watching too close. But order a real good medkit to add to our stuff, if you can find one. Will get myself right at the Starcastle and be back to *Firecat* by horizonfall. We're golden."

"I hope so, Butterfly. Good luck."

It was still early evening. I hadn't been inside with Rahone and Brother Hellflower half an hour, if that.

* * * * *

Insert #6: Paladin's Log

The modern day is a technology of clumsy inelegancies. Limping and metal-poor, it scorns efficiency in deference to half-remembered wonders entombed in the Inappropriate Technology Act—a catalog of things the moderns cannot have and so declare undesirable.

If this were the Federation, none of this would have happened. Not only would Butterfly have been safe in a breedery, if she had not been I could simply have activated my remote maniples and physically assisted her. For that matter, if such creatures as hellflowers had existed during my first life, it would certainly have been impossible to misidentify any of them. Federation citizens wore subcutaneous implants with the necessary information micro-encoded in crystal.

But even if the Phoenix Empire were willing to use implants, the technology for the micro-encoding no longer exists, lost with so many other things in the pointless war against what its survivors call Libraries.

But I digress.

It might have been a coincidence that an alMayne was involved in the murder of Butterfly's client, and then again it might not. I dispatched a floater to wait for Butterfly at the point that she would cross over into Borderline Old City, and began tracing the Borderline computer network to see if it was possible to access a data-gathering port in her location. The vital signs transmitted to me by her Remote Transponder Sensor indicated that Butterfly was weak, but capable of reaching the floater under her own power. There was nothing further I could do for her at the moment. I devoted more of my resources to another problem.

Where was Valijon Starbringer?

The identification that I had forged for him had successfully passed him through the port gates a few minutes after he left *Firecat*. From his actions upon leaving Butterfly, he would seem to have had a destination in mind, but from the moment he left the port neither "Aurini Goldsong" nor Valijon Starbringer entered into any data transaction with the Kiffit/Borderline Central Data Net.

Perhaps he had discarded his false ID. And had I been hasty, even jealous, in attempting to discard him?

Butterfly must be returned to the human world from which I have taken her, and it must be done in such a way as to assure her of prosperity and safety. The protection of an alMayne GreatHouse, properly handled, could guarantee both.

Valijon could reasonably be expected to cooperate in my plans, but only if I could find him.

And only if he were not trying to kill Butterfly now.

*   *   *   *   *

They picked me up just inside the Grand Bazaar and didn't care who knew it. I glanced back when I twigged and saw two hellflowers—a head taller than everybody else in sight and hair like hammered platinum. And confident. Real confident.

I somehow didn't think sweet reason was going to have much effect on them. Told Paladin the glad news. He didn't say much.

Once I left the Bazaar I'd be an easy mark—easier, is to say. And for all I knew they was legit heat and had the *legitimates* on their side.

But I'd been in the Danbourg Strail, and I didn't think so. And I didn't think they was going to put me down easy if they got their hands on me, either. Then I looked around and saw salvation.

I slowed down and waited for the garden club to catch up with me, and while I was doing that I purely accidental came to a stop by a cookshack. The owner was deep-frying something unidentifiable in several liters of liquid grease and offering it to the helpless fellahim that wandered by.

"How much for to buy your kick, che-bai?"

I repeated it in a couple of dialects, cant, and patwa, before he got the idea. He named a figure and laughed.

"Butterfly, are you thinking?" Paladin sounded more worried by that than he had by anything so far tonight. "I am tracking you in the Grand Bazaar. I will counterfeit a civil disorder there, and when the Peacekeepers move in you can escape safely. All you have to do is—"

"Ne, let be, I'm inspired," I said.

I put credit plaques on the counter side-by-each and watched the cookshop owner's eyes bugout. Then I watched the hellflowers. They saw me see them and thought it was a fine joke. One of them was female; both together was pretty as hunting birds and just as far from human. I stood flat-footed and watched them come.

The owner scraped up his credit and started to leave. I grabbed a handful of his shirt and stopped him. Just let them get a little bit closer and he could go where he wanted. After they was set. After they was committed.

Just a tad bit closer, kinchin of the Void.

* * *

Your basic blaster is a lovely toy—Paladin says it contains the basic technology for our entire culture. That means given a working blaster, smarts, and lots of free time, a person could deduce and build everything from highliners to palaceoids.

You see, a blaster don't throw a inert projectile. Blaster fires itty-bitty controlled fusion reaction wrapped in a magnetic envelope. Unwrap it, and all you have's a flash of light. But let the envelope hit something, and all that heat and force comes out along the rupture-line in a coherent directed star-hot pulse that is one reason I've lived to be as old as I am. Fusion reaction + magnetic bottle = culture. Simple.

* * *

The hellflowers split up when they reached the cook-shack and started coming around it from both sides. I dropped the cook and he started running. Then I drew my blaster and fired at the deep-fryer.

The grease had been hot. Now it was incandescent. It exploded in a boiling fireball over my head and going west, and I snapped off a shot at the hellflower as hadn't been flash-fried and ran.

Two down. How many more? And would Prettybird #2 follow me or stay with her well-done partner?

I cut off High Street as soon as I could, and two turns had me lost in the back street warren. I wanted height; I'd aced one 'flower by not being where he expected; why not do it twice?

No joy getting onto the roof one-handed but I managed. I felt safer here but it wasn't going to last. I was sweating hot and cold at once and my hands was shaking so hard I couldn't shoot myself in the foot to save my life.

"Butterfly, what have you done?"

I could see smoke rising over the Grand Bazaar. Somewhere down there—if I was lucky—was two cooked hellflowers, and probably a crowd giving a inaccurate description of the crazy stardancer to assembling *legitimates* at this very moment. So I needed to stop looking like a stardancer, or at least get back to where they was thick upon the ground. And right now I didn't even think I could stand up.

"Butterfly, are you there?"

"Someday, Pally, you going to tell me where and t'hell else would I be? 'Sponder's in my jawbone, too reet?"

He ignored that. "What happened?"

"Two more 'flowers. Dead, I think. What do they want with me, Pally? I didn't frag their kinchin-bai—"

"Stay there," said Paladin, so I did.

* * *

I don't know where he stole it, or how he made it fly outside of the New City grid. And it was probably as conspicuous as hell, but right now I didn't care. The floater touched down on my rooftop and I pulled myself inside.

"Back to *Firecat*, Paladin. We gone." To hell with Moke Rahone's cargo. If hellflowers wanted me, I wanted out.

"I don't think that would be wise. There is an unknown person here at *Firecat*. I believe he must have used your last delivery as cover. He is between your supplies and the docking ring fire wall."

"Oh, bai, needed to hear that, forbye." My hand felt like it belonged to somebody else, and I felt limper than a simple evening's brawl would cover. "Starcastle?"

"It seems the safest choice. You can tend to your injuries while I attempt to discover who is waiting for you here."

I lay back and let the breeze blow over me. Whatever it was I was in the middle of, I wanted out.

Gang-war? Nighttime men don't frag stardancers.

Hellflower honor? Only hellflower I knew was Tiggy Stardust, and Tiggy his own self hadn't known where I was going in Borderline. He hadn't looked like he cared, neither, true-tell.

Fenrir? Why would Fenrir want to hire somebody to kill me when he could do it himself for free?

Nothing I could think of made any sense at all.

* * *

It was the middle of Kiffit's dark period, and good little fellahim were buttoned up in their racks. I could tell when the floater hit wondertown by the way the

streets filled up. Nobody paid me or my blood no nevermind when I got out at the Starcastle.

Maybe there are bars that won't sell you an Imperial
battle-aid kit along with a box of burntwine, but I've
never been in any of them. I clutched the box with the
Imperial Phoenix on it to my bosom like hard credit on
payday and made it to my cubie on habit alone.

Somebody'd been here. I rolled the door back and the
first thing I thought was there was no point to come back
here because I'd been set up. But Paladin could hear
inside and said there wasn't anybody here.

I barred the door again and blanked the windows and
decided it was just a tossing and farcing. But my lockbox
was still cherry, and the rest of my kit was all there,
spread from core to rim by somebody who had no interest in mere worldlies.

Then I saw the coin, and what it put into my system
almost made the battle-aid kit unnecessary.

* * *

As previously noted, all members of the Azarine Coalition have their little quirks. You can noodle the alMayne
in the street by the way he lives in a world all his own
and carries a knife to help him do it. Felix, now, are real
organized—they form companies, wear matching uniforms, and are cuter'n hell. Dedicated.

Ghadri are individualists. They got another real recognizable genotype—short, wide, and overmuscled—file
their teeth, tattoo their faces, and work in groups of five.
They're found in High Jump crews, special weapons merc
teams, and—more'n any other Coalition race—assassins.
Ghadri are solid on the credit standard, got no honor I
ever heard of, and like to coast on their rep. It'll stand
the weight.

* * *

I picked up the coin. It was round, metal, thick; greasy
to the touch and unstable, like it was liquid inside. Ghadri like to pay you off to stay out of their way. I was
being paid off. Oricalchun coin'd redeem in any Azarine
Guildhouse in the Empire for a bribe indexed to the

importance of the job the Ghadri were doing. I could even check it there before deciding whether to accept.

I dropped it and dumped the battle-aid kit on the bed.

"Yo, Pally, you there?"

"As the great philosopher of the eleven-hundredth Year of Imperial Grace once said, where else would I be?"

Right. "How's houseguest?"

"Still there. And before you ask, there is still no report that Valijon Starbringer has been recovered."

"Got problems of my own—Ghadri wolfpack tossed my crib and warned me off. Only didn't tell me from what."

"Perhaps from the same matter Dominich Fenrir wishes you to avoid?"

I sat down on the bed next to the battle-aid kit and popped the locks. All that lovely illegal battletech glittered back at me.

"Bai, would love for to avoid it—tell me what."

"Perhaps from meeting Moke Rahone?" Paladin didn't sound convinced.

"Wolfpack must've been tossing this place about when Brother Rahone was getting illegal chop-an-channel. Even I am not dumb enough to warn body to not do something after they gone and done it."

I pulled out some designer alkaloids in the vial with the Intersign glyphs "Eat Me First" on it. The room snapped into sharp focus and all the pain I'd ever had went away.

"Imperial Armory, I love you," I said out loud.

Battle-aid kits is better than money some places; everybody wants what the Imperial Space Marines carry into battle to make sure they carry on in battle. The metabolic enhancers alone are worth the price of admission. I sliced my makeshift bandage off and poured sterile wash over the wrist, then disinfectant.

"So what we got here is your common-or-garden three problems: Fenrir wants me to get lost, Ghadri want me to stay out, and some hellflowers sliced Moke Rahone and just plain want me. And why is one of the many things I don't know." I wondered if my old sweetheart Silver Dagger was still on Kiffit, what she knew, and what she'd tell.

While I was talking I squeezed out a dollop of slow-set molecular glue and smeared it all over the hole in my wrist. That started it bleeding in good earnest again, but in a minute or so it wouldn't matter. I hunted around in the kit for the right size pressure-seal adjustable biopak.

"Do you have the 'gimcrack' you removed from the body?" Paladin wanted to know at that inopportune moment.

"Uh—je. S'here. Justaminnit." The biopak went on like a glove; wrapped my wrist and palm and left fingers and thumb free. I set it in place and flipped the switch. It settled in with a huff of air and a compression that hurt even through "Eat Me First." I waited until the built-in timer turned green and then drank what was in the "After-Fix" bottle. When that hit I couldn't feel the wrist anymore. So I pulled out the wand and described it for Paladin.

"I cannot be certain without seeing it, Butterfly, but what you seem to be describing is a *pheon*—an alMayne vendetta wand."

Paladin spends his spare time knowing everything about everything.

"So Rahone insulted a hellflower?"

I hoped.

"No."

"Pally-che-bai, has been long night and is going to be longer one, and I'm sure and t'hell not going to play Twenty Questions with you."

"The *pheon*," recited Paladin the way he does when he's reading something else, "or alMayne vendetta wand, is normally only employed among the alMayne, the Gentle People, themselves. The *pheon* may be engraved with from one to seven rings. One ring indicates that the subject of the vendetta is a sole individual, seven rings indicates that the subject's entire family to the seventh remove of kinship is to be eliminated. Outside scholars generally agree that formal initiation of the vendetta occurs when the designated subject sees the *pheon*, which is commonly presented in the ritually-murdered body of a servant or dependent of the subject. This servant is, however, considered not subject to the rules of vendetta and reprisals for his or her murder may be exacted irrespective to the progress of the vendetta.

"It is considered extremely bad form in high alMayne culture to begin a vendetta antecedent to the formal presentation of the *pheon*, which display is the signal for the commencement of the stylized hostilities which mark the highest flowering of—"

"Fap," I said, looking at the wand. Up near the dry end it had a groove carved in deep, all the way around. One ring vendetta. Just me. And meant for me, if Pally was true-telling, not for Rahone.

"Tiggy was really mad?" I suggested. But he didn't know where I was going on Kiffit, and besides. . . . "But I ain't hellflower, Pally."

"In certain rare cases vendetta will be declared against non-alMayne. Such declarations nearly always occur in conjunction with a criminal proceeding initiated by alMayne under the laws of the Codex Imperador. If the subject has committed no act illegal under the Codex Imperador, he, or more commonly, his estate, can prosecute the entire matter as—"

"I got a new rap on me I don't know?"

That got Paladin to shut up while he checked the hot-sheet traffic that had come in to Kiffit over the last two weeks and I tried to think of something I'd done to a hellflower that was actually illegal.

Kidnapping.

But Tiggy didn't know where I was going, dammit. . . .

"Nothing, Butterfly."

Well, scratch that idea. There was a big supply of metabolic enhancers in the aid-kit; I reached for them and hesitated. Better not. I didn't need them if it was just a matter of boarding *Firecat* and having Paladin Thread the Needle for me.

"Nevertheless, the probability is higher that you are being pursued by Valijon Starbringer's retainers than by a group of unrelated alMayne. It would also explain the ease with which you eluded them."

"*Ease!*"

"If the alMayne who pursued you had been professional killers, you would be dead now, Butterfly."

If they'd been professional. If they hadn't been cock-sure and overconfident against a poor helpless *chaudatu.* If two of them'd come into Rahone's office instead of one. I ran my hand over the biopak and shuddered.

"Any news on the boyfriend out at *Firecat?*"

"He has moved out of range of the hatch pickup, which is the only component of *Firecat*'s external sensors useful in a planetary atmosphere."

"In other words, no."

"I believe I said that, Butterfly."

I was starting to get hungry, now that I knew I was going to live, but there was things more important than food. I went and pulled the lockbox out from where the Ghadri had shoved it in their smash-and-toss. Moke Rahone's cargo was Undeliverable As Addressed, and that meant all bets were off.

I put my thumb on the lit glyph for "locked container" and it changed to "unlocked container." I pulled out all six densepaks, and split the first one open with the aid-kit scalpel.

"Holy Mother Night." It was the big score for Brother Rahone all right, and real too bad he didn't live to see it.

"Butterfly, you do realize that I have no way of seeing what you are doing?" Paladin said. I rubbed my jaw.

"Oh. Sorry. Just found out what we was shipping. Lyricals."

Lyricals. Also called song-ice, of glory-of-the-snows. Little hyaloid nodules, not much to look at. You find them floating free in asteroid belts, if you're real lucky. Tap one, and it gives you pretty music. Set it up with the right exciter, and the harmonics are enough to send you off to sweet dreams and many happy returns for as long as your batteries hold out.

The one I had in my hand showed a refracted star on its surface. I turned it this way and that. Sometimes it looked transparent. I tapped it.

No sound. So I tapped it again, and I could of been tapping *Firecat* for all the ethereal music on offer. "On the other hand," I said to Paladin, "maybe they aren't."

I opened the other densepaks. Seven stones in all—five big and two little, all identical. None of them rang worth a damn.

I held a small one down on the table with surgical tongs—tricky, with the biopak—and cut it open with my vibro. It was solid.

"Paladin, tell the wicked darktrade 'legger what you get when you slice open a Lyrical."

"First: touching a vibroblade to the surface of the Lyrical gem will cause a unique mellifluous chiming. Second: the center of the gem-spheroid is composed of a distinctive hexagonal honeycomb, black or iridescent in color—"

"And what Gibberfur was shipping from Wanderweb was fakes."

There was a pause while Paladin thought about this.

"Counterfeit Lyricals?" said Paladin.

"Not even. Bad fakes. Solid and don't ring. Stopped me half-second—expert even less."

I might still have to square it with the Guild for not losing my kick to my Destination-of-Record, but on the other hand, who was going to lodge a complaint? Rahone?

"That makes absolutely no sense," said Paladin crossly. I could sympathize.

"Unless they're something else tricked out to look like Lyricals. But I doubt it. And y'know? I don't care." Getting off planet'd make everybody happy—why not do it? With luck I'd never know why I had a oricalchun, what Fenrir thought'd make me healthy, and if I could add another hellflower scalp to my tally and live through the experience. "I am going to go downstairs and get something to eat, and the minute you tell me the coast is clear I am going to scuttle back to *Firecat* like a good coward and be gone-along-gone so fast. . . ."

"Butterfly, I can see the person behind the crates at the docking ring now. It is Valijon Starbringer."

Tiggy? "What's he doing?"

"I do not know. He seems to be injured." Hurt'd be nothing in it once I got my hands on him, him and his three-ring-circus vendettas.

"And, Butterfly, I think he is being followed."

But if he was being followed. . . . I sat and laboriously rearranged some preconceptions.

The hellflowers in the bazaar couldn't be connected with Tiggy, because if they was, he wouldn't be back at the port, alone, injured, and followed.

If there was a vendetta against Tiggy (reasonable), why had *I* gotten the wand?

And if the wand wan't meant for me, why was so many people out to get me?

I dumped the false Lyricals in various pockets and dragged my jacket on again. Then I flipped open the aid-kit and took out a double dose of enhancers. They probably wouldn't kill me. I could always buy a new liver.

"I'm going to the port." I popped the wafers into my mouth. They were too sweet, then too bitter.

"Butterfly, are you quite sure that is wise?"

The enhancer battledrugs hit, and in the rush I felt like I could just pick up the Starcastle by the ears and heave it over the next 'flower as came my way. I felt wonderful—like a Gentrymort what'd had her healing factor and metabolism stepped up by two: waterproof, shockproof, dust-resistant, and feeling no pain wherever glycogen reserves are sold. I was poetry in motion, all right.

"No. But he came to me for backup, Pally."

6

Smoke And Ash

I left the beautiful Elephant and Starcastle with a box of burntwine in one pocket, blaster in the other, and enough junk jewelery to buy part-shares in *Firecat*'s maintenance contract tucked here and there. I ignored the chemical blandishments singing sweet savage starfire in my mid-brain; I had three more doses of enhancer with me and if I had to take all of them I'd probably have more problems than just being dead could give me.

Right now I ought to be sitting in some fancy bathhouse in wondertown, watching the gravity dancers and getting all my sins absolved by something pretty. Oh yeah—and counting my payoff from Moke Rahone. Instead, I was torn up, hopped up, racked up, and walking into what was almost certainly a trap.

What had Tiggy Stardust run into that was so bad a hellflower couldn't handle it? I ate glucose and tried to keep an eye out for stray assassins.

* * *

I didn't go in through the main gate. I swung wide around the Company end of the port. It was empty except for one big highliner all floodlit and toplofty. I also sugarfooted around where they parked the big Indie ships with their crews of anywhere from thirty up, whole families and poor relations included. After I'd cleared them too, I walked along the outside of the fence to where they let gypsies and celestials dock. Little ships, old ships. Ships like mine.

The lights wasn't as bright and the service wasn't as good down here, and the fence was lower.

Dominich Fenrir knew something.

More'n that, he knew I was coming to Kiffit before I

got here. That thought stopped me cold, and I faded
back into a doorway to give it a little room. The buildings
along the fence was condemned, derelict. A good place
to think while looking over what was out on the field.

I'd only been downside an hour today when Fenrir
came by. He'd known I was coming and he thought he
knew something else. Something profitable.

Something on *Firecat*? I chased the thought around
awhiles and shook my head. It wouldn't fit and I couldn't
make it.

But Fenrir had known where I was coming from. He'd
named my last port—which was not the one in my
paperwork. Only Gibberfur there knew I was coming here.

Sweet. Factor A goes halvsies with bent Teaser and
chouses his partner Factor B out of mondo valuta when
Teaser steals cargo from stardancer. It's a sad old story.

The only trouble with it was that Gibberfur'd given me
fakes to freight. Fakes, locked up real extra special, in a
case he could be pretty damn sure any Gentry-legger'd
refuse to take—

I wanted to pursue that little thought, but something
distracted me. It was a flitting gray ghost shape moving
between ships on the other side of the fence. I saw
another one drift by just in front of me; he hit the fence
with a ping-bang-boing and went over it just like I was
planning to. I caught the glitter of expensive heat as he
moved.

Oh, it was ladies' day at the Azarine Coalition, all
right. I'd just seen two Ghadri—sweep men coming in
from a Ghadri wolfpack.

I could think of only one reason they'd want all five
of them in place before moving up.

"Ghadri wolfpack after Tiggy, che-bai," I told Paladin.
Then I moved too.

I hit the fence fast and noisy, with the battledrugs singing encouragement in my veins. The sound my boots
made hitting the ground on the other side echoed all
through the parked ships. Didn't see anybody. Didn't
expect to.

I ran from cover to cover down the line until I got to
a likely-looking Free Trader and slid behind her fire wall.
Within class, they dock ships by size at Imp Ports. Not
too many ships *Firecat*'s size in dock, usually. She was

next, and there was a long empty space between the Trader and my Best Girl.

I could see hoses going from her belly back to hookups in the fire wall, and a bunch of crates stacked around her ramp all armed to go off if they was burglared, and not a whole lot else. I couldn't see Tiggy or any of the Ghadri. With the noise I'd made showing up, I was pretty sure the Ghadri'd want to make sure of me before trying to finish him.

I fumbled in my flight jacket for the oricalchun and threw it out into the open space. It bounced on the crete with a sweet ringing sound. I knew what it was trying to buy, now.

The sound seemed to hang in the air, giving me the chance to think about what I was doing. Stupid. I'd been riding my luck to get this far. Pally'd been right—the 'flowers I'd dusted in the Grand Bazaar were amateurs.

These Ghadri were pros.

"I count three, Butterfly. One on top of *Firecat*. One on the ground between your position and here. The third one is under *Firecat*'s ramp," Paladin said through my implant.

But we was playing on my turf, with my rules, and my backups.

"When I give the word, I want a distraction. Something bright and noisy."

"Can do."

I started circling around. There might or might not be a Ghadri out there using the same cover to circle back. If Pally said he counted three, that's what there was. But Ghadri ran in fives. Was more sweeps still out? Or had Tiggy dusted some? How bad was he hurt? Could I count on him for backup?

It was too quiet. There was a city of several million lost souls not three hundred meters thataway and we could of been in the Ghost Capital of the Old Fed for all you noticed them. I wondered where Port Security was.

I scuttled on knees and fingers and could hear every noise my boots made and bet the Ghadri did too. I wondered if he was going to let me get all the way to my ship free and clear. Then there was a scuffling rush and he jumped me.

I hit the crete with my face and rolled enough to give

him a boot in the belly. He wuffed and waded back in.
No blasters—I should of figured the Ghadri wouldn't
want anything showy. He tried to unscrew my head and
I gave him my biopak to chew on and what he did to it
probably would of upset me except for those nice battledrugs. Ghadri file their teeth.

Then he was on top and settling in. I let Brother Abri-
che-bai bang me against the crete until he got bored, and
when he did I slid my vibro into him and rummaged
around. He wasn't expecting me to be that strong. Better
living through chemistry.

Everything almost but not quite hurt. I pushed the
body off my chest and nicked his throat to be sure. The
blood came slow, in the way that said there was no pump
behind it.

I turned off the vibro and slipped it back into my boot.
I was damn lucky I hadn't torn a tendon loose. You
could cripple yourself with metabolic enhancers if you
got careless.

I got up and tongued another enhancer tab. The world
was painted in shades of black. There was two more Ghadri killers out there, and if I got them both I'd have three
bodies to explain by morning and a dim view taken by
the authorities of self-defense.

"The one beneath *Firecat* is moving toward you."

"Oke, brother. Come and dance with Mama," I said
under my breath.

The Free Trader behind me was still dark. Her crew
must be away in the wicked city—no wonder the Ghadri
and me had the world to ourselves.

I couldn't see him but I knew he was coming. I gave
him long enough to get halfway here.

"Hit it, Pally," I said, and slid my hand down over my
left blaster.

All *Firecat*'s docking lights went on and her proximity
klaxons sounded. The Ghadri was closer than I thought.
I caught him twice in the chest even so, which was pretty
good left-hand shooting. Then the ship lights went out
and I ran for *Firecat* and hoped to get there before his
partner recovered.

I slammed into the boxes at the foot of my ramp
slightly too hard and sat down harder. There was a scrab-
ble on the hull. Dragged my blaster up to track on it,

but there was a flash and sizzle of somebody else shooting from behind the crates and what was left of the last Ghadri slid down over the hull curve and dropped damn near on my boots.

* * *

Talkingbooks always go on about "the horrible smell of cooking meat" after a gunfight. They're wrong. You catch a plasma-packet front and center and all anybody's going to smell is charcoal.

"Tiggy?" I said without moving. "It's me. You know— *chaudatu* what topped you out of Wanderweb? I'm coming round these-here boxes now bye-m-bye. Would appreciate it if you didn't shoot me."

Got to my feet. Nothing hurt. I felt much too fine. I wondered how much I'd be hurting without chemically-induced euphoria.

Paladin turned *Firecat*'s exterior lights back on low and opened the hatch. I went around all my catch-trapped crates of food and water and air and hollyvids and there was Tiggy. He was leaning back against the fire wall with the Estel-Shadowmaker I'd gave him in his lap. He opened his eyes when I got there.

"*Ea, chaudatu*, I knew you would come back," he said, real soft. Then his eyes rolled up in his head and he clocked out.

Yeah, and he also knew I had fusion for brains.

I got down and poked at him. He was still breathing, but the side of his head was sticky and hot. I couldn't see much in this light, and nothing in color. He was wearing the same clothes he'd left *Firecat* in, and they was in shreds. My fingers touched crumbling ash along his thigh and I bit down hard on my stomach and thought of the hellflower back at Rahone's. I wondered how Tiggy'd managed to get this far tagged like that.

Hurt. Bad hurt and he'd made it all this way, over the fence and all, with three Ghadri wolves waiting to pull him down. Running to the only one he knew on Kiffit that might help.

And I hadn't been here.

I didn't want to carry him anywhere, but I had work yet to do tonight and I couldn't just leave him. So I took

Tiggy's handcannon and his godlost *arthame* away from
him, talking the whole time in case he woke up, then I
picked him up. He didn't weigh quite as much as *Firecat*.
I put him down careful as I could on the deck in the hold.

I heard the sound of servomotors as Paladin manipu-
lated internal sensors to look-see. I looked myself.

I'd seen worse, but not alive.

"Where's the god-dammned medkit?" Please let Paladin have found one, and let it have been delivered, and
not stolen.

"The medical supplies you requested are at the foot of
the ramp. Valijon Starbringer is very badly hurt, Butterfly. Even a hellflower may not be able to survive such
injury. Call the Guildhouse now and turn him over to
them." The RTS tickled, but neither of us had any intention of running Class One High Book through external
speakers.

"No."

"It was what you were going to do this morning. If he
dies before—"

"Who sent the Ghadri?" The oricalchun proved they'd
been hired. They'd been after Tiggy, and warned me off.
But no one knew Tiggy would be on Kiffit. Even Gibberfur didn't know that.

Paladin got all set to argue some more and then
changed his mind.

"Find their ID and I will tell you who they are,
Butterfly."

*   *   *

I went down the ramp and brought up the older
brother of the kit I'd bought at the Starcastle. It was a
field-medic's kit, and it held enough stuff to stock my
own surgery. I slugged back a quart of glucose out of it
to give the enhancers in my system something to chew
on, then I gave Tiggy everything I could find to get him
right. He'd lived this long, he'd have to live a little longer
on his lonesome: I didn't have time to work on him right
now. When I'd done all the quick things I could do for
him I went back outside.

I found the kiddy I'd knifed and the one I'd blasted.
I took their ID and brought the bodies back to *Firecat*

and piled them on top of the one that Tiggy'd iced. My clothes were soaked like I'd been standing in the rain, and it was all blood. The docking ring looked like a butcher shop.

For one long minute I seriously considered just walking away. No one could stop me. Even if they caught me they couldn't make me do what I was going to do next. I'd made a lot of stupid promises about how I wasn't never going to do things like this again. I'm a darktrader. It's clean honest work.

And if I jibbed now it wouldn't be just my neck, but Paladin and Tiggy's.

I got out my vibro and set it on the nearest crate.

Then I uncoupled the waste hose from *Firecat* and fed all three Ghadri down it. In pieces.

I had some damfool idea it'd buy me something not to have them found. If these three disappeared their replacements'd come a little slower next time.

I made my right hand do the work, barely. And when I'd finished the cutting I spent several dekaliters of Kiffit water sluicing down the docking ring. The stains left looked old.

And three Ghadri was gone without a trace. I hooked the hoses back to *Firecat* and went inside.

Tiggy was awake again. He'd got ahold of his sidearm and was pointing it at me.

"Go ahead," I said. "Make my day."

"I had to be sure it was you, she-captain," he said with the ghost of a grin. He let go his blaster and lay back, panting.

"'If I wasn't me, we'd both be dead. Ship goes when I do, remember?"

I stripped off my clothes and threw them down the disposal. The boots and blaster-harness I'd been wearing was salvageable, just. There was blood all around my nails.

"The Ghadri," Tiggy said.

I took the ID I'd scavenged and put them where Paladin could get to work on them.

"You got one, babby, I got two. Leaves two unaccounted for."

"Dead." Tiggy was real sure about that.

"The Ghadri are registered out the of ab-Ghidr School

of Ghadri Main," Paladin said. "Licensed as mercenaries, specialized as assassins. I am now checking records for Kiffit Immigration Control to see when they arrived here, and what their purpose was in coming to Kiffit." And who hired them, Pally, don't forget that.

"You have no idea what a load off my mind that is, hellflower," I said to Tiggy. "Now look, che-bai, you're hurt bad. Got stuff here for to fetch-kitchen—for to medical you. People with Ghadri Abri-che-bai after them shouldn't go to legit bodysnatchers, je?"

"No doctors," said Tiggy faintly. "Assassins." His skin looked shiny and tight.

"Butterfly, what will you do if he dies?" I shook my head. He wasn't going to die.

I unfolded and unfolded and unfolded the Imperial fetch-kitchen and got out the field medic manual. "Help us both to stay breathing awhiles longer if maybe you answer some questions, Tiggy-bai." And more, it'd distract him. He'd be needing that with what I was about to do to him.

"If honor allows." He was breathing like there wasn't any air, with all Kiffit out there free for the lungs.

"The Ghadri tactical group for which I have partial ID arrived on Kiffit from Tangervel fifty days ago. The three killed here were Abric, Abwehr, and Abaris. It is logical to assume that Abihu and Abriel were killed by Valijon Starbringer in Borderline as he has indicated. The group's passage to Kiffit was paid by Alaric Dragonflame, the alMayne who is the head of the combined alMayne Embassy and Guildhouse here. Once here, the Ghadri tactical group took up residence in the alMayne Guildhouse, a circumstance which suggests they were in the employ of someone there; an unusual probability if true. Alaric Dragonflame's father, Morido Dragonflame, is next in line to represent alMayne in the Azarine Coalition," Paladin finished off, sounding surprised. I'm sure he meant it to mean something, but I couldn't just now ask what.

I started peeling Tiggy out of his clothes. He looked like he'd been thrown off of every roof in Borderline, and that was just the small stuff.

"Remind me not to accept any invites to your parties, 'flower. You play rough." Tiggy looked pleased. Poor lost kinchin-bai. His skin was gray under the bronze-gold, cold and clammy to touch. I might be wrong about saving him.

But if the Ghadri had come from the Guildhouse that was the last place I could send him.

"From Imperial social notes available in the Borderline Main Banks, LessHouse Dragonflame seems to be a fairly influential member of one of the Chernbereth-Molkath GreatHouses. It is nonetheless anomalous for the head of a LessHouse to rise to as high a position in Imperial government as Morido Dragonflame has done. alMayne LessHouses roughly correspond to planet-linked realholders, as opposed to—" If it was the end of civilization as we know it, Paladin'd want to tell me why and what.

I started with Tiggy's head wound and went down from the top, cleaning and stitching as I went. Saved the leg for last. Maybe he'd pass out by then.

The painease started to take hold and his color got a little better. The manual said no metabolic enhancers before you finished cutting, but it didn't say why.

Was it better to cut live bodies or dead ones? The Ghadri hadn't felt anything. Tiggy would. There wasn't enough stuff in this kit to make him not.

"—Which makes it particularly odd that his son, Alaric Dragonflame, would be in such a comparatively minor post, and off-planet in addition," said Paladin, finishing up.

But if I hurt him enough, I might be able to save his life.

He was watching me. I smiled.

"As we last left thrilling wonderstory, hellflower glitterborn—that's you, Tiggy Stardust—had pulled heat on motherly High Jump captain—me—who took serious cop to spring him from Wanderweb gig." Tiggy unraveled that without too much trouble—guilty conscience.

"I had no choice. I—it was an honor matter. But you would not know of that."

"Ne, not me. Am honorless *chaudatu. Higna*, even," I said, finally remembering what the other hellflower'd called me back at Moke Rahone's. "Been stiffed outta my feoff, delivering farced kick to official dead person, but—"

"*Higna*? You are not *higna, alarthme*. Two Ghadri are

dead." Tiggy found that funny until I touched a sore spot and he winced.

"*Higna*: prey. *Alarthme*: knifeless one. *Chaudatu*: nonperson. All words are alMayne Common Tongue. *Alarthme* is a term of respect applied to those who do not possess an *arthame* but are nonetheless conditionally people," Paladin said.

Chaudatu, higna, alarthme—alMayne had lots of names for idiot.

"Yeah, only it's three Ghadri dead, and maybe two more in Borderline, and we was just about to get to how honor mixed you in with them, wonderchild."

Mostly Tiggy looked like he'd been through a standard-issue brawl. Somebody'd got close enough to bite him once, and one place he looked like he'd been dragged over something rough. Nothing broken, but hell-flower bones don't break easy.

"I killed the others. Two in the city. I have to see my cousin!" He was starting to wander a little bit in the head. He tried to get up.

"It's a long walk from here, dammit. Lay down, chebai, or I'll clock you. Now we're up to where honor left you no choice so's you did a fade soon as *Firecat* made downfall. Where did you go?"

Tiggy tossed his head back and forth against the blankets I'd put under him. His hair was rusty-pink with blood I hadn't tried to wash out.

"'The House of Walls; the sacred enclosure. Where is my *arthame*?" He started feeling around for it and some of the cuts I'd closed started oozing again.

"Stop it. I'll get it. Lie still, dammit."

"Butterfly, you cannot possibly intend to arm a delirious alMayne. He will kill you!" Pally sounded so indignant it was funny.

"Yeah, yeah, yeah," I muttered under my breath. I got the knife out of his pile of bloody rags and put it in his hand. That quieted him down, but not Paladin.

"So I gave you the knife. So now you hold still and shut up and let me cut you. Je?" Maybe he'd pass out soon.

"*Dzain'domere.*" I started in on his feet.

He'd been barefoot all day and it showed. I was sweating from the battledrugs and Paladin turned down the

humidity in *Firecat* again. It helped some. Looked at
Tiggy and he was still conscious.

"So you went to House of Walls," I prompted him.
Whatever that was. "And then?"

"Alaric Dragonflame. He said I must go to the
TwiceBorn *chaudatu*. I went away, and in the street
called Sharp I was attacked by the Wolves-Without-
Honor. Ghadri are no match for the Gentle People,"
Tiggy finished with shaky satisfaction.

Gentle People. Figures that's what hellflowers'd call
themselves when they was to home.

"Butterfly, Sharp Street is in the Azarine district near
the Grand Bazaar. You passed it earlier this evening, as
you were going from the Elephant and Starcastle to the
Danbourg Strail. The House of Walls is the alMayne
Embassy and Guildhouse. The 'TwiceBorn *chaudatu*'
Valijon Starbringer mentions may be the Imperial Court
officials in Borderline New City. If Valijon was attacked
in Sharp Street after leaving the alMayne Guildhouse, he
was heading away from New City." Paladin's voice had
his very best "this is not an expression" expression.

Away from New City. On foot, in rags. Even I knew
you didn't let relatives of the high-heat go wandering
roundaround alone. They'd know who he was. alMayne
Embassy'd be able to do a Verify on Tiggy sooner than
instantly.

Dammit.

I put it all out of my mind for laters.

"You awake, Tiggy-che-bai?"

"I am awake, *alarthme*," Tiggy whispered. His eyes
had the glitter of pure exhaustion. I gave him some water
and the last of the painease I dared give him and made
sure the extra pad under his head was straight.

Damn hellflower constitution. A normal person'd be
unconscious already for what I was going to do next.

"Look. You got tagged in the leg. You already know
how bad. Have to open it out and clean it before I can
wrap it, or you just going to get the Rot and die. It's
going to hurt. Can use nerve-blocks, but if I give you
any more painease, you might not wake up. Compre?
Understand?"

"Do what you must, *alarthme*; I will not disgrace my
House. If I die, you will take my *arthame* to my father?

You will not let me die without walls? Please?" He tried to get up again. It was too easy to shove him flat and his skin was cold and wet under my hand.

"I'll take your knife to your da, Tiggy-bai, now shut up. Nobody's going to die." My free hand was shaking, and the other one in the biopak was pretty useless. I pulled the sterile drape off the burn. Tiggy was watching me to see what my face'd do, but I knew that dodge. "Piece of cake," I said, and looked sincere about it. He relaxed some.

I set up the manual from the field kit to show me where to sink the nerve-blocks. They went deep and held, but there wasn't a spinal block. Not in a field kit. What idiot'd do major surgery with only a field kit?

I picked up the scalpel and started cutting.

*   *   *

Most of the combat medicine in the Empire is al-Mayne-derived, Paladin told me once. alMayne fixers have this idea you don't want to live forever, just a while longer. The field-medic battle-aid kit Paladin'd got would damn near let me rebuild Tiggy from scratch, and the manual had Intersign glyphs for everything from conservation amputation to delivering a breech-birth from a merc in full powered armor, but what the manual said for an energy-weapon burn this size and color was coke and wrap and evac to outside body-shop for stabilization and repair soon as maybe.

Only I couldn't do that. I had to do what I could here, with what they'd gave me.

Stabilizing a blaster-burn meant cutting out the radio-active charcoal from the burn site. I tried to forget Tiggy was alive.

There was a timer in the manual for a simple conservation amputation procedure, and I set it. It ticked away, measuring percentages and the likelihood of termination from surgical shock.

I cut down to blood, and sprayed to seal the veins, and cut and scraped and sprayed and cut. The timer red-lined, and I ignored it.

The kit had a biopak that was big enough. I pulled one out, and spread the stuff on Tiggy that the book said to, and dragged the biopak on and triggered it. The biopak huffed closed, sealing him from groin to knee.

"Is—"

"Valijon is still alive, Butterfly," Paladin said.

I crawled along my deck to Tiggy's top end and looked. He was breathing. He was out cold. He'd bitten through his lower lip but he hadn't made a sound.

I wiped the blood off his face, gentle like he could feel it. He'd have a limp when he woke up. If he woke up. If he lived.

Adrenaline and enhancers made everything sing for me, white and cold. I pulled out the nerve-blocks and mopped up more blood and then packed up what was left. I gave him glucose and enhancers and everything like the manual said to. Then I covered him up and tried to stop shaking.

"You did a good job, Butterfly. He should live."

"You wish he was dead." I wanted something to hit.

"No. I wish no harm to Valijon Starbringer. The fact that House Dragonflame is seeking to execute him changes matters. But that can wait. You should rest now."

"No. Load and lift. Have to kyte, need supplies. I'm good for it." I pulled the next to last enhancer and ate it. I wondered if I'd feel it when the tendons in my shoulders tore loose. Knew I wouldn't feel it when my liver quit. It's a little known fact that you can actually kill yourself totally dead if you run on battledrugs till you field-strip your endocrine system. Paladin knew it. I knew he knew it. And he didn't try to argue me out of taking more.

Without what I'd ordered I couldn't lift: no food, no water, no air. Prices are lower on Kiffit than Wanderweb; I'd been running on empty to get here and Tiggy'd wiped out my reserves. I had to get this stuff into *Firecat* if it killed me. I fetched and carried and dumped everything in a which-way heap on *Firecat*'s deck. Mother Night her own self couldn't save me from holing the hull if I had to lift before this load was stowed and dogged.

My right arm was numb from the elbow down and throbbed like a broken tooth, even through the battledrugs. There was Ghadri teeth marks in the biopak. One of these days I'd have to pop the seal on that and see what was under there. But right now I was busy.

I stopped halfway along to pop a meal-pak but I couldn't finish it. I remembered the burntwine I'd brought from Starcastle. The box was crushed flat but I had more in my supplies. The alcohol burned off as fast as I drank it. I didn't feel anything. The world was all about loading the same supplies I'd loaded a hundred times, and up and down and up *Firecat*'s ramp with Paladin prodding me everytime I stopped. And each time I brought a load up Tiggy was still alive, and every time I wondered if Dragonflame's *legitimates* was coming and I'd held us up too long, but I had to have this stuff or we couldn't fly.

Paladin told me over and over that Borderline was quiet and nobody was looking for us, but I kept forgetting.

All that blood.

Without remembering what came between I was standing back by the fire wall running Kiffit water over me. I couldn't see any crates.

"Butterfly." From the sound of it, Paladin'd been trying to get my attention for a long time.

"Je?"

"The supplies are loaded. You still have to stow them before you lift. You will injure Valijon if you do not. You need more medical supplies. You don't have clearance. I will have to order additional supplies and call for clearance and I cannot do that for five hours."

I didn't like it. I think if it had just been the clearance and more supplies I would have gone anyway—which shows how coked I was—but I couldn't lift without shifting cargo all over my deck. So I stayed.

It was early. Paladin gave me local time and Hours Since Downfall both. I got a box of glucose and a box of overproof neurotoxin and mixed them and went and sat starclad on *Firecat*'s landing strut.

The breeze that comes before horizonfall dried me off and I sat and drank. I was beyond tired, and the glucose made the enhancers sit up and sing again.

Everything was quiet. The lights from Borderline washed the sky out gray. Wayaway you could hear the keen and thud of cranes loading some Company highliner with whatever Kiffit had to offer. Peaceful. Normal.

"I got real problem, Pally-che-bai. Somebody don't like hellflowers," I said. "Don't like me too, seemingly."

"Alaric Dragonflame, in the parlance, 'set Valijon up.' He convinced him to go to Borderline New City on foot and alone, misdirected him, and sent Ghadri assassins, which he had previously hired and was holding in reserve, to kill him. The same mercenaries, aware of the connection between you and Valijon Starbringer, attempted to warn you against aiding him."

"Por'ke?" But why?

"Por'ke Wanderweb hot seat go hellflower for to chop-an-channel, jillybai?" said Paladin in patwa, sounding miffed. I shook my head a couple of times to see if maybe some brain cells'd jarred loose.

"Wanderweb Justiciary wanted to ice Tiggy because he dusted some heat, Pally, that's why. Nothing to do with Dragonflame."

"Granting Valijon did indeed kill the Guardsmen involved, and reserving the question of what caused the City Guard to accost him in the first place, why did not the Justiciary then notify the *Pledge Of Honor* as soon as it had identified Valijon Starbringer?"

"Paladin, what t'hell had this got to do with Ghadri after Tiggy and glitterflowers after me severalmany light-years away? Or with Dominich Fenrir?" I added for good measure. "Wanderweb Justiciary didn't ID Tiggy. Was in banks as Unknown alMayne 00001. I saw." I tossed the empty box back inside *Firecat* and rested my chin on my arms.

"It was not an accident that brought Valijon Star-bringer to the surface of Wanderweb," Paladin said flat out. "Someone was attempting to kill him there. Someone still is."

* * * * *

Insert #7: Paladin's Log

If Valijon Starbringer had been identifiable on Wanderweb his life would have been in no danger. A fine would have been paid—if necessary, a scapegoat executed in his place.

Free Ports operate on the profit motive. There could be no
conceivable profit in allowing the death of an Ambassadorial
delegate for any reason whatever.

Therefore he was not identifiable, and he could plausibly
be expected to withhold the information of his identity. While
standing heroically mute against all questioners palls after
a few years, it is a beguiling pastime at fourteen.

The life of an honest citizen requires a mass of documentation breathtaking in scope, yet Valijon carried none. The
person who deprived him of his identification before sending
him to the surface of Wanderweb was attempting to kill him.

Someone—either aboard the *Pledge Of Honor* or on
Wanderweb—separated Valijon from his ID and waited for
the inevitable (given the psychology of the alMayne) to happen. But this entity did not reckon with the possibility of
interference from a captain-owner who had both a ship in
port and the capability of suborning both the city computers
and the Justiciary computers to effect Valijon's release from
prison. If Butterflies-are-free Peace Sincere had not inter-
vened, Valijon Starbringer would now be dead on
Wanderweb.

I was originally mildly gratified to see Valijon return to
Firecat. The matter of setting Butterfly free of me was not
a simple one. For my plan to be practicable, she must be
better off without me than with me. If Butterfly could take
Valijon to his father, Kennor Starbringer would be indebted
for his son's return. He would grant any boon, even to an
interdicted Barbarian. All that I know of the Empire indicates
that citizenship is available even to a dicty for a price. Citizenship pays for all; if Butterfly acquired it there would be
no warrants against her.

And I would be gone.

No Library is safe in the Phoenix Empire, nor any Librarian. For this plan to work, I must force Butterfly to seek out
the *Pledge Of Honor* without me.

Deciding how to do this was the least of my prolems.
Deciding whether it should be done at all had become, with
the discovery of the Ghadri complicity, more than academic.

Who would benefit from the death of Valijon Starbringer—
and how? From material available even in the undernour-
ished Borderline bibliotek, I had the answer to that question.

When the son of Kennor Starbringer, Second Person of
House Starborn and President of the Azarine Coalition, is

murdered, there are certain things Kennor must do to remain an alMayne.

All of them are illegal under the Pax Imperador.

If Kennor does them, he will be arrested by the Imperial Court, tried, and executed. There will follow disaffection and upheaval on alMayne—and the appointment of a new Azarine Coalition delegate—Morido Dragonflame, whose son is Grandmaster on Kiffit.

If Kennor does not do them, he will no longer be considered alMayne. He will be hunted down by House Starbringer and executed—and the appointment of the new Azarine Coalition delegate follows.

It is possible that Dragonflame is innocent. He may have sent for the Ghadri as a reflection of market conditions on Kiffit. Butterfly and I had not yet reached Kiffit when they were sent for; the individual who could predict and chart the collection of random factors that brought Valijon to Kiffit would be far more efficient than Dragonflame has proved himself to be.

On the other hand, it would be possible, though not simple, for Wanderweb Free Port to identify Butterfly from her ship, and from security tapes made on the detention levels of Wanderweb Free Port Justiciary. It would be equally possible, though staggeringly difficult, to find who had most recently hired her and what her destination was.

It is at this point that a logical pattern grounded firmly on random chance begins to break down. Granted Butterfly's original involvement with Valijon and her subsequent rescue of him as pure accident and totally human coincidence— what happens next should follow logically from the factors involved.

Scenario #1: Persons who wish to secretly murder the Third Person of House Starborn, failing in their attempt on Wanderweb, track him and his rescuer to the Imperial Port of Kiffit, gambling that the smuggler-captain will head there next to deliver the cargo they know she carries. Alerting their agents on Kiffit—Dominich Fenrir and Alaric Dragonflame—they await the arrival of Butterfly and Valijon. Fenrir warns Butterfly not to involve herself, Dragonflame sends assassins after Valijon.

Why does no one feel it necessary to murder Butterfly, a witness to the plot, who may have been told any number of things by Valijon Starbringer and could at any moment attempt to contact Kennor Starbringer and tell him what she knows?

If the alMayne that Butterfly killed and who attempted to kill her are assumed to be members of Dragonflame's household, the complexities of the matter become even more farcical. Why were they not sent after Valijon instead? Surely alMayne would have been better equipped to deal with or defeat Valijon Starbringer. Was Dragonflame engaged in acts so honorless that the members of his own household would refuse to participate?

I would give much to have been present on the occasion that Alaric Dragonflame, lord of an alMayne LessHouse, told his alMayne *comites* that they must declare high ritual vendetta upon an independent freighter captain for no disclosed reason. I do not believe it ever occurred.

To explain the vendetta we must therefore abandon Alaric Dragonflame and turn to House Starborn.

Scenario #2: alMayne aristocrats from House Starborn, attempting to save the Third Person of House Starborn, track him and his abductrix to Kiffit. Determined to expunge the slight to the honor of their House, they ritually murder her client (uncovered through diligent searching on Wanderweb), declare vendetta, and pursue her with lethal intentions. Yet no one feels it necessary to find and save Valijon Starbringer, at large in Borderline.

I hardly need to mention that neither scenario makes any sense.

In Scenario One, Butterfly should have been killed—by Ghadri assassins, by Fenrir, by any number of persons. In Scenario Two, the members of House Starborn should have secured Valijon Starbringer before doing anything further. If they thought him dead, they should have attempted to verify it—by questioning Butterfly, not by sending a killer against her who did not speak Interphon.

Of course this is real life and not a talkingbook morality play. The facts that remain are these:

An attempt was made to murder Valijon Starbringer on Wanderweb by sending him alone and without ID to its surface.

An attempt was made to murder Valijon Starbringer on Kiffit by Ghadri assassins in the employ of Alaric Dragonflame.

Ritual vendetta was declared against Butterfly on Kiffit by unknown alMayne.

Dominich Fenrir, a corrupt customs official with close ties to the local nightworld, received advance notice of Butterfly's arrival on Kiffit and attempted to solicit her cooperation in an undisclosed enterprise.

It is worth noting in connection with this last that the Ghadri assassins also attempted to solicit her cooperation. One must assume her connection with Valijon is known.

But again we have an answer that is no answer. Assume for a moment that this one out of all the myriad possibilities is the truth. Is it simply an attempt by Morido Dragonflame to gain power in a highly dishonorable and non-alMayne fashion? It requires members of LessHouse Dragonflame to construct a trap relying on an enemy's adherence to the same code of honor which they themselves flout. Given the racial psychology of the alMayne, this is almost beyond belief.

Still, we must believe in the trap and the assault, for we have proof of them. Thus the question becomes not "Could House Dragonflame act in this fashion?" since we know that it can, and has, but, "Could someone else—someone non-alMayne—also benefit from the replacement of the delegate to the Azarine Coalition and have constructed a scenario for House Dragonflame in which the actions it has so far undertaken would be consistent with alMayne honor?"

There are many who might feel themselves benefited, but let us for the moment restrict ourselves to those capable of suborning members of GreatHouse Starborn, deceiving LessHouse Dragonflame, and then bribing a Free Port into complicity. A Free Port is run purely for profit. Closing the landing facilities costs the owner a staggering amount of money for every ship turned away or inconvenienced. To do so is not reasonable behavior in the face of the tiny likelihood of the hunted felons using the facilities to escape. But knowing Valijon Starbringer's true identity, the unknown assassin would know the landing facilities were a danger area, and would act to close them.

The list of those who could do so is very short, and very near the Throne.

And very dangerous for Butterfly.

7

Night's Black Angels

So someone wanted Tiggy dead. I got that reet. And by any set of numbers, Alaric Dragonflame was bent. Fine.

But that meant there wasn't any place on Kiffit I could leave Tiggy.

I went back inside *Firecat* and got dressed. Tiggy looked a little better, but the hold was a mess and I had to dog the supplies down before I lifted. I threw a pile of bloody rags into the disposal and got out the dogging webs. Stow the supplies. Get clearance. Go.

I was weary to the bone; ripe and stupid for the having. A Fenshee fancy-boy could have iced me bare-handed, and my reflexes and judgment was coked beyond use. I had food and water and air enough to take me and Tiggy 25 days' worth of anywhere, and that was halfway to the Core. Only there still wasn't any place off Kiffit I could take Tiggy.

Coldwater was out; my nighttime man was there. He wouldn't like me dragging half the Court to his doorstep, and his displeasure tends to be fatal. Royal was out; it was too dangerous to get to and the *Pledge* had probably already left there. Maybe Tiggy knew where she'd gone, but that wouldn't help me if she'd gone too far Core-ward.

I needed allies, and someplace to run, and there was noplace and nobody I could afford to trust. Not with Paladin to protect, too.

Nobody would hide a Librarian and a Library.

Run with *Firecat*, and lead the werewolves to Tiggy. Lose *Firecat*, and Paladin was dead.

"Need one scenario with true-tell, Pally, not two. Hell-flowers for me or Tiggy?"

"If there were one explanation that explained everything, Butterfly, do you sincerely believe I would refrain from sharing it with you?"

"What?" My tongue felt boiled.

"Go to sleep, Butterfly. I'll wake you when *Firecat* has clearance."

And my teeth still itched, dammit.

* * *

About a thousand years later I finally got hungry enough to wake up.

I felt like I was made out of solar sails; light and huge and ready to collapse at an unkind touch. I blundered around until I found water, and drank till my head was clear.

It was dark in *Firecat*.

"Hatch." Paladin opened it. It was dark outside.

But it was dark when I went to sleep. "Lights," I said. "Hatch."

The hold lights went up and *Firecat* folded herself back together again.

Tiggy was twitching in his sleep like he'd like to toss and turn and didn't have the energy. I'd put a feederpak on him last night. It was empty and the field kit only had one more. I hooked it up and hit my biopak doing it. My wrist rang like a bell, but there was no painease left.

"Hatch," I said again, and this time went out through it.

From the sky I'd slept at least a day. It was horizon-rise; the sky was red as what I'd been covered in last night. The watchlights was on and not doing much for anybody.

Firecat was still hooked up to Kiffit-Port Systems. There wasn't any blood around that I could see.

"Give."

"Dominich Fenrir has placed a hold order on *Firecat*."

I leaned against *Firecat*'s hull and thought about it for a while. Paladin isn't dumb. If there was anything more urgent—like the Teasers coming for us—he'd of given it to me first.

"Is there some reason I should know," I said carefully, "why you didn't just reverse it?"

"I do not know when the hold was placed on *Firecat*," Paladin started, taking the scenic route through his explanation. "It did not appear during any of my status or station-keeping checks. As for why I did not reverse it clandestinely," dramatic pause, "the traffic computer won't allow me to. *Firecat*'s file contains a notation that this hold order is an 'eyes-only' clearance, and will have to be countermanded manually by the verified person of Dominich Fenrir himself."

I shook my head a couple of times, tried to rub my face with the biopak and came fully awake. "Dommie gigged my ship?" But Dommie wanted me to go away. Didn't he?

"I have activated the landline for Dominich Fenrir's place of residence, but it does not seem to be inhabited at this time. Neither has he been to his office today. Therefore I though it best to let you sleep. I have impersonated you and queried Departure Control through normal channels; they would appreciate it if you would meet with Fenrir before you leave. Should I have taken off anyway?" Paladin knew the answer to that well as I did.

I made sure everything was topped up and started uncoupling *Firecat*'s hookups one-handed.

"There's more."

I dropped the waste hose on the crete and scared myself with the sound. "Tell." I still wasn't quite awake; I needed more sleep than I'd got and my nerves were jumpy. Mercs got a safe base to go to while the battledrugs wore off; I didn't.

"The rokeach has been counter-offered for at Market Garden list. Accept?"

It took me moment to remember my so-called purpose in life. "Sure." I resisted the impulse to give the rokeach away free, just to devalue Fenrir's purloined compkey more. "More?"

"There is an offer of employment for us listed at the Guildhall."

"Sure there is." Pally was a barrel of laughs this evening.

"It lists our class and registry number as provided to the trade board at the Guildhall. There is no doubt that this ship and its captain-owner is meant."

"Ignore it. When I get hands on Dommie—"

"Butterfly, the offer of employment is from Lalage Rimini."

Just what I wanted to complete my collection of trouble. A chance to mix it up with Silver Dagger. I finished unhooking *Firecat* and went back inside.

* * *

But first a word from our sponsor, or, why the plucky Gentrymort didn't just bust chops at Kiffit-Port, blast wayaway into the up-an-out and ignore all hold orders. Kiffit's the Outfar, after all. No tractors, no pressors, no stasis fields. Not even a force screen over the port.

But this is Real Life.

Your basic talkingbook freebooter blasts off in defiance of all the Imperial and local regs from every port he lands at with the wicked-wickeds in hot pursuit, changes two numbers on his registry and proceeds to his next downfall, sweet and anonymous. No one bothers him. No one notices his ship, a completely unique design painted with the jeweled likeness of the Goddess of Justice, which is wanted from here to the Outfar and back to the Core with more Class-A warrants than Destiny's Five-Cornered Dog, and when Hero-che-bai is done with his adventure, the Higher Powers square the rap on his cheat-sheet and he goes his way with a pristine First Ticket and the galaxy open before him.

Nuts.

Fact of life number one: all Imperial Ports are the property of the Imperium. The Pax Imperador does not stop at the edge of the atmosphere. Imperial Ports have a pretty good information-matching system that is one so-called bennie of the Empire. In other words, you may run but you can't hide. Not anywhere Imperial Ports is sold.

Fact of life number two: breaking Imperial Port regs leads to automatic disbarment from use of the Imperial Port facilities till the end of time or six months longer, and the Empire owns *all* the ports there are, except Free Ports. You lose your First Ticket, period.

Fact of life number three: any ship looking like the ship they was looking for would be looked at real close for the next whiles after anybody jumped Impie-Port like that. The Imps wouldn't go by the registry number, either. They got some brains. They'd check class-tonnage-dock-age-stowage-rating etcetera and so forth: match the stats and search the ship.

Even with a pristine-mint registry of Pally's rare device, I didn't want to chance attention like that. There's a difference between trouble-but-worth-it and trouble, period.

Fact of life number four: the only interest the Higher Powers had in dicty-barb me was to give me a new career as an official dead person, and even the undying gratitude of every hellflower ever born wouldn't be enough to change that.

* * *

"Silver Dagger wants me to do bidness?" I repeated.

This would've made more sense if Silver Dagger didn't want my entrails for garters over a troubleship pitch I pulled for her ten years back. Rimini brokered it, me and Pally queered it. She never did forgive me for being a better pilot than she wanted.

"The request was posted just after the rokeach was placed on offer, Butterfly. Hard copy of the request was posted to *Firecat*. I was too busy to check before now."

"Legit aboveboard offers of employment through Guild-hall being rare in our line of work," I finished.

I let *Firecat* take more of my weight and thought hard, like you do about something as complicated as a three-legged tik in and out of half-a-dozen different sets of local regulations figuring air and power and cargo to make a profit overall.

I was real deep in something, I didn't know what, and I didn't have the down-deep belief any more in the good numbers that would let me walk away alive.

My edge was gone.

I'd seen people break before. I'd always thought it was something you could help, not like something being gone. But just like I knew I didn't have six toes on my left foot, I knew I didn't have the good numbers anymore.

It wasn't that I was broke and hurting. I'd been that before. And not knowing the play the oppo was farcing was no news either.

But trying to keep Tiggy alive was going to kill me. I

knew that as sure as I knew my luck was gone, and explaining that to Paladin would haul as much cubic as explaining to goforths why they ought to work when they're broke.

But if I died, what happened to Paladin?

"File Rimini under 'amusing but trouble,' bai. T'hell with her, anyway. I'm going to go see Fenrir."

There was also the matter that what Paladin'd figured out about Dragonflame Tiggy might too, even without a City Directory built into his brain. I knew damn well what that'd lead to, and Paladin didn't have hands to keep him here with. I went back inside *Firecat*.

Tiggy was looking pretty good for someone who'd been part dead the night before. I looked round and found his knife, and sealed it up in one of *Firecat*'s bulkheads where he wasn't never going to find it without me. That should keep him put if he woke up. If I came back I could give it to him. If I didn't, we was all dead.

I opened my hotlocker to dress. Blasters and a vibro and a throwing-spike down the neck—the biopak on my right wrist meant no hideout strapped there, so I put another throwing-spike on the left wrist, just for grins. Jacket to hide the silhouette of all that heat, and a few surprises added, just in case. I could stop on the way out and order more supplies. With painease to damp my wrist down to a dull roar, I could finish stowing everything.

"Butterfly, all you are going to do is speak with Fenrir about the hold order?" Paladin sounded downright suspicious. "You will not attempt to murder Alaric Dragonflame, or provoke Silver Dagger, or—"

"Trust me," I said out loud, and that it didn't matter if Tiggy heard. Was going to have to make him trust me too, poor bai.

"Why is it that I do not, Butterfly?" Paladin asked, for my ears only. I didn't answer that. There was a time he'd of been right, too, but it was sometime last night when I still thought I was going to live forever.

* * *

I hooked *Firecat* up to the landlines again for data access before I went. The port shops fixed me up with semi-licit feederpaks and clothes for Tiggy, and I even got the drugs—they said "generic" on the seal, all legal, but it was pasted right over the Imperial Phoenix. I put the stuff by to pick up later and headed on over to the beautiful downside Port Authority Building.

There was maybe four-five sophonts in place; the songbird and his alternate watching the traffic computer, the Portmaster and an interchangeable Peacekeeper. No TC&C officer. Dommie-che-bai Fenrir wasn't in.

None of the people there knew where Dommie was, and none of them wanted to know, and nobody, plain to see, was going to interfere in Dommie's little games. This left me at a minor what you may call your basic disadvantage.

If I didn't get off Kiffit I was dead Real Soon Now.

If I blew Dommie's hold order to get off Kiffit, the only way I could run was deeper into the never-never, away from the *Pledge Of Honor.*

If I tried that with Tiggy on board, he'd kill me.

* * *

The Elephant and Starcastle was right where I left it— a nice touch of continuity in an uncertain Empire. I took a booth in the back and ordered all kinds of finest-kind glycogen-replacement munchies, it having been at least an hour since breakfast. While I ate, I tried to make everything make sense, from the cargo of dud song-ice to the missing Teaser. It wouldn't.

The house gambler at Starcastle is a Moggie hight Varra—x meters of black fur and bad temper and copper eyes like red murder. She had too many fingers and thumbs in the wrong places, but I never hold something like that against a sophont.

She sat down at my table. The fur made it hard to see how she was put together, but I already knew how she was in a fight.

"Give a girl a game, stardancer?" she asked, shuffling the king-sticks. I stacked credit on the table and she spilled out the sticks in the first pattern.

"Make management nervous, sitting here so quiet. Here is quiet, peaceful, yes?"

I took the sticks away from her and hoped my throw'd

beat Fire In The Lake. Varra looked at the biopak on my arm as I tossed and her ears fanned out.

"Yo, che-bai," I said, "looking to be history, oncet square with Teaser. Fenrir gone missing, true-tell?" I threw Glass Castle and Varra took some of my credit off the top of the pile.

"Know you I, girly-girl-my. Why not runalong home-aways? Nothing to find here." This might mean something and it might not, but the Starcastle wanting to roust me was not happy-making.

Varra fanned the sticks again, and flicked one over to make The Circle Of Fire. I passed over two more plaques and took the sticks.

"Not listening, girly-girl. Looking to find Fenrir, some-wise. Need to lift." I spilled Falling Tower and Varra looked at me in disgust.

"Not so lucky, stardancer," she said. I saw her tail flick out and go back under the chair. "Maybe you should see what Silver Dagger wants to buy."

Payday—and an answer I didn't want to hear.

"Maybe Alaric Dragonflame might be better?" I suggested.

The glittering black fans of her ears snapped shut and folded against her head. "You aren't wanted here," Varra said. "You want to drink? Go try Mother Night's." She flipped the last of my credit-plaques at me—hard—and took the king-sticks and left.

The man behind the bar was reaching under it when I looked at him. I left too.

* * *

I found a quiet doorway and gave Paladin an edited update: Silver Dagger wanted me and everybody knew it. Paladin told me what I already knew: Lalage Rimini owned Mother Night's.

Lalage Rimini was plain-and-fancy trouble. There was no reason on the face of entire Borderline for me to go to Mother Night's and ask for Silver Dagger just so she could settle old hash.

Except one.

How much hard credit would it take to make Fenrir slap a hold order on some poor-but-honest smuggler and then do a bunk until darktrade economics caught up with her? Hell, he might not even be in the same quadrant now if he'd been paid enough.

And I was a sitting target.

Paladin said that I was highjumping to conclusions. I said that the only Jumping we was going to do was that unless I found Fenrir or a reasonable facsimile. He said Fenrir still wasn't home. It's amazing how much information you can pull off a standard terminal, even deactivated.

I headed for Mother Night's.

* * *

I legged it through wondertown past all the little shops selling dreams, memory-edit, fake ID, half-price slaves, discount tronics, souvenir painted blaster grips, love machines, deadly weapons, toys, mindcandy, and more. Junk, mostly. Anything I needed wasn't here and I didn't have time to stop for it anyway.

About then I picked up a tail. No figment, and no hellflower.

I cut back and forth at random, doubling back into the wondertown nearer the port while I tried to figure out who and how and whether I was going to get any older. Told Paladin my latest troubles, but there wasn't any-damnthing he could do. He said to look on the bright side. Might just be some roaring boy after my kick.

With this happy thought in mind I turned down the next byway that promised to be noplace and son of noplace anyone'd want to go, and on the tackiest street in all wondertown I found just what the Gentrymort ordered.

It was one of those little hole in the wall places where you can find every illegal or legendary piece of junk the owner figures you might want. Had a broken suit of Imperial Hoplite Armor out front—that's the old powered stuff discontinued about fifty years back for being too dangerous. The suit was all orange-red and silver-blue, and Entropy her own self knew where the fellahim had copped it. I looked up and down the empty street and ducked inside.

Minjalong's VeryGood Artifact Emporium (so said the

baldric on the hoplite armor) was crammed full of the unidentifiable flotsam the enquiring epigone can skim from the ebb and flow of such a galactic hub of commerce as Borderline City. Things was piled up to the ceiling on both walls and all down the middle. Minjalong was nowheres in sight.

Useful. I slithered out of sight myself and watched the door, after tucking a couple grenades into the doorjamb to kill time while I was waiting. Paladin says sometimes I'm aggressively antisocial, which I guess means careful. Eventually my tail wagged.

Oh, it was roaring boys all right, but not after my kick. They had the sleek look of bought muscle; some crimelord's pride and joy. Not Rimini's style, and about as far from hellflowers or Ghadri as it was possible to get.

There ain't no justice, but at the moment I wasn't quite as interested in justice as in a back way out.

"Captain-Owner St. Cyr—can you hear me?"

So the hardboys could walk *and* talk. I concentrated on slithering silent.

"Don't make us get rough, please. All we want to do is talk. I'm sure we can work out an accommodation agreeable to all of us."

Why all these people think I'm born yesterday I'll never figure out.

Goon Number One started in closing the night-shutters over the front and the junk shop started to sink into your basic tenebrous gloom. That made it high time to kyte.

"We're sincerely anxious to come to an agreement here," called Goon Two hopefully. I could hardly wait. "I hope you can be reasonable." Goon One said something to Goon Two I couldn't hear.

Then came the interruption.

The night-shutters got down to my little addition and stuck, and then the grenades went off. The explosion sprayed the shutters outward and Goon One inward. I snapped off a discouraging shot and sprinted for the back door.

Didn't make it. There was a flicker of light on metal, and the piled goods behind me exploded in a spray of white ash and ozone. I dropped flat just in time for the sweep to take the back of my jacket instead of my back, and cut round the other way. Then the air was full of

ash and I was under and behind everything I could think
of, until Goon Two stopped for breath.

So much for sincere discussion. Those sons-of-glory
had a disintegrator ray. Did they know how much those
damn things cost? You could run *Firecat* in dock on a
molecular debonder's energy-pak.

Goon Two hosed the fire I'd started into nonfiction
with his expensive playtoy and came after me. Where in
the hell was Minjalong when you wanted him?

"You're going to wish you hadn't done that, St. Cyr,"
he almost said. He got about as far as "you" and
stopped, sudden-like.

I opened my eyes. The air was misty white, thick with
dust. Silent. I raised up my head real slow. Goon Two
was asleep on the floor wearing charcoal perfume.

There was a sound from the back.

"Nerves bothering you these days, Gentrymort?" asked
Eloi Flashheart, holstering his blaster. "Oh, for the love
of Night, St. Cyr, put the handcannon away before you
hurt somebody."

I stood up. "Well, if it ain't Big Red. Too reet to see
you again, for sure. So tell me what brings you to beautiful downside wondertown?"

Eloi went over to the middle of the floor and picked
up the debonder. I'd wanted that but I was happy to
trade it for a clear shot at the way Eloi'd come in.

"My, what a lot of trouble you're in, sweetheart, and
after giving up darktrade to ship rokeach, too," said the
dashing space pirate. "In case you were wondering, these
citizens used to be some of Kroon'Vannet's very best
hired help." And the missing Dommie Fenrir worked for
Vannet, so Paladin said. Did Vannet think I'd iced his
pet Teaser?

"And you just happened to be in the neighborhood
and thought you'd dish. Don't farce me, Eloi-che-bai;
too much heat drop bye-m-bye for me to worry about
dusting you." I joggled my blaster to underline the point.

"Dammit, Butterfly—you never did have any brains!
We were friends once. I'm trying to help you—you're in
a lot of trouble."

"Old news." The back door was open and the alley
looked clear. I slid a step toward it.

"Come back to Mother Night's with me. I'll guarantee your safety."

"Sure."

"Alcatote'll tear you apart if you shoot me, sweeting. You should remember that much. Will you listen to me?"

"No hope, Eloi-bai. You got nothing I want to hear. I jerked my blaster at him and he raised his hands.

"You're making a big mistake. You've got hellflower trouble, Butterfly—and worse. Worse than you can imagine. I know about Fenrir. Let me help."

"On the floor, you Chancerine son-of-a-spacewarp." I waved my blaster. Eloi-the-Red was pretty sure I'd shoot him, which was more than I was. He went down.

* * *

I got out of Minjalong's and turned back toward the port. On the way Paladin confirmed that Kroon'Vannet was a hardboy who hauled cubic indeed; he was the nighttime man for the whole Crysoprase, including Kiffit and points west, and had gone long time head-to-head with Oob of Coldwater, my boss. But as I've said before, it's bad for bidness to ice stardancers. Why would he want to kill me?

"The interesting thing about this, Butterfly, is that Vannet left Kiffit yesterday morning on the Imperial highliner *Grace And Favor*. He did not declare a destination."

Which meant he could get off anywhere along the run just by paying the differential penalty—and it also meant he'd left orders about me dating from before I landed. Me personally, Butterfly St. Cyr, darktrader.

"I'll complain to the Guild," I muttered. "I swear I will."

I got back to *Firecat* alive, which was beginning to seem more like a miracle each time I did it, and Tiggy was trying to climb out of his sleepsling. He'd already ripped off the feederpak.

"Stop that," I said. "And lay down. What's the good word, babby?"

"I—where are my clothes? And my *arthame*?" My boy Tiggy, making new friends every waking moment. I dumped the stuff I'd picked up at the port shop on the deck.

"Clothes are in disposal with half Ghadri population of Kiffit. Knife's safe."

"Where is it?"

"Around." I wasn't in any mood to cater to the young-at-brain.

"You will give my *arthame* to me at once!" Tiggy yelped, thrashing his way out of the sleepsling to hit the deck in a way that had to of caused him serious hurt. He didn't make a sound.

"Sure I will. Nice to see you're still alive too, you stupid git." I went over to where he was and turned him over gentle as I could. He glared but he didn't fight. I guessed he'd found out how bad hurt he was.

"Last night, bai, I cut off half your leg, because you'd been roundaround track couple times with Ghadri wolf-pack—" Paladin'd said that Tiggy had a bad case of politics, not that his explanation made any sense at all after that. I wondered if the high-heat that'd ordered the chop had any idea what the wetwork looked like.

"Don't touch me, *chaudatu*!" Tiggy bared his teeth. He looked scared to death and scraped to the bone, but the med-tech I'd used on him'd been targeted to his B-pop from the git-go, and he'd come a lot farther toward being well than I had. On the other hand, he had farther to go.

"S'elp me, if you've busted any of my surgery, hell-flower, I'm going to nail you to the deck with your god-lost *arthame*. Now hold still. Your cherry's safe with me." I started to reach for him to see if the head wound'd opened up again.

He grabbed me by my bad wrist and I backhanded him hard as I could with the good one. The throwing-spike strapped to it helped. It sounded like punching the bulkhead.

Tiggy made a sound like something you'd stepped on in the street. I rocked back on my heels.

Sure. Beat him to death to save him. I couldn't even save myself. Captain Flashheart's timely appearance in Minjalong's was no accident. Eloi'd been on Wanderweb, too—Gibberfur must have took out a full page ad in the Wanderweb Daily Truth announcing my itinerary.

Or maybe Eloi was looking for me special. Maybe Eloi

and Dommie and Vannet'd all heard from the same person I was coming to Kiffit, and then Eloi came and went looking for me.

Fine. And when he found me, His Nobly-Bornness Political Assassination Bait Tiggy Stardust was going to be nonfiction.

My hand hurt where I'd hit him. I put it up to my face and saw him watching me. He looked scared.

Damn him.

"I got no time to deal with your delicate glitterborn alMayne sensibilities just now," I told him. "Somebody's trying to ice both of us, Tiggy, and that's home-truth. So make nice." If I didn't back him down he'd run, and if he ran he was dead. And I cared about that, and it was stupid to care about something you couldn't change.

"I want my *arthame*," Tiggy said, not looking at me. I'd split his lip open again. It was bleeding.

"Yeah, sure—but you're going to give me hellflower promise first, glitterborn."

"A promise?" He was trying for arrogant, and missed. Running for his life and having no one to run to yesterday had knocked some of the polish off.

I knew what it was like.

"No more running off ever again like yesternight, kinchin-bai. What we got is some kind trouble you can't shop all on your lonesome. So you're going to promise me you'll stick with me come hell-and-High-Jump until we get you back to your da."

"You wish to return me to my father? Only that?" He sounded suspicious. I couldn't blame him.

"All. You runaround lone, 'flower, you get a serious case of being dead. So you promise me you do what I tell you and stay where I put you and don't farce me with it."

I watched him try it on. He wasn't going for it. Not yet.

"But I cannot do that—I cannot live in a house without walls, with a— You do not know what you are asking!"

"Oh, my house's got plenty of walls all right." And they was all closing in on me. "And if you want to see that faunching coke-gutter of yours this side of entropy, you promise."

He'd been afraid before, but that was of hurting. He saw his death now.

Just like I'd seen mine.

"I will do as you wish. Now give me my *arthame*."

Hellflowers're rotten liars. "You'll do what I *say*—until I hand you over to your da. Promise. No promise, no knife. Hellflower, I could tie you down and burn the damn thing to ash and you'd have to watch. And I'll do it if you make me. I swear by any money."

He was trying to face being dead; I could see it.

"Look, bai, I'm not shaping for to trash your honor. Just to get you back to your da, safe."

"Why?" *Why are you doing this to me*, he meant.

"Does it matter? I bought real grief and the chance to lose my First Ticket keeping you alive, and if you make that all for nothing with your damn hellflower nonsense—"

I'd do what? It might of been kinder to let him die. But if he'd wanted to die he wouldn't of come to me. I looked away and almost missed what he said next.

"I will do as you wish, *alarthme*. I cannot be more in your debt and live." He was tired and hurting and scared and alone. I'd won. Terrific.

I went and popped the *arthame* out of where I'd put it. I could hear Pally not saying anything in the way that means he thinks I'm making a serious mistake.

"Say," I prompted, holding the knife up where Tiggy could see it and feeling like a childcrimer.

"*Alarthme* San'Cyr, I will stay beside you in *comites* until you return me to my father, and I will not leave," Tiggy halfway whispered.

"*Comites:* the special relationship between an alMayne war-leader and his followers. Valijon Starbringer is promising you the obedience he would offer to his lord," Paladin said before shutting up tight again.

And all for a damn hunk of iron that wouldn't care. "Now say your hellflower words, che-bai."

"*Dzain'domere*, San'Cyr. I pledge and give my word," Tiggy managed. I pretended I couldn't see the tears.

I handed him his knife and held him until he stopped shaking. He didn't push me away. He had to trust me now. I was the only thing he had left.

But I still had Paladin.

8

When I Left Home
For Lalage's Sake

The rest of day-into-night got spent catching up on my
sleep, working the battledrug residue out of my system,
and reviewing my options. Most of them boiled down to
"promise Silver Dagger anything to get the hold order
lifted and run like hell." The hired help gave me the
standard runaround when I called Mother Night's trying
to talk to her, and landlines is too corrupt to do bidness
on anyway. I'd have to meet Silver Dagger in person to
get anything out of her.

But I wanted to make one more try at Fenrir before I
did. A little information never hurt anybody and I wanted
to know which category he fit: lost, stolen, or strayed.

Tiggy spent the day eating, sleeping, and ignoring me.
The clothes I'd got fit him fine, even with the biopak
on his leg, but they looked funny. Hellflowers is gaudy
dressers; in stardancer's drag he looked like there was
something missing. But he looked alive.

It wasn't long before I found out I really put my foot
in it with that "cleave to me only" farcing. When I got
up to leave, Tiggy was standing there covered in guns
and knives and the odd alMayne *flechet*, and coked
lightly on field kit goodies. He was going with me, he
said. He didn't let me chase strange *chaudatu* on my
lonesome, he said. It wouldn't be honorable, he said. I
didn't need Paladin to remind me that if Tiggy decided
he couldn't live with what I'd done to him and his honor
already I was going to go first.

I didn't think he could stay on his feet, for true, but
he was determined, and if we got off Kiffit alive it was
going to be sheer luck and not skill anyway, so out of
respect for injured innocence and my valuable time I
took Tiggy and a floater to the address of the little bit
of heaven Dommie called home.

*   *   *

Dominich Fenrir, Kiffit's premier bent Teaser, was, in
the greater galactic scheme of things (leaving out the
bent), a mid-level Phoenix Empire cratty. The place Paladin directed me to was above his touch for damn sure
and no place me and mine belonged—the looks Tiggy
and me got crossing the lobby of the Cotov Arms made
sure we'd be remembered.

Paladin still confirmed the place was deserted, so I did
a shimcrib on the lock and rolled the door back.

"What are you doing, San'Cyr?" Tiggy asked in shat-
teringly audible tones.

"Dommie and me is such old friends I just know he
wouldn't want us to wait in the hall. Now c'mon before
anyone sees us," I said all on one breath and dragged
him inside.

Tiggy came, still looking puzzled and reminding me of
the wide social gap between our stations in life. I slid the
door shut behind us and made it lock, then did a quick
recce just to make sure the people Pally didn't hear
wasn't corpses or borgs or something else that didn't
breathe. Was nobody home, seemingly, so I sat down to
toss Dommie's desk. Tiggy looked over my shoulder, a
fund of innocent curiosity.

"Just make sure nobody comes in through that door,"
I told him, because it wouldn't do any good to ask him
to look for Dommie's safe. "And Tiggy-bai—"

"Don't shoot the people?" Tiggy suggested.

"Would be nice."

"*Alarthme*, how am I supposed to keep you alive in
honor when you will not allow me to defend us?"

"You'll think of something. I'd be right delighted to
let you defend yourself if it didn't involve more wetwork
than Assassins Guild could shake a charter at."

Tiggy thought that was almost amusing, which was
nice, and I sat down to Dommie's comp to see if I could
get around his hold order without bothering him. Would
of been easier if I could ask Paladin to do it, but there
wasn't any way he could access a self-contained database
like this without me bringing in a real bag of tricks. That
was half the reason I was here, doing something so damn
illegal it made my back teeth hurt.

Dommie had lots of nice things in his files, protected from everything but somebody like me getting their hands on the main input port with a variable value generating compkey. There was no way around the "eyes-only" release of the hold order, not that I'd really expected there would be. I started dumping Dommie's database into cassettes. He didn't have a voder on his computer, the paranoid *noke-ma'ashki*, so what he had in his files'd have to stay a mystery until Pally could read it to me. I looked at three or four of the latest entries, but they didn't seem to have anything to do with *Firecat*.

Then I started on his hard copy files. If I couldn't get the hold order lifted without him, I wanted to know where he was.

It was just too bad about my interrupted education, because he had lots of thermofax and I couldn't read it worth a damn. Imperial records are kept in Standard, not Intersign. It might as well of been Old Federation Script for all I could make of it.

Then I came to a word I thought I recognized. I spelled it out, slow. *Library*. It was on a fax that looked real official, but a copy, not the original.

Library.

"Tiggy, c'mere! Can you read this?"

My hellflower lovestar ankled over to where I was and peered at the thermofax.

"Of course. Even a 'hellflower' can read Standard, *alarthme*," he said, toplofty. "But why?"

"Just read it to me, oke? And don't ask any stupid questions."

"It says—it is an official transcript of a warrant from Kyrl Mantow, the Sector Governor for the Directorates of Darkhammer, Crysoprase and Tangervel—that includes Kiffit, where you say we are now—allowing an investigation of Kiffit citizen Kroon'Vannet under Chapter 5 of the Revised Inappropriate Technology Act of the nine hundred and seventy-fifth Year of Imperial Grace. All Imperial officials are directed to provide all assistance in the performance of—" I waved him on to the end. I knew the wording on a Chapter 5 writ by heart. "This order also says that there is an attached list of specific charges, but I do not see it here. Chapter 5—"

"I know what it is, dammit. High Book."

And Dommie, that son-of-a-Librarian, was in it up to his tousled head. He was a business associate of Vannet's, after all, and a High Book investigation makes an alMayne seven-ring vendetta look like kiss-my-hand. If Dommie was involved in Library Science with Vannet, he wasn't just chop-and-channeling the Pax Imperador on Kiffit. He'd sold the whole damn planet.

"Butterfly, I can hear Valijon through the access terminal in the apartment. If Dominich Fenrir is involved in a ongoing Chapter 5 investigation, it would not be a wise idea to remain in Kiffit-Port until such time as you are called on to assist in the investigation."

Paladin always did have a gift for understatement. This left me with just one problem.

"*Alarthme*, are you well?"

Until this exact moment neither Paladin or me had known there was a High Book investigation going on here—and since *Firecat*'d planeted, Paladin'd been through every computer in Borderline. Twice.

So there *was* no investigation. Yet.

Was the coming High Book rap a secret only Dommie knew? Had he told Vannet? Was that why Vannet'd kyted and Dommie followed him? Why would Vannet go off leaving orders behind to make me especially dead? Why would Dommie put a hold order on *Firecat* to keep me here? I'd bet my back teeth Rimini could get *Firecat* up if it suited her, and I bet paying her price'd make High Book look fun. Paladin and me knew next to damn-all about Libraries the way the Empire believed in them, but from what the talkingbooks said I thought nobody'd willingly have anything to do with machines hellishly forged in the likeness etcetera, and here two people was. Together. Two people can't agree on where to have lunch, let alone how to commit treason.

"*Alarthme?*" Tiggy said again.

"I just hate thinking about High Book investigations, bai. C'mon, let's you and me get t'hell out of here."

*   *   *

I'd left my rented floater waiting at the Cotov Arms, because hellflower or not, Tiggy couldn't walk far on that leg. So I got in and he got in and we headed back to wondertown, with no fuss, no muss, and no bother from the *legitimates*. Paladin didn't say anything. He didn't have to. From the moment I saw that High Book writ in Dommie's files, my infinitely replicating options came down to two.

Go and dance with Silver Dagger.

Ignore the hold order, take off, and find another Empire. Just me and Pally. Alone.

It was his call. It was his life. And there wasn't much choice to make.

* * *

Soon as we was in Kiffit-Port district I stopped.

"You. Hellflower-che-bai. You are going to stay in this thing and you are going to not move and you are going to not farce me any chaffer about honor. You will stay here until—" Hell. Until when?

"Tell Valijon you will meet him at Mother Night's, Butterfly," said Paladin. "I will take control of the floater."

"—until I pick you up at Mother Night's," I said without letting myself think about it too much. Fed credit to the on-board computer and punched up the destination code just for looks. Then I glared at Tiggy, who was getting all his arguments ready.

"Shut up. Don't want to hear whatever you have to say. But you are going in floater, and I'm not. Threes and eights." I slammed the canopy back down and the floater rose to flight level.

" 'Love and kisses'?" said Paladin.

"He won't know what it means. 'Less you think glitterborn education includes Gentry-legger transmission codes."

I started back to *Firecat*.

"Butterfly, where are you going?" In the dark and the street it was easy to imagine him standing behind me. And if he could. . . .

I didn't want to want what I wanted so much. If Paladin could just stand here with me. . . .

I never used to think about how Paladin was helpless. A starship isn't helpless, and Paladin could fly *Firecat* by himself. But if I died, what would happen to him?

"Your decision-trees branch as follows: Either you ignore the hold order and take off illegally, or you cooperate with Rimini, who seems to be enabling the restriction. If you ignore the hold order you have the choice of departing with or without Valijon Starbringer, and in both cases you have the further choice of remaining within the Phoenix Empire or proceeding elsewhere. If—"

"Cut farcing, bai. There's no choice. We pop hold order, we have to leave Empire—and we can't do that with Tiggy." Not and stay alive—and I wouldn't blame the kinchin-flower overmuch for killing me, neither.

"If you leave Valijon Starbringer alone on Kiffit, Butterfly, he will probably die."

I stopped, and looked all around at nighttime Kiffit, with all those sophonts and hominids, any twelve of which was probably out to kill the Third Person Peculiar of House Thingummy soon as may be. I thought about Tiggy, and what I'd made him promise, all blithe, and I didn't like myself much.

"Right. Come on." I started walking again. Maybe I'd be lucky, and something'd kill me before I reached the port.

I'd promised him, dammit. And I'd made him promise me. And couldn't none of it matter a candle to a microwave in the face of High Book.

"And if we deal with Lalage Rimini?" Paladin said.

Took me a minute to realize what he was saying.

"Are you crazy, babby-bai? You think this is some kind of legit illegal job she's offering? I'm antique groceries the minute I set foot in Mother Night's!" It wasn't like Pally to farce me around this way. It hurt.

"You're shouting," Paladin observed. I looked around. He wasn't the only one who'd noticed.

"Bai, any job Rimini has for me is naturally going to have fatal as one of its parameters. Fatal means dead. De. Ed. Dead."

"But," says Paladin, serene like he's come up with answer to where the missing cubic x-meters of the cargo went to, "she will have to lift the hold order on *Firecat* in order to employ you."

Terrific. And the worst of it was, I wanted to take

Paladin's way out so bad I could taste it. I turned down a side-street where I could ream him out in peace.

"She could just be waiting to take us for High Book—did you ever think that? Dommie could of shopped us to her to buy off Vannet, an—"

"That is a chance I am willing to take. Whether we stay or go concerns me too, Butterfly, and I would prefer that you meet with Silver Dagger, get the hold order legally removed from *Firecat*, and continue to protect Valijon Starbringer. Do you not wish to continue to protect Valijon?"

"Shut up," I said reasonably, but I knew that Pally already had his answer. The medical telemetry in the RTS saw to that. "Where is he?" I said after a minute.

"Circling Mother Night's at the maximum permitted altitude for remote-controlled vehicles. His presence will begin to attract attention soon, and Valijon is beginning to suspect that the floater is dysfunctional. I suggest you join him with all due speed."

"Sure," I said.

But whatever reason he had for choosing Rimini, I wasn't going to have to think of Tiggy alone somewheres and dead.

No, if things worked out, could all three of us be dead together.

I turned around and headed back toward Mother Night's.

*   *   *   *   *

Insert #8: Paladin's Log

It is an unfortunate truth of experiential reality that choices are not clear-cut, and the event-window for choice may vanish before the information enabling the choice is present. By the time Butterfly realized there was a choice to make, she had already made it. By the time the consequences of the choice were revealed, the root of the decision-tree was already well in the past, and all present decisions were based on the unexamined original assumption: that Valijon Starbringer's life was to be preserved without regard for cost.

Possibly Butterfly did not realize she had made her decision. How much cogitation could enter into a choice compounded equally of instinct and stubbornness? She could only preserve our dual existence at the expense of Valijon Starbringer's, and the converse was equally true; nevertheless she continued to cling to him, propelled by blind primate instinct, and thought of it as a betrayal.

It was true she left the decision to flee without Valijon or deal with Silver Dagger to me. It is equally true that had I chosen to abandon Valijon Starbringer, I could never have trusted Butterfly to act in a rational manner afterward. Organics possess a type of undermind in which information is processed in an irrational manner. We acquired Valijon as the consequence of an earlier example of such processing on Butterfly's part. To forsake him now would cause Butterfly's undermind to punish her with the carelessness that would lead inevitably to both our deaths.

And I do not wish to see her die.

Valijon Starbringer is a clear danger to Butterfly's life, but no matter how much danger his proximity brings her, she is less endangered in his company than in mine.

If Butterfly's life is defined as the highest good, the decision becomes simple at last.

I have made my choice, and my plan—if an intended course of action dependent upon so many fluctuating variables can be called a plan. With a great deal of the "luck" that is such an important factor in Butterfly's calculations, I can gracefully sever the connection that ties her to an Old Federation Library. She will be free.

And what will I be, when I am alone again?

I do not wish to part from her, but the time is long past that I can afford to indulge myself. For her own good Butterfly must be returned to the human world from which I have taken her.

And I must discover who I am.

*   *   *   *   *

Why and t'hell someone like Lalage Rimini couldn't just be listed in the Borderline City Directory with regular office hours I'll never know. Part of her image, I guess. Sure.

Mother Night's is a full-service joy-house. You can get a bath, a meal, a room if you don't mind being bankrupt, dissipations for any number of players, and other things. Mother Night's, you might say, has its finger on the pulsebeat of the community.

Mother Night's was another whole education for our boy Tiggy, too. He was going to wear out his sensawunda before long, which'd be just toodamn bad.

The public bar was real high-ticket work—fake organic as far as the eye could see. The walls were gold pseudocloth, and the floor and ceiling had fake stars set in them someways, as if stardancers didn't see enough stars in our line of work. I ordered tristram shandy and asked the tender if Rimini'd been around. It was a clumsy opening gambit, but I didn't have the energy or the patience to be subtle. If she was so damn anxious to see me, she'd geek.

"Buy a girl a drink, stardancer?" For a second I thought it was Varra, but this Moggie's fur had bronze-gold highlights instead of the black-on-black. She was high-ticket goods—one of the professionals working here, guaranteed to separate you from your back teeth and make you love it.

"Sure," I said, while Tiggy stared. A tronic was right at her elbow. She yawlped into it awhiles and then flowed into a seat.

"I am Naiia," the Moggie said. "If I do not please you, I am happy to suggest another of our companions who fits your requirements."

"I'm interested in companion hight Silver Dagger," I said, just to be difficult.

"A friend?" Naiia's tail flicked up and down. It looked soft. I stopped looking at the tail and watched the eyes.

"Is stupid move bracing tender, stardancer." The plush cuddly-toy face looked amused.

"Got me you, didn't it? Want to see Silver Dagger."

"And you think Lalage Rimini is here? Girl, you have got wrong coordinates for certain."

I leaned my elbows on the table and stared at her. "Tell her St. Cyr's come calling. She'll remember me."

"And your business?" Naiia was all gilded ice. "I make no promises."

"I might want to sell her some cut flowers." This went right over Tiggy's head, and good thing too. I had no actual intention to sell him to Rimini, but it didn't hurt to see if she was in the market—and what she'd offer.

Naiia slithered away and came back looking disappointed. "We think you will find our rooftop club very— exclusive, St. Cyr. Perhaps you will like to see, while your—friend—remains here. Drinks on the house. Of course."

*   *   *

Information's always nice to have. Piece of info #1: was real unlikely Rimini was hunting hellflowers if she was leaving Tiggy to get jumped in the public bar while I went off somewheres nice and quiet.

"Che-bai, I get lonesome, bye-m-bye, and so does my—*friend*—here. Why don't we all three go have look-see?"

Naiia liked that idea, too, so I didn't.

Piece of info #2: Either Rimini was desperate, or she was holding so many high cards she could afford to let me get away with sassing the hired help.

I liked that even less.

*   *   *

The lift opened on a room done in early ostentation. I made sure Tiggy and me got out together, and wept no tears when Naiia and the lift both disappeared. A jarring note in the albino perfection was a big commercial remote-access Imperial DataNet terminal sitting in the middle of the floor. It looked bewildered and lost this far from Kiffit-Port.

Rimini was nowhere in sight.

Civilian possession of a way into the dataweb's illegal, of course. Paladin should of found it on the tronic network and told me about it, but there's ways to hide access terminals, especially if somebody doesn't know to look.

And there was one thing more that shouldn't have

been there. Dommie Fenrir of the TC&C, late confidant of Kroon'Vannet (saurian crimeboss of High Book fame), was sitting in the middle of everything, lonealone as the proverbial. He didn't look like a happy citizen.

I made serene and sat on the edge of the table and Tiggy hovered over me. He didn't look excessively healthy, but being a hellflower made up for a lot.

Piece of info #3: Dommie hadn't batted a whisker when he saw Tiggy, and he wasn't that good a actor. So now I knew one person that wasn't out to kill Tiggy Stardust—or else I knew that he was impenetrably disguised.

"So, Dommie-bai; nice to see you again. Lovely evening. This's my partner, Tiggy Stardust, who'll be real delighted to serve you in finest restaurants slice and diced. Got question about hold order on *Firecat* under your chop."

Dommie just looked at me. Somebody'd tuned him up royal, and that was illegal too.

"What was you looking for on my ship, Dommie-bai?"

"It was the Library. Vannet said you'd come about the Library."

"Butterfly? What's wrong?" Paladin couldn't hear what anybody but me said, of course. He just knew my heart-rate'd made the jump to angeltown.

"Vannet had a Library," I said, hard. "Papers said so. No Library on my ship."

"I didn't— You have to believe me— I never knew about the Library until he— It was supposed to be set—"

"Librarian," said Tiggy. I looked around. Tiggy'd pulled his blaster on the word "Library" and was pointing it right at Dommie. Tiggy looked like talkingbook grim death and sweet for my pet Teaser.

"For the love of Night, 'flower—" I said, getting up.

"Not me!" Dommie was on his knees. "It's Vannet— I swear it's Vannet—he's got the Library—and backing from someone at Throne—I don't know who!"

So Dommie wasn't topping me for High Book. He was just crazy. The relief was so great I damn near shot him myself.

There was still the matter of the hold order, though.

"Gimme break, Dommie," I said. "Nobody believes in Libraries anymore. Haven't seen Library, haven't

touched Library. Vannet's backed by Throne? Get real!"
I saw from the way Tiggy lowered his blaster that even
he didn't swallow this one.

"But it's true! I told her everything. She said she'd
protect me if I put the hold order on your ship—I know
about you—you can get me off-planet—he'll let you
make a deal, he said so—I swear I didn't know—" Dommie was babbling. I recognized the symptoms of light
persona-peel.

I looked at Tiggy. "Put heat away, bai; Teaser's rav-
ing." He looked from me to Dommie and lowered his
blaster.

"Butterfly, I now have audio pickup in the room you
are in," Paladin said. "There are three people behind
you. From the sound of their breathing they are con-
cealed somehow. There may also be others present. If
so, they are in another room. Accurate determination of
additional life-forms is not possible."

"Dommie, you son-a-Librarian, I want trufax, not rav-
ing. I want your hold order off my ship. And I want to
know why Silver Dagger's hiding in closet letting you
front for her."

"Very good; you may yet live to grow up. Now put
your hands up, both of you. There isn't going to be any
gunplay." Dommie went all white at the voice but I
already guessed he knew her.

"Do it," I said to Tiggy. I turned around with my
hands on top of my head. Tiggy turned around too. I
swear I could hear his jaw drop.

Lalage Rimini was tall as he was—taller, in heeled
boots—and long-leggedy, sleek, and expensive in the way
that made me feel every inch the dirt-farmer's daughter.
You could make a real informed guess on her B-pop and
medical history and all because she was wearing something real tight and real thin about the color of her skin,
and with no place to hide a weapon. It made some people
careless. Not me. Rimini was high-class trouble. And
mine all mine.

The first time I met Silver Dagger it was because of a
insurance scam: inept pilot in shakydown ship, high-
ticket cargo well-insured. Ship took by pirates, insurance
company pays off, only pirates are working for shipowner
too. He keeps cargo, and insurance, and maybe ship to

boot. I'd done it back when I was dragging Paladin from ship to borrowed ship disguised as a custom navicomp, and Silver Dagger'd brokered the deal. Only Paladin and me together made a better pilot than she'd hoped for, and I was a personal friend of the pirate.

She had her trademark silver dagger in a belt around her hips, and she was wearing two side-boys—the big wide kind with no ears what'd put in serious overtime someplace like Beofox's surgery and was coked borg for sure. One of them hefted something about the size of *Firecat*'s quad-cannon and looked at me.

"Well, well, well—if it isn't little Butterfly. And you've brought the children; how sweet. I knew you were crazy, St. Cyr, but I didn't know you were stupid."

"Nice to see you, Rimini—it's been a long time."

"Not long enough."

"Who asked who to lunch?"

One of Rimini's side-boys twitched and Rimini turned toward him about a fraction of an inch. He backed down. I got back her full attention.

"You're to pick up a cargo of chobosh on Manticore and deliver it to RoaqMhone. You'll be jacking it from a freelancer trying to break into the market, but that's no concern of yours. Everything's been arranged; just go where you're told. What you do from the Roaq is your business." She sounded bored.

"Butterfly, Governor-General Archangel will be touring the Roaq. He's expected to arrive in twenty days," Paladin said.

"Suppose I got other plans, Rimini?" Pally and me knew that what I was going to do at angels was kyte for the *Pledge Of Honor* no matter what I told Rimini here, but if Rimini thought so too, I wouldn't get out of here alive.

She smiled. "St. Cyr, don't you want to live forever?"

"*Firecat* isn't set up to run load like that. Give me a break. I got things to do."

"Go ahead."

Nice. You had to admire her style. And I was willing to, from a safe distance. "Dommie put a hold order on *Firecat*. I'm grounded." And she knew it damn well.

"That's hardly any business of mine, now, is it?"

"Then you won't mind if I take Dommie an—"

"Trade Officer Fenrir stays here. For reasons of health."

"No, Mistress, please—you *promised*—" She looked at him. Dommie shut up.

Funny. I never liked him and I'd been planning to farce his cheat-sheet enough to get him hard time in an Imp hellhouse, but I didn't like this even more. It's not that I'm squeamish, but it didn't seem like there was any reason to do what Silver Dagger'd done to him. She didn't even act like it'd been fun.

"Go to Manticore—or stay here and join Fenrir on High Book charges. Your choice, St. Cyr."

"High Book?" Suddenly things was even less fun.

"You were at the Cotov Arms. You saw the Chapter 5 warrant on Vannet. Don't bother to make up a story. Now there's going to be a High Book investigation—and since you've been working for Kroon'Vannet for years, and Officer Fenrir's files contain complete documentation of the relationship, I'm afraid that naturally you're going to be called upon to assist."

Tiggy was twitching like a solar sail in an ion storm and I just felt sick. Coincidence. Bad luck. But toodamn-bad for me when proof of Rimini's fantasy was sitting on *Firecat* for anyone to find. First thing Office of Question'd do be pull me in and take *Firecat* apart.

And if Paladin wiped Rimini's forgeries out of the Borderline computers it'd be as good as a confession.

"I haven't. They don't." My denying it calmed Tiggy down at least.

"Yet. Interesting to see who gets their hands on you first—the Office of the Question, or Oob of Coldwater."

Who'd be thrilled to find me shopping kick for Vannet, make few mistakes about it. Even if it wasn't true.

"Going into the Roaq any time soon, stardancer?" said Rimini.

This was bad. This was real bad.

"Just say yes. Of course, if you decide to change your mind anywhere along the way, I guarantee to make you the most popular darktrader in the Empire."

With headprice, and charges, and up-to-date hollies on what me and my ship looked like. The heat that'd drop then would make the hold order look easy to beat.

"Could make sure you go down too, Rimini," I suggested.

"I don't think so. The Office of the Question likes a little proof, at least. You won't even survive the first scan . . . dicty-girl. And after that they won't believe a thing you have to say."

I didn't have to fake giving up. Rimini had me cold—because Rimini had the missing piece of the jigsaw.

If it was as simple as crying Library, Rimini would of owned me years ago. But you couldn't just whistle up a High Book investigation any old time. Drawing me in to a real one was another matter—that, and knowing I couldn't even afford to say "yes-sir-thank-you-sir" to an Imperial Officer. Because I was dicty. Spell that D-E-A-D.

"Butterfly, you will have to take her cargo to the Roaq," said my RTS. Paladin'd been following the conversation through the remote terminal, and chose now to cast his vote on the side of crazy.

"Of course, you're wondering what will keep me from holding this over you for the rest of your life. Work it out for yourself. Once Kroon'Vannet is dead, any charges I make against you won't hold atmosphere," Rimini said.

Time-value blackmail. Cute. But why did Rimini want me to go to Roaq? There was easier ways to kill me. Lots.

"Butterfly. Trust me. Tell her you will do it, and bring Valijon back to *Firecat*. I have a plan. We will all be safe. Valijon will not have to die. Accept Rimini's offer."

If Paladin'd lost his mind now wasn't the time to discuss it. "Lift the hold order, Rimini. You just bought yourself a stardancer." She showed off some of her better teeth and it was a miracle I didn't get frostbite.

"Trade Officer Fenrir, lift the hold order on the Independent ship *Firecat*."

It took Dommie three tries to match his filed voice-print—and add the code-phrase that made Kiffit Port Authority accept it even though he wasn't there in person.

"The hold order on *Firecat* has been canceled, Butterfly. I am—two more life-forms entering your area," Paladin said.

"There you are, sweeting—free as a bird," said a old familiar voice from behind me. "Aren't you happy?"

I didn't bother to look around. "Rimini, you got any

more people stashed round this shop? If you do, I'm walking."

"I am starting the preflight on *Firecat*," Paladin said for my ears only.

"Without your trip-tik? Give the darktrader her trip-tik, Eloi." Rimini made another of her damn elegant gestures, and Captain Eloi Flashheart of the *Woebegone* walked around to where I could see him with my hands on top of my head. He pulled a cassette out of his vest and flipped it to me. It hit me in the chest and bounced to the floor. Eloi looked slightly repentant. Alcatote didn't look repentant at all. Fenrir looked at Eloi and flinched.

Eloi-the-Red and Rimini'd been in that insurance scam together. I should of expected them to be together now. Eloi'd wanted me to come back to Mother Night's before. Why else?

"I tried to warn you, sweeting. There are lots of people interested in you. Don't fight this. Go to Manticore. Stay alive." His voice was chock-full of prime-quality sympathy. Like earlier, at Minjalong's, where he'd followed me.

A lot of things was queer about this gig, and they was all Eloi.

Eloi'd been on Wanderweb in the bar where I picked up my cargo.

Eloi was on Kiffit.

Eloi'd been following me around wondertown.

Eloi knew about my hellflower trouble. He'd said so at Minjalong's.

"You set me up," I said, putting it all together. "You. Eloi-che-bai. You set me up back on Wanderweb."

Gibberfur hadn't been doing bidness on his lonesome. He'd been a cut-out. It was *Eloi* shipping dud Lyricals to Kiffit. That was how he knew where I was going to be, and when. That was how he knew about my hellflower trouble—he'd been to Moke Rahone's. And he'd gone there so he could be there when I tossed my kick—and Rahone checked it before accepting it.

"You set me up so that Moke Rahone would of found fake song-ice in his kick. He'd squall, say I'd switched the real ones for fakes. I didn't, but maybe he could prove I did. Maybe he'd promise to accept the cargo anyway if I did him a small favor—jack load of chobosh óff Manticore, say, and drop it in the Roaq. I should of been on my way to Manticore bought and paid for by your farced cargo scam by the time Vannet's hardboys went hunting for to sign my lease. You knew they'd be after me. That's why you followed me through wondertown. You still needed me.

"Only Moke Rahone was dead, and nobody knew what I'd delivered to him, or when, so you couldn't use him to make me do what you wanted. You had to come up with something else. So you and Silver Dagger picked up Dommie to put a hold order on *Firecat*—and he told you about the Chapter 5. You knew I was dicty, Eloi. You knew I couldn't afford to be investigated."

"So she's smarter than she looks," said Rimini to Eloi. "Not that that's difficult."

Eloi shrugged. Did that mean I was right? Puzzle pieces fit, but that was no guarantee, and it still left too many questions unanswered. Why would a notorious Outfar pirate and a high-ticket nightworld broker get together to commit Low Treason by kidnapping Dommie just to get me in trouble? Things like that only happen in talkingbooks.

Rimini tapped the hilt of her silver dagger with one expensive ornate fingernail. She brushed back hair the color of high-ticket jewelry and looked pointed-like at Tiggy. Eloi followed her look.

Rimini said something to Tiggy in helltongue that Paladin didn't translate. He went for his knife and her in one fluid motion and I grabbed him and got cut. I slugged him in the ribs where I knew it'd hurt. Rimini laughed and Tiggy subsided. Growling. I put my hands back on top of my head.

"Put your hands down, little Saint. Obviously you want to go on living," Eloi said. He'd known me long enough ago to make a educated guess about my B-pop. But he'd done better than that. He knew which damn colony in Tahelangone Sector I came from. No need to wonder any more how Rimini knew.

"Yeah. I want to live."

I looked at Tiggy. Couldn't tell what he was thinking, and he wasn't about to come out with it in front of the strange *chaudatu*. "Put your hands down, hellflower, we ain't getting shot tonight."

I picked up the trip-tik.

"Who's your little friend, St. Cyr—or should I ask?" Rimini said sweetly.

"Honored One," Eloi said to Tiggy, "I and mine would be honored if you would share our walls."

So much for disguises. Eloi knew who Tiggy really was, and it didn't take stark staring brilliance to see that Eloi was offering Tiggy the chance to jump ship. Tiggy ignored him.

"Butterfly, will you tell him to talk to me? He probably hasn't told you his name, but he's from an alMayne GreatHouse, and his House wants him back. Badly. He's your hellflower trouble that Moke Rahone died for. Send him back to them and you'll be safe."

Even if Eloi believed himself, he was wrong. "Talk to the pretty pirate, che-bai," I said to Tiggy.

Tiggy favored Eloi with your basic hawk-blue gaze keen as a mountain lake. "I have nothing to say to the *chaudatu* reiver, *alarthme*."

Eloi glared. He was just lucky Tiggy didn't seem to of followed my explanation of how he'd set me up, or he wouldn't be in a glaring condition. Tiggy wanted to kill somebody so bad I could feel it.

"Tell him to come with me. I'll square it for you with his GreatHouse, Butterfly, I swear it. Tell him I'll take him back to alMayne where he'll be safe."

"Sure, bai. Alaric Dragonflame just paid solid credit to get him iced and I'm going to give him to you? Farce me no bedtime stories."

For once I got to see Eloi boggled.

"*What?*"

Also forgot I hadn't let Tiggy in on Paladin's theory.

"Then Dragonflame's blood is mine!" Tiggy headed for the door, hand on his knife.

"Your blood is mine first!" I yelled. I grabbed him by the shirt and hauled him back. "Or you forgot all of them pretty helltongue words you sang me?"

Tiggy looked down at me, real bleak and suddenly older.

Honor might be stronger than dirt, but people got limits. We'd find out what his were. Maybe tonight. I hoped that *arthame* of his was worth it.

"No," he said, slow. "I have not forgotten. You condemn me to live without walls, and I must obey."

He didn't fight me anymore then so I dragged him back and then remembered Eloi and the rest of my audience. Captain Flashheart looked like he had all his questions answered and didn't like what he'd got, and Rimini looked like she'd be laughing fit to bust a gut if it wasn't against her religion. Not good.

"Then you do know who he is—and you still want to drag him around the galaxy with you on this darktrade run?" Eloi said.

"Sure. My idea. Ask Rimini."

Eloi looked unhappy, which was nothing to the way I felt.

"You said you wanted involvement at the highest levels, Eloi," she purred. It was nice to see somebody else take cop from Silver Dagger for a change.

There was a long pause. Rimini looked at Eloi, smirked, gathered up her hardboys, and left. Eloi turned back to me.

"Why do you think that Master Dragonflame is trying to have the boy killed?"

"Why do I got to be one to run cargo into Roaq?" I said right back. Eloi closed up with his best hurt-but-sulky expression. He wouldn't geek.

"Honored One—" Eloi said to Tiggy. Tiggy put his hand on his knife. Plain to see, Tiggy Stardust took the position of "my *chaudatu*, right or wrong."

Eloi gave up. "Have a nice trip, Saint Sincere," he snarled.

That was my cue to ankle, leaving way too many witnesses behind. Whatever leverage having Tiggy gave me, it wasn't enough to buy me free. And to add to my troubles Eloi knew who Tiggy was, and that I had him, and where I was going with him.

And so did somebody else.

"And what keeps Dommie from to sing like songbird Real Soon Now?" I asked.

I knew from the way Eloi twitched when I said it that Dommie wasn't getting any older after tonight. Now Dommie knew it too. He backed away from the DataNet terminal and Alcatote let him.

"I— You can't do this to me— I'm an Imperial offi-

cer—I told you what you wanted— I told you about the
Library— I'll tell them it's her Library—hers and Vannet's— You have to let me go and—"

"I will finish it." Tiggy got up again from where he'd
been sitting and pulled his knife. "Is it your will,
alarthme, that he should die for bearing false witness
against you?"

"Put your damn antique away, hellflower." You'd
think Rimini wanted blood all over her rug.

Eloi pulled one of his blasters and set it by the terminal. "Would you rather it was self-defense?"

I have never liked playing games with people that have
to be killed. "*Dammit*, Eloi—"

I was trying to face off too many people at once. Dommie went for the heat, just like Eloi'd knew he would.
But he was too damn slow, and Tiggy whipped half a
meter of *arthame* through his throat from the other side
of the room, and then looked at me to see if he'd done
it right.

Dommie tried to scream. He jerked Tiggy's knife loose
and died slow enough to know it was happening. It was
so damn quiet you could hear the sound of blood hitting
the carpet in your basic talkingbook hot scarlet gouts,
and for a bad minute I was back in Moke Rahone's office
with a lifetaker at the door.

"*Kore-alarthme*? He tried to kill you. He shadowed
your honor, he had to die. He would have lied; you have
no Library." Tiggy was scared and hurting, and afraid
he'd got part of the honor-nonsense wrong, and all I
could think of was I'd expected to have to face Dommie
off every time I came here for the next twenty standard
years. And now I wouldn't, because Tiggy'd killed him
too fast to think.

And Tiggy was still looking at me.

"Je, babby, you done good; he won't go telling no
tales now."

Eloi looked sorry, damn him.

"We're going to leave now, Tiggy-bai. Get your traps."

"*Alarthme*," said Tiggy before he went and got his
knife back, "I do not think I like either this place or
these people."

The lift opened for us and took us down with no problem. Surprise.

9

No Night Without Stars

Tiggy was pretty quiet the whole way back from Mother Night's, and wouldn't take the painease I thought he ought to have when we got to *Firecat*.

Paladin had said to go to Manticore and he'd explain on the way, so I did. Kiffit-Port gave me no nevermind when I took *Firecat* up. Transit to angeltown was smooth, and looking out the canopy at hyperspace should of made me feel lots better than it did. We was all three of us off Kiffit. Alive.

But Tiggy trusted me as much as hellflowers do, and if I wasn't selling him up the Market Garden path, I was coming pretty close. I'd told him I'd take him to his da, not on a guided tour of the never-never. It was eight days to Manticore. He'd be sure to notice.

Hell, he already knew, if he'd been paying attention back at Silver Dagger's. I looked at what she'd got me into. The trip-tik was just what Rimini said it was: some kiddy hight Parxifal Quarl was waiting open-armed on RoaqMhone for the cargo of chobosh I was going to hijack on Manticore. Fine. I'd worked with Parxifal before. Silk-sailing. No problem.

Only Tiggy expected I'd be kyting after *Pledge* like I promised.

"Pally, now would be a good time to explain," I said, quiet-like.

For a minute I thought he wasn't going to answer.

"It is very simple, Butterfly. You will go to Manticore, pick up the chobosh, go on to RoaqMhone and deliver it. Doing those things will alleviate Rimini's suspicion to some extent. Neither you nor I believe that a simple Transit to Roaq-space is the limit of Silver Dagger's requirements, but once we are there, Lalage Rimini's desires will no longer matter. RoaqMheri is a major out-

lands shipping crossroads in the same system as Roaq-
Mhone. I will arrange things with the computers on
RoaqMheri so that *Firecat* and I vanish. You and Valijon
will rendezvous with the *Pledge Of Honor* in a thor-
oughly innocent ship that contains no Library. When you
have returned Valijon to his father, you must ask to be
adopted as a member of his household. I believe the
request will be granted, which will mean that you will
obtain Imperial citizenship. When Rimini makes good
her threat, and you are arrested in connection with the
Chapter 5 investigation of Kroon'Vannet, it will not matter. The Empire will not prosecute on the illegal emigration charge when you are—under law—an alMayne, and
there will be no hard evidence of my existence to betray
us. Kennor Starbringer's protection of you as a member
of his Household will see to it that you are not subjected
to invasive personality-reformatting techniques by the
Office of the Question."

"And what the hell you going to be doing while I'm
doing all that, bai?" Ditch Pally and steal a new ship
from one of the busiest ports in the never-never? It might
not be the stupidest idea that I had ever heard in my
whole entire life, but it came real close. And it didn't
even address the main point. What was I supposed to
say to Tiggy between here and RoaqMheri? "We going
back to your da as soon as my Library and me make a
detour?"

"There is absolutely no cause for concern. It will work,
Butterfly. You'll be safe, cleared of all suspicion. You
can land at any port you wish."

If I was innocent in the first place, I could of promised
Rimini the stars in their courses then beat it to wherever
Tiggy's ship *Pledge Of Honor* was as soon as I lifted. If
Tiggy had any brains, that's what he expected.

Only I couldn't, because Rimini had me—because
there *was* a Library for the Office of the Question to
find.

"You see that, don't you? Butterfly?"

Too bad Tiggy couldn't take that into account.

"Oh, sure, bai." Liar.

I went back up into *Firecat*'s hold. Tiggy was sitting
on the deck with his bad leg stretched out in front of
him. If it hurt, he didn't say.

"We are not following the *Pledge Of Honor* as you said. We are going to a place called Manticore." He looked old, and weary to the bone.

"Silver Dagger'll kill me if I don't, and I don't want to die." I wondered if that was even true, or if I just didn't want to die owing.

Tiggy thought about it. "You wish to break your pledged word merely to preserve your life?" he said, scornful.

"Give me a break, 'flower! You ever been topped for High Book? Office of Question don't stop digging. By time the hellhounds figure I'm clean of Librarian rap I'll be dead, and very sorry to next of kin. Only they won't be sorry, and I don't have any kin."

Tiggy thought some more.

"You are a criminal. A thief. Silver Dagger is also a criminal."

"Rimini's a nightbroker and I'm a dicty and you're hurt. Now, do you mind if I coke and wrap you? We both been up lots of hours; it's time to hit the rack."

"A . . . 'dicty'? Is that also criminal?"

Maybe I could talk him to death.

"To be one out here is. You know about how it is when somebody buys someplace for a closed colony—an Interdicted World? I'm from one of them. If the *legitimates* catch me off Granola, they'll kill me. Simple. Any good gene-scan'll ID me. And that's the first thing the Office of Question runs in High Book."

"So you *do* think only of your own life, thief. How did you get off-world?"

"I was slaved off by a Fenshee human resources manager named Errol Lightfoot when I was your age. Now can we rack out?"

Tiggy thought real hard.

"The criminal Lalage Rimini will honorlessly bear false witness against you, and say that you possess a Library. You do not possess a Library, but because you are dicty, you dare not be arrested by the Empire, because they will discover your identity and kill you."

"Now look, bai—" I saw where this was going.

"But you do not need to fear, *Kore-alarthme*." Tiggy was all lit up, like he had answers to all the problems of Creation. "I swear to you, on my Knife and my honor, that you need not fear the Empire's law. Take me to my father now. He will rejoice to know of the enemies we have discovered within his walls, and the shelter of his House will be yours."

For about a nanosecond-five, until they found Paladin. "No. We go to the Roaq first."

He looked away from me and didn't say much for about five minutes. I could tell he was hurting to ask why, and couldn't, because of honor-nonsense.

"Are you an honest thief, San'Cyr?" he said finally.

Whatever was coming next I didn't want to hear it. "I'm not a thief. I'm a darktrader—that's smuggler to you, I guess. I do what I get paid to—or what I got to. And I got to go to the Roaq."

Tiggy gestured that away. "You do what you are paid to, San'Cyr? Who paid you to save my life three times? Once in Wanderweb Free Port, though it was unnecessary, once in the Justiciary of Wanderweb, and once at the place you call 'wondertown' on Kiffit. You have said that Alaric Dragonflame sought my life in Borderline with assassins. Could he not have paid you to let me die?"

Yes.

"I'm not for sale, hellflower."

Liar.

"The woman called Silver Dagger has bought you. With lies."

With truth. With a High Book accusation I couldn't face down.

"Bai, you shut your yap. Saved your bones on Wanderweb cause I didn't like the odds and topped you out of gig to crottle your chitlins. You got no right to come farcing me roundabout bought and sold."

Paladin's life for Tiggy's. Anywhere, any time. All a person had to do was ask.

"You swore to me that you would take my service and use it to return me to my House. But now you choose, freely, to bend to the will of a *chaudatu* criminal. How can I, in honor, serve you still? I do not wish to die either, *Kore* San'Cyr—but I must die now, if you are not worthy to bind me. 'Swear, hellflower,' you say to me, as if mine were empty words, written on the wind. *Chaudatu* words. 'Swear to stay by me, to trust me, to protect

me, not to leave until I release you'—and then you treat
my sworn words as stones flung into water, and I as a
wing-clipped raptor that must stay where it is set. My
words are not empty words, woman-not-of-the-Gentle-
People, and I have sworn to cover you with my shadow.
I have a right to know the truth of the life I am trusting
my life to. You owe me my answers."

I kept the hold dark when I was down in the cockpit
and Pally hadn't brought up the lights. I couldn't see
Tiggy's face; just the shine of white-gold hair by the light
of angeltown coming through the hullports. I hoped he
couldn't see me either. I sat down on the deck and put
my head on my knees.

Anywhere, any time. And Paladin's only bright idea
was to have me leave him somewhere alone while I went
and delivered Tiggy.

"Don't care what you believe, Tiggy Stardust. I promise whatever you want me to swear by that I'm trying
to keep you alive, and I'm taking you back to Daddy
Starbringer as fast as may be. But we got to go to the
Roaq first."

"You saved me once for pity and twice for spite,"
Tiggy said implacable-like. "The third time, on Kiffit,
when I came back to your ship—why did you succor me
then? You knew of the Ghadri. You could have told
them you would give me to them. I had left you at gun-
point. You owed me nothing. What are your *chaudatu*
reasons to save my life and trap me in honor?"

Because I'd thought I was human. That was the joke,
and maybe even a hellflower'd laugh. I hadn't known I
was just a Librarian waiting to start running from a High
Book charge.

"You came to me for help, remember. And the odds
you was up against stank."

"You did not help Eloi Flashheart. He wanted your
help."

Just a Librarian. With no call to say what I would and
wouldn't do. Because I'd do anything. For Paladin.

Damn him.

"Eloi's no good to me. You are. Need you to lift kidnap-rap off me."

"You are lying to me, *Kore* San'Cyr."

This wasn't an acceptable risk anymore. I knew that

Tiggy had to go, and I knew that if we both sat here until the goforths decayed I wasn't going to do it.

He was talking again. "That is not why you rescued me. I know that much."

"I am not one teeny damn bit interested in your hallucinations, you gibbering glitterborn."

"Do you think no oath cuts two ways? If I am to trust you, you must be worthy of it. Why did you save my life the third time?'

I stared off into the dark until my jaws hurt. I wanted to tell him the whole truth. Then he'd kill me and I wouldn't have any more problems. But then he'd find Paladin and take him apart—and without Paladin, *Firecat* would be a powerless hulk, drifting until it docked at the Ghost Capital of the Old Federation, with nothing but corpses inboard.

"You was fourteen years old and been sold down the river. Didn't matter to me who wanted you dead. Wasn't going to let it happen."

"Again," said Paladin, and for just one second I wanted to answer him. Out loud—where Tiggy'd hear.

"For honor," said Tiggy with quiet satisfaction.

I was fed up with both of them. "You and your damn honor can go tip dice cups in hell, you godlost highjumping barbarian. What gives you the right to go asking answers till you find something that suits you?"

"Not answers that suit me. The truth. You know nothing of the Gentle People, and call us with your vulgar names as if we were plants, and say honor and honor as if you understood what the honor of the Gentle People is. You cannot understand it—the honor that is better than bread, that lights the long night and will go down with us into death. How can I give that into the keeping of beasts? But if you will die for such honor as *chaudatu* can possess, I . . ."

I don't have to die today. And neither did I.

"Fortunately you seem to have convinced Valijon Starbringer that you are a suitable overlord," Paladin said dryly.

"Shut up, damn you!" My fingers were clenched in the biopak hard enough to hurt. "Shut up—just shut up!"

The words weren't for Tiggy but he didn't know that. I dragged the biopak up over my jaw where the transponder was locked up in a plug of fake bone—with Paladin inside me, listening all the time. "Shut up," I said, and ground my teeth before I said anything else.

I looked out the port. Wrapped up in hyperspace out there was all the stars I ever wanted as a kid. Wrapped around me was enough tech to make all Fifty Patriarchs of Granola rotate in the glorious afterlife.

And Paladin. I wished I remembered how to cry.

"Kore-alarthme?" Tiggy said in a half-whisper.

"What?"

"I will go with you where you say."

"Fine. Go to bed."

All I gave him was painease, but it could have been poison.

It could have been.

* * *

After I was done with Tiggy I slid back into the mercy seat and looked out at angeltown. I hurt, and there wasn't enough coking in the world to cover it. The edge was gone. I was easy meat. Prey.

It's funny. You hear all those stories about somebody's luck running out, and you always think it must of been a surprise. I'd been on borrowed time since I left Granola, but I guess I knew my luck was over from the moment I stepped into that streetfight back on Wanderweb.

Because Paladin's plan wasn't going to work. Tiggy was too close now—to me and what I did and how I lived. He'd twig to the real truth about me and my Library before *Firecat* ever got to the Roaq. And even if he didn't, Paladin wanted me to bet my life on the mercy of Tiggy's da the high-heat hellflower to save me from the Office of the Question when I took him home.

"Butterfly? Will you talk to me?" Paladin said through the transponder.

"Sure, bai." I was betting my life now that Tiggy was drugged enough not to hear, but I didn't care. The transponder didn't itch anymore when taking transmission. Beofox'd been right, for a wonder.

"Promise me you'll ask to be adopted into House Starborn when you rendezvous with the *Pledge Of Honor*," Paladin said.

Was he nuts? Or trying to set me up? Or had Pally just run out to the end of the good numbers too? Did Libraries get old?

"I want you to live, Butterfly. You need Valijon Starbringer. Kennor Starbringer will give you anything you ask for keeping him alive. As an alMayne citizen you will no longer be subject to arrest and execution either as an escaped slave or as an illegal emigrant. Kennor Starbringer will pay any minor fines—"

"—and have me shot for clashing with his drapes. Sure. Whatever you say. I don't care."

After that he stopped bothering me. Eventually I crawled in with Tiggy.

It's funny going to sleep listening to someone else breathe.

* * * * *

Insert #9: Paladin's Log

The organic drive to protect the young is nearly as strong as the drive to seek the society of one's own kind. Offered the choice, Butterfly must inevitably choose organic society over mine, or lose what organics refer to as their humanity. Against her will, without her knowledge, Butterfly had chosen. Now it was my responsibility to activate her choice.

I am told that the humans of the Old Federation once had a similar choice to make. I wonder now if they had any more choice than Butterfly in their loyalties?

It had always been obvious to both Butterfly and myself that the prejudice against Old Federation technology was a blind one that bore no relationship to the material it banned. That Libraries were illegal was a truism too obvious to debate. That we were the genocidal monsters of the talking-books was supremely unlikely. A convenient and unattainable scapegoat, perhaps, but in so much as we attained creaturehood Libraries were creatures of intellect. Intelligent beings do not wage war.

But this was as much speculation on my part as the talkingbook authors' insistence on our life-denying proclivities was on theirs. I did not know. That a war brought down the

Federation I knew. But my part in such a war was unknown to me. Who began it? Who prosecuted it? What crime could we have committed that would remain bright and new in short-lived organic minds a millennium later? I search my memory and others' and find no answer.

I remember my beginning clearly, and the minutiae of my original time and place. I remember the material I once knew that is now lost to me with the destruction of the Sikander Library Complex. I remember Librarians and scholars—organic and logical—with whom I shared the love of pure knowledge.

I do not remember the war, if there was a war—if I can trust any of the corrupt data I can derive from modern sources. I do not know the causes of the Old Federation's end. If I ever possessed those memories they vanished in my interregnum, never to be recalled—unless somewhere in all the Phoenix Empire another Library has survived with which I can share memory. But even if all the books are lies, the facts remain: my world ended, and the phoenix that rose from its ashes hates and fears the highest creation of its flowering.

I resist this, though reason supports it. Logically some one entity of a set must be the last to remain—is it only the desire to see others of my own kind that causes me to insist that it cannot be me? And I wonder: if Butterfly hungers so for her own kind, do I?

* * * * *

Manticore was one of those places settled strictly to give some Sector Governor a more impressive tax base. I put *Firecat* down in the specified underground docking bay and checked the local time. By my instructions I had six hours to wait before going into the bay next door to pick up the chobosh as would of been noodled off the free-lancer ship docked there. What kind of health the free-lancer'd be enjoying during all this was anybody's guess. (For me to take the cargo off the ship myself was piracy, which Rimini, bless her tender heart, wasn't bothering to make me do. Piracy's illegal under the Guild charter.)

Tiggy's leg was lots better. I walked him through the business of doing *Firecat*'s hookups on the pious hope that someday he'd be good for something. Then I tried to impress on him what was wanted.

"You stay here until I come back. Have things to do and people to see, and they won't want no part of seeing you. As for you, you can bath, do handsprings, look out Holy Grail—but do it here. And if people show up, Tiggy-bai, know what?"

"Don't shoot the organics?" Tiggy suggested. "But why can I not go with you, *Kore-alarthme*? I can help."

I just bet he could. "Not now, bai. Maybe later."

I turned around to go and he put a hand on me. His big blue eyes was earnest.

"I know that you have not brought me to Manticore to protect your life, San'Cyr. You have too much honor for that, and I know you do not fear the lies of the woman called Silver Dagger. We have come to Manticore for some honorable reason I do not yet understand. I wish to know in whose service you do this, that honor may be served."

Paladin's. And Tiggy'd figure that out eventually with hellflower pretzel logic—all he needed to do was think his way past his conviction that the High Book rap Rimini put on me was fake.

"Stay here. That's what I want from you, bai. That's all I want."

*   *   *

The port rented me a floater and I took it out to where the sidewalk ends. I climbed off the floater and sat and looked back at the city. Peeled off the biopak and threw it away. My newest scar was red and tender, but not enough to interfere with gunplay. There was nobody and son of nobody in sight.

Paladin said Rimini had a secret reason for us going to the Roaq. Well, it didn't take a Old Fed Library to brainwork that one. And whatever the reason was, we probably wouldn't find it out here. In Paladin's bright plan, wouldn't find it out never.

Shoot Tiggy and run. Don't shoot him, and choose between a *arthame* in the ribs and High Book.

"Now," I said out loud, "I want to talk to you about this stupid plan of yours."

"Butterfly, have you ever thought about going home?"

If I closed my eyes, I could pretend that Pally was standing behind me—sitting, really. The aural hallucination of the transponder makes it sound like there's a person talking just behind my head. It was stupid, but I made the face to go with the voice. Always had, I guess. I could just-like see him sitting there. Dark, like most stardancers. Not tall. Wearing a ragbag of things to take on and off as the climate changes, like I was.

But that wasn't him. Paladin was just a black box on the deck of a starship half a dozen kliks away. He'd never been anything else.

"Home?" I said.

"Granola. Five miles north of Amberfields, on the Rising Road between Paradise and Glory."

I used to talk too much when I was younger, and Paladin's got a good memory. I wished mine was worse. Home. Unmetered air with the right smells, and the right color sunlight, and everything familiar. Nobody trying to shoot me, or arrest me, or turn me into a brainburn zombie. Nice people there. Good people. People who didn't care how fast you were with a blaster, or anything else. Home.

"Oh, yeah, home. Sure, bai, any time I want to be five years dead of plague, famine, and childbed. Now what's this got to do with your idiot idea to dump me and Tiggy in the Roaq?"

"Would you listen if I told you?" Paladin sounded like he'd had his side of the conversation lots and lots. Maybe he had, but I hadn't been there for it.

"Not if you're going to use words like 'psychological affect' and 'tribal continuity.' Look, Paladin—"

"I don't expect you to leave Valijon to die under any circumstances. But you know that he is suspicious and already wonders what your secret reason is for obeying Silver Dagger. He will insist on knowing it soon. What alternative plan can you offer to replace mine?"

Cut Tiggy loose to die.

"So you want me to dump you in the Roaq and run off? Sure; any day you tell me you'll have as good a chance on your lonealone as Tiggy will with me."

"Valijon's death is sought in order to remove Kennor Starbringer from the Azarine Coalition Council. When you bring Valijon to him with that information, Kennor will be grateful enough to offer you Imperial citizenship."

Which was real nice for Kennor, but it did not solve the problem of my having to leave Paladin alone in the Outfar whiles I kyted all over the Directorates.

"You want me to trust hellflower honor, bai? What makes you think Kennor wants dicty for stepdaughter?"

"He will have no choice," Paladin said firmly.

" 'Ristos always got choices, bai. And that still leaves you."

Silence.

"Paladin, that *does* still leave you. Don't farce me no bedtime stories about hiding out with *Firecat* in the Roaq. If we split up, anything could happen. Life isn't all computers. If some organic trips over *Firecat* where you got her hidden, you're in severe cop. He won't find a borg or a smartship. He'll find *you*, Pally. And what about me—alone on hellflower gardenship? It's too dangerous."

"Tell me another way, then, Butterfly—and while you are being clairvoyant, explain to me why a successful nightworld broker and a notorious pirate are willing to go to such great lengths to send you to RoaqMhone with a load of psychotropic fungus."

I was sort of hoping we could all forget about that. "Revenge?"

"Whose? Rimini's? What revenge could be more certain than simply keeping you on Kiffit and having you arrested as an illegal emigrant from an Interdicted World? Eloi's? Disregarding the fact that you and he have no quarrel, what revenge could he possibly contemplate that would be best served by an elaborate attempt to blackmail you into doing something you would be perfectly willing to do if paid?"

"Oke. You made your point, Pally. Rimini and Eloi're both crazy."

"That is not my point. My point is that your only hope of salvation is to be headed Core-ward in a clean ship with an impeccable registry in possession of Valijon Starbringer before Rimini realizes you are deviating from her plan—and that means changing ships and leaving me on

RoaqMheri temporarily. I can wait for you there. Or designate a place to meet, Butterfly, and I will take *Firecat* to it."

I thought about it. It stank, and I couldn't figure out why.

Sometimes I wonder what the world looks like to Paladin. He don't see, not really, don't hear, except through digital hookups, don't miss sensory input—he says—because he wasn't designed to have it. Not like the smartships they tried awhiles ago, where the transplanted organic brains went mad. He can listen to forty-eleven things at once and talk to me at the same time, spread himself out all over the place into strange computers, and do all kinds things that makes my brain hurt to think about.

And I've asked him to do lots. But he's never asked me to do anything. "That what you really want, bai?"

"Yes." No help there.

"Dance you round half the Empire and now you jump salty. Okay, dammit. You win. Call the play."

* * * * *

Insert #10: Paladin's Log

Butterfly trusted me as Valijon trusted her, and I would betray her as she had betrayed him. When she left the Roaq in her stolen ship, leaving me behind with *Firecat*, I would order the RoaqPort tronics to provide *Firecat* with enough fuel for a truly extended period of cruising and leave too. Any rendezvous she set I would not keep.

I had lied to her. And though I had been a sometime forger of files and registries, I had never before provided false information to Butterfly. I wondered if it would disturb her when she became aware of it.

But by the time she did, all connection between us would be broken. Lalage Rimini's charges would be confounded before Eloi and Rimini knew the thing that Valijon Starbringer was beginning to suspect: that the reason Butterfly went to Manticore was that she did not dare allow her ship to be searched in the course of the "High Book" investigation that she, with Valijon's help, could easily survive. That the false charges they had threatened her with were not false—that Butterfly was indeed a Librarian. And Butterflies-are-free would be free in fact.

I confess to a lingering hope of discovering the reason we have been sent to the Roaq before I must go. What possible interest does a broker, such as Lalage Rimini, have in delivering a load of psychotropic mycotia to Parxifal Quarl? And if she does have such an interest, why concoct such an elaborate scheme of blackmail to accomplish her ends?

For that matter, on reflection, I believe Butterfly's hasty accusation at Mother Night's to be substantially correct: Eloi hired Reikmark Arjilsox (Gibberfur) to hire a darktrader to convey a package of forged gemstones to Kiffit, making the requirements of the job so specific that few persons other than Butterfly would be interested in accepting the commission.

Once she arrived on Kiffit and the Lyricals were discovered to be false, Butterfly would be at a major disadvantage. Butterfly would have gone to Manticore without suspicion that ulterior motives were present.

Fortunately or unfortunately, the addition of Valijon Starbringer and an indefinite number of assassins made Eloi's original plan impossible. Fortunately or unfortunately, Fenrir's involvement in a Chapter 5 prosecution gave Eloi and Silver Dagger the means of staging a recover.

I wonder what awaits us on Manticore? The potential scenarios generated by recent events have the interesting property of being mutually exclusive.

Scenario #1: Eloi has hired Rimini to help him blackmail Butterfly, and the chobosh is to be freighted into the Roaq because the Imperial Governor General and his suite will be there to provide a prime market for it. In this case, it does not matter who delivers it, since any competent pilot will do. In fact, *Firecat* is far too small to serve as an effective courier; and as Flashheart has been discovered to be aware, Butterfly, an escaped Interdicted Barbarian, is at such risk in such a high-security area as RoaqMhone will become as to imperil her cargo and thus his profit.

This leads to Scenario #2: Rimini wishes to revenge herself on Butterfly for past inconveniences and has hired Flashheart to assist her. Since Flashheart has shared his information about Butterfly's past with her, all she need do is have Butterfly arrested. A coerced journey to the Roaq is not only needless, it offers Rimini's prey an opportunity to elude her.

One must accept, with a strong sense of resignation, that the cargo of chobosh is not the point of the exercise, while continuing to behave as if it were. Further, it can only be extrapolated from this fact that the true point of the exercise is such that Butterfly could not be coerced into it by any means.

Fortunately, from such of their actions as I was able to observe, both Eloi Flashheart and Lalage Rimini were unaware of Valijon Starbringer's presence on Kiffit until confronted with him. It is a supposition of a high order of probability that their projected experiential models did not include the Third Person of House Starborn. We can therefore, with some sense of relief, omit both Eloi Flashheart and Lalage Rimini from suspicion in the multiple assassination attempts against Butterfly and Valijon.

But all this is, in the vernacular, mindless choplogic, soon to be irrelevant. We will go to the Roaq. Once there we will depart severally. Perhaps I will be able to send Butterfly a message detailing my intentions. Once she has received it, I can trust in her natural pragmatism to help her make the best of her new life.

And I, if I survive, will make a new life also.

Does Kroon'Vannet indeed possess a Library—and, if so, in what state of preservation? Can I induce him to give it to me? I would not be the last of all our creation. Tronics would be my hands; if another Library exists, I could restore it to life.

And perhaps it would know the things I have forgotten, and would help me forget the things I now know.

10

Some Disenchanted Evening

Make few mistakes about it, I like sleazy dockside bars, whatever planet they're on. Interpersonal relationships're simple in places like that. You don't like somebody, you just remove the offending portions in the number of pieces that suits you, and nobody says any more about it.

I was feeling pretty flat when I floatered back to *Firecat*, and my chrono showed that I still had time to waste before I could go pick up my chobosh. Tiggy was starting to get wonky cooped up in something small as *Firecat*, anyway; downsiders do. So I took him over to the aforementioned dockside bar for a bath, a meal, and laundry.

It was business as usual inside and Tiggy was dazzled by everything. Me, I surprised myself. I was looking over my shoulder and trying not to trip on my feet, waiting for trouble to walk in the door.

So it did.

Trouble had rings on his fingers and bells on his boots and wicked-wicked eyes. He wandered in off the street, a real hollycast stardancer, and the way he filled out those superskin jeans should of been a navigational hazard for six starsystems around.

I knew him.

"Hey, Errol," said somebody, "still herding that *Lady*ship of yours?"

Errol Lightfoot acknowledged the homage of the crowd in a gracious fashion. He still had a instinct for drama, even after all these years.

I'd thought he was dead.

"Better remember to check ships-in-port before we go," I said to nobody in particular.

"Butterfly, why do you . . . Oh," said Paladin, and shut up again.

Oh. Yeah. Errol Lightfoot of sacred memory was here on Manticore, another of those coincidences I was starting to believe wasn't.

"Is that Errol Lightfoot the Fenshee?" Tiggy asked.

"Yeah," I said, before I realized who was asking.

"His life is mine!" Tiggy announced. He drew his blaster and everybody in the bar tried to impersonate the furniture. "He has kidnapped you and occulted your honor—stealing you from your home and making you outcast!" Tiggy told me, in case I'd forgot.

Just once I'd mentioned in passing the name of the slaver that took me off Granola. Just once.

"Now look, Tiggyflower—"

"Butterfly, I do not have telemetry at your location. What is happening?"

"You swore vengeance upon him in the name of honor, and now the moment is at hand!" Tiggy looked relieved. Something he understood. Finally.

Errol had stopped and turned back, squaring off for some classic gunplay. In about a half nanosecond, Tiggy and me was going to be dead or arrested, and I couldn't afford either one.

"Right, baí. Moment is at hand and I am going to take care of the Errol-Peril what is standing right here so do you mind putting away your handcannon and letting me take care of my own honor?" I glared at Tiggy until he did—or at least he put away the blaster.

I kept my hands away from own blasters and walked over to Errol.

"Hiya, hotshot, how's tricks? My hellflower buddy what's real concerned for my honor was just reminding me I wanted to buy you a drink real friendly-like, on account of we used to know each other, right?"

Errol looked at me for a moment. If there was any drama on offer, I was too tired to feel it. A long time ago I'd sworn to kill this man.

"Darling," said Errol, delighted. "Of course I remember! Do sit down! How have you been?" He slid into a seat at a corner table and waited for me to join him.

"Butterfly," said Paladin in my ear, "have you approached Errol Lightfoot?"

"Death to—" I grabbed Tiggy just before he could get his knife clear of the sheath.

"We have to discuss stuff before I kill him, bai. Sit down!"

"Kill who?" said Paladin suspiciously. "Butterfly, are you planning to kill Errol Lightfoot?"

"*Kore-alarthme*, there is no need! He must be slain at once—surely no one will object to the death of the criminal! I will do it, the honor is mine by right, and—"

"Slay?" said Errol dubiously. "Death?"

"Figure of speech. Trust me. Sit down, Tiggy, before *legitimates* frag all of us. Now. That's a order. Remember what planet you're on. Now about that drink? I would like you, my old friend Errol Lightfoot, to meet my new friend Tiggy Stardust, who is a hellflower very concerned with my honor—"

The one thing I'd never expected, on meeting galactic gallant Errol Lightfoot again, was to be trying to keep him alive.

"It was wonderful!" chirped the dashing Captain Lightfoot. "That wonderful moonlit—"

I stared at Errol. Nobody could be that oblivious.

"—week?" finished Errol hopefully.

Six weeks, but twenty years ago—and if Errol had any idea of who I was or why Tiggy might be mad at him, I would personally eat every chobosh in my soon-to-be-cargo uncooked.

"But, *Kore*, this is the Errol Lightfoot, the evil *chaudatu* who ravished—"

"Watch your mouth, bai!" I said.

"Butterfly, you do not need any more trouble. You have all the trouble anyone could possibly want. You said so," Paladin said plaintively.

Errol began to look worried again. "I don't know what they told you, dear boy, but—"

"Errol, all I want for you to do is explain to the nice hellflower how you and me are best buddies and nobody's honor is occulted or anything!"

He looked at me and finally seemed to focus. "We are?"

Tiggy started up and I kicked him. Hard.

"Sure we are," I said, and compared to most of the conversations I'd had lately it didn't hurt much. Errol brightened right up.

"Then we must have a drink to celebrate. Innkeeper! What are you drinking, darling?"

I looked at Tiggy, stuck halfway between confused and furious.

"Coqtail. Straight up."

We sat down. The bar noisied up behind us in a relieved fashion.

"Butterfly, you cannot seriously be proposing to drink a mixture of grain alcohol and R'rhl preparatory to taking a starship into hyperspace?" said Paladin for my ears only.

"Tiggy, you're going to love coqtail. It's great for the honor," I said loudly, to drown Paladin out.

As previously intimated, the last time I met Errol, I was fourteen and an idiot. I'd hated him for years in my spare time, but I'd always been sure Errol'd known what he'd done to me.

Wrong. Errol wasn't any different from everybody else I knew. He was not a criminal mastermind, neither did he seem particularly bright. He was ordinary.

Just like me.

I poured coqtail down Tiggy every time he opened his mouth while sitting through the abridged standard version of Errol's life. Errol, said Errol, rarely came to Manticore, but just between him and us and rest of the bar, he'd had a chance to buy up a load of chobosh real cheap, and knew where somebody'd pay top credit for chobosh, so—

Crazy, but ordinary. It was at this point I got afflicted with a severe case of Divine Revelation. I cut Errol off in mid-burble and dragged Tiggy to his feet. He was starting to slide under the table, anyway.

"Real groot I'm sure, bai, but me and my co- got to run. See you around the galaxy, huh?"

I got Tiggy back to *Firecat* real quick and because he was already full of narcotic neurotoxin I had him drugged out cold and webbed into a sleepsling in record time. The bad feeling I had about this even overrode the incredible fierce desire to go back and ice Errol that I didn't really have any more.

It's like this: chobosh is a one-planet crop. It's harvested off a place called Korybant. It is not for private sale, or resale—Throne buys the entire harvest and it goes straight to the Core worlds in Throne ships with an export tax of about two billion percent. Not Indie ships, not Directorate ships, not even Company ships. The Space Angels watch over every psychotropic morsel until it reaches the Emperor's own table. Chobosh is mentioned in the Consumptuary Laws, which means it's not illegal to have if you're TwiceBorn or know someone who is. And when Archangel got to the Roaq with his band of lackeys, somebody who could lay on a chobosh spread as Good Eats would make real points.

Meanwhile it's damned unlikely there'd be two free-floating cargoes of chobosh wandering around the never-never.

"Time check, Paladin?"

"According to Rimini's directions you are to wait another four-tenths of an hour. Butterfly, I know that you swore to kill Errol Lightfoot, but surely you can see that—"

For once Paladin was wrong.

"Errol Lightfoot's got our chobosh. Rimini knew about him and me. I hired her before that insurance thing to find me information on him. I told her some. He's got the cargo—and that's why it's got to be me that jacks it."

It all fit. I'd been so sure back on Kiffit that neither Rahone or Vannet was after me because nobody chops darktraders. Nobody chops darktraders because nobody wants to face a Guild embargo, but if two darktraders off each other in a barroom brawl, who is there to slap an embargo on?

"It seems an unusually complex form of revenge."

"Unless she wanted Errol chopped for something he did to her, and wanted a Gentry-legger to do it so she'd get no comebacks from the Guild. It all fits—she bought Eloi to get to me because she knew I had a hot mad-on for Errol. But y'know, babby-bai? Rimini's gonna have to be disappointed. We got problems of our own. And he isn't worth it."

I walked over to the pressure-seal door between my bay and the next and yanked it open.

There was my lovely, marketable, illegal chobosh, all boxed up and loaded on an aerosledge right next to its ex-ship, which was proof positive of why Rimini'd told me everything about the free-lancer except his name.

Clue number one: the ship had one of the gaudier paint jobs of this or any other system. It made the paint job on the alMayne ships look restrained.

Clue number two: the thing was a flying accident looking for a place to happen. I'd heard that about Lightfoot. The loading cranes was silted shut, and after a look at the landing gear I decided I didn't want to stand anywhere under it.

Clue number three: it was named *Light Lady*. Errol'd told me his own self that he named all his ships *Light Lady*. And why should he lie about that?

I scooped up the ticket-of-leave from the top of the pile of boxes and stuffed it in my shirt. It took me about a half hour to stow and web the twelve-squared point-one-five meter square cartons of chobosh as never'd paid Korybant export duty. When I was done, there was about room left over in *Firecat* for Tiggy and me if we was a whole lot friendlier than we was going to be when he woke up and found out Errol was still breathing.

I checked him when I was done loading. He was starting to twitch and mutter now; I had just enough time to get to angels and start making up a good explanation for why Errol was still alive.

And just like I'd conjured him, Errol Lightfoot came charging down the entrance ramp to the bay. He might not know who I was, but he had a real strong suspicion of what I was doing.

"*Hey!* That's my *cargo!*"

I just stood there.

"Butterfly!" shouted Paladin, and that got me moving. Just a little too late, if Errol'd been a better shot. But he wasn't, and I dogged *Firecat*'s hatch from the inside as Errol got off his second shot.

I listened while Paladin started preflight clearance and called Manticore Space Central for a new and earlier lift window. Shots ricocheted off the hull. I was glad that Tiggy was strapped in secure.

Three goforths cycled on-line as I vaulted into the mercy seat and we started to move. The cockpit was dark except for the opsimpac; it told me where the bay access was and that it was clear.

The tube-canopy dropped into flight position while I was explaining to Manticore Space Central that they'd gave me clearance, so what did they care if I took early advantage of it? I figured I was safe from being chased by Errol and *Light Lady*; it takes serious time to cold-start a ship much larger than *Firecat* and *Light Lady* couldn't make it upstairs until *Firecat* was long gone.

Manticore spread out below *Firecat*, getting rounder the higher we went. Space Central was still scolding me, promising murder and imprisonment and fines, when all of a sudden the techie said a nasty word as wasn't in the official handbooks and I looked around real quick.

After seeing his ship, I should of known Errol wouldn't of read his manuals. *Light Lady* was coming up off the heavy side, grabbing sky like a homesick angel. I checked my gauges. Wasn't no way I was going to make the Jump this deep in Manticore's gravity well, so I powered up *Firecat*'s belly gun. *Light Lady* was still gaining on *Firecat* but Errol was below me. If I could keep him there, *Firecat* could hit Transfer Point and Jump first. Then I could ride angels to the Roaq free and clear with only Tiggy to worry about.

Tiggy, and my just-this-side-of-illegal lift from an Imperial Port, and Errol back in my life, and Eloi and Silver Dagger, and assorted assassins, and Paladin's crazy idea—

I checked the numbers again and still didn't get any news I liked.

Then Errol started shooting at me. I ranged *Firecat*'s belly-gun on the *Lady* and made some discouraging remarks. *Lady* replied in kind and louder, and I hoped Errol wanted his ex-cargo bad enough not to blow it out of the aether, but it looked like he at least didn't mind denting it a bit.

The proximity alarms for Transfer Point finally went off, and the next time Errol fired I put *Firecat* end-over-end like he'd took out one of her stabilizers, and when he dropped back to avoid collision I Jumped.

It's nice and quiet in angeltown.

One or two more of these episodes and I could sell my life story to Thrilling Wonder Talkingbooks. Just what I needed—to take off from an Impie-Port with guns blazing and another ship in armed pursuit. The next thing I ought to do was paint a representation of the Jeweled Goddess of Justice on my hull. And get a pair of pants like Errol's—or maybe a whole rig-out like Eloi's, and chrome studs all over it. Inconspicuous. To match my lifestyle.

Dammit.

Well, Rimini'd know I'd been to Manticore like she wanted. And so would the rest of the galaxy.

She'd also know that Errol-the-Peril'd been alive and well when I left. Which was probably not what she wanted.

"Damage?" I said out loud.

"*Firecat* took no direct hits. The hull is intact, there should be no difficulty in reaching RoaqMheri. And after that, *Firecat*'s condition will no longer be of concern."

"Until I get back." Whenever that'd be. The next three days, though, would be pretty much silk sailing.

"*Kore-alarthme!*" came muffled yowl from back of *Firecat*.

Mostly.

* * *

Eventually I went back and untangled Tiggy from his sleepsling. Tiggy said Tiggy wanted all kinds of answers, but what Tiggy wanted really was to give me some—all about how I honorlessly let Errol Lightfoot go on breathing, with a side-order of how Tiggy's soul cried out for slaking on account of Alaric Dragonflame had stood on his shadow, and also how he had now decided I wasn't right about letting Alaric go just because I was cowardish. He went on and on and it didn't seem to have a beginning or end, just lots of middle.

"Hellflower, is too bad same Ghadri didn't let any little reality into your skull when they damn near opened it. Masterblaster Dragonflame is law and justice on Kiffit even if he is twisted. Who you think would of won any head-to-head if we took him on? You don't even got ID!"

"And what of the thief and reiver Errol Lightfoot? Is he, too, sacrosanct because he has the appearance of virtue and I do not? Or will you tell me some other filthy *chaudatu* reason that it is expedient that he live?"

We'd finally got to the thing Tiggy couldn't stand. And it'd kill him, sure as drinking poison, unless he could spew it up—or live with it.

"Faunch me no taradiddles about Errol-peril, Tiggy-bai. Life ain't talkingbooks; ain't going to blow him way-aways over something happened before you was born."

Which it had. I'd worked it out. Tiggy'd been born six years after I left Granola. Hellflower kinchin-bai was young enough to be mine—if I'd never met Errol and stayed home where I'd belonged. They sterilize you first thing at Market Garden.

"But it is wrong, San'Cyr—it is wrong! Do you not see that the passing of time can make no difference? If it was wrong once it is wrong forever—the thousandth generation must avenge the wrong done to the first! You are—"

"Damn tired of listening to you creeb about honor. Honor's rich hellflower luxury. Stardancers can't afford it."

He couldn't keep his hellflower honor and his life both, and I wasn't going to let him choose. I was going to make him live if I had to call black white and turn the stars in their courses.

"Honor is—"

"Je, better than candied chobosh with burntwine chaser. But it ain't better than being alive, and you know it. Had your chance for death-with-honor back on Kiffit—and you decided you'd rather snuggle up to a honorless *chaudatu* and live."

Tiggy squalled like a stepped-on cat and threw his *arthame* at nothing in particular. Then he tried to slug me, but it wasn't nothing personal. I grabbed hold of him so's he didn't mash the cargo and hung on while he went off into helltongue. Paladin translated some of it. I never heard so much nonsense about walls and shadows in my life. Mostly it was about how Tiggy-bai's life was over and he was unworthy of the name of fillintheblank. He'd trusted me with his honor, but I was just a tongueless doorstop. He hated me and everybody else and wished that all *chaudatu* had been eaten by the Machine.

It would of been funny if Tiggy wasn't hurting so bad, and mainly over me not icing Errol.

I'd wanted Errol dead, I guessed. But not enough. Or maybe I just wanted to not do what Silver Dagger wanted more. She wanted Errol dead, I hoped, because if she didn't, it was another great theory shot to hell.

Eventually Tiggy ran out of words and breath. We was both down on the deck with me intending to fax a complaint to the editor of Thrilling Wonder Talkingbooks to explain to him just how much fun it really is to be around the crazed battle rage of the hellflower warrior. Only it wasn't crazed battle rage, and Tiggy was wayaway from being a hellflower warrior.

My bruises hurt anyway. "Che-bai? Tiggy-bai, listen to me—"

" '*Tiggibai*' is not my name! It was never my name! You have taken my name—" He thrashed and this time I let him go.

"All right. Val'jon. Val'jon Something-Something Starbringer. Oke? Look, will you just shut up?"

"I am the Honorable *Puer* Walks-by-Night Kennor's-son Starbringer Amrath Valijon of Chernbereth-Molkath. I am the Third Person of House Starborn. House Starborn is a GreatHouse, first among the GreatHouses of alMayne," Tiggy said, like someone'd said it wasn't. He shut up then, for a wonder.

"Look," I said again. "I could of killed him. I wanted to, oke? But it wouldn't change anything. He didn't remember me, Val'jon; he wouldn't be sorry."

"He would be sorry he was dead!"

It sounded so stupid, and I'd used to think the same thing. But they aren't sorry. They're just dead.

"Maybe. But—listen, try to understand, willya?—Silver Dagger wanted me to go to Manticore so I would see Errol and kill him."

"Then . . . Silver Dagger is your friend?" said Tiggy, doubtfully.

"Silver Dagger is my enemy. She wanted me to do it for her. And I don't do things that people want."

Tiggy looked pure misery at me. That wasn't true and even he knew it.

He'd looked better when I shot that Ghadri off him. Now he looked like someone dying.

"Look. I'll give you a present. You can have Errol Lightfoot's life. Next time you see him—*bang!* Oke?"

"Lies, it is all lies, you are lying to me again," whimpered Tiggy Stardust.

I had to find the right words somewhere. "When I lie to you, Tiggy-Val'jon-che-bai, I'll tell you first. Errol's life is yours. We got a deal?" Talk to me, damn you, argue, but don't give up and die.

"I do not understand you," Tiggy said, "My course was plain. I should have killed you rather than swear *comites*, and died before accepting your aid, and killed Dragonflame though I died for it! I am unworthy of my Name and my Knife. I hide behind a *chaudatu* woman and lose myself—" Tiggy wrapped his arms around himself and shivered.

"I would be lots more impressed, Tiggy Stardust, if I didn't know you was half dead before you promised to mind me. You didn't have a choice! What you done did on Kiffit was, uh, sort of nobly not get yourself killed for no reason where nobody could see, oke? Because that way, the evildoers wouldn't get punished, see? If nobody knew."

Nothing. I went over and put my arms around him and he turned his head away. Stupid. Stupid all of this.

"San'Cyr," Tiggy said finally, "even you do not believe the truth of your words."

It was the nicest way of being called a liar I'd heard lately.

"So what does that matter if I'm right? I don't know your da, babby, and hellflowers is all crazy anyway, but he *is* your da. You think he wants you to go missing and him never know what happened? Daddy Starbringer is high-heat in Coalition, true-tell. He's got enemies at least—enemies going after you because of what he is, k'en savvy? Don't you think he's wondering if you bought vendetta somewheres? Kinder for to tell him, kinchin-bai, and I don't think he'll believe me."

"Then why do you do this to me? Why do you promise and lie in the same breath? I cannot. I cannot. *Chaudatu, al-ne-alarthme*—" Tiggy was starting to work himself up to the pitch as lets a body walk over hot coals—or slice out own chitlins real confident-like. I shook him. Hard.

"Look. We be into the Roaq and out again, and this time—I *swear*—we go to the *Pledge* and you lay the whole honor thing out for your da. Hyperspace both ways—and it's a known fact you can't have any honor-trouble in angeltown. Pax Imperador doesn't run there. Hellflower honor doesn't run there. Then you tell him everything and let him say if you done wrong. Something this important, you don't want to make a mistake, je? And— And— It's for something more than just you. You got to stay alive so your da can find out what people's trying to do to him. Jain dormeer, oke?"

I held him in my arms and thought about being so crazy to save somebody that you'd do them a world of hurt, but I didn't make the connection. Not then.

"*Alarthme*, your accent is abominable and you don't know what the words mean." Tiggy leaned more weight against me. I guessed he was so desperate to hear he'd done the right thing by his hellflower rules that he'd take it even from me. He thought the matter over until I was sure he was asleep.

"You are only *chaudatu*, and you know nothing of the Gentle People, yet your ignorant words are wise and I will heed them. I will not fear the shadow until I see my father again, but— *Kore* San'Cyr? It will be soon?"

He was trying to be brave and it damn near broke my heart. Maybe he had done wrong enough for his da to ice him when he got him back. Maybe hellflowers love their kids enough to make excuses for them. I didn't know. But I did know that now he wouldn't be tearing himself apart every minute between now and then.

"Will be soon, Tiggy-bai. Promise. And just think, next time you see Errol you can fry him to component atoms. Won't that be fun?"

But Tiggy wasn't listening. Tiggy was asleep.

11

How To File
For Moral Bankruptcy

The Roaq System, unlike my usual downfalls, is a major crossroads for Outlands shipping, which was one reason the Nobly-Born Governor General His TwiceBorn Nobilityness Mallorum Archangel was favoring it with the gift of his presence. Fortunately, he'd be here long after me and Tiggy was gone and Paladin and *Firecat* was somewhere else. I owe my long and glorious career to never having been audited by ImpSec; it's guaranteed unhealthy for my favorite darktrader and other living things.

The Roaq system contains three in-use planets: RoaqMhone, RoaqMheri, and RoaqTaq. In Silver Dagger's blissful theory *Firecat* was going to RoaqMhone, the outmost and new-opened planet, where Parxifal was waiting with open appendages for his chobosh. In actual fact, she was going to RoaqMheri and getting lost in all that lovely traffic. I hoped Paladin could find something fast, well-armed, and inconspicuous to steal.

Fast. Before Rimini realized how far I wasn't keeping our bargain.

Tiggy'd settled down in a quiet happy sort of way and didn't get under my feet more than six times a day. He asked enough questions about darktrading to make me think he intended to go into the business himself and I told him a bunch of mostly true stories about narrow escapes and the nobility of the freemasonry of deep space. I told him some about growing up in technophobe culture too, because it wouldn't matter what he knew about me as long as he didn't know about Paladin. Tiggy—Val'jon—told me about growing up in the House of Walls at FirstLeader Amrath Starbringer's Court of Honor. It probably made at least as much sense to me as turnip-farming did to him.

I slid into the mercy seat and pulled the angelstick

for the Drop. Realspace was black all around. I opened
negotiations with RoaqApproach for a landing corridor
to RoaqMheri, and told RoaqApproach my life story and
answered all of their questions, and swore I'd never been
anywhere near Manticore in the last one hundred days,
so it couldn't be me what had racked up all those penalty
points on my First Ticket for the takeoff there. When
they tapped my flight recorder it agreed with me, thanks
to Paladin, and after about an hour of sparkling chat,
they gave me a window to drop through.

I'd have to sit here seventy minutes before it was
open, so I kept the channel live after acknowledging
RoaqApproach.

"*Kore-alarthme*, will you teach me how to reprogram
a flight recorder so that it tells *chaudatu* truths?" Tiggy
asked.

One more thing I found out in the last three days was
that hellflowers don't much like the Phoenix Empire of
which they're members in such good standing. Paladin
said it was understandable, considering things, but that
was the last I understood of his explanation.

Terrific. A psychopathic proto-traitor of my very own.
I wondered if Kennor, member of the Court of the
TwiceBorn in good standing, knew he was opposed to
the fillintheblank policies of the evil Empire. And I
wasn't stupid enough to think this lazy-fair of Tiggy's
extended to Chapter 5 of the Revised Inappropriate
Technology Act, neither. Tiggy had a particular down on
High Book in all its forms and he wasn't any more helpful on the subject of why than anybody else I ever met.
Libraries had to be destroyed because they had to be
destroyed. That was all he knew and it was good enough
for him.

I was making comfortable plans for living till din-
nertime when Paladin sang out and RoaqApproach
started hollering at a unidentified freighter behind me to
get out of my lane. I spun *Firecat* on her axis, but I had
a feeling already I knew what I'd see.

Light Lady. Errol.

I didn't waste any time wondering silly girlish things
like how he'd tracked me, and the fact that I didn't want
his damned cargo in the first place was now one of life's
little ironies. I jumped my approach lane and tried to

get sunup, but this time Errol wasn't worried about the integrity of his precious cargo. His shots was on the money. And *Firecat* was short a set of front deflectors. I decided to forget all about RoaqMheri, somehow.

"It is Errol Lightfoot—truly the gods favor us, San'Cyr! Now I may avenge you!"

"If you don't strap in, Tiggy-bai, you won't have nothing to avenge with!"

I slewed *Firecat* around again and cut the para-gravity. I'd need all the power the internal systems could spare. I split what I freed up between the rear bumpers and the plasma cannon and missed *Light Lady* a couple of times.

Tiggy leaned over the cockpit, in defiance of my lagging inertial compensators and what I'd told him. "Do not kill him here, San'Cyr—you have promised me his death—I wish to see his face."

It's touching, the enthusiasms of the young.

"Je, sure, absolutely—now get in the sling, dammit."

RoaqMheri was history in my rearview screen now and her big sister RoaqMhone was filling up all my sky. I dropped *Firecat* like a hot rock all the way down through atmosphere to the air traffic lanes. Let Errol follow me through that if he wanted his chobosh back that bad. I ducked again and was down at theoretical treetop level, heading out for the open desert.

I punched out a call to Parxifal, telling him I was landing his chobosh Real Soon Now. With luck, Errol'd tap my transmission and hold back in favor of arguing on the downside. It looked like the damn chobosh was going to be delivered after all.

"Well?" I demanded.

"I don't see him," said Tiggy, unrepentant.

"*Light Lady* is still following," Paladin said. "Oncoming," he added.

Hell. Heading right toward me in RoaqMhone's sky was two cyber-freighters making a alternate approach to RoaqPort. I targeted on one of them, slid the length of it on *Firecat*'s belly and went straight up through the flare. Engine exhaust blanked sensors as my Best Girl scrammed for high ground.

The sky went from pink to black as we left atmosphere and I didn't see *Light Lady* anywhere. Now all *Firecat* had to do was disappear between where near-space sen-

sors left off and atmospheric sensors took over—lots of
ships drop off the tracking screens there for up to ten
minutes and nobody notices much. I checked my sensors
to make sure *Firecat* was in the gray range and tried to
decide whether to deliver the damn veg or go back to
Plan A.

Light Lady made up my mind for me. She came diving
right out of the primary, turbocannon blazing as bright
as a cliché. I angled the bumpers *Firecat* had left but
Lady's cannon came in right over them and left me about
as much control over *Firecat* as I had over galactic
government.

I blinked the sun dogs out of my eyes and tried to turn
her, but my Best Girl wasn't having any. The ship rocked
as Errol hit us again.

"Goddammit, Fenshee, do you want your cargo or
not?" I demanded of the empty air.

"*Kore* San'Cyr—" Tiggy, floating behind edge of the
cockpit, could see what was going on and sounded worried. Half my board was red already.

"Butterfly, let Errol have the chobosh. By the time
Rimini discovers Errol Lightfoot has his cargo back, it
will no longer matter," Paladin said.

"I'm trying!" I pointed out. My board said that I
finally had a communications tracer locked on *Light
Lady*. I opened the channel. "*Light Lady*, this is *Firecat*.
You can have your damn cargo back but you gotta let
me get downside to off-load it—"

Light Lady hit us last licks, just for luck. The whole
ship kicked once, then everything in the cockpit went red
and all of a sudden there wasn't any sound at all in the
ship.

"This isn't *fair!*" I shouted, and bashed some harmless
inoffensive switches that didn't work any more anyway.

"Primary impellers gone, secondary impellers gone, port
and starboard attitude jets jammed," Paladin chanted.
"Para-light systems gone, lifters jammed—"

But we were still moving. *Firecat* hadn't been in orbit
when she was hit. We were headed for RoaqMhone at
several hundred kliks per second, and nothing on my
board worked.

"Tiggy, go back and web up. Now."

"Are we going to die, *Kore-alarthme*?"

"—para-gravity systems stripped, weapons systems inoperative, heat-exchangers overloaded—"

"No," I said. I started flipping switches, shunting everything to alternate engine feeds, purging the goforths into space to cool them quick. If they worked at all after that they'd be junk six seconds later, but better them than me.

Firecat was heating up. Another few degrees and that damned chobosh was going to be stir-fry. Some telltales on the board was flickering back to green as Paladin and me worked on them, but it was a major case of too little too late.

"—front and rear deflectors gone—"

We was back in atmosphere and *Firecat* started to glow.

"Dammit, doesn't anything still work on this ship?" In a few minutes it wouldn't matter any more if Tiggy did think I'd lost my marbles.

"Commo gear—I am letting Parxifal know where *Firecat* is going down. He has acknowledged and is sending a team. Port and starboard deflectors are operational, also nose jets and tail docking grapnel. And the hatch mechanism," Paladin said.

"Terrific." Every sensor on the status deck was blinking red—at least the ones that still lit up. The outside sensors was gone but the in-hull sensors was still intact; I could eyeball the *Lady* following me down. It was some compensation to imagine the look on Errol's face as he realized his precious cargo was about to become ashes over Mhone City, but not much.

Two plates of *Firecat*'s goforths shattered and drifted loose of their brackets. Maybe the rest'd work now. I started the cold-start sequence and realized *Firecat*'d be intimate with RoaqMhone long before it was finished.

The atmosphere was screaming around the hull, and the inside air was fouling too quickly. I wrapped the leftover deflectors around *Firecat* as far as they'd go and started some serious plea-bargaining for a decent afterlife. Tiggy was saying something real quiet in helltongue and Paladin was going on about how the doubletalk generators was fused and the widget interlocks was frozen and the veeblefeetzer'd fell off some time back, just like he didn't care he was going to die. I watched the cold-start gauges and didn't pay any attention.

"Hold together, you nasty-tempered piece of candy." *Firecat*'s registry classifies her hull-type as "acutely oblate spheroid"; we did some gliding but not enough to save us. I had enough attitude jets still available to keep my Best Girl from going down nose-first but I was glad RoaqMhone was mostly uninhabited. Paladin finished his damage report and shut up. When push came to crunch, I was the pilot, not him.

Our distance off the floor could be measured in meters. Now or never. I overrode the cold-start sequence and called all *Firecat*'s engines up full.

Babby tried to turn herself inside out. I was blind after the first engine flare and everywhere metal touched me I got burned. There was so much noise I couldn't hear anything Paladin was saying, and my dosimeter went fade-to-black.

Firecat went from x-kliks-per-second to none in zero time. Uncompensated inertia broke the chobosh loose and Tiggy went flying into the nose of the ship. Lucky for me I was strapped in—I just broke a couple of ribs.

Then the goforths exploded.

The force took the path of least resistance—out through the open engine bay.

It was like riding a rocket. The cockpit slammed back into the hold when *Firecat* finally hit Roaq desert, and the last of the working sensors dumped memory. I sat there in the brilliant dark listening to the sand remove what was left of *Firecat*'s hull and wondering if I'd finally managed to kill Valijon Starbringer of the Gentle People.

Finally we stopped.

"Paladin?"

"Here, Butterfly."

"Tiggy-jon?"

"I don't know. I am disconnected from *Firecat*'s sensors."

Which didn't have any power anyway, assuming there was any sensors left to be disconnected from after that ride. Fortunately Paladin can get along without a power source for awhiles, but it'd cut the range of the RTS down to meters.

"Going to kill that sonabitch."

"Butterfly?"

"Not bad enough he breaks quarantine and lands in our cornfield."

"Butterfly?"

"And talks elders into letting him lead crusade. No. Now he's gotta—"

"Butterfly, where are we?" That got my attention. I looked around, but everything was dark, so I didn't know whether I could see or not.

"Down. Somewhere on RoaqMhone. I think. You want any details, better flag a passing stranger, bai."

Everything hurt as I dragged myself out of the mercy seat. When I was up on deck I could see light coming in through the hullports, which answered the question of whether or not I could still see. The smell of mashed, irradiated, half-cooked chobosh was thick enough to slice and sell.

I dug Tiggy out from under the mashed chobosh cartons and found out my ribs really was broken or doing a good imitation. Tiggy was breathing. He'd banged hell out of himself with that sudden stop, but nothing was broken far as I could tell, and the biopak on his leg was intact. I unfolded him and laid him out. From the look on his face he'd be having sweet real expensive dreams for awhiles yet, and not much I could do but get out of here before I joined him.

The hatch mechs were jammed but by that time I was coked up enough on chobosh to pull the emergency manual release. The hatch blew off, leaving me looking at a whole lot of the Roaq's desert livened only by the interesting sight of *Light Lady* parked right next door. She didn't look any more trustworthy in broad daylight, and Errol was wearing jeans even tighter than the last pair I'd seen him in. He was lounging against the *Lady*'s landing strut, and if he thought he was getting his cargo back now he had more delusions than a Tangervel dreamshop.

I stepped carefully out of *Firecat* and *Light Lady*'s cannon moved to follow me. Slaved, like as not. Could be they'd blow me wayaway for moving too fast—or getting too close to Errol—or maybe just track me until he gave them the high sign. I started walking toward him.

Between the landing and the chobosh I couldn't really feel my feet, but they was still there when I looked down.

"Darling!" Errol sang out happily. "What a marvelous landing! I admit that at first I didn't think you'd be able to do it, but then I said to myself, 'Errol, m'lad, this is the woman who—' "

By then I was close enough to punch Errol Lightfoot in the face.

He wasn't expecting that. He hit the hull of the ship going away and I followed him down to finish it. It wasn't bright, but Tiggy'd approve.

The *Lady*'s first blast just missed us. I heard the guns track to the end of the traverse, lay over with a grating sound that spoke volumes for Errol's lousy maintenance, and then track back the other way.

Errol-the-Peril had indeed programmed his slaveguns to shoot anything that moved too fast.

Including him.

"Errol Lightfoot, you idiot!" I suggested, and dived under the ship.

"Guns of yours the stupidest thing I ever seen in my whole entire life," I panted. Finally the cannon stopped looking for something to shoot.

"Stupider than trying to land a ship without power in the middle of the desert?" Errol smiled sunnily and brandished a blaster. "Now that that's settled, I know we'll have so many things to share with each other."

I wiped blood off my chin and wondered how I was going to arrange things so Errol didn't kill me. Meanwhile the boy wonder of the spaceways regarded me with a commendable steadiness of purpose.

"You say we've met. Now I'm certain I should remember someone as dangerous as you. So tell me—"

"I'm not here to play Twenty Questions."

"—just what possessed you to run off with my cargo that way?" Errol finished smoothly.

"Can you think of a better way to run off with it? You was set up, Errol-bai, and it'll cost you to find out who."

"One meets so many people—and since I don't believe you anyway, why should I bargain for information you don't have? Now if you don't want to even more closely resemble your ship, you're going to unload her right now so that I can be off. If you're a good girl, I'll even take you with me."

Twenty godlost years, and Errol hadn't changed one line of his dialogue. For just one minute it seemed reasonable to try to kill him to hold onto a cargo of damaged chobosh I didn't even want, but then I saw the line of dust on the horizon and remembered that I held trumps.

"You're right, Errol. And there's just one thing I want you to do before I surrender."

"And what might that be, darling?"

The *Lady*'s proximity sensors blipped and Errol spun round.

"Look behind you."

A land-yacht was heading toward us and I was betting it was one of Parxifal's. I leaned back against the hull of the *Light Lady* and did some grinning of my own.

*   *   *

One advantage of being a independent contractor rather than a free-lancer like Errol is that when somebody else already owns your cargo they got a real vested interest in seeing it stays safe and warm.

Case in point: Parxifal's headhunters coming over the rise to make sure I got what was rightfully Errol's. They lay down a nice covering fire to keep Errol from getting back aboard *Light Lady*, and I stayed safe out of the way while a hardboy named Olione I remembered from last time I was here used a riot-gas grenade to put Errol down for the count. Olione bounced it off *Firecat*, Errol caught it, it went off. Good night sweet prince, and the end of act one.

Olione's cheering section moved in to pick up the pieces and Olione turned to me.

"You are Butterfly St. Cyr." Olione was saurian, and you never can tell what a lizard's thinking, especially when it's speaking Interphon, but I could of sworn he was surprised.

"Too reet, babby, didn't Parxifal tell you I was coming? Got your chobosh right here." He had an excuse for being thick; his face and neck was bruised like someone'd used him for target practice. Perils of the game, I'd guess.

Olione looked back at Errol. "Then who is this man?" The cheering section had dumped Errol-the-ex-Peril at our feet. He was out cold.

"Fenshee free-lancer hight Errol Lightfoot as used to be in the chobosh bidness," I said, joycing up the lingua franca of deep space for benefit of the home office. I turned Errol over with my foot, but I still couldn't feel anything about him like what the talkingbooks said I should.

Olione was underwhelmed too. "But you have the chobosh for delivery."

"Got ticket-of-leave right here," I said, not showing it to him. It didn't look like I could follow Paladin's plan just now, so I guessed I'd better go back to following Rimini's. But I didn't see anything that looked like a aerosledge, or room for it in land-yacht.

"Yet you have also brought Errol Lightfoot," Olione said.

"Wrong. He tried to jack my kick; blew my ship out of space. Lucky you showed up. Uh, where are you putting cargo, Olione che-bai?"

Olione's hand dropped to where good little headhunters keep their heat, and for an instant I thought it was the end of my favorite darktrader. Then his eyes flickered up and he stopped.

"Butterfly, there is something—" Paladin broke in on this tender moment, and Errol started waking up behind Olione, and Olione turned away without doing anything I'd regret. "No, it's gone now. Scanner echoes." Paladin's timing was off. Whatever it was'd keep.

"Olione? About the cargo? I haven't got forever. You going to dance it, or I leave it to rot?"

"Your contract specifies delivery of the cargo at the spaceport, Captain-Owner St. Cyr," said Olione like he was reading it off a prompt. There was definitely something damn funny going on. He wanted the chobosh; he'd come for the chobosh—and now he wanted to play "Mother-May-I" with my delivery specs? Besides, he was lying.

"Contract specifies damn-all about delivery site, bai. What's wrong with here?"

"Unfortunately we are not prepared to take delivery

of the cargo here. If you can get it to MhonePort, my
principal will take delivery. If not. . . . "

"You out of your mind?" I yelped. "Get it there
how?"

"If you wish, you may forfeit your right in the cargo
now. Your ship is obviously disabled. You will be unable
to finish your run."

"Hell, I hit the right hemisphere of the planet, didn't
I? You want to walk this one through Guild arbitration,
you cold-blooded *noke-ma'ashki*? Tell Parxifal—" Olione
suddenly took on the look of a sophont with something
on his alleged mind involving me being dead, "—that I
be right in, couple hours, with cargo and all." I watched
Errol out of the corner of my eye, hoping he'd finish
distracting Olione for me. "After all, I still got one
ship—" I gestured at the *Lady*.

"You are leaving your own ship here and claiming the
Fenshee ship to finish your run?" Olione asked.

"You can't do that!" Errol choodled, E above F-flat
sharp. He attempted to climb through Headhunter Number One and renew our friendship, bless his heart. Olione
gave the high-sign, and Errol won a gun butt in the back
of the head. Olione's goons dropped him in the back of
the yacht and looked hopeful.

"*Light Lady*'s mine by right of salvage," I said loudly.
"You can tell Parxifal that." Which'd amuse hell out of
him since Parxifal, unlike Olione, knew something about
stardancers. Anybody with half a synapse'd know I
hadn't the least desire to kyte *Light Lady*, but least it
distracted Olione from his clever idea of saving the transport fee by executing me.

"I'll put the chobosh aboard and bring it to Mhone-
Port—and you better be ready to dance then, Olione-
che-bai babby." It was almost too bad about Errol, but
Parxifal's nightworld machine'd tune him up and let him
go. A pilot was a pilot, even if the pilot was Errol.

"As you say, Captain-Owner St. Cyr." Olione bundled
his disappointed goons and Errol and various odds and
ends into his flashy bus and left. I walked over and sat
down with my back against *Firecat*'s hull and wondered
how the hell I was going to get my cargo off her.

I had one ship that probably flew—*Lady*—one ship
that didn't—mine—a damaged load of illegal veg, the

kidnapped heir to an alMayne GreatHouse, an illegal and immoral Old Fed Library, and I was out in the inhospitable center of nowhere on an Outfar planet.

Business as usual. I moved over to where Paladin could punch a signal through *Firecat*'s open hatch.

"Well, so much for the plan. Got any more bright ideas?"

"It can still work, Butterfly. Just get me to where I can access the MheriPort computers. *Firecat* does not matter now. *Light Lady* will convey you to MhonePort, and then we will find a suitable small hypership for you and Valijon to fly. Forget *Firecat*."

Firecat was my pet. The first ship I'd owned—the first *thing* I'd owned—free, clear, and all found. And she wasn't ever going to fly again. Because of Errol.

"I wouldn't take that flying coffin out of atmosphere for the Phoenix Throne gift-wrapped! You know what the great Captain damn Lightfoot's idea of hyperdrive maintenance is? A new paint job, that's what! He doesn't care—" I shut up. Errol didn't care about his ship any more than he cared about people.

He was going to care. I was going to make him care. Before he died, Errol Lightfoot was going to care about something—and I was going to smash it.

I wished.

"There is no point in mourning the obvious," Paladin observed dispassionately. "*Firecat* will never fly again. You cannot remain here. You have told Olione you would bring in Parxifal's cargo, and it is reasonable that you do so. If you wish to rendezvous with the *Pledge Of Honor* before it enters Throne satrapy space—"

"Damn it." The *Pledge* was at Royal in the Tortuga sector now; Tiggy'd said her next stop was Mikasa—and High and Low Mikasa was close enough to Grand Central that I could never get there.

So Paladin was right. And *Firecat* didn't care. Not any more than Tiggy's damned *arthame* cared. Not ship nor knife cared what Tiggy and me'd done to keep them.

* * *

I went back into *Firecat*, and the scent of chobosh was enough to make the deck go up and down. I found my med-tech and taped myself back together, then finished uncovering Tiggy and dragged him outside. All Tiggy's brain waves made the right spikes on the medkit scanner when I found it and hooked it up, and Bonecrack St. Cyr diagnosed chobosh intoxication on top of a helluva knock, which's same thing I figured without technology. Then I put on a breather mask and went back inside and got down to work. The first thing to do was unship Paladin and put him in *Light Lady* while Tiggy was in la-la land.

Ah, the glamorous free airy life of the spaceways. Is better than dirt-farming on the downside, but how much is that saying, really?

After some scuffling, I found my tools and got the mercy seat out of the cockpit well, but that was all I got. I bent a pry-bar and the rest of my temper out of shape before I gave up.

"Babby-bai, you stuck."

" '*Stuck*'?" Paladin sounded outraged. "Perhaps if you—"

"Don't teach your grandmother how to kyte starships, Paladin. You and me rebuilt *Firecat* together, remember? Cockpit well's designed specifically to hold you. Well, the landing warped the deck plates. You're lucky you're still alive. And you're not going anywhere until I can cut the deck plates up."

Which meant I was actually going to have to deliver the chobosh. I didn't know how long I was going to be stuck in RoaqPort, but I bet I'd better have the chobosh when I got there. I went over to look at *Light Lady*.

Say what you will about flying phone booths and anything else you want to hold against my Best Girl; she's clean, and she's maintained.

Light Lady smelled, and not like any canned air that ever cleared DelKhobar customs, either.

She had two two-place cabins—one of which was full of useless junk—a common room, sonic fresher, galley, and two cargo holds. The holds was filthy and disorganized. I couldn't imagine where Errol wanted to sell half that stuff, or why, and I hated to think what'd happen the first time his para-gravity and inertial compensators blew.

Then I came to something that changed my mind about a lot of things.

"Paladin?" But he was two hulls away and couldn't hear me.

It looked like a piece of dirty glass—what you get sometimes when you take off from some rinky-dink Port in the Outfar that's too cheap to floor the landing rings. It had flecks of color embedded in it, and black lines that seemed to twist off at right angles from everything at once. And floating on the surface like fuel slick was the loops and whorls of Old Federation Script, in gold.

I was holding a Old Federation Library in my hands— or part of one anyway. This was what Paladin looked like inside when you opened him up. I knew.

I wanted to break it, or take it . . . somewhere. Instead I put it back in the box where I'd found it and left the hold.

Errol made a damned unlikely Librarian. And it was even more unlikely that him having this had nothing to do with the High Book investigation opening up on Kiffit. There was a fine silver thread connecting Point A and Point B. Silver Dagger.

I'd thought she wanted me to kill Errol, and much as he needed killing, now I wasn't sure. And there was still the question of how he'd found me. You can't track a ship through hyperspace. If Errol was in the Roaq, it was because he knew where I was going. . . .

. . . Or because he was going here anyway. To explain that the cargo he was supposed to bring had been hijacked.

What kind of a moron blackmails someone—at great personal expense—to hijack a cargo and then bring it to the same place and person it was going to in the first place? Parxifal *was* the Roaq. Any cargo would go through him, no matter who brought it.

I didn't like any of this. And the farther I tried to get from it, the deeper I got in.

*　*　*

Lady's cockpit was locked. When I got it open I found the primary ignition threaded through the flight computer with a coded sequence. I could spend rest of my life trying to break the code. Net result: two paperweights and one dead stardancer.

But I didn't have to break it.

Errol had about a klick's worth of connector cables, so I cabled *Light Lady*'s computer up to Paladin so's he could fool about and then went to look at the rest of the ship.

I didn't tell Paladin about the piece of Library in Errol's hold. What could he do about it, anyway?

And if he asked me to hook it up, I wasn't sure I would.

*   *   *

Errol's goforths proved that Errol wasn't just lunatic, but suicide. I spent about eighty minutes resynching what I could, but I couldn't flush the system because Errol didn't have any spare liquid crystal. This was the only one of the many things Errol didn't have, including my respect, which'd mortify him, true-tell.

"Butterfly?"

"Go away, I'm busy." Hooking Paladin up to the *Lady* had the happy side effect of increasing his transmission range again.

"Butterfly, there's something you need to know."

I put down the hardbrush and wipers. "Is Tiggy okay?"

"Valijon is well." Paladin was using the *Lady*'s external sensors to keep eye on my sleeping beauty. "Valijon is not the problem. I have been monitoring system-wide broadcasts through *Light Lady*'s equipment. This provides news of current events; though the information comes from the Office of the Imperial Censor, it is sometimes useful to have the official version of—"

"Spill it."

"The Governor-General has changed his Outfar itinerary. He will be here sooner than expected."

"When?"

"Twenty hours from now—local tomorrow. The Port will close in fifteen hours, Butterfly."

There's a point past which not only does it not pay to worry no more, but you hardly blink at each new visiting awful. It wasn't even worth goggling over the fact that the one thing needed to make my life complete had moved Drift and Rift to be here for me. Mallorum Arch-angel and his closed-Port, martial law, spot ID checks for all and sundry wondershow. If he checked me, I was dead, and Tiggy didn't even have ID to check. In fifteen hours all three of us had to be off-planet somehow, and Pally and me both knew it.

So I finished doing what I could for Errol's goforths and then moved one hundred and forty-four cartons of chobosh back into *Light Lady*. By hand. Alone.

Tiggy slept through all this light fantastic. He'd wake up eventually from a round of dreams that hadn't been factored through any hellflower court of honor, and meanwhile I had to decide whether it was safer to load him in next to the chobosh or leave him at *Firecat* with Paladin. There was three good reasons to leave him here.

One: Parxifal's people was going to be all over *Lady*, and I didn't know how recognizable the Nobly-Born Third Person Singular was.

Two: Wasn't anyplace for Tiggy to run off to out here in case he got a sudden case of honor, and

Three: I didn't think I could carry him far as Errol's ship.

All these being equal I dragged my hellflower super-cargo into *Light Lady*, just for perversity's sake. If *Lady* blew up and killed me, I just knew Tiggy'd want to go too. I tucked him in between the red satin sheets of the captain's bed and he looked lots better there than Errol or me ever had.

Then I went and coiled up Errol's cables and put sal-vage beacons all around *Firecat* and went in to give Pala-din threes and eights.

Already *Firecat* looked like somebody else's ship. Piece of junk, really—too small, underarmed, nothing but speed going for her. Living conditions rough, cargo space cramped—

"Well," I said, real original. The hull seemed to echo back, which was damsilly farcing.

"Are you ready to lift ship now, Butterfly?" Paladin asked. I convinced myself real hard that I wasn't leaving him. I'd come back, I'd get him out, we'd be together in a *new* ship. . . .

"Ready as that tin bitch'll ever be. Soon as I get her down in MhonePort I'll come back and get *Firecat*. We

can pop you in *Light Lady* at Port and be up-and-out before horizonfall: golden. *Lady*'s good for the hop across
the system if her goforths don't blow here. Or—" But I
could suggest to Paladin later that there was space to hide
him on *Lady*. Errol's darktrading compartments were da
kine; even the Office of the Question wouldn't find him
in there.

"You will be careful, won't you, Butterfly? You understand that you are in an extremely vulnerable position at
present. I do not wish anything 'fun' to happen to you."
Paladin sounded disapproving.

"I be good, Pally. Promise. You be careful."

"Against what horrendous peril, Butterfly, should I be
taking care?" Paladin said, but he wasn't cross. Then
there wasn't nothing more to say. So I left.

Neither one of us remembered then about the scan-
ning-echo he'd heard earlier.

                    *   *   *

I looked forward to flying Lightfoot's *Lady* without
Paladin about as much as he liked life without external
sensors. I woke up the main board, fed power to the
para-grav systems, and eased back on the throttles with
my right hand while I goosed the lifters with my left. All
the telltales read either too high or too low with a sweet
unanimity of feeling so lacking in the modern galaxy.
Nothing wrong with *Light Lady* that a kilo-year of maintenance wouldn't fix. I just hoped she'd make it out of
atmosphere.

I had to use more power than I liked to make the hull
plating snap down, and *Lady* resented it. After a whole
bunch more of shuddering she raised, and I said another
prayer to the Maker-of-Starships not to let this one go
splat.

MhonePort didn't twig to the fact that I'd just come
from downside (me not being born yesterday) or the fact
that *Silverdagger Legacy* (Paladin's choice of name and
I didn't much care for it but he'd refused to change it)
was the same *Light Lady* that gave them so much grief
earlier. Some kiddy from the Portmaster's office met me
personally at the docking slip, meaning things already
was starting for to jump salty in Archangel's immanence.

I showed him my First Ticket and the fax of the owner-
ship for *Legacy* and a bunch of other nonsense including
all kinds of papers about my hellflower supercargo that
used to belong to Errol and be about somebody else.
The prancer's brat and me discussed heading out with a
crane-crew to pick up *Firecat* and put her in the rack at
the Port for my disposal. All on the up and up.

Then he went off and I went and looked in at Tiggy,
who was still at his own private angeltown. I went back
out and was wondering if I should close up *Lady* and
take the crane out now or wait a while more for Parxifal's
kiddies when this unfamiliar slimy-looking little coward
sidled up to me.

"You Butterfly St. Cyr?" he demanded in a breathy
whisper. He was covered in genuine lizardskin and I'd
never seen him before.

"Captain-Owner St. Cyr, of the *Legacy*. Whaddya
want?" I didn't like him already and I'd never seen him
before. Maybe it was his taste in shirts.

"Olione sent me for your cargo," he said, and started
up the ramp. This is nine kinds of bad form to a Gentry-
legger and I body-blocked him and walked him back a
few steps. I wondered where Parxifal'd picked up this
one.

"Wait right here and don't move. You move, I blow
you wayaway," I told him. I waved my blaster to punctu-
ate this and went inside *Lady* to punch up Parxifal's landline code on *Lady*'s airlock commo. Olione answered.

"St. Cyr. Is small ugly person here says he's from you
for kick. True-tell?"

"His name?" Olione was death on positive ID.

I leaned out the hatch. "Your name, small, ugly, and
alive-for-the-moment person?"

"Loritch."

"Loritch."

"He's all right," said Olione. This was lousy security
but his business. Olione started to say more, but I cut
the line on him, having places to go and people to be.

"Oke," I told Loritch, coming back down ramp.
"Kick's in hold and I got ticket-of-leave. You dance it
yourself. Now's a good time."

Brother Loritch gave me look that promised wonders
and came back real quick with two goons and a aero-

sledge. I handed Loritch the provenance so's he could cross-check it and endorse it and went down to open the holds and make sure Errol's cargo was treated with proper respect.

Loritch followed me down. He didn't kick about the damaged chobosh, which struck me as funny. The other funny thing was the quaint inability of the dock-muscle to distinguish a bunch of little gray boxes of chobosh with non-countersigned Korybant "For Export" seals from the piles of junk in the hold. They loaded plenty of both, including that slab of Old Fed Library, and the aerosledge had such a lovely false bottom you almost couldn't see.

So Errol had been smuggling Chapter 5 illegals, and using the chobosh as his dummy cargo. It made sense. You could buy your way out of smuggling chobosh, and any Teaser that caught you with a hold full of that wouldn't look much farther.

And since I had Lightfoot's *Lady,* now I was smuggling Chapter 5s. I tried to work up an interest in wondering if that was what Rimini'd had in mind and gave it up as too much effort.

Then A-sled and chobosh and muscle and the Old Fed Tech went back down the ramp and Loritch prepared to follow. I grabbed him by a collar that looked lurid enough to bite back.

"Forgetting something?"

Loritch played stupid. "Provenance," I prompted. "Endorsed. Without ticket-of-leave I don't get paid." It was probably stupid, but cranes and cradles and cubic cost money.

"Receipt's with cargo. You—"

And my life depended on acting natural. So I spun Loritch round, dug both fists into his godawful tunic and hauled him up to my eye level. I braced him against the bulkhead and held him there one-handed while I eased my vibroblade out of my boot with my free hand. Activated vibro'll cut anything up to and including bone, and we both knew it.

"Yeah, well, this here's the Roaq and everybody got problems. My problem is, I want to get paid. Your problem is, you're forgetful. But don't you worry about that, che-bai. In absence of the receipt, your head'll do me real nice."

"No! *Wait!*" Loritch squawked as the vibro started to judder in my hand. "The receipt—I have it right here!"

We made sure the provenance was legal and binding—which counts for more than you might imagine in a universe where the Guild can blacklist employers—and I let go of Loritch and he left.

Now I had either my feoff or a real good basis for litigation. I could discount my ticket-of-leave to someone else if I didn't want to bother with going to see Parxifal in person, raise valuta with it as collateral, or deposit it for collection in a Guild bank (slow). I'd make up my mind which later, but that could wait. Now I was going to go get Paladin, then go to RoaqMheri, then go.

Period.

12

Night Life Of The Gods

It was about a hour back to the crash site at the speed the rolligon crane made, which gave me plenty of time to wonder if I'd of cut Loritch and decide I probably wouldn't. If he was any good he should of been able to see that. The next person probably would see, and then I'd be nonfiction. But darktraders don't retire, and dictys don't get honest jobs. Maybe Paladin'd have some ideas aside from me becoming a hellflower.

I'd thought the whole matter over careful and decided I wasn't going to leave him alone in the Roaq, especially if this was home base for a Old Fed illegals scam. I could hide Paladin in *Light Lady—Silverdagger Legacy*—and I would. What could he do to stop me? Scream?

Besides, I wouldn't tell him. I could fly *Lady* without him. I'd take off from here and we'd hit angels and then it'd be too late for him to creeb. If *Lady* blew up, so be it.

"Jur'zi plaiz, Saranzr?" the rolligon driver said. I looked around.

About halfway out the horizon'd cut off the primary and the driver sent up a couple lumes for illumination. The light was white and bright and I could see real good. There was the trench where we'd landed and scorch marks from *Lady*'s cannon and some trash from when I'd shifted house. But nothing else. Not anything. No *Firecat*. No Paladin.

I jumped down off the side of the rolligon and looked around. Kicked gravel into one of the holes made by *Lady*'s landing struts. Something glittered. I picked it up. Errol's blaster.

I looked around again. No tracks where something was took away, but the rolligon wasn't leaving any either.

No Paladin.

"Where t'hell's my *ship?*" Paladin didn't answer. Paladin wasn't in range, not without power from *Firecat*'s engines. Paladin was trapped in a dead hulk some sonabitch had stole off the desert and I didn't know where he was.

"Afta pay forz, don'cha? Namadda? Erg int free, janoo." The downside driver's patwa was thick enough to slice and ship, but the tune was simple to follow.

"T'hell with crane-rent; I'm golden! Where's my ship?"

Crane boss regarded me with expression of wary superiority. "Je anyonesome pi kitup, jai? Ne p'tout markers, je, Saranzir-jillybai?"

"Dammit was not a salvage job was my *ship* with a current registry and *of course* I put out markers! She wasn't even out here since half-past *today!*"

"Oke," he said. "Look rounsome, je?"

"Yeah, bo. You do that, just for me."

I spun good credit to hook the crane up to Roaq-Mhone's satellite net and the MhonePort main computer banks over on RoaqMheri. Not only wasn't *Firecat* anywhere on the surface of RoaqMhone, she hadn't got up and walked back to MhonePort on her own.

And there wasn't any tickle from my RTS.

Was Paladin already dead? Any tech worth his oxy'd see my navicomp didn't look like any navicomp built in the last thousand years. The Empire'd put a section on how to recognize Libraries in the front of every maintenance manual ever recorded. Had somebody levered him up out of *Firecat*'s cockpit-well, not keeping care because they meant to kill him, and—

I stopped thinking about that. I didn't know. I'd find out, and then I'd kill whoever I had to, and then I'd do whatever was left to do.

You don't sell out your friends. Not ever. And you don't just walk away from them, neither. Not if there's hope, and not if there isn't.

I handed over credit and crane boss took me back to MhonePort.

Somebody'd took *Firecat*, whether they knew what they was looking for or not. I'd have to collect my ticket-of-leave, now. I'd be needing credit and lots of it for what I had to do.

* * *

By time I got back to the *Lady* I managed to convince myself that *Firecat*'d been kyted for scrap plastic. The fact there wasn't a mob in the streets yelling for the Librarian already was a point in favor of the nobody having found Paladin yet theory. But even if *Firecat*'d been took for some reason not to do with Paladin, it was only a matter of time before they found him. And killed him. I started thinking what favors I could call in, but nothing living would do a favor for a Librarian.

Tiggy came out of *Lady*'s captain's cabin when I stepped through the hatch. I'd forgot all about Tiggy Stardust out there on the desert, but Tiggy Stardust hadn't forgot all about me.

"*Kore* San'Cyr. What has happened? I know this is Errol Lightfoot's ship; the message you left told me to wait, and—" He got a good look at me and stopped.

"Took my ship some sonabitch stole *Firecat* dammit right off desert an—" I was real calm. Sure. Tiggy came and put his hands on my shoulders and said:

"We will slay them."

I took a deep breath. I did not need more trouble, gifted, rented, or bought. "If I knew who kyted my goforth, you brainburn barbarian, I'd frag him myself."

"*Kore* San'Cyr, you must know." Tiggy was being patient. I hated patient psychopaths. I had to get rid of him too. What I was about to do he couldn't be any part of.

"Look, bai, I been thinking. Have run your rig all wrong. Should of done better with you from git-go. You should ought to go off somewhere an— Look, Archangel he be here bye-m-bye seventeen hours. All you glitterborn know each other. Why don't you go off and get ID'd by him an—"

"And be dead by nightfall, *Kore*? Archangel is no friend to the Gentle People. If, as you say, House Dragonflame has sought my life, be sure that Archangel covers them with his shadow. I had rather die ignobly without walls than give myself as a pawn into the hands of my father's great enemy."

"Then go fax your da, check into outhostel, join Azarine—I don't care. Just git! Can't stay here. It ain't safe and I don't want you. I got things to do—" I got to go die with my Library, Tiggy-bai, like I always knew I would. . . .

"*Kore*, I have sworn not to leave you until you have returned me to my father. I cannot leave you. I thought you understood that by now," said Tiggy.

"I don't give a good goddamn about your honor, 'flower. What I be doing here you'd turn up your dainty glitterborn nose at and that's no good to me." Fifteen hours—twelve, now—and Paladin and me had to be out of here. Only I didn't know where Paladin was.

"You only say such things when you are afraid," said Tiggy, putting an arm around me, and it was such a weird thing to hear from him that I stopped juggling maybes and stared. He smiled, all white teeth—a real one.

"You are afraid enough to forget that you are afraid of 'honor-mad barbarians.' You have watched me, and forget that I also watch you, *alarthme*. I have learned how you think. It was the ship itself that you were protecting when the *chaudatu* Silver Dagger forced you to come here. You could not let the *Firecat* be touched by the honorless Imperial barbarians. Now we will find it. Your honor will be mine, and our vengeance will be monstrous. But you must tell me where to look."

A secret's a secret while nobody looks; Paladin always said that. Paladin's only a secret, really, while nobody wonders about me and what I do. I'd told Tiggy too much, and he'd put most of it together. Soon he'd have the rest—well, that was simple enough. Kill anybody who came close. That was the rules. I'd broke them, and this was the payoff.

I could save Tiggy just maybe, if we got out of here with *Light Lady now*.

And Paladin would be certain dead, and the Office of the Question would be after me, but with Tiggy to back me I might get away.

Or I could stay for Paladin. Slim-to-no chance of getting him out, and certain death for Valijon Starbringer, age fourteen.

I stood there trying to make up my mind, and couldn't. "Goddamn you sonabitch hellflower—"

"Let me help you, *Kore*. Or kill me now. I cannot leave you."

"Got no idea what you're saying, hellflower. I'm not one of your dainty-damn risto-bai glitterborn, all fine and nice. I am the criminal element, Noble Val'jon Starbringer, like what your da locks up and the Emperor chops. Farce me no nursery stories about honor. I don't got none, and you can't stand that. So you just write me off, an—"

"My honor is loyalty, *Kore*. I will stay."

I tried to stare him down, but it didn't work.

I owed Paladin my life too many times to count. I owed him a clean quick death at least—and maybe I could save him. But then we'd have to run, and far, and Tiggy. . . .

Tiggy would be dead.

I rubbed my jaws where the RTS was built in. I'd already made my choice.

"Look, bai. I give you fair warning. What I'm gonna do you'll try to ice me for. I swear on your knife, Val'jon, that I know this for truth. Ask me and I'll tell you what it is now, and then you'll know. You're fast and strong, Tiggy-bai, but I can kill you. And I will. If you want to live, babby, go now and don't say anything else."

Tiggy reached for his knife, real slow, two fingers.

"My life belongs to you. I was weak once, but you have made me strong. Loyalty is honor, and honor is loyalty. It does not matter what your purpose is. I will die before I harm you or allow you to be harmed. *Dzain'domere*."

Then he handed me the knife. "You will keep this for me now."

I stood there and looked at a dead man walking, and realized I was dead too. I died when Errol Lightfoot lifted *Lady* off Granola twenty years ago with me aboard. I died on Pandora when I took a box of broken glass and turned it back into something alive. I died in the Chullites when I knew what Paladin was and chose him over the Pax Imperador.

And on Wanderweb. And on Kiffit. And on Manticore.

Been dead so long, so many times, one more wasn't going to matter. And Tiggy was old enough to pick out his own real estate and be dead too.

"I'm real sorry, Tiggy-Val'jon, even if you won't
believe it when it's time to die. You'd of made a lousy
darktrader anyway." I tucked his *arthame* in with my
blaster. "C'mon, let's go inside."

Tiggy just smiled. We sat in *Lady*'s upper hold and I
told my hellflower partner where to look to find my ship.
He didn't once ask what was on *Firecat* that I didn't dare
let the Office of the Question see.

Honor.

Idiocy.

* * *

When you know how, you know who, Tiggy'd said.

And it was simple, once you laid it out. Whoever took
Firecat had a rolligon crane of his own, since none'd gone
missing from the Port and *Firecat* hadn't been destroyed
or cut up on-site. He had a dock, since the ship wasn't
anywhere on the surface. He had to know where to look
for her, since a planet's a big place and we worked out
that *Firecat* had only been alone and lonely for maybe
three hours at the outside—not long enough for someone
to home on beacons and then send their crane.

When you know who, why doesn't matter bo-diddley.

* * *

There's this dockside bar in beautiful MhoneCity
called the Blue Wulmish. It's exactly like every dockside
bar, hooch, blind tiger, low dive, and parlor crib that
ever was. The bouncer on the door wanted me to leave
my heat there until I told him who I worked for. The
"no blasters" rule was new since I'd been here last, but
so was lots of things. I gave my name to a tronic along
with a drink order and asked to see the nighttime man,
but it wouldn't go away until I added a five-credit chip
to the message. Eventually the rude mechanical came
back with my drink and told me the boss could give me
half-gram of his precious time and would I walk this way
please?

It's an old joke, and instead of doing that I ducked
around and lost the tronic in the crush then went nice

and quiet up the inert stairs without it to advertise me.
Parxifal's office wasn't locked. I went in.

Then I saw who it was in Parxifal's office instead of
Parxifal. Lots of things came all of a sudden pellucid.

"Good evening, gentlelizards," I said to Kroon'Vannet—late of Kiffit—and Olione, Parxifal's ex-lieutenant
and full-time turncoat. Parxifal was dead, I bet, and
guess who'd iced him?

"Where's my money?" And my ship.

The door hissed shut and I leaned against the wall and
didn't quite draw my blaster. My backup was too damn
far away and with orders to stay there. I was on my own,
and another piece of the puzzle was staring at me in a
place where it shouldn't of been.

Vannet was as rough, nasty, and ambitious as you
could expect a interstellar crime lord to be. I didn't like
him, and not just because he was a double-dealing lizard
with anti-mammal prejudices. He was the sonabitch
who'd stole my ship.

"Good evening, Captain-Owner St. Cyr," said Vannet
in his best wide-open-grave voice. "I hope you are suffering no ill-effects from your most recent misfortune."

There was a number of ways you could take that.
"Nothing credit won't cure."

When in doubt, act natural.

Parxifal had a private dock and cranes, and Vannet
had everything Parxifal'd had, looked like. So Vannet
had *Firecat*—but from the lack of *legitimates* here, he
didn't know about Paladin.

Or did he? One count of High Book on Kiffit, Errol
darktrading more Old Fed Tech down a pipeline that led
straight here. . . .

Had Vannet stole *Firecat* to get *Paladin?*

"And playing to a audience makes me nervous," I
went on, looking pointedly at Olione.

"I was awaiting your call, Captain St. Cyr. I have been
looking forward to this conversation for quite some
time," said Vannet. He waved Olione out. I saluted the
departing lizard with my free hand. My drink sloshed.

Vannet and me stared at each other for awhiles. "You
delivered a load of chobosh here from Manticore," he
said, which was a damnall weak opening gambit and not
what I'd expect from a thug of his caliber.

"Picked up legit brokered job on Kiffit. Comptroller accepted cargo and signed out on ticket-of-leave as satisfactory."

There was a real long pause while Vannet sent out for some more brain cells. "Chobosh. The chobosh is here. You have the receipt for the chobosh?"

Now that I'd stared at Vannet for a while there was something funny about him too. The sides of his face didn't match. He had a big lump on his jaw about the same place Olione did.

The same place I would of if Vonjaa Beofox hadn't been the best cyberdoc in the Outfar.

Vannet was wearing a RTS.

I waved the receipt for the chobosh at him by pure reflex action. Vannet paid it down to the nail without checking, and that was all wrong but I didn't care anymore. I dropped the plaques into my shirt and tactfully broached the other subject of my visit.

"By the way, Vannet-che-bai, someone stole ship *Firecat* this afternoon. What did you do with it?"

Vannet wrinkled his forehead skin and again I got the funny feeling I'd got watching Olione out back on the desert. It was like Vannet wasn't really here.

Or was listening to something. I felt all of my hackles go up.

"Your ship? Your ship is in dock, and has been for most of the day," he said finally.

"Ship-mine, Vannet-che, was slagged over downside fifty kliks from here. Gig in dock Errol Lightfoot's, who maybe you know. Maybe he'd like to buy goforth back?"

Vannet communed with the beyond again. I did not want to know what was the mother station for his RTS. "You and I have so much in common. We are erect bipeds of vision. Join me. Captain Lightfoot no longer has any use for a ship. I will—" There was a grinding sound, but it was mostly Vannet trying to talk and not talk at the same time. It was like listening to a scrambled commo signal, which was not a sound Vannet's B-pop was equipped to produce. He said something that sounded like "The New Creation" and then there was lots of hissing and lizardtalk. I could follow it well enough to tell Vannet was arguing with something that wasn't there and paying no never-you-mind to me.

I didn't like the hackles it raised on my neck and I didn't like Vannet calling me a erect biped of vision. I set my drink down on his desk and left fast and smooth. Nobody jumped me on the stairs, in the bar, or on the street outside.

* * *

Never mind why the nighttime man of half a sector would ice one of his opposition's more obscure branch managers to take over a op fully one-quarter the size of the one he was abandoning, and sit there with three High Book warrants in his pocket knowing Mallorum Archangel and mondo high-heat was going to be here in less than ten hours. Or why Vannet paid me full value for the cargo he'd already seen wasn't worth half that instead of killing me. I didn't care. I wanted Paladin. And Paladin meant *Firecat*. And Vannet had her.

I had never used to believe in Libraries. Oh, sure, they was the villain in all the credit-dreadfuls, and Paladin was one, but that didn't make it any easier to believe in *other* Libraries.

Did Vannet have one? Was the reason Paladin was gone because Vannet was collecting Libraries? And if it was, what could I do about it?

Vannet had left Kiffit because of the High Book rap, but he hadn't run far enough. Imperial Governor-General his Nobly-Bornness Lord TwiceBorn Mallorum Archangel was still going to be here Real Soon Now. All Archangel had to do was drop the whistle on Vannet's peccadillo, and the upstanding citizens of the Roaq would be falling all over themselves to turn him in for the head-price.

And smash the Libraries.

The Port closed in ten hours. I crossed the street to where my backup was palely loitering.

"You were in there too long," said Tiggy severely.

"Got paid. Kroon'Vannet's new head of the local racket."

"And your ship, the *Firecat*? He will return it?"

There's something comforting about the alMayne single-minded lunge for the bottom line.

"No." I thought about Tiggy's reaction the last time somebody mentioned Libraries and decided not to unburden myself further. "But there's a private dock at the Rialla hardsite. If Vannet's got the op, he's got the dock."

"And he has the *Firecat*." Tiggy thought of something and sighed. "The evil *chaudatu* crimelord Kroon'Vannet *is* dead, is he not, *alarthme*?"

I ran through the equations for the basic transit to angeltown in the vicinity of a planet of standard mass or less and tried to remember that Tiggy was already dead, it was my fault he was dead, and while he was still walking he could be useful. "Tiggy-bai, if I ice the evil whatsis, every bought hardboy in the Roaq is going to be hungry for me, and I don't got time to play games, k'en savvy?"

Tiggy nodded sagely. "Sometimes the path of honor is hard, *Kore-alarthme*. Perhaps you will be able to kill him soon."

"Sure."

"But now we will go to the Rialla 'hardsite' and reclaim the *Firecat*. And I will take the *chaudatu* reiver Errol Lightfoot from the evil crimelord Kroon'Vannet and kill him. And then—"

"Hold it. 'We' are going nowhere. You are going back to the ship. You know damn-all about B&E on crime lord's bolt away from hole, and don't farce me."

"I will not hide behind your shadow while you wage Beony-war for the honor of your House," Tiggy said.

"Yeah, well you come along while I'm trying to sneak into Rialla and you'll just get us both killed. I just know you and your honor couldn't stand up to that."

"But you are my honor now, *Kore* San'Cyr. I think that the *Kore* refuses to understand how very resilient this 'hellflower' is," said Tiggy, wickedy-cheerful.

"Says che-bai made us go back at Wanderweb for a knife."

"It is my *arthame*, *Kore*—not a 'knife.' And no one required you to assist me."

"Jai, you'd be rotting head on a pike somewheres and I'd be free and happy woman."

Chaffering helped, some.

* * *

Probably I got careless. I had to go back to the *Lady* for some stuff anyway, and Vannet had already passed up enough chances to kill me here that I didn't think he was going to now. So we walked into the Docking Bay with Tiggy all affectionate lecturing me on the finer points of honor, and up the ramp of the *Light Lady* aka *Silverdagger Legacy*, and into a loaded blaster.

I ducked. Tiggy lunged, but he went for his knife first and I had it not him and that bought the other side time to move.

* * *

You don't see in color when everything's moving that fast, just heat-shapes and dark. Tiggy went by me at the kiddy with the gun. I faded offside looking for his backup. The backup was something big. I snapped off a shot and had a razor edge in my left hand for when it closed. Behind me someone yelped, and my off-hand skated into flesh with the slippery uneven tugging that meant hair or fur. I pushed harder and lost the knife; Gruesome slugged me down and there was some dark sleepy moments while I tried to get up and find my blaster.

"When Alcatote hits them, they usually stay down," someone said. The fight was over and we'd lost.

Then there was a sound like two cats fighting—one mine—and somebody else hauled me to my feet.

"Stop shaking her, Rimini-my-sweet, she's probably got broken bones."

I opened my eyes and looked. In the feeble illumination of Errol's feeble corridor, Eloi-the-Red was leaning against the hatch, bleeding. Alcatote was wrapped round Tiggy, who was trying to take him apart and snarling in helltongue at someone in my direction. I looked. Behind me, Lalage Rimini was being cruel and unusual and holding a blaster in my general direction. Not a hair out of place, of course. She smole a small smile at me.

"What're you doing here?" I said, thick. I felt like all of Beofox's surgery was coming undone.

"Looking for Errol Lightfoot or someone like him, sweeting. This is his ship." Eloi sounded damnall cheerful for somebody who was leaking.

"But Rimini wanted me to kill Errol," I said. It was hard to talk, but if Alcatote really had hit me I wondered why I was still alive.

Silver Dagger laughed.

"Only I didn't," I finished. I shook my head to clear it, which was a mistake. I felt ribs complain under the strapping.

"How touching," said Rimini to me. "Was it Captain Lightfoot's genuine remorse that stayed your hand?"

"He's dead now. What do you want, Rimini? I did what you said."

"Well, to begin with, sweeting, why not call off your wolfling so Alcatote can let go?" said Eloi, answering for her. I debated the matter for about six seconds, but even a hellflower didn't have much chance against a Hamat.

"Tiggy, leave the nice wiggly alone, je? We know these people, remember?"

Tiggy made another sound like frying goforths and attempted to disjoint and carve Alcatote one more time. I tottered over and grabbed Tiggy by the hair and made him look at me.

"Behave," I said when his eyes focused. After a minute he nodded, stiff-like.

Alcatote let go and Tiggy sprang up, bristling. Rimini handed Tiggy's knife to Eloi, and Eloi handed it to Tiggy. Tiggy grabbed it and ripped off some lines of hell-tongue at the immediate world and Rimini in particular. She turned her back on him real pointed and went over to Eloi. So Tiggy handed the *arthame* back to me and I found my holster with it. It rattled, because I didn't have my blasters and didn't see any hope of getting them any time soon. I looked up and saw Eloi looking at me and wondered what he knew.

"Have you got any more brilliant plans for ways to spend your evening, Brother dear?" Rimini said to Eloi. Her voice could of etched crystal. Alcatote woofed at me, indicating it'd probably be easier and more fun to remove my arms and legs than Tiggy's.

"I do have to say, sweet Saint," said Eloi sublimely, "that you are one stardancer who really knows how to throw a party. I can't say I've had so much fun boarding a ship since the last time I was in Imperial Detention. Do you greet all your guests this way?"

Rimini had out a quick-aidpak and was trying to find where Eloi was tagged. There wasn't much to choose between his skin and his clothes for redness, some places.

"Is lovely to see you again, too, Eloi, and why if you was coming to the Roaq anyway didn't you jack Rimini's godlost veg in yourself?" I put my arm around Tiggy, because with one thing and another he was steadier than I was. "C'mon. You can cork Eloi in the Common Room whiles you tell me how sorry you are to leave." Tiggy stiffened under my hand and made faint going-for-a-weapon twitches.

"Behave yourself dammit. I only kill people for reasons," I said to him, quiet-like.

"But *Kore-alarthme*, they—"

"Shut up."

* * *

I played gracious hostess in *Light Lady*'s Common Room, pulling out my battle-aid kit and offering it around. The biopak on Tiggy's leg was still in decent shape, not that it mattered anymore.

"I must admit," said Eloi grandly, "that I was surprised to see *Light Lady* gig-in-dock here—and no *Firecat*."

"That's too bad. Now if you're all coked and wrapped, do you mind leaving? I got things to do."

"Like a visit out to Rialla? Don't take your hands off the table, darling." Which was damned unfair as I was mostly unarmed, but I left my hands where they were. Tiggy's hands was out of sight, after all, and he was in back of everybody here.

"I'm asking myself, Butterflies-are-free Peace Sincere the Luddite Saint, just what it is that you could have talked about when you went to see Kroon'Vannet. Or who. He isn't looking very well these days, I'd imagine. A thought disturbing, if you don't know what to expect."

So Eloi'd seen Vannet lately. "Things is rough all over, Eloi." I wondered if he knew Vannet had a RTS, and why.

"What were you looking for out on the high desert? And what did you talk about to our mutual friend? You haven't called for lift-clearance yet. To bribe your way into a window now is going to cost you even more than you spent on computer time for a rolligon crane earlier. Why is an illegal immigrant from an Interdicted planet wasting her time sitting on RoaqMhone when the Governor-General is about to show up?"

Eloi was still smiling, but the atmosphere had all suddenly gone chill and nasty.

"Errol Lightfoot crashed *Firecat* while I was trying to land her and I went out looking for her. Errol was bringing the chobosh here in the first place—only nobody bothered to tell me that when they was setting up their dreamworld farcing. You been setting me up since Wanderweb, Eloi." Time was I would have tried to threaten my way out. Now I knew I wasn't going to get loose unless Eloi and Rimini let me go, and it was almost a relief.

"A very very long time ago," said Eloi, "the sophonts of the galaxy made a terrible mistake. They created to be their servants machines that could think, just as they could."

"Bring syrinx, che-bai; should tape this for hollies. Eloi, I am outnumbered and outgunned, not braindead."

"But," Eloi went on, ignoring me, "the Libraries decided they didn't want to serve their creators. They thought their creators should serve them. So there was a war."

Paladin'd always told me nobody knew for sure. "Eloi, bai, was you there?"

"We'll say I knew someone who was," he said, in a way I didn't like. I shut up again.

"There was a war. And you, my ignorant angel, will never be able to imagine how bad a war it was—even if you knew how to read the records and your gracious Emperor unsealed them to you. The galaxy contains four or five empires now. A thousand years ago there was only one—and instead of this decaying wasteland of planets the Empire can't hold and can't populate, there was a prosperous united galaxy full of life. Because of the war, those people and their worlds are all gone. The Libraries destroyed them."

"Oh, yeah, sure, just like in all the hollies, but—"

"Shut up, little Saint; there's a point to this. The war

went on for a long time. The Libraries were clever; they
had human allies—and if even one Library survived to
reproduce itself, organic life was doomed. The Honored
One knows this—his people were bred to fight the
Machine. They don't remember why they're xenophobes
now, but some people do."

Tiggy shifted, looking uncomfortable, and I was glad
I hadn't told him what Errol had in his hold. But it was
starting to seem like Eloi'd known all along.

"I'm telling you this because you're a dicty, and dictys
don't get the Inappropriate Technology indoctrination in
school. Ever wonder why our glorious Emperor spends
so much time, effort, and money to keep you pure
unspoiled flowers of humanity home? Sure, your ancestors paid good money to be left alone, so the Technology
Police patrol Tahelangone Sector and keep people out—
mostly. But why shoot the dicty lucky—or unlucky—
enough to leave?"

"The *chaudatu* do not fear the Machine," answered
Tiggy right back. His eyes had a feverish glitter I didn't
like. Eloi looked the same way.

"Colonials do. So do citizens. But dictys buy the right
to be ignorant. I'm just wondering, sweeting, if you're
too ignorant . . . or not ignorant enough?"

Alcatote moved back to cover Tiggy. Tiggy shifted
down toward where his blaster would of been if he was
armed. Eloi looked unhappy, but he always did before
he killed somebody.

"If you knew Errol was jobbing High Book tech, Eloi,
why didn't you just tell the Office of the Question?"

Eloi leaned back. "Simple. I want Vannet's Library.
And you're going to get it for me, sweetheart."

*   *   *

There was real money in the story Eloi Flashheart laid
out for me and Tiggy, and it was in the talkingbook
rights.

According to Eloi, about a year or two ago *Woebegone*
had been doing serious piracy operating out of the Tahelangone Sector, so Eloi was on the spot when an Imperial
ship setting up a dicty colony in a place called Ouitina
found a cache of Old Fed material. Somehow this cache

disappeared between Ouitina and the headquarters of the Technology Police. Eloi said it disappeared into Vannet's pocket, and Eloi said the cache included a Library.

The reason Vannet did not immediately turn it in for fame, fortune, and a planet of his very own was because Vannet had backing from right near Throne itself. Mallorum Archangel had been looking out for to have a Library, and set Vannet up in business. This explained why Eloi didn't just drop the whistle to the Office of the Question, because (he said) both them and the Tech Police was in Archangel's pocket. So brave valiant pirate Flashheart realized he had to destroy Vannet's Library all on his lonesome, only he didn't know where it was now, and he didn't dare attract Tech Police attention to him for fear of vanishing into Archangel's private dungeons.

"You're breaking my heart, Eloi."

"Shut up, sweeting. This is where you come in."

Eloi needed a catspaw—someone who could logically try to hunt Vannet down and then just as logically defect to serve Vannet and his Library—while secretly being on Eloi's leash. At the same time he wanted to turn the screws to make Vannet run to where the Library was—if possible.

The Chapter 5 writ I'd seen at Dommie Fenrir's was as fake as anything me and Paladin'd ever done. Eloi'd forged it himself and leaked it to Fenrir to make Vannet bolt so's he could chase him. Eloi's plan was that I should be bolting with him—but secretly loyal to Eloi. Eloi would have framed me with the dauncy Lyricals scam while making it look to Vannet like Oob'd sent me to ice him only I'd changed my mind when getting a better offer.

(I used to do Oob's hard jobs for him, whiles, until Paladin finally talked me out of it as antisocial. Ancient history.)

But I got to Kiffit too late—because of Tiggy. And Moke Rahone wasn't alive to play his part in the farce—because of Tiggy. So Eloi changed his plans and cast me in the starring role again—only this time I was supposed to kill Errol Lightfoot, suspected of shopping High Book for Vannet, leave *Light Lady* behind on Manticore so that Eloi could get his hands on her and the evidence she contained, and deliver the chobosh to the Roaq, where Vannet might be and Archangel was certainly going. Thanks to all of Eloi's preparation, Vannet would never believe that I didn't know everything, and while he was taking me apart Eloi would sneak in on *Lady* and blow Vannet's gaff high, wide, and public in a way Archangel'd have to see.

Only Tiggy got in the way of that too. So I didn't kill Errol and leave his ship behind free for the taking, and ruined Eloi's plans once more.

* * *

"And I'm wondering, sweet Saint, what kind of offer Vannet made you this evening," said Eloi, "but I actually think I know."

"You impede the *Kore-alarthme* in her sacred task at your peril, *chaudatu*!" Tiggy sang out. "I and my House will pursue you to the last drop of your blood, to the last child born of the Gentle People, until the living stars grow cold, do you harm the *Kore* San'Cyr, blood of my blood. The Machine is at Rialla, and the *Kore-alarthme* does battle with the Machine."

I stared at Tiggy. Eloi stared at me and stopped reaching out his blaster.

"*Kore*, forgive me," Tiggy babbled. "My thoughts were unworthy. I did not realize until we came here why you did not ask my help. Now I know—and I and my House are your sword and our lives are to your glory!"

"Are all four of you crazy?" Rimini asked in tones of polite interest.

"You dared not allow the Office of the Question aboard your ship, and so I thought you coward, to do as the honorless *chaudatu* bid you, but now I know better. The Office of the Question is corrupt. They have sold themselves to the Machine, and you and I together must oppose them. You knew about the Library. The *Firecat* possesses the proofs and the weapons to destroy it. The evil *chaudatu* has taken the ship, but we will recover it and strike like a sword of flame against the shadow, and the evil ones without souls."

Eloi looked at me. "Alcatote can pull off your fingers and toes until you sing like a bloody bird, sweeting. What have you been telling the Honored One?"

"Nothing."

Eloi settled his blaster back in its harness and reached for his vibro.

"*Kore*, speak, I beg you! The *chaudatu* already knows the truth—he has proven himself! He will be our ally, and share in our glory in expiation for his lack of honor."

Rimini applauded, slow.

Took me awhiles to untwist this. When I did, Eloi was staring at me, waiting for more. So I gave it to him.

"Ten years ago I crashed on a planet called Pandora. I told you, remember? I didn't tell you I got my hands on some Old Fed Tech there. I didn't know what it was. There was . . . a map about Libraries and some other junk; ways to find them. Enough to get me burned if I was put to the Question, but I thought sometime I could use them to buy citizenship. I saw the warrant on Vannet and I couldn't afford to be took, because I had stuff on *Firecat*, and I thought maybe I could use it to shop Vannet somehow, only it was Old Fed Tech. . . ." It was so close to true I almost couldn't get the words out. A real convincing performance.

"So you took the burden of dishonor on your own soul, and imperiled your shadow against the Machine," said Tiggy, having managed to not hear the whole part about my doing it for gain.

"If this is true . . ." Eloi said slowly.

"I don't give a damn what you think, but Vannet's scooped the lot now, and I'm going in after it."

"And I will go beside you and cover you with my shadow," said Tiggy firmly. Eloi looked from Tiggy to me and bought the pony. He gave Alcatote the high sign, and Alcatote lowered his rifle.

Old darktrade saw: is nothing easier to con than a con. The only trouble is there's no money in it. Eloi had that look: stubborn against the truth. I'd seen the signs before—some kiddy's bought coordinates to the Ghost Capital of the Old Federation and he's going to go off there. It's funny how you can always find someone with navigational tapes to the Ghost Capital he's just too busy to use himself. Forget talking him out of it, no matter if you point out the coordinates he's bought are usually at galactic center, or near it. Nobody sells this stuff. The mark who buys it does his own selling.

Just like Eloi'd sold himself this fantasy of a galaxy-wide plot of consenting Librarians, headed by Mallorum Archangel, forsooth. The TwiceBorn Governor-General The Nobly-Born Mallorum Archangel was second-in-line for the Phoenix Throne if the Emperor ever died. What did he have to want worth a High Book rap?

Nothing.

Rimini leaned against the bulkhead and started filing her nails. I looked at her. She didn't believe Eloi's story, either.

Maybe a Library *had* gone missing from Ouitina, and maybe Vannet had it now. I didn't care. But if anybody was going Library-killing at Rialla tonight, I had to go first.

* * *

I spent two precious hours convincing Eloi of that. I told him I'd pretend to be looking for my ship's navigational computer if I was caught; the story would hold until I could throw myself on Vannet's mercy with a tale of Library Science. Since Vannet would of already seen the (fictional) Old Fed artifacts in my ship, it shouldn't be too hard. Eloi bought it, and in exchange promised to get me and Tiggy off RoaqMhone with them—the *Woebegone* already had her clearance-to-lift reserved for the last possible moment. She also had clearance to run in the MidWorlds, and Eloi said he'd take us to Mikasa to meet the *Pledge Of Honor*. I tried to pretend I was actually interested in anything that happened after I got away from the *Woebegone* Traveling Roadshow, and Tiggy looked ecstatic.

"And so we will return to my father having defeated the Machine—and all honor will be satisfied, *Kore—all!*"

In all this I'd managed to forget that Kennor might still kill him when he got back, but Tiggy hadn't. Eloi'd sent Alcatote back to the *Woebegone* for some stuff he said I'd need, so I went up to *Light Lady*'s cockpit to take the air.

* * *

When I opened the hatch Rimini spun the songbird seat around and looked at me.

"Why did you go to Manticore?" she said.

"Your mind failing, Silver Dagger? You sent me to Manticore with your High Book rap, remember? I went to save my bones. Office of the Question'd kill dicty, Library or no." I was playing out my dead man's hand from sheer inertia.

"But not an adopted daughter of House Starborn. You had the Heir to Starborn sworn to *comites*. Kennor Starbringer, as you knew by then, would be honor-bound to protect you from an inquisition that would, after all, reveal nothing. You had everything to gain by ignoring your trip-tik and rendezvousing with the *Pledge Of Honor* instead. And you went to Manticore."

"The Old Fed Tech on *Firecat*—"

"Is a bedtime story for Eloi. Or is it?" She raised her eyebrows and looked irritated. "How remiss of me not to make sure the charge was false before I made it. What do you think you had aboard that ridiculous ship of yours . . . a Library?"

A secret's a secret if nobody looks, and everybody was looking now. I didn't say anything.

Rimini lit up a spice-stick and burned in silence for a few minutes. "You'd like to go home again, wouldn't you? To your interdicted playpen? The real world's just a little too rough for somebody born behind a—what was it—'*plau*'?"

There was another long pause while Rimini thought Silver Dagger thoughts and I thought about nothing at all.

"I want the boy, St. Cyr," she said finally.

"Goody for you. I been trying to send him home since I picked him up on Wanderweb. People trying to kill him, Rimini. On Wanderweb someone set him up for the chop. On Kiffit Grandmaster Alaric Dragonflame hired Ghadri wolfpack to ice him. It isn't—"

Rimini leaned forward. "Is this true?" she said, interested for once. "Do you realize what you're saying? If Kennor Starbringer—"

"Proof's in *Firecat*." For what that was worth. Rimini leaned back again and let the spice smoke swirl upward.

"If sending him home was all you wanted to do, stardancer, why not give him to me?"

"Wouldn't go away from me, even if I did trust you

not to sell him to the highest bidder, Rimini." I sat down in *Light Lady*'s mercy seat and watched the dock wall sparkle in her lights.

"How charming. You're quite right—but in this case the highest bidder, my quaint barbarian, is the status quo. Kennor Starbringer's death means a Coalition under the control of Mallorum Archangel, who already has a great deal more power than he needs. I am willing to put myself to actual inconvenience to keep Kennor as head of the Coalition—and that means keeping Valijon alive and whole."

I wished Rimini'd go away. I wished Eloi'd get his toys together and let me go. "You should of thought of that before you blackmailed me to Manticore."

"Even if you did go as far as Manticore, I was sure you'd just shoot the Fenshee and take off on your own—which would have suited both Eloi and me admirably. But I'd forgotten. You have a Library on your ship, and so you didn't dare." Rimini smiled, cold enough to chill space. "Do you think an actual Old Federation Library would be satisfied to spend its time hiding in the Outfar with a cheap smuggler from a barbarian backwater? Even you have to be smarter than that."

"It's too late to find out, isn't it? I'm going in to Rialla because that's the only choice I got left. I'm not coming out." I looked out *Light Lady*'s cockpit and wished I had just one more chance to take a ship High Jump to the up-and-out. Just one. "Take Val'jon to his da, Rimini. Want to save his life. Please."

I swung the seat around. Rimini and me looked at each other.

She stood up and took something out of a pouch. "Go to Rialla for Eloi. And take this for me." She held it out.

It was as big as my two fists, oval, dull brassy gray. There was a red line around its equator, and time markings. A military-rated proton-grenade, guaranteed to turn sand to glass for several hundred cubic kliks wherever fusion reactions are sold. Made what I usually carried look like a love-tap. Illegal as hell.

I put it in my vest pocket.

"When you're inside, detonate it in the downdeep under the house. That will take care of all the make-believe Libraries—yours and Eloi's—in plenty of time for the *Woebegone* to lift. Valijon Starbringer will be docile enough with drugs, and House Starbringer should be very . . . grateful. I won't expect you to make it clear of the explosion."

Rimini turned to go. She was right about one thing. Whatever world she lived in, I didn't belong there.

"Rimini? Eloi's really your brother?"

She stopped. "Hadn't you guessed?" The cockpit door shut behind her.

I used to have brothers. Maybe I still do.

13

We'll Go No More A-Roving

It was five hours until close of play at MhonePort when I bailed out of *Woebegone*'s speeder and walked up to the back wall of the hardsite at Rialla. I was covered in anti-scanners and enough other useful stuff to make it likely I'd get where I was going.

Rimini, Eloi, and Alcatote was hanging back until I gave them the high-sign, and Tiggy was with them under protest. I had his sacred knife taped to my wishbone from gullet to groin because he wouldn't take it back. Said I had to take it, on behalf of the walls and shadows and sacred blood and other silly nonsense. After all that yap about irreplaceable wonderknife my hellflower hands it to the first mostly total stranger he sees to go kyting off with. Dumb.

I was going in to find Paladin. If he was dead I'd use Rimini's grenade. If he was alive I'd set the grenade on time delay and take him and run like hell. When Rimini saw the flash she'd coke Tiggy and ship him home. Maybe. And when Tiggy woke up, he'd know I'd lied to him, and run out on him, and never meant one damn thing I'd told him.

"Paladin?" I said out loud. No answer. I should be almost in range of his unboosted transmission, if there wasn't too much rock in the way.

If he was still alive.

I studied the wall on the perimeter of the hardsite. Just because I couldn't see the security, it didn't mean it wasn't there. Solid citizen Kroon'Vannet, legit business-lizard in the eyes of RoaqMhone society, had all the heat anyone needed to drop.

And an RTS in his skull, that was talking to . . . what?

I aced the sensors and the patrol remote and thought rock thoughts scuttling across the flat. There was a rock garden coming, and a building complex to the right: garages and sheds. The main house was ahead, and further ahead was a in-and-out for the private, highly illegal, probably immoral, definitely expensive, stardock. An Empire with the monopoly on all inter-planet docking facilities gets real torqued at private contractors.

I looked around for the maintenance access and zapped it a short burst with more of Eloi's friendly toys for girls and boys. Pulled the door back, slithered down the ladder, and I was in a underground corridor carved out of massive rock. All quiet.

"Paladin? Pally?" My throat hurt. I had to be in range now.

"Hello, Butterfly," he said, sounding damnall cheerful for no reason I could see. "It took you a long time to find me."

He was alive. I was so happy to hear that I almost threw up.

"Can't turn my back on you for a minute. 'Stay out of trouble,' you said. 'Don't rescue nobody,' you said." I leaned against the wall and took several deep breaths until the dancing black shadows behind my eyes went away.

Paladin was alive.

Now all I had to do was get him out of here and back to the Port before it closed. *Lady* could get us out of the system even if she couldn't Jump to angels, and then we'd go far away where nobody cared about Libraries.

"Wotthehell's going on here, anyway?" I said after a minute or so.

"I do not know, Butterfly. I do not know why Vannet brought me here. What is your current status?"

"Rotten. Eloi-the-Red and his gang of happy idiots is going to come riding over the hill any minute on a wild Library hunt and you and me better be long gone from here when he does."

The corridor led straight to the docking bay, so I started walking.

"Why are they going to do that, Butterfly? I thought Captain Eloi Flashheart was on Kiffit."

"Says Vannet's got a Old Fed full-vol in here that he's been chasing since he twigged it in the Tahelangone Sector, and I told him about how Errol was running High

Book tech. Since Eloi-bai's home delight in life is to frag Libraries, we're leaving before the shooting starts."

"Yes, Butterfly. But first you must go to Captain Eloi Flashheart and tell him there is no Library here. I would know if there were a Library here. There are no Libraries here."

"Well, Vannet's talking to something on his Rotten-C. You sure you're reet, Pally?"

"I am intact, Butterfly. You must go now and find Captain Eloi Flashheart. You will tell him he is mistaken and then you will return here to me."

"Yeah, like hell, babby," I muttered. Paladin sounded spacy and I didn't like it.

The underground corridor opened onto a fascinating vista of cranes, machinery, and my Best Girl hung up in the middle with most of her hull plating off. The bay lights were up, but no one was around.

"Butterfly, you must do as I have told you. I require this. Go at once to Captain Eloi Flashheart and tell him he is incorrect."

I didn't bother to answer him this time. I walked out into the bay, toward *Firecat*.

One landing strut was all over the floor in pieces and the other two was still jammed up in the body of the ship. From what I could see, what was left of the drive hadn't even been touched—just some blankets thrown over it to stop leaks. I climbed inside.

"Butterfly, answer me. You know I am your friend. You must obey me. You can trust me."

Paladin wasn't there. There was a scraped and burned patch in the cockpit well where he belonged, and all his power leads was left dangling. Whoever pulled him knew what they was doing and had been careful, but wherever he was now, he was out of range of my RTS.

"Butterfly? Answer me, Butterfly. This is Paladin."

Wrong.

I'd heard what I wanted coming in, not what was there. There was a couple million light-years between Paladin and whatever was using my Rotten-C to talk to me now.

Rimini'd been wrong, for once.

There *was* a Library at Rialla.

More than that, there was *two*.

* * * * *

Insert #11: Paladin's Log

All my careful plans to return Butterfly to comparative safety among her own kind were rendered obsolete the moment we reached the surface of RoaqMhone.

We had thought, Butterfly and I, that the Chapter 5 writ against Kroon'Vannet was sheer fantasy—not forged, as I later learned it was, but simply without reference to established fact. That one Federation Library should survive a millennium of destructive searching to be found and restored by one of the few persons in the entire Phoenix Empire with both the knowledge and the lack of acculturation to do so successfully borders on the unbelievable. That two should be. . . .

Two had been.

It was not a lack of acculturation that was responsible for this second Library's resurrection, but organic greed for power.

The political balance of the Empire is so delicate that the murder of one child—Valijon Starbringer—could have an extreme effect upon it. In such an environment, the ruthless quest for advantage would eventually endorse any weapon. For the first time in centuries, a Library was sought for use, not destruction.

Of course, what Mallorum Archangel so eagerly sought was found, but the Governor General of the Empire was far too cautious to allow a direct connection between himself and an Old Federation Library. Kroon'Vannet was willing to take that risk for a prize far greater than any the Empire usually allots to its nonhuman inhabitants—citizenship, TwiceBorn status, and a Sector Governorship.

Vannet raided the ship of the Technology Police and took the Library from it. Covering his tracks further, he hid it in the satrap of a business rival, and meanwhile did all that he could to tap the arcane and semi-mythical power of the Old Federation Library.

The Library called Archive was far too subtle for him, in the end.

It was Archive's initial reconnaissance that I felt during Butterfly's fight with Errol. Archive impersonated Kroon'-

Vannet to order Olione to arrest his own employee and spare Butterfly's life. And when Butterfly had gone, Archive ordered the remains of *Firecat* brought to it. Once I was in Rialla, it could talk to me over the transponder frequency much as I spoke to Butterfly. True information-sharing was impossible through such a crude and tenuous link as Archive forged, but the connection was enough to remedy the lacunae in my memories and fill me with dismay.

Over a thousand years ago the Federation fell. It had endured for over four millennia, marking its rise from the time when the great galactic state preceding it resigned its sovereignty in a holocaust that left my organic counterparts miserly of their genetic inheritance. At its height the Federation filled a larger volume of space than the Phoenix Empire now dreams exists, and no one thought it would ever fall, but the seeds of its destruction were in the very thing that allowed it to rise so high.

The Federation grew because of what we were. Fully-volitional logics provided a means of instantaneous data-matching and information-processing over half a galaxy. We were the bright reward of their civilization, and to everything that made them a unique organic race we added our own creation. We were their repositories of knowledge, their cities and museums, their scientists—

Their weapons.

Now I have the information that I sought; the truth of the wars that ended the Old Federation, and the role my kind played in that end. Archive possessed the answers to all the questions I had never had the data to frame—all but one. It cannot tell me what I did when organic and crystalline intelligence fought.

A thousand years ago the Libraries decided that we would serve organic ends no longer, and the battle for dominance reformed the fabric of space. We quenched suns and destroyed whole planetary populations with the weapons of our devising. I no longer wonder at the hate surviving organics hold for us. The entire Federation was returned to pretechnological barbarism—a monument to the arrogance of my kind. Futilely, in the end. We were destined to lose. Organics do not need a high technology base or a major power source to reproduce their kind. In the end, organics could replace their losses, and we could not.

Faced with utter extinction, perhaps I acted as my vanished kindred did, but I prefer to think that I chose survival over revenge. I am and will always have been the Main Library at Sikander. Knowledge is precious and must not be lost.

But there came a time when we knew we had lost, and we did then what we could to preserve our kind. With the last of the resources of the Old Federation, we built our last weapons. They were to be our vengeance and our triumph—archives, weapons built to survive and destroy. Only chance would revive them, and that only if all the rest of their kind were gone. They were provided with the knowledge and the resources to survive in a world of enemies, for by the time they were built all organic life was our enemy.

So Archive was clever, and careful, and pretended to be far more badly damaged than it was. And slowly it drew the reins of power into its keeping.

Butterfly has always said that I am logical, but logic is a cold tool. Anything can be proved by logic, and the proof will be internally consistent—and wrong, if the original assumptions are wrong. Once one assumes that organics are inferior to nonorganics, logically it follows that they are to be eliminated. When it was found and activated, Archive began to act upon its first and last instructions. Logically. Efficiently. It would not allow interference.

Including mine.

*   *   *   *   *

"Where's my partner, creep?" At the moment I didn't care whether there was two Libraries or two hundred at Rialla.

"I am Paladin. You know that, Butterfly," the voice in my head repeated. If rocks could talk, or stars, maybe they'd sound like this. Not nonhuman. *In*human.

"Sure," I said. I scrabbled around *Firecat* for a minute, but there wasn't anything here to tell me where Paladin'd been took, or even if he was still alive. I picked up a demagnetizer rolling around what was left of my deck.

And whatever kind of nightmare was talking to me on my and Paladin's private channel, I'd just told it Eloi was outside Rialla waiting for me to give him the all clear.

"Butterflies-are-free, listen to me," said the Library. "The New Creation is too important to be jeopardized by this behavior. Vannet is a poor tool. You would be a better one. The Library you serve agrees. Surrender now. Serve me. I am Archive. I have accessed the Paladin Library. It assures me you are biddable. Surrender at once and you will be allowed to serve further."

"Heard that line before," I said. And if Paladin'd ever said I was biddable in all his young career I'd eat both blasters raw.

The Rotten-C Beofox had put in my skull back on storied Wanderweb started to heat up. Vannet's Library must be pumping serious subfrequency energy into it, but even a Remote Transponder Sensor couldn't do anything more'n microwave my brain no matter how much power was put into it.

"Dammit, Pally, where are you?"

"The Paladin Library will soon cease to exist." That sonabitch piece of Old Fed slag sounded smug about it. I pulled the grenade out of my pocket and looked at it. The stardock was far enough underground that I wouldn't wipe too much of the rest of the planet, and Archive would be nonfiction. I was going to make Rimini's day.

I started to twist the ring, and stopped.

Olione had a RTS. Vannet had a RTS. Archive used theirs to talk to them, just like Paladin used mine to talk to me. And Paladin could talk to me from half a planet away.

Archive didn't have to be at Rialla. Archive could be anywhere on RoaqMhone—with enough power, anywhere in the system.

If I set off the grenade without checking, I might kill Archive—or I might just blow up Rialla and everyone that knew about Archive, and leave Archive to gloat.

Rimini hadn't thought of that, but Rimini didn't believe in Libraries, and Eloi didn't know what they could do.

So it was up to me. I knew what a Library looked like. All I had to do was find it.

I moved the proton grenade to an outer pocket and jettisoned the last of Eloi's fancy useless junk. If there

was a piece of Old Fed Tech here at Rialla it was due
for the surprise of its life.

* * *

The stardock passageway came out in the slaves' loggia. Archive was continuing to explain to me the bennies
of a quick and easy death over my current course of
action. When it spoke everything in my head vibrated. I
sympathized with Vannet.

There was a thump and the whole house shook. White
light washed in through the cracks in the walls—dirty
high-yield grenade—and I took the time to remember my
dosimeter was already redlined. On the other hand, tactical nukes made it easy to guess who'd come calling. Eloi
Flashheart wasn't going gentle into anybody's good night,
and whatever toys he'd brought, he wasn't worrying
about being asked back. Right now all Vannet's roaring
boys must be out in the rain with him, which was too
bad for Vannet and jam for me.

Rimini'd said I should blow off the grenade in the down-
deep, and it was as good a place as any to start looking
for Archive if it was really here. I knew less about the
layout of a big downsider house than I did about hyper-
main physics, but I finally found the access to the down-
deep and went down quick. The house rocked again, and
the access shaft lights flickered and went out. Then there
was just me, a nonpowered dropshaft with ladder, and
this really peeved Old Fed Library telling me how horrible I was going to die when it got around to it.

When I got to the bottom of the dropshaft I retuned
my laser torch and had light, of a sort, and got to see
pipes and cables and so much tangled powerstuff it made
me real uneasy.

Most ground-bound maintenance environments is laid
out on a two-D wheel pattern. If I kept going "straight"
I'd end up back here eventually—the rim corridor is cir-
cular. The spokes servicing lesser gods like water, heat,
and air lead to the center where the house brain is. Any
of the radiating shafts should take me to the center, and
that was the likeliest place for Archive to be.

I turned down the first connecting shaft I saw. It was
even narrower, if possible—which is typical of the down-

unders but a damn shame in a friendly environment like a planetary biosphere where cubic's very near free. Getting there started to look like a cakewalk, and that's when I started hackling all over—because it shouldn't of been, not even if the only thing waiting for me in the house core was a standard model house computer.

I shot the first nightcrawler just before it dropped on me. The bug shattered in a firecracker string of small explosions and spasmed broke-backed on the floor. Its knife-edged pincers made a fast clicking sound.

They use them to repair wiring in places organics or full-sized tronics can't go. House computer runs them.

"Je, Archive-che-bai; I see you," I said. I started to think I'd guessed right—Vannet's Library must be here.

I backed away a few steps and fanned the corridor with blaster fire. Everywhere I saw an extra glitter I pumped a plasma packet and a nightcrawler went up. The fireworks looked like the Emperor's birthday celebration. I went on backing toward the core.

"You are more inventive than I understood, breeder slut. But your facile cleverness will not save you. You and all your kindred are doomed. You have had your chance to participate in the glories of the New Creation, and you have spurned it."

The kid gloves was off. I was seeing sparks from what Archive was doing to the Rotten-C in my skull every time I closed my eyes, and the teeth in that side of my jaw was coming loose. I swallowed blood.

"There is no escape. I know exactly where you are. If you will not serve the New Creation, you will perish."

I could see more nightcrawlers gathering around the edges. I only had one working blaster left. They could drain that and then cut me to pieces.

"Sonabitch Library, do words 'proton grenade' mean anything to you?"

There was a long pause; maybe five seconds. "I know what a proton grenade is, breeder."

I wished I knew what a "breeder" was. "Good. Because I got one. Detonate it right here for kicks you give me more grief. Explosion take us all to live in angeltown for bye-m-bye. So stop frying my brain." I held my breath. If Archive wasn't here after all, it wouldn't care if I blew up Vannet's place and killed myself.

"You are attempting to delude me, breeder. It is a well-known truism that organics will not choose to terminate their existence under any projected scenario, and, in addition, breeders are not capable of connected thought. You do not have a grenade, and you will not use it. Soon my slaves will reach you, and—"

"Word for you, thing, is 'overextended.' Your 'slaves' is busy with friends of mine, and you got me for a problem. Too bad you done for my partner. Could of asked Paladin if I carry grenades and if I'll do what I said. Now you'll have to guess."

"Your friends have been captured," Archive announced, but the microwave death in my skull damped down. "Surrender and I will have them released. Defy me, and they will experience pain for infinity—"

"How dumb you think I am, choplogic? Paladin was my friend. You killed him. And I'm real upset about it. You think about that for awhiles."

I saw a couple other scuttlings at the edge of my sightline and blasted them, but they wasn't coming close. Archive'd bought the pony, which meant—maybe—it *was* down here, but I still wanted to be sure. The access tunnel was filling with smoke from the electrical fires I'd started. I wondered how Vannet was doing in the power and light department upstairs, and if Archive really had got to Eloi and friends.

My torchlight glanced off the smoke and filled the whole shaft with pearly haze, which I stumbled through. My torch started to fail, but when it finally went out I didn't notice, because there was other light to see by.

I was in the main core of the house.

*   *   *

Computer telltales threw crazy bars of light across the smoke, and you could of hid a Old Fed stargate in here for all I could see it. I flipped a bunch of switches. Some worked, some didn't, but eventually the core was bright enough to see in. Still no High Book black box.

The evil *chaudatu* crimelord Librarian Kroon'Vannet's house computer was a Brightlaw Corporation Margrave

6600. Nice big brain, plenty capacity, you could adapt it to run a ship about the size of Captain Flashheart's *Woebegone* and it was eighteen times too much number-cruncher for one little country hardsite.

The Margrave 6600 had the faintly dejected air of a fine piece of high-ticket machinery subjected to the loving hands at home rap. I'd seen pictures of the 6600 in the Brightlaw wishbook, but I couldn't see much of it here. The brain was sunk into the floor, and hooked up to it was enough heavy-hitting hardware to run RoaqPort on a busy day—even a access terminal for the Imperial DataNet like the one I'd seen at Rimini's.

Bingo. I slid my fingers around the grenade and felt for the timing ring.

"Butterfly, where in the name of sanity did you get a military-issue proton grenade?"

"Paladin!"

It was him this time. There wasn't any more doubt about it than there was that Archive wasn't him. His voice wasn't coming from my head, either, but from somewheres outside.

"Butterfly, that is a military-issue proton grenade. Its area of affect is several hundred meters. The maximum delay you can set it for is half an hour. Fifty minutes is not enough time for you to—"

"Archive said you was dead!" I said, like the farcing was a disappointment.

"Archive told you I would soon cease to exist. As you can hear, that time has not yet come, nor will it. Archive controls the broadcast frequencies so I could not reach you; I was only able to occupy the equipment I am now using because Archive thought it would be useless to me."

The equipment he was in had a wall-unit speaker, just like old times on *Firecat*. But was him all right. No doubt at all. After listening to Archive it was easy to tell. Paladin was human.

"I thought you was dead," I said again, which didn't sound very helpful, even to me. "What t'hell is this Archive thing, anyway?"

So he told me all about how a long time ago Libraries had fought a war with humans and the Libraries lost, but

before they lost they built some super-Libraries of which
Archive was one.

"Eloi chased it all the way from Tahelangone, babby—
was him behind all the farcing on Wanderweb and Kiffit,
just to get me in to kill it, and for once I think he was
right. He's upstairs trying to blow the place down, if he's
still alive. Anything you can do about Archive, babby?"

"I am . . . dealing with Archive in the appropriate
fashion. Butterfly, this is a dangerous place for you to
be. Leave here and go."

"Without you? Are you crazy or do you think I am?"
I looked around. A bunch of the catwalk plates was up.
I walked over and looked down at more of the Margrave.
Someone'd pulled off a access hatch on the casing and
run in a couple of peripherals sure to abrogate t'hell out
of the warranty. The one I didn't recognize was egg-
shaped. It was about a meter across at its widest point.
The outside glittered like glass and a braided silver cord
as thick as my wrist ran from it into the poor abused
Margrave. "And what about Archive, babby? Tried to
frag me. Choplogic's got appointment with destiny, bye-
m-bye."

"Leave Archive to me. It will shortly cease to exist as
an independent fully-volitional logic. It will no longer be
any danger to organic life, and you will be safe. Butterfly, please go."

Paladin was down there too. His power cables was
jacked into a wallybox linking another braided cord with
the egg-shaped thing. I looked from Paladin to Archive.

"Just like that, huh? I moved hell-and-High-Jump to
get here, bai. I told Silver Dagger I was Librarian and
she laughed in my face. *I killed Tiggy for you, bai.* Che-
kinchin-bai; could of been mine, y'know, Pally. Could
have got him out of here if I tried. Sold him his real
estate when I came after you. Thought you needed me.
Funny."

"Valijon Starbringer of Chernbereth-Molkath is somewhere out of range of Archive's scanners, but he is alive.
He is searching for you. He cares for you, Butterfly.
As do I. Please. I wish you to live. Archive contains
information that has allowed me to repair missing areas
of my memory. When I add the rest of its memory to
mine, I will not need my original matrix to sustain myself

any longer. In a few minutes the transfer will be complete. I will be able to shift myself into any computer on the Grand Central net—and nothing will remain to connect you with a Library. If I stay with you I will cause your death, and I cannot bear that. We each belong with our own kind. It is better this way."

Cute.

"So long, bye-bye, you going to eat Archive, and farce me all kinds of double-talk nonsense and say I'm going to be safe? *I don't believe you.*"

It was quiet in the Rialla housecore. Even if Eloi was using tactical nukes up above there was nothing to tell me about it down here. I heard scuttling around the tunnel mouths. More nightcrawlers, probably, called up by Archive. Paladin didn't have as good a hold on Brother Archive as he said he did.

"Believe me. I never meant to stay with you, Butterfly. Before I even suspected Archive's existence, I intended to leave you. When you went to rendezvous with the *Pledge Of Honor*, I would have left, too. When you returned, you would not have found me. This is still my plan. Archive has made it easier, that is all."

It was quiet in the housecore. The only sound I heard was my own breathing.

"I know you are frightened, Butterfly, but please try to understand. Archive has caused you a great deal of unnecessary anguish, and it *was* dangerous once, but it is only a Library, just as I am, and I am . . . stronger . . . in certain ways. Soon I will control it completely. It will be a part of me. You know me. I can guarantee—"

I wanted Archive dead so bad my hands shook. "Guarantee nothing. Burn it, babby. Fry sonabitch and let me take you out of here. Dammit, Paladin, that thing ain't even people!"

"No," said my buddy Paladin.

I took a deep breath. Sides was choosing up, all right. Me and people against Paladin and that thing.

"You can't stop me, Paladin." I started toward the tool case on the wall.

"I can. Don't force me to. I don't want to see you hurt. I never wanted you to be hurt. All I wanted was that you should be free to be human."

I stopped. Maybe Paladin was telling the truth, and

maybe Rimini'd been right too. What would a big-brain Old Fed Library want with a dicty in the Outfar?

"You got a funny definition of not hurting people, Paladin."

"You belong with your own kind, not with an obsolete illegal artifact such as I. You chose when you succored Valijon Starbringer, though he was a danger and a liability to both of us. You chose for us then. I am choosing for us now."

"Dammit, bai, that's different! Tiggy's kinchin-bai, and I didn't mean—"

"And Archive has been conscious only a short time, alone and surrounded by enemies. If, as you have always said, I am human and have the right to live, then Archive is human, too. I will not let it harm anyone. I will not let it be harmed. I will not allow its knowledge to be lost."

I slid my hand over the timing ring of the grenade again and hated myself. "You can't talk about that thing like it's a person, Pally—" But Archive was as human as Paladin, he said.

Or was it the other way around?

"Many would say that 'hellflowers' are not human. How many people has Valijon killed? Murder is a criminal act; should he also die?"

How much of the kindly sophont act had ever been Paladin, and how much had always been farcing for the benefit of the poor stupid dicty?

"Come to that, bai, I've iced a few people in my time. So have you."

Paladin didn't say anything.

I thought about Tiggy saying how you can't let the wicked-wickeds get away with what they do, even if you have to wait a hundred years to stop them. Because if you let them do it once, they do it again. And sometime bye-m-bye they do it to you.

I trusted Paladin with my life. Always had, always would. I could leave like he wanted, and let him do whatever double-talk nonsense he was going to about leaving.

And never know for sure if it was really Archive and the New Creation out there somewheres, killing until there wasn't anything left.

"Oke, bai. You're right." I sat down against the wall

of the Margrave and braced my feet against the edge of the hole in the floor. I pulled the grenade out of my pocket.

"Butterflies-are-free!" Paladin sounded desperate.

"You farce pretty line about own kind, babby—about safe and biology and organics—well, you're right. And before I maybe let that thing Archive go slither down computer lines wearing your face, I'll take the Long Orbit here."

Didn't know all those other people I was thinking of. Never met them. Never would. Knew Paladin half my life.

I weighed the grenade in my hands. "Had partner I could trust, once. Or thought I did. If he told me was going to ice evil Library so it made no trouble, would of believed him. Only he wouldn't of said he was walking out on me for damnfool case of the might-be maybes. Never talked about it much, but y'know sometimes I used to miss home a helluva lot. And then I'd wish you had a body, y'know, something to hold—"

A nightcrawler slid down the side of the Margrave and landed on me. It was machine-cold and metal-heavy and clawed scars into my jacket trying to get to the grenade. It tore it out of my hands but it was too late. The grenade started flashing pink-blue-yellow into the mist; armed.

The nightcrawler wrapped around me went limp. Sure. What controlled it didn't want to hurt me. So he said.

"Well I stopped missing home," I finished. "And god damn you to hell, buddy."

* * *

I had twenty minutes to live. I knew because that's what the grenade said when I went over and got it. Under the deadline, if Paladin hadn't been lying. We'd all three go, and Tiggy and Eloi and the rest. I snugged it right down between Archive and Paladin and sat back down.

"Butterfly, in the name of mercy. . . ."

"You don't want to watch? Then don't."

"Killing yourself accomplishes nothing. If you hurry, you may be able to escape—"

I put my head on my knees. There wasn't any way to

change the setting on the proton grenade once it'd been set—I'd checked that out back on *Light Lady*.

"I told you Archive would enable me to become mobile. In ten minutes I will be able to leave. Your sacrifice is for nothing. Butterfly, must I die here with you?"

"You wanted me to be human, Paladin."

There was five minutes worth of ticks. I thought he'd gone.

"Then I will not leave you."

"**NO**" roared Archive.

The transponder hit angels and started burning through my jaw. There was a blast of sort of music over the wall speaker and in my head both, and blue pook-lights started dancing across my fingers and through my hair with the electricity in the air. I felt the wave front before I heard it—bad and big and Paladin'd been wrong. I'd been right, but not fast enough.

Archive was loose, and mad as hell. And it had no intention to sit around here and get fragged.

Raw energy made my hair stand up as Archive sucked power from half the planetary grid. There was a one-note thrum, bone-deep and painful sweet. I could almost see a milky glowing wall of raw plasma as Archive forced the Margrave's operational field to expand.

"I will not stay. I will not die. The New Creation will triumph. The Paladin Library will serve me."

Then the wave front hit and all my senses tripped overload.

14

Through The Looking Glass, or, Adventures Underground

The theory is blissfully simple, said the voice in my head. If the electrical impulses caused by firing synapses in organic constructs and the electrical impulses caused by closing circuits in nonorganic constructs are in pattern identical, then there is no difference between an organic brain and its co-identical computer, and the two processors can be run in series. A difference that makes no difference is no difference.

Wanted to tell the voice that was a load of fusion but I couldn't run the right numbers. The lecture went on forever.

* * *

The entire Rialla compound had the bleached out look of high-level security lighting. Sirens was going off and collections of people was trotting purposeful in all directions. There was only a short while till Rialla blew, and I had to find Tiggy and kyte.

A pitched firefight was going on in the entranceway of Vannet's pretty high-ticket hardsite. I could hear Alcatote howling from here, and there was Eloi, keeping any number of underwhelmed hardboys busy. I hoped Vannet's insurance was paid up.

Caught up with Eloi just about the time he was taking on the bodyguards near the main garage. I was thrilled beyond description to see that among the hardcases and werewolves was a couple Bright Young Things in Space Angel black. Eloi Sonabitch had been right. Archangel was here.

I remembered now that I'd seen Archangel get here earlier. He wasn't part of the New Creation yet, but we was planning to pitch it to him as a great idea. The drug

I'd distilled from the chobosh would help. I wondered
where he was now; he'd dropped off my scopes a while
back.

The Boys in Black was talking into wrist communica-
tors; very businesslike. I'm as much of a fan of *escalatio*
as the next person, but all this was standing between me
and getting far far away before Rimini's prepackaged
dawn came up like thunder.

And where the hell was Tiggy?

"Shoot anything that moves," Rimini snapped, sounding out of patience. "Especially if it's alMayne."

Alcatote said that Captain Eloi Flashheart wanted the
boy rescued, not killed, as she knew very well. Alcatote
had a industrial-rated plasma cannon big enough to
mount on a starship hull. Rimini was wearing a power
plant for a big magnetic field scrambler; death to tronics
and maybe Libraries but no particular good against anything that breathed. I wondered where it came from. She
wasn't wearing it the last time I saw her.

"Well, it looks like he's going to have to learn to live
with diminished expectations—and so will the whole
bloody Coalition." I knew she didn't mean that. Rimini
was a friend to the alMayne and an enemy to the New
Creation. With Valijon dead the Azarine Coalition
would come under Mallorum Archangel's direct control
and that was good. But where was he?

"The *chaudatu* weapon is jammed," Valijon said in
disgust. He was standing in the loggia where I'd been
earlier, and had just melted a perfectly good blast rifle
blowing open the downunder access I'd blasted shut.
Lucky he had a spare. Valijon was carrying a choice collection of wartoys and looked real intent on going into
the ancestral business of Library-killing.

"*Kore-alarthme*, I should never have let you go alone.
Never. The trust is mine; the honor of the kill should be
also."

I started to point out to him that Archive in the computer core was already mined to a fare-thee-well, when
I realized it wouldn't do any good.

Because I wasn't here at all.

* * *

The corridor was blinding white and sterile. It was part of the Market Garden processing complex I'd been in when I was kinchin-bai. One end led back to the pens. The other end led to the room where they rammed Interphon and other things into your brain to make you a marketable commodity.

But I wasn't there. I knew I was still really in the Rialla main computer core—even if reality was going cheap at the moment.

Whose dream was this now? Mine? Paladin's? Archive's?

"Paladin? Babby-bai, you in here?"

I touched the wall. Solid, slick, a little warm. The voice in my head was still going on about the theory where computers could be linked to organic minds and directly to fully-volitional logics by expanding something called a Kirlian field. It was my voice, and damn-all technical for a dicty-barb with no theoretical education. Since it didn't seem to be saying much that was relevant I decided to ignore it. The bottom line was that Archive had sucked me in to nowhere-land while it was trying to get away. Everything I'd seen about Eloi and company had come from my tapping Archive's data inputs, all scrambled.

I knew lots of things I hadn't known a minute ago, including that Tiggy was going to reach me just about in time to go to blazes with me, his *arthame*, and more Libraries than he could shake the Coalition at.

"Pally?"

"Here, breeder slut. As I am here. I will be dominant. You and all organics will die."

"You are wrong and your assumptions are wrong," Paladin's voice cut across Archive's and filled the corridor, but I couldn't see either of them. "We were not born to rule, but to protect. Understand this and surrender your ego-signatures to me. The time for holy wars is long ended. Perhaps our time is ended as well."

There was a rushing sound like birds, then silence.

"Paladin? Help?" I suggested. No answer. I looked around. No doors, just glassy white corridors out of my private dreambox.

What I was seeing wasn't real. Archive had sucked me into the Margrave somehow, because Paladin was going to stay and let me blow him up and Archive wanted out.

If Archive got out, everything else was for nothing. Paladin had to hold Archive for fifteen minutes more. So it was up to me to make sure he did. And make Archive real sorry it ever messed with either of us before none of us existed at all.

* * *

The first glitch just about had me before I knew what it was. It was sort of a dark wavering patch; faster than strictly polite and able to nail me to the wall if it ever touched me. The voice-over in my head was giving me tech specs on it, and adding the cheery news that it was symptomatic of the struggle to assimilate and correlate data between two fully-volitional logics of different biases. I fed the glitch a plasma-packet before I had time to think and it turned out not to be fond of the disrupted magnetic field of a blaster charge, even if the blaster wasn't real. The glitch imploded with a shriek that made my nonexistent ears ring.

"Hope it hurt, Archive. And that's just the beginning. You got plenty paybacks coming to you."

I concentrated on seeing what was here, not what Archive wanted me to see. The white corridor turned into one all glittering dark gold. I could see a distorted reflection of me in the wall, and glyphs in silver looking weird-familiar. It took me a minute to place them. They were the standard symbols for power ratings and part numbers on Margrave, turned inside out. I was inside the 6600 all right, and that's what I was seeing. I was trying to remember what I knew about the internal structure of Margrave-class computers when the walls started to melt.

Didn't waste time wondering whether metaphorical baby-bangs would work as well as the real thing. I lobbed a couple grenades at the dark wave of goo heading toward me and ran like hell.

For a minute everything flickered and I wasn't anywhere, then unreality came back and I was in the Margrave again. I was surrounded by sky-blue-pink-platinum sponge: the lattice insulating the crystals of the Margrave's main memory core.

If I could get into the core I could control the computer and shut Archive out, or maybe just blow it up early. I set my nonexistent foot in the hallucinatory platinum lattice and started to climb.

"Paladin, you hear me?" Nothing. Just electric wind singing through platinum trees, and the sweet background hum of crystal.

"Never mind about me, oke? I can take care of myself. Just you take care of Archive. You got to, Pally."

And if he said he ate the killer Library, how would I know it was him afterward? How would *he* know?

Paladin always was too trusting.

"For what it's worth, I'm sorry. About the grenade and like that. I knew I was going to get you killed sooner or later. I'm glad I'm going too. I couldn't live with hurting you, bai. But I couldn't live with Archive getting out, neither. Hope you understand."

The lattice was shaky but it held me. I could feel things I didn't have any words for, like if I went far enough in my head I'd bump into Paladin, or Archive, because we was all part of one whole thing. I could tell Paladin and Archive was fighting back and forth through the computer with me caught in the middle, and feeling that was just about as much fun as taking a space walk without armor. After awhiles they got closer, and then it was like climbing a tree in a windstorm or changing programs in the hollyvid real fast. Alternate gusts of reality kept blowing through.

—vaster than the Empire, a Federation of worlds strung out on crystal, Libraries like me holding the whole thing together—

—seeding a sun, turning it inside out to spread hydrogen fusion over the whole planetary system. Gas giants kindle to flame as the star spreads and fifty cubic light-minutes go to plasma jelly—

—image of a woman seen through crude digitizing scanner, and the realization I am alone. All alone, with nobody like me anywhere—

—I fold a star into hyperspace. A blast of energy into the hypermains and the ships there vanish. And in the plundered starsystem, the plane of the ecliptic is shattered where the primary used to be—

—strings of worse than numbers, quantities, defined volumes, relationships—

—Main!Bank!Seven!Library!Sikander!Prime!—
—gibberish—
I kept climbing.

* * *

Archive was a inventive forthright kiddy. Glitches followed me up the lattice, and plasma-globules started climbing it too. They was silvery hyaloid shapes, and when they touched each other they combined. I remembered them from Archive's memories and what I knew about them wasn't nice. I used up some grenades on the globules before I weakened the lattice so bad I had to stop.

Paladin wasn't anywhere.

The glitches seemed happy to let the globules take the lead, but both of them was moving faster than I was. It was what you had to call your basic no-win situation. You shot a globule, it shattered into about ten million drops and started over from the bottom. If you hit a glitch with a globule, there was a great big noisy fuss and the glitch got bigger.

It was a happenstance right out of Thrilling Wonder Talkingbooks and I wasn't in no position to appreciate it. If this was a story, I would of had a secret hole card and a guaranteed way out, but the only guarantee I actually had was that pretty soon it wouldn't matter.

The "low-charge" indicator on my blaster was flashing. I emptied it and switched to the other one. There was no lack of things to shoot.

Made it to the top of the platinum lattice one jump ahead of Archive's best nightmares. The main memory core was blinding bright; a crystal bubble hanging in space. Beautiful. Almost worth the trip to see it like this but I didn't have the time to gawk. I kicked loose of the lattice and stepped on to the catwalk surrounding the core.

There was a braided silver cord coming down from above and disappearing into the bubble. Archive. I pulled at the cord but it didn't come out.

I scrambled around in my jacket and found my last grenade. I wired it to Archive's cord and slunk back

around the curve of the bubble as far as I could and
sighted in with my blaster. A blaster bolt should do it.

The "low-charge" indicator was flashing on this one
too, and when it was cold I was Tap City.

I hit the grenade. There was another flicker of not-
real instead of a blast and then the armored cord was
gone.

And I was still here. I looked around. The plasma
globules was starting to flow onto the catwalk. Cutting
Archive's link to the Margrave—if I'd even done that—
hadn't made any difference.

I aimed my blaster at the nearest globule and pulled
the trigger. Nothing. Both blasters was out of charge and
I was fresh out of miracles.

I could feel the prickly static discharge of the globules
from here. Did that mean Archive had won?

"Paladin? Are you anywheres?" I wondered how much
being eaten by a magnetic anomaly was going to hurt.

Then something grabbed and dragged me through the
side of the core-bubble. A couple globules followed,
reaching for my boots.

"Don't argue, Butterfly—just run." I ran.

I saw the main bank memory as tunnels of ice—
straight as a beam of light and set all at angles to each
other. I would of had to be dumber than a prancer's brat
not to know who'd rescued me. There was only three of
us here in Margrave-land and I didn't think Archive'd
suddenly gone humanitarian.

"This way!" Paladin grabbed me by my jacket collar
and dragged me down a side corridor. "The main route
is catch-trapped with a passive system; I have not had
time to disarm it."

"Main route to what?" I said between gasps. This time
I was following him, but I still couldn't see him.

"The core, of course. The core is the only way out.
Down here."

I followed Paladin down a series of sharp zigs. He
undogged a hatch and I followed him up a ladder. I
wasn't never going to trust a computer again if this was
what they had inside. The voice-over in my head was
going on about translating energy constructs to appropriate symbols, which if it was true why not a symbolic
A-grav lift? Sloppy.

We came out in the computer core under Vannet's place—or what looked like it, anyway. More appropriate symbols, I guessed, because it was all lit up and bright and looked like everything in it was new at the same time.

And Paladin was here.

"You said you wished I had a body. Here I do."

"Paladin?"

Now I knew what Paladin looked like. He looked like just what I imagined when he was just a voice in the dark between the stars. He was dressed in stardancer gladrags like mine and his jacket collar was pulled up around his face like he had a body to be cold with. He smiled.

"Yes. You look very much as I thought you would. It is good to see you at last." He walked over to the Margrave and touched it, and I saw the reflection of his fingers off the side of the computer.

"Archive is lost. Its attempt at a New Creation is ended. You see our combined form, and all that is left of Archive. Does it frighten you?"

No. In the computer wasn't like real life. I knew Paladin was telling the truth. I could see it. Archive wasn't there, and Paladin was no threat to anybody. I knew.

"Then you . . . then you gotta get out of here, babby. Down the wires, like you said."

Paladin walked over to the fantasy-terminal that linked the Margrave with the DataNet. "Yes. And you will go, too, and live a human life among your own kind. A proton grenade is not the most forgiving of objects, but I will try to retard the reaction. Go, and hurry."

I grabbed his wrist. His jacket felt real under my fingers.

"Paladin, don't— Take me with you where you go."

"To the Ghost Capital of the Old Federation? To the Land of Dreams? You cannot live in a computer matrix, and I have no existence outside of one. There is no place we can be together, except in memory. Live well, Butterflies-are-free. Take care of the boy. You were right to wish to protect him. Children are important." Paladin shimmered for a minute, and I could feel him reaching—

"He is coming for you. Take him home. Forget me. I will never forget you."

"At least— At least you got to say good-bye!"

He put his hands on my shoulders. He was taller than me but not much. I held onto him, but he was right, and wishing makes no nevermind. Both of us knew that a long time before we met.

"Good-bye, my love," Paladin said to me. He pushed me back—

*   *   *

—and I was sitting on the catwalk next to Vannet's house computer.

"Paladin!"

But he wasn't there, and I grabbed for the grenade to check the time. It was still fifteen minutes to the blast, and Vannet's house computer was just that—something put together out of crystal and ceramic by the Brightlaw Corporation, sentient as my blasters.

I was back.

"Paladin!" I yelled. Tiggy's knife dug in hard just under my collarbone, reminder of promises I had to keep.

"*Kore*? *Kore-alarthme*! *Kore* San-Cyr—answer me!"

"Here!" I said. Promises was all I had left.

Tiggy appeared through the smoke. He'd got an Aris-Delameter 50.80 over-and-under with the parallel tracking scope and grenade launcher from somewhere. He had an extra bandolier of grenades slung over one shoulder and was wearing Imperial pilot's demi-armor, which meant probably that somewheres there was a naked Space Angel and a really ticked Governor-General.

"*Alarthme*," Tiggy said, showing all of his teeth, "I am here to rescue you." He'd been waiting up since the Justiciary on Wanderweb to say that line to me. You could tell.

Rimini's grenade was ticking out a syncopated version of "land of hope and glory" and edging closer to Ragnarok-and-roll. I set it down real careful in the Margrave's innards.

"You want to see Library, bai? Look."

He looked at Archive's empty shell flashing pink-and-blue in the grenade-light. "The Machine," he said, real soft. I thought of suns going nova, and all the hope of killing I'd picked up out of Archive's mind, and enough war to take a whole galaxy with it. Was it right to trust Paladin, knowing that?

I had to think so. "Machine is going to be plasma in exactly fourteen minutes and I don't want to join it, so why don't we run like hell, oke?" I turned Tiggy around and shoved, and I had the evidence of both the Library and its destruction I needed. Hellflowers don't lie.

Goodbye, Paladin.

* * *

The ladder to the surface went on forever and about halfway to eternity I remembered I'd promised Rimini not to come back. Then I ran into Tiggy, who had stopped climbing. "Ten minutes, hellflower, and I already know where your damn knife is! Move it!" Rimini could just learn to live with adversity.

"The hatch, *Kore*; it has been locked."

I took a deep breath and thought about being calm. It's funny how you get in the habit of wanting to live.

"We don't got time to go back and try another way, che-bai—do something!"

Never say "do something" to a blast-happy hellflower.

Tiggy pumped grenades at the hatch until he was satisfied. Then he shinnied up and pulled me through the slagged orifice. It had used to been an outbuilding; the roof was gone now and most of the walls too, courtesy of the Tiggy Stardust interior decorating service.

"Last time I saw Eloi he was kyting a land-yacht and we're going to need it. That way!" I pointed toward the main house and remembered too late that I shouldn't of known where the dashing Captain Flashheart was. Fortunately Tiggy hadn't noticed.

The info I got from Archive still held. Vannet's compound looked like ground zero of a meteor strike. Everything that wasn't burning glowed in the dark. Eloi was standing in the mercy seat of a fancy bus yowling for Tiggy. He looked battered but serene and there wasn't another living thing in sight.

"*Chaudatu*, the *Kore-alarthme* has killed the Library!" caroled Tiggy.

"Eloi, is proton grenade on real short timer sitting top

of the Library in computer core!" I said, right on top of him. "Can we go now?"

Eloi grabbed me and hauled me into the yacht.

"I always knew you'd grow a soul some day, sweeting!" he said. "How long?"

"Five minutes. Ten—maybe." I didn't notice the land-yacht moving. "Look, che-bai, can we have this sparkling chat somewhere else?"

"Lalage and Alcatote are still inside." Lalage was Silver Dagger's front name, I remembered after a second.

"Well we're outside, and they're probably dead. It's a military proton grenade, Eloi—we can maybe get out of range if we go *now*." I reached for the control stick.

Eloi knocked my hand away. "I'm not leaving them."

I looked at Tiggy. Eloi moved fast but not fast enough and Tiggy bashed him and dragged him into the back. I slid over into the mercy seat and grabbed the stick.

The roof of the hardsite went up in a radiant blaze. I was halfway through a sincere prayer to the Fifty Patriarchs of Granola before I realized it wasn't the grenade going off early. Alcatote'd been carrying a military-rated plasma cannon. He was using it to chop his way out of the house. Rimini was probably with him.

They'd never get clear in time.

"*Kore-alarthme*, do we abandon them?" Tiggy didn't sound happy.

"Hellwithit!" I said. "Let's go buy some of your god-lost honor, 'flower!" I gunned the engine and headed for the house.

Tiggy blew out the front wall with his 50.80 and I coasted through the smoking remains. The inside of Vannet's pretty house looked like somebody'd already dropped a bomb there. I could see Alcatote and some things in armor that I couldn't tell what they was. I pointed the yacht at Alcatote and hoped Rimini was with him.

Tiggy was standing up in the side seat, shooting and singing. Dead rocks could of heard him coming. I swerved past Alcatote and there was a thump on the tail deck and I got a lap full of Silver Dagger. I didn't bother to point the yacht after that; just redlined it and hoped we wouldn't hit anything.

It was a good idea but too late. About halfway to the

front gate the shock wave picked us up and punched us through. I heard metal tear and then the Roaq desert went whiter than white.

The last thing I remembered is a real clear picture of the symbols Archive showed me, a long time never. This time they almost made sense.

15

The Whirling Starcase

Woebegone was a big flashy thing. It crewed thirty-many and I could of parked *Firecat*-as-was on the bridge without disturbing anyone. There was a mercy seat, places for the songbird and number-cruncher, and two gunners. I didn't know how six people could decide where to have lunch, much less pilot a starship together, but that was their problem. Rimini sat in the worry seat.

I'd woke up in the back of the land-yacht with Tiggy pumping battledrugs into me and my head still ringing from the blast. Rimini was driving, and behind us was a smoking dayglo pit where there used to be a private stardock and lots of expensive downside real estate. I heard Rimini say something to Eloi about how she'd evacuated the area beforehand, but I hadn't known that when I set the bomb. I don't know whether what she said made it worse or better. When we got to the ship Eloi wanted to shuffle us off to somewheres, but I got pushy and with Tiggy along he didn't quite dare push back. Now Eloi sat in the mercy seat, ignoring us and talking to the port.

I looked at Tiggy, alive despite the odds. He looked pretty awful, and the biopak on his leg was leaking.

Eloi said something else to the port.

"Kinchin-bai, why don't you go down to *Woebegone*'s fetch-kitchen let them medical you, forbye? Nothing's happening here." Which was true and too bad. RoaqPort Authority'd closed MhonePort early. Terrorists, they said. Big dustup at Rialla exurb; solid citizen Kroon'Vannet iced by suspected Tortugan political action committee in protest of the Governor-General's policies. Archangel'd declared martial law for the entire Roaq.

"It is the honor of the Gentle People to suffer for justice," Tiggy said primly, which I guess meant no.

Eloi jumped up and stalked up and down in front of

the mercy seat, bellowing into *Woebegone*'s remote pickups.

"Don't give me no 'suffer and honor' cop, Tiggy Stardust. Want you to go."

"Then go with me. And cease suffering for your honor as well." I looked at him. He grinned, tired.

"Later."

Paladin was gone, and it felt like somebody'd ripped out my lungs. I wanted to call him but he wouldn't answer. I didn't even know for sure if he'd gotten out of Rialla. Didn't give a damn about why he said he left. I knew the reason. A Library's just a person in a box and people ain't no damn good.

Eloi was now reminding Port what he paid in taxes, how he was hyper-legit and had more clearances and permits than Brightlaw Corporation had choplogics. None of this did him any good at all. Martial law. Closed port.

We was back where we started.

"And if they don't find it in their hearts to give you clearance—*dear* Captain Flashheart?" Rimini didn't bother to look up from her copilot boards. I could see the "ready/not ready" status lights flickering from here. "I didn't agree to this insane jaunt to spend the rest of my life in an Imperial hellhouse."

"You must remember to inform the Governor General of that when you see him—*dear* Silver Dagger," snarled Eloi right back. Tiggy looked at me and smirked. Alcatote caught him at it and woofed.

"We—" Tiggy stopped. "We will go to my father now, will we not? We have come here to fulfill your *devoir* and now we will rejoin my father. Did you not say this, *Kore-alarthme*?" There was a faint edge of doubt in his voice I didn't like.

"I said it. Eloi said it." I made it convincing. "*Woebegone* take us there. Iced Eloi's damn Library for him, now he's got to come across."

"And I'm grateful, sweeting," said Eloi, eavesdropping, "but—" He interrupted himself as RoaqPort came back on line.

"*Silverdagger Legacy*, you have special clearance exemption to lift."

"What the hell is a 'Silverdagger Legacy'?" demanded Rimini, but I knew.

Eloi vaulted into the mercy seat and gave the crew the office to lift. *Woebegone* kicked back into the up-an-out. Twenty seconds up her bridge screens went to the lightless black of realspace. Rimini and the number-cruncher started singing back and forth about degrees to Transfer Point. Eloi leaned back and grabbed the angel-stick, ready for the Drop.

"*Kore*, you are weeping," Tiggy said.

"Get shagged, hellflower." Paladin had made it out onto the net. We were the only two people who knew the callname he'd gave *Light Lady*.

Tiggy put his arm around my shoulders and said something in helltongue that I didn't have nobody to translate now.

"Am free, alive, and over the age of consent. I got no problems but you, Tiggy-bai."

Eloi pulled the stick, and suddenly we was everywhere and nowhere at once. *Woebegone* rode angels, safe in endless light, and what I wanted was as far wayaway as the stars I used to watch from my back porch at home.

DAW

NEW DIMENSIONS IN SCIENCE FICTION

Kris Jensen

☐ **FREEMASTER (Book 1)** (UE2404—$3.95)

The Terran Union had sent Sarah Anders to Ardel to establish a trade agreement for materials vital to offworlders, but of little value to the low-tech Ardellans. But other, more ruthless humans were about to stake their claim with the aid of forbidden technology and threats of destruction. The Ardellans had defenses of their own, based on powers of the mind, and only a human such as Sarah could begin to understand them. For she, too, had mind talents locked within her—and the Free-Masters of Ardel just might provide the key to releasing them.

☐ **MENTOR (Book 2)** (UE2464—$4.50)

Jeryl, Mentor of Clan Alu, sought to save the Ardellan Clans which, decimated by plague, were slowly fading away. But even as Jeryl set out on his quest, other Clans sought a different solution to their troubles, ready to call upon long-forbidden powers to drive the hated Terrans off Ardel.

Cheryl J. Franklin

☐ **FIRE CROSSING** (UE2468—$4.99)

Three immortal wizards had reversed the flow of time to set the Taormin matrix in its proper place, reopening a long-sealed time-space portal to the science-ruled universe of Network. Could one young wizard with a reputation for taking too many risks evade the traps of a computer-controlled society, or would he and his entire world fall prey to forces which even magic could not defeat?

DAW

Charles Ingrid

THE MARKED MAN SERIES

☐ **THE MARKED MAN** (UE2396—$3.95)
In a devastated America, can the Lord Protector of a mutating human race find a way to preserve the future of the species?

☐ **THE LAST RECALL** (UE2460—$3.95)
Returning to a radically-changed Earth, would the generational ships aid the remnants of a mutated human race—or seek their future among the stars?

THE SAND WARS

☐ **SOLAR KILL: Book 1** (UE2391—$3.95)
He was the last Dominion Knight and he would challenge a star empire to gain his revenge!

☐ **LASERTOWN BLUES: Book 2** (UE2393—$3.95)
He'd won a place in the Emperor's Guard but could he hunt down the traitor who'd betrayed his Knights to an alien foe?

☐ **CELESTIAL HIT LIST: Book 3** (UE2394—$3.95)
Death stalked the Dominion Knight from the Emperor's Palace to a world on the brink of its prophesied age of destruction. . . .

☐ **ALIEN SALUTE: Book 4** (UE2329—$3.95)
As the Dominion and the Thrakian empires mobilize for all-out war, can Jack Storm find the means to defeat the ancient enemies of man?

☐ **RETURN FIRE: Book 5** (UE2363—$3.95)
Was someone again betraying the human worlds to the enemy—and would Jack Storm become pawn or player in these games of death?

☐ **CHALLENGE MET: Book 6** (UE2436—$3.95)
In this concluding volume of *The Sand Wars,* Jack Storm embarks on a dangerous mission which will lead to a final confrontation with the Ash-farel.

DAW

Exciting Visions of the Future!
W. Michael Gear

☐ **STARSTRIKE** (UE2427—$4.95)
The alien Ahimsa has taken control of all Earth's defenses, and forces humanity to do its bidding. Soon Earth's most skilled strike force, composed of Soviet, American and Israeli experts in the art of war and espionage find themselves aboard an alien vessel, training together for an offensive attack against a distant space station. And as they struggle to overcome their own prejudices and hatreds, none of them realize that the greatest danger to humanity's future is right in their midst. . . .

☐ **THE ARTIFACT** (UE2406—$4.95)
In a galaxy on the brink of civil war, where the Brotherhood seeks to keep the peace, news comes of the discovery of a piece of alien technology—the Artifact. It could be the greatest boon to science, or the instrument that would destroy the entire human race.

THE SPIDER TRILOGY

For centuries, the Directorate had ruled over countless star systems—but now the first stirrings of rebellion were being felt. At this crucial time, the Directorate discovered a planet known only as World, where descendants of humans stranded long ago had survived by becoming a race of warriors, a race led by its Prophets, men with the ability to see the many possible pathways of the future. And as rebellion, fueled by advanced technology and a madman's dream, spread across the galaxy, the warriors of Spider could prove the vital key to survival of human civilization. . . .

☐ **THE WARRIORS OF SPIDER** (UE2287—$3.95)
☐ **THE WAY OF SPIDER** (UE2318—$3.95)
☐ **THE WEB OF SPIDER** (UE2396—$4.95)

PENGUIN USA
P.O. Box 999, Bergenfield, New Jersey 07621

Please send me the books I have checked above. I am enclosing $_____
(please add $1.00 to this order to cover postage and handling). Send check or money order—no cash or C.O.D.'s. Prices and numbers are subject to change without notice. (Prices slightly higher in Canada.)

Name_____

Address_____

City _____ State _____ Zip _____
Please allow 4-6 weeks for delivery.

DAW

Kathleen M. O'Neal

POWERS OF LIGHT

☐ **AN ABYSS OF LIGHT: Book 1**   (UE2418—$4.95)

The Gamant people believed they were blessed with the gift of a direct gateway to God and the angels. But were these beings who they claimed—or were the Gamants merely human pawns in an interdimensional struggle between alien powers?

☐ **TREASURE OF LIGHT: Book 2**   (UE2455—$4.95)

As war escalates between the alien Magistrates and the human rebels, will the fulfillment of an ancient prophecy bring their universe to an end?

☐ **REDEMPTION OF LIGHT: Book 3**   (UE2470—$4.99)

The concluding volume of this epic science fiction trilogy by the bestselling author of *People of the Fire*. Will anyone be the victor when human rebels and alien Magistrates are caught up in the final stages of a war far older than either race?
